MY LIFE IN BLACK AND WHITE

MY LIFE IN BLACK AND WHITE

BLACK AND WHITE

A NOVEL

KIM IZZO

HARPER
PERENNIAL

Published by Harper Perennial, an imprint of HarperCollins Publishers Ltd

First published by HarperCollins Publishers Ltd
in an original trade paperback edition: 2013

This Harper Perennial trade paperback edition: 2014

HarperCollins books may be purchased for educational, business, or sales promo-
tional use through our Special Markets Department.

HarperCollins Publishers Ltd
2 Bloor Street East, 20th Floor
Toronto, Ontario, Canada
M4W 1A8

www.harpercollins.ca

Library and Archives Canada Cataloguing in
Publication information is available upon request

ISBN 978-1-44342-247-5

Printed and bound in the United States

RRD 9 8 7 6 5 4 3 2 1

For my sisters, Jackie and Janis

FADE IN

Police Station—The Town of Cirencester, Gloucestershire, England

I was dressed like a film star at a movie premiere in four-inch heels and a gold satin evening gown. Only the flashbulbs that popped in my face weren't paparazzi, just your routine mug shot. And in lieu of gliding along a red carpet, I marched down an austere hallway with cops for escorts.

Most people would have been scared witless, all things considered. Instead, all I was was cold. The trench coat draped over my shoulders like a cape wasn't doing much to fix the problem, just made me long for its owner. I kept picturing his face and the sensation of his hands on my skin. Having been intertwined with each other only an hour before, there had been plenty of body heat to stave off the damp.

When the cops deposited me in the tiny airless room, I shivered, but the police officer seated at the metal table with a yellow legal pad on it didn't seem to notice. He was too fixated on surveying the outline of my figure beneath the satin.

"I'm chilled to the bone. Can you turn up the heat or something? Get me a cup of coffee?" I asked, drawing the line at smiling.

The cop lifted his eyes—nut brown and blank—to my face. "Why are you wearing a nightdress?"

A corner of my mouth lifted into an involuntary smirk. "It's a slip dress."

"A what?" he asked accusingly, like I was trying to pull one over on him.

"An evening gown. You don't sleep in it. It's for fancy occasions."

He examined me carefully, the kind of close-watch inspection that was meant to unnerve. I just stared back. "I can't do anything about the temperature, but I will get you a hot tea." He stood up and strode to the door. It was pale green, like hospital scrubs, with a small window. Other than the yellow pad of paper, the green was the only real colour in the room. The walls were a dull shade of grey. The metal table and chairs were silver, like brushed nickel. Even his uniform, though I knew it was dark navy, appeared black beneath the sole light source—a dim bulb that shone down from a metal pendant fixture in the ceiling.

He opened the door and muttered to another cop, then stood there, waiting like a sentry. Within minutes there was a knock at the door, and I saw a Styrofoam cup thrust towards him by an unseen hand. The door was shut once again, and the cop stepped to the table and placed the cup in front of me. It was steaming. The tea bag had been left in it but there was no milk or sugar to be seen. My instincts told me to shut up and sip the tea. But I hated strong tea, so I grabbed the string and lifted the bag out. I let it hover over the cup, dripping, and looked up at the cop. "Is there a garbage can handy?"

He sighed audibly and took the string from me and held the dripping bag away from his clean uniform as he crossed the room to the green door and opened it. There were more mutterings, urgent and irritated, and then he was back. He took a pen from his pocket and tapped it on the table. It had a tinny sound.

"Name please," he ordered brusquely.

"Clara Bishop." I kept looking at him as he wrote my name down.

"Occupation."

I contemplated for a moment, then said, "Screenwriter."

This seemed to pique his interest. He looked up at me with a hint of life in his face.

"Anything I've seen?"

It was the usual question. "Not yet, but one day," I gave him the usual answer. Then it was my turn, "How long do I have to stay here?" I gripped the Styrofoam cup, letting its warmth bleed into my fingers.

"Until I get a proper statement!" he snapped, and I saw the hint of life had vanished. "When there is an alleged crime, especially one that involves foreign nationals, particularly Americans like you, all loose ends must be tied. And the entire lot of you has been uncooperative." He picked up the yellow pad to slam on the table for effect, but when he let go it fell to the floor. He dove down for it, flustered.

The smile came back to my lips. I replaced it with a scowl. "Maybe that's because there's nothing to say." I shoved my hand into the pocket of the trench coat and felt the familiar cigarette case—his case—and took a cigarette out. I held it to my lips, parting them just enough to show my top teeth. "Got a light?"

"You can't smoke in here!" he snapped again, this time seemingly aghast at my audacity.

"Can't I?" I asked, even though I knew he was right. I made do with clenching the cigarette between my teeth like a soother.

"You shouldn't smoke," he added, like being a propagator for the anti-smoking brigade was part of his job description.

"You're right." I took the cigarette out of my mouth and tossed it onto the table.

I noticed a calendar on the wall. Its pages were as grey as the walls and lacked the vivid photography normally used to make the passing of time appear less monotonous—just look at the April shot of . . . insert animal, car, bikini model, etc. The numbers were stupidly small, but if I squinted I could make them out. The year was what it ought to be. Obama was still president and for the second term.

"Look here, Miss Bishop, Clara, whichever you prefer . . ."

"Miss Bishop, please. Let's see how we get on before we go to first names." I leaned forward to read the name tag on his uniform. "Officer Hooper."

He fidgeted awkwardly, like he was insulted that I wouldn't let him call me Clara, and that amused me. "Sergeant Hooper. Tell me, Miss Bishop, do you always act like you're a character in a film noir movie?"

I bristled. "No," I answered and picked the cigarette off the table and sucked on it a moment as he watched. Then I smiled what I hoped passed for a droll smile and said, "You're not the first man to ask me that. And if by character you mean the femme fatale, then I take it as a compliment."

He fidgeted some more.

"I take it you're a movie buff?" I asked him. "Not many people would make a comment like that unless they were."

"I've seen a few."

I tossed my head back so my hair fell across half my face. "Do you like film noir?"

There was no answer. Then I continued, "I love those movies."

His patience was at an end. "This situation, this crime . . ."

"Alleged crime," I corrected him. I'd seen enough television police procedurals to know the drill.

"This alleged crime," he repeated. "This isn't a movie."

"It isn't, is it?" I leaned forward.

"No."

"There was no crime," I said.

"Assault is a crime."

"Like I just finished saying, there was no crime, no assault, no anything," I told him firmly.

"You need to tell me what happened, what you saw," he said.

"I didn't see a thing," I lied. I'd seen everything and then some.

"Then I'm afraid you'll be here for quite some time until it all gets sorted out."

"Where are the others?" I asked.

"They're here too. In equally cold rooms with black tea and no smoking."

"Now who's talking in noir?" I asked sarcastically.

"Just tell me what happened," he said.

I stared past him at the calendar on the wall. The room spun a little and I felt weak. I wondered what was in that tea.

"You want the long or the short version?" I asked at last, the veneer of brazen defiance cracking. Or maybe I was finally coming to my senses. The reliable, predictable Clara Bishop.

"Up to you."

I shuddered and crossed my arms tightly. "I don't know where to begin."

"What about the other American woman, Amber Ward?"

I smirked. "Let me guess, you're a gentleman who prefers blondes."

His features softened, like he was remembering all the girls he'd ever loved all at once. "I like all hair colours. Including redheads."

That made me smile. He was flirting with me. It was probably a tactic, but I liked it more than the bad-cop routine.

"Is Amber a friend of yours? Did you travel to England together?"

"Not exactly," I said.

"What do you mean by that?" he asked firmly, the bad cop returning a little.

I twirled the cigarette between my fingers like it was a cheerleading baton, faster and harder until it broke in half.

"I can tell you all about Amber . . ." I began.

"And you, I want you to tell me about you," he said pointedly, his pen poised over the yellow pad of paper.

"Don't worry, I won't leave me out of it. I couldn't even if I wanted to . . ."

TAKE ONE:
THE GOOD WOMAN

CHAPTER ONE

It started with a splatter. If this were a scene in a classic film noir, the audience would see the tall willowy brunette was shot in the chest. The red ooze on her breast would have been less lurid in black and white, but the dark circle spreading fast on her pale dress would have gotten the point across *tout de suite*. There were certainly enough gasps from the crowd to alert the entire room that something terrible had happened.

Fortunately, the splatter was no gunshot. The thick ooze had hit like a bullet all right, but it was a chopped-beet-and-baked-goat-cheese-topped potato crisp that did the damage. I was the tall willowy brunette, and it was my new dress that took the hit. This is routinely how things worked out in the life of Clara Bishop. I was the girl who never saw the banana peel until I was flat on the ground. Sure, I loved film noir, but back then, if someone had asked me to compare my life to a movie genre, I would have told them screwball comedy.

Take the first meeting I had with an agent. I was a freshly minted screenwriting graduate from USC with a pile of scripts ready to take on Hollywood. The agent was Howard Katz. By reputation, he made Ari Gold on *Entourage* seem like a puppy lying on its back for a belly rub. I was lucky he was willing to meet me. He'd heard about one of my scripts from a colleague who had taught a semester. I arrived fifteen minutes early, and not wanting to appear too eager, I waited in the lobby. I should have killed time walking around the block instead of standing there like a target, because then that girl from film school wouldn't have seen me. But she did see me and hopped over with a big grin on her face like we were best friends. I can't even recall her name, but she told me she had gotten a job as a temp at the agency for the summer. I felt proud that, unlike her, I was potentially a client, not a receptionist. It was to be a fleeting feeling. I noticed that in her hand was a banana. It had been frozen and dipped in white chocolate and she sucked on it like it was, well, it wasn't something that should be done publicly, but you get the idea.

"Clara! So nice to see you!" she cheered.

"I'm having a meeting with Howard Katz," I announced.

"He's tough," she warned between sucking sounds. Then her phone rang. "It's my boss. Can you hold this while I scribble down his lunch order?"

What choice did I have? I took the banana, which had the tip bitten off, and stood there as she sidestepped away from me to take her call. That's when he came by. How he recognized me I couldn't say. With my mousy brown hair, jeans and Converse sneakers, I usually blend into the crowd. I blame the banana.

"Are you waiting to see me?" Howard Katz boomed at me, his eyes glowering at the offending frozen fruit.

"Yes." I gulped.

"You're Clara Bishop?" he asked, not quite believing.

"Yes." I gulped again. "I'm early."

He looked me up and down, judging every inch of me. I could see in his eyes that I was just a tall, skinny brunette with a frozen phallus on a stick, not the next big thing in screenwriting. He automatically offered his hand, and I automatically shook it. Only by then the chocolate had begun to melt, and a white sticky mess was dripping down my right hand and consequently covered his palm in the melted ooze. "Oh my God! I'm so sorry!" I said, horrified. "I can get you a paper towel from the restroom."

"Don't bother. I'll take care of it." He stared down at his hand and swallowed, completely revolted. "Come up when you're finished with that *thing*." He then walked quickly away, holding his right arm as far from his body as he could. Finally, whatever-her-name-was came back.

"Ooh, thanks for holding my banana!" she cooed.

The meeting was a disaster. It was impossible to recover. He didn't sign me.

After that, my screenwriting career went nowhere. For a few years, I worked several crew jobs on independent films. I kept meeting reporters and crews that showed up on set for celebrity magazines and entertainment television shows, and I gave one of the journalists an idea for a regular behind-the-scenes feature, and the reporter said he'd talk to his editor. He did. I got the assignment and haven't looked back. Seeing my name in print was addictive at first. Now, a decade later, I was over the celebrity-reporting thing, having grown tired of chasing famous people around for a living and not creating something original. I kept trying to write scripts in my spare time, but I never finished anything. So without a handful of screenplays, or at the very least a *great idea* for one, to the entertainment industry I was just a gossip writer.

Which brings me back to the party and my ruined dress. I locked eyes with the waitress. She wore an expression that I was sure was horrified embarrassment. I knew it wasn't her fault entirely. I had been racing to the exit, anxious to get the hell out of there, when out of nowhere the canapé hit me. Navigating through a packed room balancing trays full of hors d'oeuvres can't be easy, though it seemed strange that only one managed to fly off the tray, but no matter. The waitress—a tanned, blonde, blue-eyed goddess with cheekbones so sharp you could hang a mink coat on them—looked no older than twenty.

"Don't worry about it," I said and smiled warmly to reassure her that I wasn't a high-maintenance movie mogul's wife. Then the party guests circled and began tossing out home remedies to try.

"Sprinkle baby powder on it," one suggested.

"Salt and club soda," offered another.

Instead of making for the exit, I wound up in the ladies room with my dress soaked in club soda and splattered with baby powder, like some deranged Jackson Pollack knock-off. But I never saw that waitress again. It wouldn't be until much later, reliving the moment over and over, that I realized she never apologized. And when I remember that look on her face, I recall now that it wasn't horror or embarrassment. It was satisfaction.

How I regretted my polite "don't worry." I should have punched her in the face.

Thirty Minutes Earlier

I slunk into the party feeling uncomfortable for several reasons. The first was the pale pink dress I'd bought. I'm not much for showing leg; I'm mainly a jeans type of girl. I probably have close to fifty pairs, which I wear either with sneakers or knee-high boots if I need a confidence boost, which brings up reason number two that I was uncomfortable: high heels. But my friend Sylvia insisted the dress needed heels. It was all about impact, making an entrance, owning the room and all those sorts of things women who weren't me seemed to do effortlessly. But despite my best attempt, I was more Molly Ringwald than Megan Fox, for here I was standing in the middle of a room having made an effort and no one noticed. Least of all Dean. I'd had a crush on him since university, when crushes were appropriate. Now that I was thirty-five, I still swooned when I saw him, though it was more controlled. Dean was right over there, within eyeshot, and I swore he looked right at me once, but he might as well have been across the room or even across the country for all the attention I got. I was about to shove my chin up and walk over to him like the life of the party with a bit of hip action here, a bit of hair tossing there, except as I began to approach, he turned his back to me to speak to another guest. Instead of a swagger, I began to stagger on my four-inch heels, from nerves at first, then a loss of balance. It wasn't good. I needed to sit down. I told myself I would connect with Dean soon enough. After all, we had a lifetime of connecting ahead of us. I knew this because Dean was my husband. This was his wrap party.

My husband's a reality television producer who, like most men in Hollywood in his position, would rather be directing films. But he got his big break, if you could call it that, as a producer's assistant on a show that pitted dwarfs against giants in a race to find a pot of gold out in the desert. I wish I were making that up.

Disappointed my unexpected appearance at the party didn't get better results, I headed to the food. The craft table was stacked with the expected variety of snacks from the humble carrot stick to classier fare like beef sliders topped with foie gras. If no one bothered to talk to me, at least I wouldn't go home hungry. I normally avoided wrap parties. If you didn't work on the production, then you were seen as an outsider at best, or at worst, a groupie. Dean preferred me to stay home on nights like this, too. He said he had to focus on the guests, particularly if there were television network honchos in the mix, or if he was really lucky, a movie studio executive or two whom Dean would want to schmooze in the hope he could at last escape the reality television racket. But tonight was different. It had the whiff of a going-away party attached to it, and I had taken a risk that he would be happy to see me.

"Are you Clara?"

I was midway through a beef slider when I heard my name. I turned around and found myself face to face with Kiki, the "break-out star" of Dean's latest hit. Her looks were what tabloid reporters referred to as "plastic fantastic." Her skin was plump from strategically placed filler, and if I wasn't mistaken, she had cheek and breast implants. I wondered if she got a two-for-one special. Her eyes were large, almost Kewpie-like, and she had a sweep of platinum hair that Gwen Stefani would envy. Kiki was the poster girl for reality TV: a standard-issue blonde with big assets and a mouth willing to say and do anything.

"Yes, I'm Clara."

Kiki giggled but her face barely moved. Botox *and* filler, then. I bit into the slider.

"Clara Bishop who writes for *Hollywood Hush?*"

I swallowed. I had no idea how she recognized me, but I didn't have to wait long for an answer.

"They ran your photo a few times when you were doing Emmy picks," she explained. I nodded but said nothing, because her interest in me meant one thing. I was a celebrity journalist at a top weekly glossy that could make or break a star, or at least extend the run after a series finale, and it wasn't unusual for D-list celebrities to ask for my help. Some even tried bribing me. I never took bribes; never slept with a source either, but I was happily married. That didn't stop reality contestants. Even the girls. Oh Lord, maybe Kiki was a lesbian. It wouldn't be the first. Clearly Kiki wanted me to write about her.

"I want to ask you a favour," Kiki purred, flashing her Chiclet teeth in the process. Here it comes.

"Sure," I said cautiously. It took chutzpah to ask someone you just met for a favour.

"I'd like to buy you a coffee," she began and paused nervously.

Cripes, maybe this was a come-on. "I'd like to pick your brain because I've always wanted to be a writer like you."

This floored me enough that I stopped myself snatching a second slider off the tray. I took a closer look at her. She was busting out of her dress like an escaped convict. Her platform pumps were ridiculously high, but given my own shaky gams I gave her points for balance. Her expression said fun-loving party girl, no serious thought detectable beneath the thick layer of foundation and lashes of lipstick. She looked like a writer about as much as I looked like Santa Claus.

"You write?" I asked in a tone more snooty than I intended.

"I'm a poet," Kiki enthused. I grabbed another slider and shoved it in my mouth whole. "But I want to switch to journalism."

I continued to chew on this bit of information and the slider. "That's a big switch," I said as sincerely as I could.

"I know. That's what I keep telling myself." She shook her head like she was discussing giving up an opera career at the Met. "But no one's buying poetry."

"Sadly, no one's reading it either," I interjected.

"Riiight?" she agreed in a high-pitched voice. "But I know all about how this reality thing works, and I could write inside scoops and do post-mortems and things like that."

She was no dummy. She knew the term "post-mortem." Magazines like *Hollywood Hush* loved first-person stories, as did entertainment television shows. A successful contestant could parlay their fifteen minutes of cavorting fame into a career if they were smart. And I never met a smart cookie I didn't respect.

"Sure, we can have coffee and chat about writing," I offered and smiled at Kiki for the first time. She beamed, which made me like her more. Smarts and enthusiasm got you places in this town, not to forget Kiki's plastic-fantastic attributes.

"That's awesome!" she hugged me. "Are you here to cover the show? I can introduce you around if you like."

I shook my head, "My husband worked on it." In these situations I preferred to be vague.

"Who is your husband?"

I hesitated as long as I could. "Dean Lapointe," I said and waited for the inevitable reaction of surprise. I was never what people expected, but Kiki gaped in a way that alarmed me. "You seemed shocked," I said flatly.

Her eyelashes fluttered like a moth trying to land on a light bulb. "I had no idea that Dean was married," she exclaimed, looking more alarmed than me.

"We have a policy of not telling people in the industry. Except for our closest friends, that is," I said politely. Liar. But what else could I say? That my husband was embarrassed that I wrote for *Hollywood Hush?* That my husband disliked wedding bands because he didn't like how his felt on his finger? Or that lately it was something more than rings he didn't like the feel of? That was enough reality for a dozen television series.

As if sensing my attempt at faking it, Kiki touched my arm, "You shouldn't worry about him."

"I wasn't," I stuttered and felt my heart race as the heels once more wobbled beneath me. Sensing my anxiety, she flushed.

"No, of course not. Why would you? He's just a man, that's all I meant. And we all know how *they* are! Riiight?"

"Riiight," I drew out the word in a perfect imitation of how she had said it, but she was gone before she could hear it.

It was time to leave. Clearly Dean didn't intend for this current crop of "stars" to know anything about me. I wondered if he *had* seen me earlier and turned his back anyway. Feeling a fool, I moved through the packed room towards the exit, past a leather sectional sofa stuffed with the men and women who had appeared on the show. The door was only a few feet away, but by then it was too late; Dean was standing in front of it like a Walmart greeter when he saw me. He was shaking hands with a man who produced a sitcom. The sitcom's star had just fallen off the wagon, and I had written an unflattering but honest story about it. This wasn't going to be pretty. Dean pasted a smile on his face, but not before I'd seen the flash of disappointment. As I walked towards him one agonizing step at a time, afraid I would topple over, I felt a desperate urge to have Kiki at my side for reinforcement. The pace was excruciating, as though the world had become a slow-motion film.

"You didn't tell me you were coming tonight," Dean said without warmth. "You know my wife, Clara?" He knew full well the producer knew who I was. I was never certain if Dean thought these types of awkward moments were funny or fodder for his next reality show idea: pitting a celebrity journalist and a furious star against each other, fight to the death!

"Clara," the man croaked my name.

"George," I said and forced a smile.

"George was just telling me about his show." Here it comes. I braced myself. "The ratings have gone up despite the negative press," Dean said, making it clear to George whose side he was on. I wanted to disappear.

"Yes, some stars are impervious to the *media*," George said pointedly. I wanted to point out how the *media* helped boost those ratings, but he kept talking. "So when do you go to London?" he asked Dean.

"I leave on the weekend," he answered and stood straighter, chest puffed up. "You know the Brits, they always want to push the envelope. And that's hard in reality TV."

Ah, London. Dean was flying to England to produce a new show called *Come to Daddy*, which brought reality TV to new heights of low. The premise was this: a houseful of buxom beauties vie for the attention of a super-rich sugar daddy who is at least forty years older than all of them. Dean insisted it was a stepping stone in his quest to direct films. Just how that worked was a mystery to me, but it paid the bills.

"They've come to the right man," George said and thumped him on the back.

"I'll be gone at least six weeks. They're putting me up in a suite at The Savoy, so I'm going to be well taken care of," Dean continued.

George turned to me and looked as if he might choke when he said, "You're going to miss your wife." Dean nodded slightly.

I had a secret. I'd bought a plane ticket to London to surprise Dean. Armed with romantic visions of moonlit walks along the Thames, inspiring nights at the theatre and afternoons spent in galleries when he wasn't shooting, he would find me irresistible all over again. Time away was all we needed. But there was another reason to go; I wanted to get pregnant. I had a miscarriage when we were first married; in fact, the pregnancy was why we got married. Not that we're old-fashioned, but we were both from broken homes and so it just felt right. Besides, I was crazy about Dean. So I was devastated when early in the second trimester it was all over. I'd never felt such loss before, never felt so incomplete. Dean was distraught too. We decided to postpone trying again until our careers were more established. I'd agreed, in part because emotionally I couldn't handle losing another baby. And at the time, I still held the ambition of being a working screenwriter, not a celebrity writer. Nearly six years had passed, and at thirty-five I didn't want to wait anymore, but all attempts had failed and my period still arrived jarring and unwelcome like an alarm clock that's been set too early.

Dean wasn't convinced that we should have a baby until he'd directed his first film. It seemed like an excuse, a reason to say no, which made me lie awake at night wondering if I hadn't gotten pregnant the first time would the man I loved be lying in bed with me. Of course, as a writer I had a vivid imagination and that wasn't always helpful. Dean was still my husband, no need to be paranoid.

But as I stood there in the midst of a party celebrating his latest achievement, it didn't seem to matter that Dean wasn't thrilled to see me. Once I became pregnant it would be different. He would be a proud father and he would realize what he had: a wife who adored him and would give him everything he wanted. I smiled and touched my husband's arm. He looked down at my hand on his sleeve and went back to talking to George. What Dean didn't know was that tonight was prime time for making a baby. Tonight would be perfect, and if not tonight, then we had six weeks in London to make it happen. Then we would be happy.

CHAPTER TWO

After the Party

I kissed Dean as soon as we entered our apartment. Gently at first. He hated it if I was "aggressive." He took my hand and led me to the bedroom. We kissed some more and I waited, limp in his arms, for him to make the next move: a hand on my breast maybe, or a nibble on my neck. Dean was restrained as usual, his arms at his sides like a tin soldier, but I kept kissing him until I could almost see the passion seep out like liquid mercury.

I didn't give up. I lifted my stained dress over my head and threw it to the floor. I kicked off those damn heels so I was a few inches shorter than him. Little, unthreatening me.

"I love you," I whispered in the hope he'd take the cue.

When he didn't respond, I glided to the bed and removed my bra and underwear. Dean undressed too. I climbed beneath the covers and he slid in next to me, my hand once more lightly touching him, only this time, the layer of protective denim gone, he swivelled his hips away, pecked me on the cheek and smiled.

"I'm wiped out," he said breezily, as if we'd come back from a hike with flushed cheeks and cold hands.

"I think we have enough energy for one more thing . . ." and I kissed him again. This time his lips didn't part.

"Clara, I'm tired," he said firmly.

"Is it me?" I asked, just as I had done many times over the past year and always with the same result.

"Don't make me feel bad about this. I'm just not in the mood. Is that okay?" He pouted at me like a child.

"Of course it is," I said with forced warmth. "I just miss you."

"I'm right here," he said, sounding relieved, as though excused from the dinner table after refusing to eat his broccoli. Then Dean rolled over and went to sleep. I lay on my back and stared at the ceiling. I felt the tears run down my face and I didn't wipe them away. Part of me wanted Dean to see me cry and feel bad or guilty, anything but indifferent. But I knew that wouldn't happen. I was playing to an audience of one: me.

The Morning After

This was what being left by your husband looked like: him standing at the foot of the marriage bed. You sitting up naked—the sheet pulled up to your chin like a deflector shield. In his hand a packed duffel bag, and a set of keys discarded on the duvet.

This was what being left by your husband felt like: an ambush.

"I love you, I'm just not in love with you," Dean explained with a note of pity in his voice. "It hasn't been good between us in a long time. You can't really be shocked, Clara."

"But I am shocked!" I cried. I couldn't bring myself to admit I knew he wasn't happy. "I believed you when you said you were just tired all the time. I didn't realize you meant you were tired of me." I grabbed my robe and leapt out of bed and threw my arms around him. "We'll be better. You have to try, Dean. You *do* love me. *You* know you love me." The words sounded hollow even to me. He didn't move a muscle; he just stood there allowing me to grasp the last breath of us before he gently pried my arms away.

"I'm sorry, Clara. It's not you, it's me."

"You're leaving me and all you can say is a cliché?" I retorted dryly.

"Your writer's criticism never leaves you, does it?" he snapped. That got me.

"What are you talking about?"

"You're always so sharp and clever when it comes to words, especially mine or my work for that matter."

"That's not true! I've always supported you. You know I think you're talented."

"You look down on what I do," he said accusingly. "You don't think it hurts me when you write about how bad reality TV is?"

I was taken aback. "I always showed you those articles before they ran. And besides, I've been off the reality TV beat for ages and you know it," I said weakly. "What's this really about? Surely you're not leaving our marriage because I don't like *The Bachelor*."

"I'm leaving because I need more."

At first I didn't say anything. What more could I have given Dean? My marriage was my proudest accomplishment, and I gave more than I got but never complained. I felt my eyes well up and prayed that when the tears fell it would be in a single dramatic stream down my face like you see in movies, the kind of tears that somehow makes the actress even more beautiful. No such luck. The tears flooded down my cheeks in uncontrollable torrents as words sobbed out of my mouth incoherently. "More than a wife who adores you? Who thinks you're talented and believes in you?" I stuttered. "What about our baby?"

Dean flinched. "We don't have a baby."

"But we were trying! You wanted to have a baby with me," I moaned, aware that my nose was running too. I grabbed a tissue from the nightstand. "You were so happy when I was pregnant the first time!"

"Let's not bring that up again," he said coldly.

The blood was pumping through me so hard that my ears were pounding. I wanted to say what I'd always feared and suspected . . . that he only married me because I was pregnant, but despite my reporter skills of being able to pull the truth from others, some truths were better left unspoken. This was one of them. I began to tremble and clutched the robe tighter around me. Then I remembered Kiki's words last night. *"He's just a man . . ."* What had she been trying to say? That Dean had cheated on me?

"Is there someone else?" I asked. "I know the rumour." I lied about the rumour, but what Kiki let slip was close enough.

"What rumour?" he said in a panicked voice.

"You forget what business I'm in," I said, making myself sound more in control than I was. "I hear things."

A very long pause filled the room, and I felt my stomach churn like rancid butter. He ran his fingers through his hair and then he said it.

"I didn't mean for it to happen," he spoke clearly, defiantly, as though it was me who had done something wrong. "But it did happen."

No wife wants to be right about this sort of thing. Suddenly, the tears stopped, as if my insides were flash-frozen.

"Who is she?" I managed to squeak out.

"It's none of your business."

"Who is she?" I repeated. "I deserve that much after all we've been through together."

"She's just a girl I met at a bar."

My jaw tightened.

"What do you mean some girl at a bar?"

"She's a waitress."

"A waitress? You're leaving me for a waitress?" I realized how snobby that sounded, but I didn't care. If he told me he left me for a successful producer or a movie star it wouldn't have lessened the pain, but I could say he left me because I was only a tabloid reporter.

"She may not be a movie star," he said as though reading my mind. "But she cares about me."

"Do you love her?" I asked, my lip quivering.

"I don't want to hurt you more than I'm doing. Do you think it's easy leaving you? I know how much you love me."

That stung—the one-sidedness of it all. "How much *I* love you? You never loved me, did you?"

"I did love you, Clara. But what we had is gone. I always felt that our marriage was a mistake. I'll go to London, and it will give you time to get your head around a divorce. It's better this way."

I heard him speak but I wasn't listening. I wanted one answer. "Do you love her?" I repeated.

He exhaled deeply. "Yes."

Then the tears returned. This time more slowly, perhaps there was only one stream, but I doubted it made me beautiful.

"What's her name?" I asked him.

"Not that it makes any difference, but her name is Amber. Amber Ward."

Amber? A reality show name if ever there was one. The irony! If my life wasn't so pathetic it would be amusing. Dean stepped towards the door. It was my last chance.

"I love you! Don't go, Dean. Stay," I pleaded. "We can work through this. Let's go to counselling or take a vacation. We've haven't been away in ages." I paused, not wanting to reveal that I'd bought a ticket to London.

"It's too late," answered Dean flatly without looking me in the eye. I gazed at him longingly, taking him in for the last time. He was wearing a khaki linen shirt and faded black jeans. We bought that shirt together on a trip to San Francisco last winter.

But I wouldn't be buying shirts with him anymore. He cleared his throat, pulling me back to earth or hell, I wasn't sure which. "Our marriage is over," he touched my cheek with his hand, and I closed my eyes longingly. "I'm not coming back."

Then he left. I listened to the door click shut. It was hell.

Police Station—Cirencester

There was only one window in the room, and I was looking out of it. It had begun to rain, and on the street below people were scattering for shelter in shops and office towers or running for a bus that was idling at a traffic light. I heard Sergeant Hooper shuffle the loose pieces of yellow paper ripped from the pad. He had filled them with my words.

"So you see, I know Amber Ward. But she's no friend."

"Indeed," he said. "If you don't mind my saying so, your husband sounds like a complete bastard."

This made me smile.

"How on earth did you end up with a bloke like that? I know you said you were pregnant, but surely shotgun weddings are a thing of the past? Especially in America, I think?"

I stopped smiling and walked slowly along the length of the room, running my hand gently across the cinder-block wall. I stopped when I reached the next corner, turned and faced Hooper.

"I always wanted a family of my own. I was almost thirty and wanted to have a child sooner than later. I wanted several children in fact. I'm an only child myself, you see. And my own family history is, well, complicated. I was hoping to avoid repeating the mistakes of my mother and grandmother. I

thought Dean was the answer. And, as I explained, I was in love with him. Crazy about him, really. You don't know Dean, the effect he has on women. He's dashing in that dark, brooding, artistic way; he has a rock-star quality to him. Remember what I said about my life being a screwball comedy? He found me funny. Men don't often like funny girls."

I waited for a reaction; Hooper shrugged. "Besides, I didn't exactly have a lineup of men outside my door. Dean paid attention to me."

"Hard to believe you didn't have a lineup of men, seeing you in that gold slip dress." He smiled kindly.

"I've changed a little." I leaned against the wall; my neck was sore so I rubbed it with my hand. "Why does anyone love anyone?" I continued. "Who can explain every attraction? Women fall in love with the wrong men all the time. And men fall in love with the wrong women just as often."

He nodded as though it was the wisest thing he'd ever heard. "I've been known to fall head over heels for girls who think I make good money or who like the uniform. They never stick around once they learn the truth or they get tired of the outfit. Been cheated on a fair bit myself."

I walked back to the desk and sat down again. "Then you understand." I ran my fingers through my hair; the soft waves tumbled down my back and shoulders. I reached into the pocket of the trench coat and pulled out another cigarette to play with. Hooper picked up his pen once more, then flipped through the pages.

"One more thing. You do realize this is an official statement. You said at the beginning you are a screenwriter. You just said you are a celebrity journalist. Which is it?"

I examined the cigarette in my hand and without looking away said, "I'm a screenwriter. Like I told you, I was a screenwriter in the beginning, then I became a celebrity reporter. I'm a screenwriter again. That clarify things?"

"Not entirely. But continue, Miss Bishop. Tell me what happened next . . ."

— CHAPTER THREE —

I spent the morning with my heart hanging by a thread and tried to recall how I'd dealt with being dumped in the past. The last man to kick me to the curb was a guy named Ralph. It was my sophomore year at college, and he was a visual art major who felt that my screenwriting program was a joke and that filmmaking was a commodity, unlike his performance art videos, and that made us incompatible. Ralph seemed a lifetime ago and he was ridiculous. I remember crying once, mostly because I thought I had to, and only once. This was different. This felt like drowning in icy water, trapped beneath the surface as Dean walked away leaving me to die.

In novels and films a broken heart always seems glamorous: the woman takes to her bed for days as friends and family gather around and bring her food, which she ignores. Unable to sleep at night, she walks along hallways or dimly lit streets or damp fields bathed in fog and weeps softly in a trance. I tried to live up to the image that first morning, treading the plank wood floors, stepping out onto the balcony like a forsaken Juliet. But in Los Angeles, there was no dim street lighting or fog to disappear into. Here the sun was inescapable, beaming shards of brightness into every shadow and crevice, including the ones on a forlorn face, illuminating eyes red and swollen. Los Angeles may be a city built on creating scenes of great romantic tragedy, but it was all make-believe. Dreams came here to die, discarded like used wrapping from a fast-food joint. Surrounded by so many broken dreams, sympathy could be as tough to find as a snowdrift. My only hope was that the desert heat would bake my heart until it was so hard it could never break again.

I collapsed on the sofa and thought about the half-empty bottle of vodka in the freezer. It was only nine thirty, but wasn't getting drunk in the morning one of life's great remedies? Before the vodka could touch my lips my cell phone rang, and I answered because it was Sylvia, she of the high-heel mantra, my closest friend in LA and a staff photographer with *Hollywood Hush*.

"How are you on this fine morning?" she asked breezily.

"Dean left me," I said and burst into tears.

"Oh my God," she said. "Are you okay? Of course you're not."

By the time Sylvia arrived, I had managed to get dressed. I left the vodka out on the counter for effect.

"You look terrible," she said.

"Thanks."

"Sorry. But you're wearing two different socks, and your T-shirt is ten times too big and has a giant stain on it."

I looked down at my feet, a red one and a grey one, and shrugged. The T-shirt was Dean's, one of the few he left. It still smelled like him.

"You smell like stale beer," she added. I sniffed the T-shirt: Dean and beer. I grabbed the vodka and flopped on the sofa.

"Are you drunk?"

"Not yet."

She flopped down beside me. "What happened exactly?"

I told her exactly, and when I was done, I took a swig of the vodka straight out of the bottle and began to cough.

"Easy there, Clara. You're not a big drinker at the best of times."

"This is the worst of times," I said and waited for her to agree.

Sylvia was silent, which annoyed me.

"What does Marjorie say?" Sylvia asked. Marjorie is my mother, and she was a minor celebrity among my friends. Marjorie insisted everyone, including her only child, use her Christian name. Marjorie was excellent at giving advice, and many times over the years my friends would drive to her house on Camrose Drive in the Holly-wood Hills for one of her famous chicken-pot-pie chats. Sort of like Roosevelt's fireside chats during the Depression, only hers included wine and dessert along with the wisdom. When it came to me, how-ever, my mother's advice burned like scalding-hot water.

"I haven't told her yet." My confession was met with widened eyes and a slack jaw.

"Why not? She lives for this type of drama!" Sylvia pointed out. "She was awesome when I ended that threesome last Fourth of July. She never judges."

"She doesn't judge you," I explained. "You're not her daughter. Wait until she hears that Dean left me for a waitress!"

"Are you sure she's just a waitress?" Sylvia asked. "She could be a med student."

I shot her a death-ray glare and she swallowed.

"He said she was a waitress, and that probably means she's an actress," I said, and then a horrible yet inevitable realization sank in. "In which case Marjorie wouldn't blame him."

"That's not true!"

"You know how she feels about my career," I argued. To Marjorie it would make sense that a producer/director like Dean would want to be with a starlet and not some hack reporter. I could hear her now: "If your screenwriting had taken off, then that would be different. You'd be in show business like he is, not merely writing about it . . ."

"She'd never say such a thing," Sylvia said as though reading my mind. "She loves you."

I shrugged. Sure my mother loved me, in her way. I supposed Dean had too, in his way. When was I going to be loved in my way?

"We were happy. I don't get it," I said.

Sylvia reverted back to silence. I knew she was hesitating.

"Say it, Sylvia," I coaxed warily.

She sniffed as if what she had to say reeked like rotting fish. Then with a toss of her hair she announced, "You and Dean should never have married. You were his favourite booty call because he knew you'd always say yes. But he was never husband material. You loved him far more than he ever loved you. Sorry, but I must be honest."

"He's just not that into me?" I quoted the title of that inane self-help book. "He did love me. We were great together, all the movie marathons we watched, shared jokes, shared dreams." As I listed the things that made Dean and me a perfect match she shook her head.

"You should have kept it at friends with benefits."

"Why are you being so blunt?" I snapped. "We had a lot of great times together once we were married. After I lost the baby he was wonderful to me, and tender and caring."

"He did take care of you, I'll give him that. Least he could do. But before you got pregnant and married him, he strung you along for years. From what you've told me, he was doing it ever since you met him in film school."

I thought back to film school. I was going to be an Oscar-winning screenwriter and he was going to be an Oscar-worthy auteur. I'd harboured my crush in silence during the first two years of university, until fate—and a student film production—threw us together.

"I'm Clara Bishop." I remembered trying to sound like a seasoned pro, which was ridiculous since we were barely out of our teens and had never worked on a real film. I knew my hand was shaking when he shook it, and worse, my palms were sweaty and he noticed.

"You must get your computer keyboard wet with hands like that," he said, then beamed his trademark smile on me. I remember feeling faint, part swooning, part humiliation.

"I'm hot," I explained stupidly and felt my face flush at what the words implied.

"I'll be the judge of that," he said and winked at me.

I wasn't "hot." If anything, I was what can best be described as "handsome." I looked like my father, complete with mousy brown hair and strong jaw. My best features are my legs, apparently, and my green eyes. I also had the good fortune to inherit the maternal side of the family's bee stung pout.

Sylvia kept talking. "You can talk a good game and write an even better one when you're working on a story. There's a reason *Hollywood Hush* loves you so much. You're a smart and funny girl, Clara. But around Dean, you become this worshipping, treacly mess. You're his biggest fan, but you aren't his partner."

I slugged the vodka again. The stinging in my throat kept me from crying. "I am his biggest fan," I said flatly. "But you're wrong. I am also his partner. We will get back together. This Amber girl is a fling."

She nodded. From her expression, it appeared she knew she'd said enough.

"I just want him back," I said miserably.

"Do you want me to go alone?" she asked. I tilted my head like a dog trying to decipher a command.

"Go where?"

"It's Saturday. We have the kids."

My eyes widened, which hurt because they were swollen. We volunteered at a weekend filmmaking program for underprivileged children. It was fun seeing what the kids came up with, and I loved spending time with them. The students varied in age from seven to twelve, before puberty turned them into cynical teenagers who knew everything.

"Well? The kids will be hurt. Today they screen their finished videos." She needn't have bothered with the guilt trip. I would never hurt a child. And being the reliable and predictable Clara Bishop, I wasn't going to be a no-show.

═ CHAPTER FOUR ═

The next three hours were spent surrounded by children's laughter. It was a tonic. They adored us because we showed them movies their parents hadn't even heard of. It was like we were part of a secret society. Plus they got to show off by playing parts in one another's short films. The parents adored us because their children went home exhausted but happy. Sylvia and I had been doing this for three years now and had even begun to raise money to expand the program to other districts in Los Angeles.

This morning we were watching final cuts of their latest assignment, which was to recreate a scene from one of the movies they'd watched in the program, and they ran the gamut from *It's a Wonderful Life* and *Mr. Smith Goes to Washington* to *The Wizard of Oz* and included loads of pets and startled siblings. Then it was my favourite student's turn—yes, I had a teacher's pet—a ten-year-old girl named Pilar who had been raised on the beauty pageant circuit. Sylvia shoved the disc into the DVD player and the video began to play on the large flat-screen television. Not surprisingly, given her skills on the pageant stage, Pilar had chosen to star in as well as direct her own movie. Her co-star was Estefan, a twelve-year-old boy with a raffish quality to him. Unlike the others, the video was in black and white, and not some child-friendly fare either. To my astonishment, it was a scene from *The Postman Always*

Rings Twice where Frank and Cora plot to kill her husband. Pilar wore a platinum-blonde wig and a very pretty white dress, and Estefan was in a beat-up leather jacket. The musical score was eerie and dramatic but it wasn't from the original. It had a decidedly Latin flair to it.

"I'm not what you think I am, Frank. I want to work and be something, that's all. But you can't do it without love. Do you know that, Frank? Anyway, a woman can't," Pilar pleaded, speaking the lines like she was twice her age. "Well, I've made one mistake. And I've got to be a hell cat, just once, to fix it. But I'm not really a hell cat, Frank."

"They hang you for a thing like that," Estefan said in a monotone. He didn't have Pilar's gift for melodrama, but since he really wanted to be a cinematographer when he grew up, it didn't matter much.

"Not if you do it right," Pilar's Cora said haughtily.

That's where it ended. Sylvia tried to contain her laughter. I elbowed her in the ribs, but in truth I was a little horrified and was worried that her parents would be descending on the centre at any moment to have us arrested.

"My God, Pilar! What on earth made you pick that scene?" I asked. She looked puzzled.

"You did," she answered. "You said it was one of your favourite movies and now it's one of mine. I love Lana Turner's hair colour."

Sylvia didn't even try not to laugh. "She's right, Clara."

"I used my dad's book and copied the dialogue from there," she said proudly.

"Pilar, your parents aren't going to be happy," I said worriedly.

Pilar shook her head. "My father picked the music."

"Your parents have seen it?" Sylvia asked.

Pilar nodded proudly. "They said it should get me a scholarship."

"It's better than a life of *Toddlers and Tiaras*," I said to Sylvia as we drove back to the apartment. I couldn't stop thinking of the dialogue

that Pilar had chosen. It could have come from my lips. I wanted
to work and be something. And I agreed with Cora that a woman
needed love to do it. Like Cora, I'd made a mistake. I didn't give Dean
what he needed and now I'd lost him. Only I doubted there was a hell
cat inside me to fix it, and I hated that about myself.

"I wish I could be a hell cat," I said to Sylvia. We'd parked the car
and were walking to the apartment. She looked at me blankly. "Like
Cora in *Postman*," I reminded her.

She furrowed her brows. "You want to kill Dean?"

"That's not what I mean. What you said earlier, about me being a
treacly mess."

She stopped at my door and waited for me to fumble about for the
key. "I shouldn't have said that. I'm sorry."

"But you're right. My whole life comes down to my inability to
fight for anything or anyone. I just let the world have their go at me
and lie down at the end of it. I'm a coward, Sylvia. And the key to
happiness is fearlessness. No wonder Dean left me."

"You really are a writer, aren't you? Save some of that dialogue for
your next script."

Inside the apartment I tossed the keys and made for the vodka. "If
only there was a next script!" I sat down on the sofa exactly as I'd done
hours before and took a giant gulp of the stuff. "I haven't written a
line of dialogue in years."

"Well, now that you're single you have time," Sylvia said, then
seeing the hurt expression on my face, quickly added, "I was teasing.
But maybe you should write about Dean."

I shook my head. "Not until I know how it ends. And trust me,
I'm going to make sure it's an old-fashioned rom-com with a happy
ending."

"Considering your family's past maybe you should stick to film
noir."

It was true; I came from a family with close connections to the shadowy world of noir. More of a visual style than an actual genre, the stark black and white lighting, fog, shadows, the snappy dialogue and the costumes were spellbinding. The stories were dark, paranoid almost, always containing a crime or a double-cross or both, and the leading men were detectives mostly but sometimes a cop or more routine things like an insurance agent. They always had a bad girl in them too: the femme fatale. She was tough-talking and morally ambiguous, but you always got the feeling that she was hiding or running from past hurt. Amazingly, even the smartest guy fell for her and would do anything to keep her: rob banks, steal jewels, even murder. She was irresistible.

My mother and I were addicted to these films and spent hours watching and rewatching the classics and the obscure. But of particular fascination for us was the 1947 film noir *He Gave No Answer*. It was special because it was the only movie that my grandmother, Alice Dawson, stage name Alicia Steele, was in. She played the other female film noir archetype: the good woman role, the nice girl that the brooding hero knows would make him happy only he can't tear himself away from the femme fatale and ends up paying for it big time. It was supposed to be Alice's/Alicia's star-making turn, but it was her last because she got pregnant with my mother and ended up working full-time as a seamstress in the wardrobe department and never walked in front of a film camera again. She died when my mother was five years old. I think because of that my mother was obsessed with Alice. I think it was the sole reason she tried to become an actress, at least in the beginning.

Yet despite wanting to surpass Alice's one-film-wonder legacy, my mother's acting career was even less successful. She had to make due with walk-on parts and extra work before she met my dad and then decided she would raise a great actress rather than become one. Such is the fate of a single child like me.

As a little girl, I felt all her hopes and dreams of becoming a star foisted on me. She tried in vain to get me into ladylike dresses and curl my hair, but it was no use. An inner bombshell wasn't struggling to come out. When I emerged from my adolescent cocoon, I was the same tomboy with dull hair and square features, only taller and with firmer opinions. But the lack of interest in my appearance wasn't the main reason I was a disappointment to my mother. I never wanted to be an actress. I skipped the acting classes she signed me up for as a teenager. I didn't like being in front of a camera. I didn't wear makeup. This was a bone of contention between us. My saving grace was that I chose to become a screenwriter. At least I was in the "family business." She still asks me how my writing is going. I refuse to answer because it isn't going anywhere.

"Like I said, I'm no hell cat. I doubt I can write a noir script any more than I could write a rom-com. I should stick to what I'm good at: penning detailed accounts of what Justin Bieber had for breakfast."

She grunted. "So you're not a hell cat. What woman is these days? Is this Amber girl one?"

"Don't give her that much credit!" I snapped.

"Just asking. Who is she, then?"

I shrugged and drank more vodka. Sylvia got busy on her iPad and it didn't take long for her to find what she was looking for. She held the tablet up for me to see. It was a Facebook page belonging to a girl who was young and blonde and gorgeous.

"Clara Bishop meet Amber Ward," Sylvia said darkly.

I cringed. "Why did you have to show me that?"

"You need to know who the enemy is," she said and scanned Amber's photo album. "Even if she's not a hell cat. Christ, she's only twenty-one!"

"Are you serious?" I asked. It made my mood sink further.

"Typical twenty-one-year-old too, loads of drunken and practically naked shots of herself. Looks like she's in Vegas."

"Vegas?" I asked. "Dean was in Vegas last week. He said he went with Jerome."

"Yup, he did," Sylvia said, trying not to sound alarmist. "There's a shot of Jerome here with Dean . . . and Amber."

"What?" I howled and grabbed the iPad. Sure enough, there was my husband with his arms around a scantily clad Amber, his friend and our best man, Jerome, on the other side. Then I couldn't stop. I kept looking at photo after photo of this blonde girl, smiling, cavorting and partying, with my husband and a slew of others. Mostly there were images of her doing shots with her friends, other nubile girls with bare midriffs and big hair. And yet there was something about her . . .

"She looks familiar," I said.

"Do you know her?" Sylvia asked incredulously.

"No, but I've definitely seen her," I said, scowling in concentration, trying to remember. I continued to flip through her Facebook photos and stopped at one of Amber in a tight little black dress with a tray of drinks in her hands. Then it hit me.

"Oh my God," I drew out the words slowly. "I have seen her."

"Where?"

"She was there last night."

"What? How?" Sylvia asked, horrified.

Like in a time machine, I was back at the wrap party, walking through the crowd, when that nasty little appetizer came from nowhere and hit me. "She was a waitress from the catering company."

"Holy shit!" Sylvia gasped.

"She was the one who dumped that beet thing on me. No wonder she looked so smug." I placed my fingers on the iPad and expanded the photo of Amber so that her face filled the screen. There was no doubt. "She didn't even apologize."

"I can't believe it. Did Dean know she was there?" Sylvia asked.

"He must have," I admitted. "No wonder he didn't want me to come to the party."

"That motherfucker!" she snapped.

I was reeling from the thought of Dean's mistress being there, watching me and throwing food at me, all the while I didn't know who she was. He had given her the advantage. Then I remembered Kiki.

"Kiki knows something," I said.

"Kiki? The girl who won the show?" Sylvia asked.

"Yes. I'm going to send her a text." I relayed to Sylvia what Kiki had told me at the party. Within minutes my iPhone bleeped. It was Kiki willing to spill it to me over a cocktail.

"Where you meeting her?" Sylvia asked as I scrambled to my feet.

"Where dreams come true," I said flatly. "Hollywood."

CHAPTER FIVE

It was November and the temperature in Los Angeles skipped around like schoolgirls playing double-dutch. I grabbed a navy cardigan in case I needed it. The drive from Santa Monica, where I lived, to Hollywood, where I was meeting Kiki, was thirty to forty minutes if traffic wasn't bad. Traffic was always bad.

Dean disliked Hollywood. I loved it. All he saw was a city with grimy streets and storefronts where the scruffy hipster residents mixed it up with tourists, lower-income families and the homeless. I saw the neighbourhood I grew up in, which had all those things he hated but more; it had a hint of magic. Hipsters were artists waiting for a break. The lower-income families had kids I went to school with and hung out with at the mall or at their houses. The homeless weren't to be ignored or pitied; my mother still volunteered at the food bank, as I once did.

When I graduated from USC, I rented an apartment on North Sycamore Drive, just east of La Brea, south of Fountain. It was a dive. But Dean moved me to Santa Monica on the west side as soon as we were married. The west side was more spacious, the roads wider, the streets cleaner, even the air was fresher. For a guy from Michigan who was accustomed to lakes and forests, it was more palatable. I went along. I always did.

So it was a comfort to me to be back in my old stomping grounds. I was meeting Kiki at the Formosa Café, a ten-minute drive from Hollywood Boulevard. It was a major hangout back when movie stars wore fedoras and even the starlets chain-smoked. I liked the shumai dumplings and half-price cocktails during happy hour, but mostly I liked the old-school Hollywood atmosphere and its walls hung with photos of real stars.

Kiki was there when I arrived. I slid into the red vinyl booth beside her. Her reality television looks were in stark contrast to the dimly lit room. It was like she glowed, all bright hair and teeth, her body was spray tanned and glossy with oil and cinched into a deep purple T-shirt dress. There I was in my faded blue jeans and navy sweater and bright red Converse high-tops. I was still amazed she wanted to write. Maybe if I looked like her Dean would have stayed.

"Thanks soooo much for meeting me and soooo soon," she cooed.

"You want to know everything I know about being a journalist," I said, not wanting to waste time. "I want to know everything you know about Amber Ward."

Despite the spray tan her face went white, turning her complexion a soft shade of beige.

"Don't worry, you didn't let the cat out of the bag, at least not entirely. Dean confessed as much this morning when he walked out on me."

"Oh my God. I'm soooo sorry," she said and looked visibly shaken. "I didn't think that would happen."

I snorted a little. "What did you think would happen?"

"I'd seen them around set. I knew they flirted, and people talked."

"Set? Why was she on set?" I asked.

"She was a craft service girl on the show. Worked for the catering company."

"That explains why she was at the party," I said. Craft service is a department on a production usually staffed with pretty girls who serve food to the cast and crew. It was one of the lowliest positions on a film set, but at the same time a beacon for the tired and hungry crew. A good craft service girl was part mother hen, part psychologist and part vixen. I had my doubts that Dean's attraction to Amber was her culinary skills.

"Did they seem like they were in love?" I asked tentatively.

"I don't know. I didn't talk to Amber much. She wasn't very nice to us. Claims she's a serious actress and takes classes and all that."

That did it for me. My mother was going to have a field day with this one. "Fancies herself a starlet, does she?"

"Well, I don't think she's ever had a role in anything."

"Except husband thief," I said tartly.

"Like I told you, none of us knew he was married. Maybe she didn't either? But she really worked on Dean. Treated him like he was Steven Spielberg. She brought him an audition script and he helped her with it. But I don't think she got the part because she was still doing craft service."

Dean would have loved that. Being admired and feted by a pretty young thing who thought he was the next Scorsese. I was just the wife who picked up his socks. My compliments were routine.

"Can I get you ladies something to drink?" The waiter stood smiling at us like we were two friends out for a night of fun.

"A sidecar, please."

"Ooooh, what's that?" Kiki shrieked with joy like a kid discovering a new type of candy.

"Our family cocktail. Brandy, Cointreau and lemon juice with a sugar rim," I explained. According to Marjorie, her father, my grandfather, Lyle, had sampled one at the Playboy Club in Chicago in the 1950s and had brought the recipe home. Frank Sinatra had been a fan. Sidecars weren't easy to get, but the Formosa made a decent one.

"Make that two," Kiki said and batted her lashes at the unsuspecting waiter. She could turn it on like a switch.

"You do that well. That flirting thing," I said admiringly. "Never been much good at that."

Kiki tore at a napkin with her red lacquered nails for a bit, and when she spoke she cast her eyes down. "You have to be in this business."

Our sidecars came in a hurry. "You're on that show," the waiter gushed at Kiki. "I thought I recognized you."

Kiki blushed on cue. "I am. Did you like it?"

"I watched every episode and you were my favourite," he squealed. "Your drink is on me."

My eyes widened. Kiki flashed her eyes at me and the waiter gulped as if realizing for the first time that I was sitting there.

I decided to give the Kiki move a try and batted my lashes at him as I tilted my head and pointed my chin to the floor.

"Did you lose a contact lens?" the waiter asked and dove down on all fours.

"Oh dear! I did that once!" Kiki said as she too hit the rug. "Careful you don't crush it!"

Not daring to admit that I didn't wear contact lenses, I faked finding it myself.

"Got it!" I called out and the two of them popped back up.

"Where is it?" Kiki asked.

"I already put it back in. I'm quick. All good now. Let's have that drink!"

The waiter and Kiki exchanged looks before he dashed off.

After the third sidecar, two of which I paid for, I had told Kiki more than she ever wanted to know about Dean Lapointe and Clara Bishop. I told more than I heard, and felt my mood shift down a few notches at the thought of going home alone.

"I can't sleep without him," I said.

Kiki rummaged in her handbag and pulled out a prescription bottle. She unscrewed the cap and took out a few tiny oblong white pills and placed them in my hand.

"Take one of these tonight. It will help you sleep, calm your nerves," she said.

"What are they?"

"Lorazepam."

Half of LA took lorazepam. I'd always avoided drugs. Hated being out of control. Alcohol had always been enough feel-good buzz for me. But tonight I wanted to obliterate every ounce of heartbreak.

"Can I take all of them?"

"No!" she shrieked in mock concern. "Just one. They've gotten me through tons of messes."

Part of me wanted to know what sort of messes a girl like Kiki got into. But not a large enough part to ask, and after paying the bill I went home to the big empty marital bed, took two of the tiny white pills and passed out.

Police Station—Cirencester

Sergeant Hooper was sipping tea. He had taken one bathroom break since I began telling him the whole truth. I imagined he was bored by now, but he didn't show it.

"So you corrupt youths in your spare time? That is, when you're not taking prescription drugs?"

"You make me sound depraved," I said gravely. "I wouldn't want people to get the wrong idea."

Hooper shifted in his chair and smiled at me reassuringly. "To be honest, from what you've told me, I think you would make a very good mother at that."

"I'd like to think so."

"Too many parents are overprotective. Kids like to be imaginative. They like to be scared. I watched all those movies too when I was a little boy. Worse, my brother and I were into slasher films."

My eyes widened in mock horror. "No!" I cringed. "I can't watch those."

He laughed. "Maybe that's why I ended up a policeman. Wanted to capture all the maniacs with chainsaws and daggers."

"You get a lot of that in this part of England?" I asked.

He laughed again. "Sadly, it's mostly break-ins and car theft. Miss Bishop, without a doubt, you are the most exciting thing to walk through this station since I've been here."

I smiled and batted my lashes a few times for effect. Apparently some of my newly discovered techniques were here to stay.

"So I take it you want to hear more?" I asked softly. He nodded.

CHAPTER SIX

I didn't understand what the woman was saying. Something about a car and junk. A junk car? A junkie's car? But she wouldn't stop talking to me. I tried to tell her to shut up but it was no use.

"Clara!" the woman shouted angrily. How did she know my name? Finally, she stopped talking. Then came a loud bang from somewhere. Normally I'd be frightened by a sudden sound like that, but instead I got mad. Especially when it kept going. Louder and louder, harder and harder, until the woman's voice was back, only she sounded different. Closer.

"Clara! What the fuck did you take?"

Hands grabbed my shoulder and shook me. Now I was really mad. "Leave me alone," I barked. "Who are you?"

"It's Sylvia! For Christ's sake, what is wrong with you? Open your eyes!"

I struggled to do as I was told and a small slit opened; it was enough to know that the woman's voice did in fact belong to Sylvia. I groaned.

"I've been calling you for the last twenty minutes. I've been downstairs waiting for you in my car," she said. "You answered the phone but spoke gibberish. Good thing I know where you hide that spare key."

"What do you want?"

"That's a fine thing to say," she said. "We have a press junket in fifteen minutes that we're going to be late for. You're not even dressed!"

Oh shit. Oh crap. I struggled to sit up. "The one with You-Know-Who in it!"

"Yup. And you know how much You-Know-Who loves you."

I sat on the edge of the bed and opened my eyes. The movie star in question was a gorgeous blonde actress who did not love me. I had been one of the journalists who had broken the story about her split from her even more famous movie star husband and his equally famous dark-haired movie star lover before it was public knowledge. I guess I reminded her of that bad point in her life because our interviews have been terse ever since. So terse I'd taken to calling her "You-Know-Who" because, like Lord Voldemort, I dare not speak her name. Being late wasn't going to win points, or worse, I'd lose the interview.

"What are these?" Sylvia held the remaining lorazepam pills in her palm. "Who gave you these?"

"Kiki," I said glumly. "Didn't think it would knock me out."

"Did you drink?"

"Just three sidecars."

She whistled. "Not smart. Go on, get into the shower and fast."

We drove to the Four Seasons Hotel on Doheny in record time. Fortunately, Sylvia had a way with PR flacks and had moved our interview slot back by an hour, so when we arrived we were still technically on time. Sylvia was going to shoot You-Know-Who before our interview in case my questions irritated the star, and an irritated star never made a good portrait. At least that was how it was supposed to go.

"Clara first, photo after," the PR woman said firmly.

"But I'd like to . . ." Sylvia began, but the woman shut her down with a wave of her hand.

"She has requested interviews first. Pictures second. Come now."

I left Sylvia fuming and followed the woman down a long hallway. I began to feel sick. Really sick. I asked for water.

"I'll get you a bottle after your interview," she said snarkily.

I was led into a hotel room with a door to an adjoining suite and told to sit down. I sat all right. But I wasn't alone. There was another journalist waiting his turn as well. He was a stern-looking fellow, not much older than me, with short-cropped blond hair. He had wide-set blue eyes, and if I wasn't trying so hard to remain upright, I'd have had more time to think of how handsome he was.

"You feeling all right?" he asked me with a clipped English accent. "Your face is a rather grim shade of green."

"I'm fine." I gulped. Normally I enjoyed speaking with Englishmen; I loved the accent, but not today.

"Are you quite sure?" he persisted.

I nodded. He smiled at me then, and stood up to shake my hand. "I'm Niall Adamson from the UK. I'm covering the film premiere for the *Daily Buzz.*"

I could barely manage to lift my hand. I knew it was sweaty, like the rest of me. I told him my name. He sat down again but he obviously wanted to kill time by chatting. He waved the press kit with a large colour photo of You-Know-Who on it.

"I've never met her before, have you?"

I nodded. "You-Know-Who's friendly to the right reporter."

He looked at me sideways. "You-Know-Who?"

I grimaced and pointed to the photo. "We call her that here in LA. It's an in-joke." It was a white lie but I wasn't about to tell him the details of my not-so-friendly relationship with her. "I take it you don't live here?"

He shook his head. "London. The studio flew a few of us over."

I really was feeling worse by the minute, but hoped the small talk would distract me, so I kept chatting. "A friend of mine lives in north London. Near Tufnell Park."

Her name was Trinity Mayberry. She was an actress I met during a semester she spent at USC. She was one of my closest friends and once stayed with me for two months during pilot season, but unfortunately she never landed a role. I had yet to visit her and I was going to surprise her when I flew over to see Dean. But that was a plan two days too old.

"That's an odd coincidence because I live in the same neighbourhood. What street?"

I didn't want to give out my friend's address, so I told him I couldn't remember.

"Wonder if she's near The White Stallion. It's the local pub. What does she do?"

"She's an actress. Mostly stage. Trinity Mayberry."

A flood of recognition came across his face. "I know her. Not personally mind, but I have seen her. Does television too. Character actress."

Trinity would agree with that depiction of her career.

The PR woman came in and escorted this Niall fellow into the inner sanctum of stardom.

It was a relief to stop talking; if only the room would stop moving. The swaying began to increase. All those doctors and rehab folks were onto something with their persistent claims that alcohol and drugs don't mix.

Then, shockingly, the door to the adjoining room opened and You-Know-Who glided in like a golden panther. The PR woman and Niall must have left through the next suite. Clearly his interview was over in a flash. Probably said the wrong thing.

You-Know-Who sat down where Niall had been and fixed her feline eyes on me and forced a smile. She was always one of the polite ones. If she only knew how much we had in common now. But I was a professional and knew I had to ask about her latest romantic comedy even if the advance reviews said it stank. Only I didn't get a chance to start asking because she fired her own question at me first.

"So Dean left you for an actress, huh?"

"Excuse me?" I asked, shocked. "How did you know?"

"You think tabloid reporters are the only ones with sources? So how does it feel? Being left for another woman?"

I swallowed. "It's hell," I admitted.

"I know. And what's worse than being left for another woman?"

"What?" I was afraid of the answer.

"Being left for another woman in front of the whole world. But that's what you do, don't you? Expose people's private lives."

"You're famous. Your privacy is never really private," I answered, but it was no use.

"Let me introduce you to some people," she said and walked to the door. "They want to talk to you."

A slew of reporters scurried in, and I was suddenly surrounded by microphones and cameras all pointing at me. A flurry of voices began shouting.

"When did you first suspect your husband was cheating?"

"He says he's in love. How does that make you feel?"

"What do you think of Amber Ward's Oscar nomination?"

"What are your diet secrets?"

"Clara?"

"Clara?"

I opened my eyes but everyone had gone. I was lying on the bathroom floor in the hotel room, my arms curled around the toilet, with no idea how I'd gotten there. I looked up to see the concerned faces of the PR flack and Niall staring down at me. It was painfully obvious that I had passed out and dreamt the whole You-Know-Who scene. Blech.

"What's wrong with her?" the PR flack asked.

"Perhaps it was food poisoning," Niall offered as a polite explanation. I nodded weakly. There was apparently no end to humiliating incidents this week. Being discovered passed out in the washroom in the presence of a dashing Englishman was beyond embarrassing. Another screwball moment for Clara Bishop. At least I hadn't thrown up.

"Well, she can't do the interview like that," the PR girl stated obviously.

"Really? You-Know-Who can't sit on the tub for a few minutes?" Niall asked sarcastically.

The PR girl glared at him.

I kept staring at the toilet bowl but could feel Niall's eyes on me.

"I'll cancel it," PR girl said.

"Give me your notebook and digital recorder and I'll interview her for you," Niall offered.

I was taken aback by such kindness but was also immensely grateful. I handed him my list of questions and iPhone. "I record on this," I muttered. Sylvia was somewhere in another part of the hotel set up for the photo, which she wouldn't get if I didn't get the interview. Then neither of us would get paid and we'd risk pissing off an editor, which meant less work.

Niall took the notebook and nodded firmly.

"He just spoke with her," the PR girl argued.

"That was for the *Daily Buzz*. This is for"—Niall looked to me. I tried to speak clearly when I said "*Hollywood Hush*."

"*Hollywood Hush*," he repeated.

"Fine, Clara," the PR girl said, annoyed.

By the time Niall was done his second brush with fame, I had managed to toss some cold water on my face and redo my ponytail. The only parts I couldn't clean up in time were my pride and my ability to make a good first impression.

"Here's your mobile. I recorded the whole thing," he said. "You look brighter. Feeling better?"

"Yes, thank you," I said and took my cell phone and notebook from him. With a slightly clearer head I saw how good-looking he was, albeit dressed a tad on the scruffy side. Typical entertainment journalist. "I appreciate it. She doesn't much like me so it was probably good that I got sick when I did. Probably a sinus infection."

He grinned a lopsided grin that gave him a mischievous look, almost boyish. "I recognize a hangover when I bloody well see one," he said, teasing. I felt my face flush. "But not to worry, *You-Know-Who* was charming. Thanks for that, by the way."

"I'm sorry. I was joking. I didn't think you'd repeat it."

"Don't worry. I'm always willing and able to help a damsel in distress."

"That's very kind of you," I said. "I'm feeling like one today."

"I see you're married," he said and pointed to my left hand. I stared at the wedding band but said nothing. "If I'd seen that earlier, I wouldn't have put my contact info in your mobile."

My eyes widened. A handsome Englishman who saw me passed out from a hangover found me attractive enough to give me his number? Why did I get all the freaks?

"Wasn't trying to be bold," he said urgently, as though not wanting me to get the wrong idea. "I thought if *Hollywood Hush* or anyone here ever needed a UK freelance reporter you could give them my name." Cleary he wasn't hitting on me, and he wanted to be sure I knew it.

"Don't worry about it. I assure you, my husband won't mind." I started to leave the hotel room to find Sylvia. "Thank you again."

"Try a shot of vodka," he called out to me. "Always works for me. Hair of the dog and all that rot."

"'Rot' is the right word." I smiled weakly.

I found Sylvia and explained what happened. We drove to my place listening to Niall's interview. Apparently You-Know-Who was in a fabulous mood and gave him loads of juicy quotes.

"Looks like the best interviews are the ones where I don't show up. Even my job is abandoning me."

"Stop it," Sylvia said. "Not even You-Know-Who is immune to an English accent, and you said he was good-looking, right?"

"Yes."

"Then she liked talking to him."

"It's weird he was hitting me up for work," I said. "There are tons of papers and tabloids in the UK."

"Maybe he wants to branch out, break into America," Sylvia said.

I leaned against the car window. "I don't want to go home to that apartment."

"Where do you want to go?"

I knew the chances were good that I wouldn't feel any better or hurt any less, but when a woman is left by her husband there is one place she inevitably ends up: back home with her mother.

— CHAPTER SEVEN —

The house I grew up in on Camrose Drive had been in my family for three generations. I was raised there when my parents divorced. Marjorie had grown up in it with her father and stepmother. But we all owed that roof over our heads to my grandmother Alice, who bought it after her role in *He Gave No Answer* and paid it off before she died.

Our house was only a five-minute walk from the famous High Tower Court, an enclave of five houses that were reachable by immense staircases built onto the hillside or an elevator that required a private key. Designed by Carl Kay in the thirties, the story goes that his wife was so fed up climbing the stairs that he built the elevator just for her. A tunnel led from a parking garage several storeys below, and only the homes' owners had a key. Other people in the neighbourhood and gawking tourists alike could stroll up there on foot, and they often did. No matter what time of day, the area held an air of mystery, creeping with vines, bamboo and twisted prehistoric-looking ferns and palms. The steep staircases that twisted up through the hills and the glow from lamps seen peeking through the foliage and perimeter fences hinted at the private lives inside the house. I used to play along the pathways and pretend it was a jungle, as my mother had done when she was a child. It was a mystical place for a kid's imagination. It might be just what I needed as an abandoned wife.

But before sober reflection along High Tower Court, I had to first take what was coming to me from my mother. The precise form of attack varied visit to visit, the only certainty being that there would be one. This time around the ambush started after wine had been poured and dinner was under way. In other words, all the trappings of a warm welcoming were in evidence, enough to lull a wayward daughter into thinking sympathy was on the menu alongside casserole. But that was foolish thinking. On this occasion, she chose as a starting point a long-standing source of contention: my appearance. Marjorie was convinced that there wasn't a problem in the world that couldn't be solved by a makeover. I felt differently.

"Have you thought of colouring your hair? Or getting a different style?" My mother had a sly way of asking such questions, like it wasn't something she'd given much thought to, when in fact she'd run the dialogue through her mind repeatedly like they were lines from Shakespeare.

I stared at my mother the bombshell, at the blonde tresses that she kept in a quasi–Marilyn Monroe style, loose curls that fell just below her chin, then flipped up at the ends. Her eyebrows were their usual pencilled-in perfection. Her lips were candy-floss pink. The trouble with glamorous mothers is that they want you to be as glamorous as they are. As usual, I fell into her trap and felt a surge of anger flush my cheeks. "What's wrong with my hair?"

"Just thought you might be ready for a change," said Marjorie as she shoved dinner in the oven. "A new hairstyle can do wonders for a woman."

"Really?" I asked and grabbed a fistful of my long hair. "I'm loyal to the mousy look. It's stuck by me all these years. Longer than Dean did, that's for sure."

When I saw the look on my mother's face, I knew I shouldn't have said it. The look meant one thing: she'd known Dean was going to leave me and why. Her reasoning went far beyond hair colour. It was fate; a life philosophy that we didn't share. Like most everything in this house, her beliefs were borrowed from another era. I waited for her to say what she had undoubtedly rehearsed.

"I discovered this new Cabernet last week," she said instead.

Maybe this time I wouldn't get the lecture. It was a false hope; still, I picked up my glass and swivelled around on the kitchen stool and took in the scenery. It always amazed me how nothing ever changed from what I remembered growing up. The furniture in the house was its usual eclectic mix of mid-century modern, art deco, and arts and crafts. The pieces were exquisite and cared for; a less discerning eye might take them for reproductions, like what you find in a Restoration Hardware store. But they were the real deal. The walls were covered with local artists' watercolours and pencil sketches. The colour scheme was taupe, white and black with the odd punch of colour in a cushion, nothing flashy. The entire effect was art directed, like a set on a soundstage.

But the most striking object of all loomed large over the entire space. It was a giant, framed vintage movie poster from *He Gave No Answer,* the film that gave my grandmother her one big role. Alicia Steele was third from the left, staring straight at me. I raised my glass to her and wondered silently what words of comfort, if any, she would have had for me.

"The house looks good," I said, hoping to neutralize the enemy long enough to escape the ambush. Besides, the house did look good. My mother had a knack for décor and it was one of the few things we had in common. I loved décor magazines and rummaging around the California antique shops. The apartment had some quality things. I didn't expect Dean to put up a fight over any of it. The fine lines of a Dutch teak coffee table never held much fascination for him. After all, that sort of thing was nothing compared to the fine lines of a blonde actress. I got up and crossed the room and stood in front of my grandmother's poster. When I was a little girl, I used to stare at the poster and talk to her, usually to complain about Marjorie. I liked to think she protected me, looking out at the world from the poster, a sort of pulp-art heaven. Imagination is wonderful when you're young, but how quickly it can turn to delusion as an adult. Like imagining Dean loved me and would come home. Such thoughts made me want to ask the question in spite of my better judgment. Bring on the ambush, I told myself; let's get it over with. I called out to my mother.

"You aren't surprised that Dean left me, are you?"

Marjorie crept up beside me. She took a long sip of wine and said nothing. The unfulfilled actress had never left her, so even everyday gestures took on a dramatic flourish. She looked at her mother's face, maybe for inspiration, and shook her head.

"You know I'm not," she paused, taking her time, drawing out the suspense like she was a character about to reveal a vital clue in a Hitchcock film, even though I knew what was coming. "It's the family curse, Clara."

It was precisely what I expected her to say. That didn't stop me from snapping "Not that again!" as though I'd hoped it would be something new.

"I know you don't believe in fate," she said disappointedly.

"You're right. I don't," I said. "Was it fate that Grandpa left Alice for Lillian? And that Dad left you for Emily? Chalk it up to fifty percent of marriages failing, not some character flaw that gets passed down generation after generation."

After my diatribe I was spent, but Marjorie was just getting started.

"It wasn't just Alice and me; her mother, your great-grandmother—she was divorced, too, in an era when that sort of thing was practically unheard of. It was quite the scandal. And if it was just the state of marriage, why haven't any of the women in our family left their husbands?"

"We believe in love?" I answered feebly.

She went back to refill her glass and I followed her, a fool for punishment.

"You know you could have tried harder," she said.

"Gotten a better haircut, you mean?" I said icily.

She looked at me with pity. I didn't much care for that either.

"You gave up on yourself, Clara. Your writing . . ."

"I am a writer!"

"Let me finish, child. I mean your screenwriting. If that didn't work out, then you could have tried something else in the business, not merely writing about movies."

"Like you should have acted in movies?"

My attempt to get in a shot went unnoted. "And yes, a little bit of personal grooming might have kept Dean more interested."

I wanted to say "fuck you" but I had been raised differently than someone from an episode of a Dean Lapointe reality show, so instead I said, "You're always so quick to tell me what I'm doing wrong. I'm sorry I let you down, Marjorie. You and Dean should go to dinner and bemoan my lack of lipstick and lack of screenwriting credits."

I snatched the bottle of wine off the counter and refilled my glass. Marjorie shook her head. "I don't mean to quarrel."

"Yes, you do," I objected.

"I only want to be honest. You have to accept the fact that you're exactly like Alice and me—your career and marriage weren't meant to be."

"I'm nothing like you and Alice. Isn't that what you hate about me?"

For the first time my words hit home. She spoke softly but defensively. "I don't hate anything about you. I've only ever wanted you to be happy."

We were both quiet. Call it fate or coincidence, the brutal truth was that she was right. Despite my rebelling against all that was glamorous and holy to them, my life turned out the same anyway. It wasn't something I could admit, not now, if ever. As if reading my mind she said, "I know how much it hurts. Look what it did to my poor mother. She died of a broken heart."

I wanted to resist contradicting her. Sometimes when she said it I was successful, but tonight, with my emotions running high on wine, it was no use. "No she didn't. Alice died in a car accident."

Silence dropped between us like a cinder block. We hardly ever spoke of how my grandmother died for this reason. The only thing we could agree on was that it was a sad and violent end to her life; one that was full of broken dreams, and yes, a broken heart. Alice had apparently kept a convertible jalopy on the road way past its prime. She was driving up near the Hollywood sign on a Sunday night in December. It had been unseasonably hot, so she had the top down. What she was doing or where she was going was a mystery that was never solved. The police report said she was speeding and lost control and went plummeting off the mountainside. According to the *LA Times* there was a witness, an actress who gave only her first name— Betty—who said she saw the car roll over and over, and with the top down, well, it doesn't take much of an imagination . . . There was zero alcohol or any other funny stuff in the toxicology results. My mother was a little girl but she still remembers the funeral. A slew of bit-part actors and fellow seamstresses from the wardrobe department where Alice worked came, and Marjorie's father, Lyle, and Lillian, who was his wife by then, hosted a reception afterwards. My mother said she stayed up late, not because of grief but simply because no one noticed her. They were too busy drinking brown liquor in cut-crystal glasses and telling stories from back in the day when everyone had hope for a happy ending. She thought they were ghosts. Part of her never believed Alice's car crash was an accident, but she never told me what she thought had actually occurred. Murder? Suicide? I always chalked it up to one too many movies. As time wore on, she seemed to give in to the police and witness accounts, except for occasional outbursts like this one.

"Yes, it was a car accident," Marjorie repeated softly.

"Well don't worry, I won't drive near the Hollywood sign until I'm over Dean," I said and felt like a jerk for saying it. Marjorie ignored me and went back to preparing dinner.

I raised my glass once more to Alice as Alicia and followed her.

"Maybe you need to get away. When your father left I disappeared for three whole weeks." An odd expression came across her face, like she was remembering something, bad or good I couldn't tell.

"I remember," I said. "I went back and forth between Grandpa and Lillian and Granny Bishop because Dad was too busy at the hospital. But I can't run away." I dipped a hot tortilla chip into my mom's homemade guacamole.

"Staying put and facing trouble head-on is overrated," she countered and sipped from her glass. "What do you have to stick around for? You don't think he's coming back, do you?"

I shoved the tortilla chip so hard into the guacamole that it crumbled in my hand.

"No," I protested a little too loudly, hoping my tone would cover any hint that in fact I was hoping very much he would come back.

"Good, because he won't."

"Marjorie!" I exclaimed. "I don't need to hear that right now."

"You do, Clara," she insisted. "You do."

═ CHAPTER EIGHT ═

Despite the usual tension between Marjorie and me, I stayed there on Camrose Drive. She had her own life and I wanted to be left alone, so in essence it was perfect. During the day, I toured the paths on High Tower Court, peered down the elevator shaft and wondered if the people who lived up here were happier than I was.

At night I curated my own film noir festival. I watched *Out of the Past*, *The Big Sleep*, *Asphalt Jungle* and *Key Largo*, to name a few. Of course, there was also *The Postman Always Rings Twice*, with Cora, the hell cat, to remind me of the kind of woman I wasn't. Eventually, I pulled out the DVD of *He Gave No Answer*. That's when Marjorie joined me. We rarely watched it because of the effect it had on her. It seemed to revive her childhood longing for her mother. For my part, it always made me wonder what might have been if Alice had lived and had broken big into pictures, how different our lives would have been.

Seeing Alice as Alicia Steele taking on a wisecracking gumshoe was remarkable. She was so young and pretty with bright eyes filled with hope and stars. Her big scene came near the end where she confronts the femme fatale. My grandmother actually gets her face slapped by the other woman.

"See to it you can take a slap as easy as a kiss. That is, if you want to get anywhere in this world and not be anybody's fool," the femme fatale told her.

Alicia Steele fought back tears and turned on her heel to leave the room, but not before stopping in front of the leading man, a tall dark-haired fellow, and slapping him hard across the face.

"I may be a fool but I'm no longer your fool," she said and stormed out. Marjorie and I applauded as we always did.

"Why don't we slap people across the face anymore?" I mused as the credits rolled. "As a culture, I mean, not you and me necessarily."

She grinned. "I think it's considered a form of violence."

I shrugged. "It's more civilized than calling someone an asshole or a slut. More satisfying too."

"No doubt," she agreed. "Though you'd probably get arrested for assault, or at the very least get sued, so I don't recommend it. Not in the era we live in now."

"Didn't Quentin Tarantino bitch-slap someone once?"

"I believe so. And I believe he was sued. Case in point."

"Point taken," I said. "But it's awfully fun to think about." I hit the menu button and replayed the slap scene again. Alicia Steele was tougher than the character she played, the so-called good woman. She wouldn't have taken Amber stealing her husband lightly, like I had. Not according to Marjorie anyway. She told me how when my grandfather had left Alice for Lillian, Alice had packed little Marjorie into her car and drove over to their place and set his car on fire.

Though when I got older and asked Lillian—we visited her once in a while after my grandfather died—she always maintained that this was a fabrication and that Marjorie was too young to remember the truth. Lillian's story was that Alice had been furious that certain items she felt were hers were taken by my grandfather, and in attempting to take them out of his car, her cigarette had fallen inside accidentally and started the blaze. I preferred Marjorie's version. As far as family legends go it was more dramatic. As for Lillian, she was a small, dark-haired woman who smelled like lavender and whiskey. She was always nice enough to me. Tried to spoil me too, but my mother wouldn't let her. I knew it wasn't because she was against grandparents spoiling grandchildren, but only that she was against Lillian.

When *He Gave No Answer* was finished, I checked my cell phone again. There was nothing from Dean. He had cut me off entirely. I had called him, sent text messages and even tried Facebook. But there was only silence.

"You have to stop obsessing over Dean," Marjorie scolded. "It's unbecoming."

"Leave me alone, Mother," I said and stomped off to bed, although since Dean left, it was anxiety that kept me warm at night and sleep was a luxury I couldn't afford. Tossing and turning, I managed a few fitful hours but was woken up the next day by the sound of something falling from a great height and my mother's shriek. I ran to find her standing over a large cardboard box that had fallen from a top shelf. It looked like it had exploded.

"Closet terrorist?" I said dryly.

"You could say that," she said equally dryly. "I thought it was time to start going through the family wardrobe department and get rid of some things."

The family wardrobe department was the in-joke for my mother's oversized walk-in closet that was really a converted bedroom. It was stacked to the rafters (if the room had rafters, but really it had fifteen-foot ceilings) with clothes, shoes, coats and accessories. There was an old wooden screen that my mother used to change behind and I used to hide behind. Marjorie kept everything, or it looked like she did. She still had her favourite dresses from high school right up to what she wore to her friend's wedding last summer. If I had been a girlie-girl, then this room would have been heaven to me growing up. But as I said, I was a tomboy, and so I avoided it like homework and Brussels sprouts.

The only part of the closet that ever held my attention was one special section that was entirely devoted to my grandmother. It was like a shrine to her style. Painstakingly packed in acid-free tissue in carefully labelled boxes were every suit, cocktail dress, evening gown, piece of lingerie and every pair of shoes and slippers she either wore when she was a struggling starlet in the 1940s or when she worked as a wardrobe assistant on film sets in the early 1950s. Marjorie had inherited the entire collection when she was old enough not to wreck them. And through the years, she had tracked the origin of most of the items, partly from Alice's notebooks and partly from her own research. It was a time capsule and probably worth a small fortune.

I found the formless clothes kind of sad, once alive with my grandmother's vibrancy, a woman I never knew except for a few flickering images on a videotape, but with no life in them now. Growing up, Marjorie told me how she played dress-up with them when she was younger; it made her feel close to the mother she barely remembered. I never played dress-up once, not a chance . . . until today. The box that had fallen and exploded was one of my grandmother's. Marjorie and I stood staring down at the spilled mound of chiffon and satin like it was pixie dust.

"You were going to get rid of Alice's dresses?" I asked in disbelief.

Marjorie kneeled down and began to fold the pile, and I kneeled down to help. It was a box full of dresses, yellow ones, pink ones, green and purple.

"There are so many great pieces but I never wear them, and neither . . ." She stopped short but I knew what was coming, so I finished it for her.

"I'll never wear them either," I said. "Another reason I'm a disappointment."

"I had hoped you would have the same passion as I did," she admitted sullenly. "Like Alice had too. But there's no point hanging onto them. I can get a pretty penny for the collection."

I wanted to shout to save them for a granddaughter, but I kept quiet and let the guilt bear down on me as it had for as long as I could remember, no less heavy for the span of time. There was little point in objecting on behalf of a daughter that didn't exist, and may never exist, like some twisted version of a hope chest. Nor was there any point arguing that my life wouldn't have turned out any differently if I had dressed better or pursued acting or any of the things that had, in effect, brought only unhappiness to Marjorie and Alice. As I watched her painstakingly handle each item, I realized that my mother, for all her vibrancy and wit, was aging. She wouldn't be around forever, and something inside her seemed to tell her it was time to clean house, especially since she'd long ago given up on me ever living up to expectations. From deep inside I couldn't let her be right, not entirely, and unlike my marriage or writing an award-winning film, feigning an interest in fashion was an easy win.

"Tell me about that one?" I asked when she held up a bottle-green bouclé shift dress. "It's so bright."

"You can't be afraid of colour." She smiled slightly. "Though I know how you love black. This was one your grandmother made for an early fifties film noir. It was worn by the femme fatale, that's why it's so sexy. She was dangerous!" My mother laughed raucously. She had folded the dress up neatly when I said something that shocked us both.

"Can I try it on?" The words came out quickly, as if whatever part of me that was willing to do it was afraid the other part would slam on the brakes.

She looked at me in amazement but didn't hesitate. "Of course!"

I could feel her beaming from behind the wooden screen as I took off my pyjamas. The dress was heavier than I expected, but given it was made by my grandmother out of natural fabrics and not a micro-fibre sewn by a sweatshop worker in China, that wasn't altogether surprising.

"I need help with the zipper," I said and stepped sheepishly out from behind the screen in the bright green dress.

Marjorie rushed to my side and zipped me as I held my hair up. She stood back.

"You need the right shoe," she said, examining me like a prize calf that needed its hoofs polished. Then she was off into my grandmother's boxes, which seemed less precious all of a sudden, and was at my side in a flash with a pair of black patent shoes with, thankfully, a thick heel that was only an inch and a half high. I slid them on. Remarkably, the three of us were all of a size, including shoes.

"Oh, Clara!" Marjorie clasped her hands together. "You look stunning."

I walked towards the strategically placed three-way mirror. In the heels my hips swung more than I'd ever noticed. "It does look pretty good, doesn't it?"

"You'd knock them dead in that dress if you wore it out," she said confidently.

I contemplated this. I could think of at least one person I'd like to knock dead.

Still wearing the green dress, I felt hours pass as we sifted through the boxes. We didn't talk much; it was mostly oohs and aahs from me and more Alicia Steele tidbits from my mother. Stories I'd heard before, some more riveting than others, yet, perhaps because I was so full of grief myself, I saw once more how bittersweet this was for Marjorie.

"You must have missed her a lot when you were little," I said softly. Marjorie's fingers tightened on a dusty rose blouse and for a moment I thought she might cry. But she didn't. Her pain wasn't new like mine.

"I missed her more when I got older. I mean, obviously I missed her when she died. Terribly so. But when I became old enough to comprehend what I'd lost, what might have been . . ." Her voice trailed off for a moment before she continued. "It wasn't meant to be."

I kept quiet as she continued to fuss about, unpacking and repacking our distaff family history, all the while wondering where the idea that wouldn't leave me alone had come from. Yet it couldn't be helped, so I said it, though it made no sense at the time.

"Would it be okay if I borrowed some of Alice's clothes?"

Marjorie stopped her folding and stared down at the garment in her hand, another satin dress the colour of eggplant. I thought maybe I'd overstepped my bounds because her expression was so serious, the kind of look normally reserved for discussions about taxes.

"You can't borrow them," she said sternly. I looked down at my feet, feeling even more rejected. "Keep them. They were always meant to go to you."

I looked up to see my mother beaming at me as though I'd just been born. And if I didn't know better, I'd even say I beamed at her for an instant.

"Thank you," I said. "I'll be very careful not to spill anything on them. I can't imagine I'll wear them." And I couldn't, any more than I could fathom why I wanted them in the first place.

"I understand." She smiled knowingly. "Perhaps you need them, like I once did." Her mind drifted off somewhere, no doubt somewhere in the distant past. Then she was back with a wide smile again. "It's time they left this closet and went out on the town for a bit."

We spent some time selecting my favourites, and afterwards I had a new wardrobe of very old clothes. Talk about dressed up with no place to go. The selection of pencil skirts, blouses, cocktail dresses, evening gowns, coats and day dresses weren't me at all. Then again, I didn't want to feel like Clara Bishop anymore. There was a tiny part of me that wondered what Dean would say. He always admired the vintage clothes my mother kept. One time when we were first married, Marjorie showed him many of the same outfits that I was going to take. I remembered he said that it took a certain kind of woman to pull off clothes like these. "Women like that don't exist anymore," he'd said, and at the time I agreed with him.

"Clara, I have just the thing you need to make your transformation complete," Marjorie announced hopefully before disappearing into another room. I wasn't so sure transformation was possible but I'd take my chances. I heard some more thumping and banging, as though she was retrieving something from deep inside a cave. She emerged carrying an enormous vintage suitcase. It was robin's egg blue with a white polymer handle and white vinyl trim and absolutely pristine.

"It belonged to Alice too. It came with a matching train case but that got destroyed in the car accident," she said sadly, remembering. Then perking up, she said, "It hasn't been used since I went away after your father left. I can't think of a better way for you to take the clothes home than in this."

The suitcase was gorgeous, and I was touched that my mother trusted me with it. The suitcase was stuffed as well as you could stuff luggage that didn't give at the seams. I practically had to sit on it to shut it and fought with the clasp until, at last, it clamped down. My mother had found the key, so I locked it up and shoved the key into my faithful knapsack. The morning had whittled by in a haze of chiffon and silk, and I'd managed to string together an hour or two without thinking about my empty apartment and emptier life.

— CHAPTER NINE —

Police Station—Cirencester

I finished my tea. Sergeant Hooper crossed his arms and stared.

"I must say, the impression you give me," he said, "that of a sad and rejected girl prone to madcap moments, is not the same as the polished, perhaps even dangerous woman I see seated across from me."

"Is that so?" I asked, silently relishing being considered dangerous.

"Which is the real Clara Bishop?"

I contemplated this. "I'll let you decide."

He grunted his displeasure.

"So where is your father in all this mess?" he asked.

"Funny you should ask," I said. "He showed up that day in time for dinner. I remember them fighting when I was little. I used to escape the house and hide on the driveway until the yelling stopped. Then one day he was gone. He'd moved to San Diego, where he still lives. I saw him every other weekend. We'd go to McDonald's and he'd buy me a Happy Meal. I kept those toys for years."

Hooper picked up my Styrofoam cup and crunched it in his fist. The tiny bit of liquid left at the bottom spilled onto the table, and worse, onto his precious yellow pad. "Bollocks!" he said.

I smiled and continued with my story. "I was shocked to see him. But my mother didn't seem surprised . . ."

It was nearly suppertime, and I was finally feeling hunger pangs, when there was a knock at the door. Naturally, my first thought was *Dean,* but my mother quickly put that to rest.

"Your father is here," she said. This was news to me.

"Who called him?" I asked.

"I did," she answered casually as she went to the door. "He had to be told. And you weren't doing it any time soon."

I wasn't very close with my father. Dr. Charles Bishop is an imposing man, a very no-nonsense, unemotional, typical doctor sort of person. He wasn't even that upset when his second wife, Emily, left him for another doctor. Though I was relieved because I didn't like her much. He always made sure my celebrity magazines were in his waiting room. He always said I'd be a great mother.

"Dad can't see me like this!" I protested.

"Like what? Hurt and abandoned? That's when a girl needs her father most."

"Since when do you two talk anyway?"

"He's been coming to LA for seminars and things," she said matter-of-factly. "We've had lunch once or twice. Now, I must open the door for him!"

I was surprised she hadn't told me about his visits, even though I shouldn't have been. We never touched on the topic of my father.

He walked into the room and I dutifully got up to hug and kiss him.

"I hear you're having a rough time," he said and sat down beside me. His hair used to be the same mousy brown as mine but now was white, though immense waves of it remained, like sea foam, with a side part that created a kind of tsunami over his right eye. His pale complexion was almost wax-like. He was a dermatologist who took his advice to stay out of the sun very seriously. He used to terrify Dean. The thought made me smile.

"I think you should go home and make a bonfire with that son of a bitch's things."

He spoke so calmly that he might have said "go home and make a pot of tea."

"Someone's phone is ringing," Marjorie observed.

It was my cell, and it was Dean.

"It's him." I felt the blood drain from my face.

"Want me to talk to him?" my father offered a little too eagerly.

I shook my head and rushed out onto the back deck and slid the glass door shut, anxious not to miss his call.

"Hello."

"Hey, Clara."

"How are you?" I asked. I wasn't breathing. All I wanted was to hear him say he was coming back home. That it had been a terrible mistake. That he still loved me.

"I'm at the apartment."

I felt my hopes rise.

"I'm getting the rest of my stuff. I just want to warn you in case you'd rather not be here while I move out."

I swallowed hard. "Are you sure you want to do it so quickly?"

"Yes. I leave for London tomorrow and I don't want my things to be in your way when I'm gone."

I wanted to say he'd never be in my way and his stuff could and should be with me forever. But all I said was "aha."

"Okay, I'll also leave you money for my share of the rent. Two months' worth for now. We can discuss the rest later." I knew by "the rest" he meant divorce. "Bye."

And he hung up. It was over so fast, part of me wasn't sure it had happened. I kicked myself for not saying something that mattered.

For days I'd waited to hear his voice, and all I could say was "aha."

I went back into the house and my parents stared at me like I had a fatal disease.

"Apparently Dean is moving out as we speak."

"Coward!" Dad snapped.

"It's better that Clara isn't there," Marjorie interjected. She brought me a cup of tea and a platter of cookies. As I bit into a cookie, peanut butter chocolate chip, I made up my mind. Why should I change my plans?

"I'm not going home," I announced. "I'm going away."

"You shouldn't run away," my father said, sounding like I had a few days before.

"Shush, Charles," my mother said gruffly. "I'm glad to hear it. So where are you going?"

I took another sip of tea and cleared my throat.

"London."

I packed in the morning, tossing the usual suspects—jeans and more jeans—into my knapsack. I decided to make do with whatever clothing I had lying around my mother's house; there was no way I could cope with going back to the apartment and seeing it empty of Dean. I looked in the mirror, the yoga pants, matching hoodie, ballet flats, banana clip in my hair, and burst into tears. Was it any wonder he had left me for a gorgeous young blonde with a name like Amber? But she was here in Los Angeles. I was going to London where Dean was, and I was going to win him back. I'd emailed Trinity, and fortunately she was prepared to welcome me with open arms and a shoulder to cry on.

I was ready to run out the door to where my father was waiting to drive me to the airport when I saw Alice's suitcase—an entire wardrobe from another era. My mother called out to me.

"Clara, get a move on!"

I couldn't let it sit there not knowing when I was coming back. The clothes would be all creased and musty, and after spending decades in my mother's carefully constructed closets, it would be irresponsible, even insulting to her and Alice. Unsure what to do and with no time to find another solution, I grabbed the suitcase.

"I'm taking this with me," I said to Marjorie on my way out the door.

She grinned. "You won't regret it!"

CHAPTER TEN

"Clara!" Trinity shrieked when she opened the door to her flat and ensnared me in a giant smothering hug. Being greeted by Trinity was like coming home to a golden retriever—complete with long blonde hair and big brown eyes—who knew there were biscuits in your pocket.

"I'm so thrilled to see you!" she cried.

Trinity was small and curvy, almost plump as if still carrying baby fat, and with her hair in two long plaits she looked about fourteen. She never wore makeup. Her skin was flawless and her lips naturally dewy and pink. High heels were only pulled out for an audition. So while people might not consider her glamorous, she was appealing, bubbly and men always found her sexy. She had the look of an Edwardian maid or a war bride, so it was not surprising that many of her biggest parts had been in BBC costume dramas.

Her flat was on the top floor of a Victorian townhouse, near Tufnell Park tube in north London. Once we climbed up the steep steps and through her door, the place opened up and the flat was airy with the extreme ceilings that make old houses so glorious. Her quirky taste stood out in every ornament and piece of furniture. Only Trinity could take a chair shaped like a giant high-heeled shoe—and in purple velvet no less—and make it work with a cowhide rug in zebra stripe. A 1950s red Arborite kitchen table and matching red vinyl chairs lifted the stuffiness from the formal dining room. The kitchen was tiny but bright and gleamed with stainless steel. Books were everywhere, on shelves, in stacks, loads and loads of books.

"Nice place," I said.

"I love it. It's home. Let me show you your room," Trinity said and, taking my hand, guided me into the tiny guest room. It seemed to be bursting with its contents of a twin bed, four-drawer dresser, nightstand, tiny desk and chair and even tinier closet space. This must be what people meant by "twee." I wasn't sure I could fit my grandmother's suitcase inside the room. I plunked it down next to the dresser.

"Sorry this room leaves much to be desired!" she chuckled. "Once you unpack we can store your bag under the bed. With that size suitcase you must be planning on staying awhile."

My ticket was for six weeks because I'd assumed I would stay with Dean for the length of the production.

"I can get a hotel as soon as you're sick of me," I said. "I don't want to impose."

"Stay as long as you like. I took advantage of your hospitality for two months, remember?"

"And you should come back to LA for pilot season next year!" I encouraged her.

"You know, I might. I'm older now. Could play someone's mum on a sitcom!" she rolled her eyes, then turned it into excitement by jumping up and down. "I can't believe you're finally in London!"

Neither could I. What was I thinking stalking Dean like this? On the other hand, it gave me comfort to know he was here in London. But it wasn't a plan I was going to share with Trinity. As far as she was concerned he'd left me high and dry, and I was here to get over him, not get him back.

"I don't suppose I'd accidentally run into Dean here?" I asked, disguising my hope with anxiety.

She waved her hand dismissively. "He's a total tosser doing that to you! London is a huge city. There's very little chance you'd bump into him unless you wanted to."

I thought about this. Of course I wanted to run into him. That was the point. I wasn't about to let Amber have Dean without a fight. I wanted a different outcome than Alice and Marjorie had ended up with. He'd see I was intrepid, spontaneous, and that I loved him so much I travelled halfway around the world to show him.

"I washed the sheets and duvet cover yesterday," she explained, jolting me from my thoughts. "Have a lie-down. I have to go run some errands, then we can go nurse your wounds. There's a lovely gastro pub around the corner."

"A what?" I asked, perplexed.

"Gastro pub, dearie. It's like a pub but with better food and a decent wine list."

"So what do I wear to a gastro pub?" I asked. Trinity was wearing black jeans, flat motorcycle boots and a heather-grey sweater, or jumper as they said here. "What are you going to wear?"

She shot me a look. "What I've got on me!"

"You look great," I said, panicked.

"Don't worry. Gastro pubs aren't any more fancy dress than regular ones, but unlike normal pubs you've got to tip the staff."

"I wouldn't know any other way but to tip; I'm from LA!" I smiled. "I'll take that nap." But as I took a step towards the bed, I tripped over the suitcase and crashed into the dresser.

"You all right?" she asked, trying not to giggle.

"I'm fine."

"It is a small room," Trinity said and picked up the suitcase and flopped it on the bed. "So what do you have in here?"

"You'll love them," I said and grabbed the key. I tried to unlock the case but the clasps wouldn't unfasten. It was jammed tight.

"Great, I brought all these clothes I didn't want to bring and now I can't even open the damn suitcase," I said, thoroughly frustrated.

"What clothes?"

"My grandmother's," I explained to her. "From her wardrobe department days." She lit up like any actress who worshipped Old Hollywood would.

"Alicia Steele. Film noir goddess!" she grinned and took a bow. She knew all about my grandmother from our film-school days. She'd also been introduced to my mother, who had forced her to watch *He Gave No Answer* at least five times.

"Wannabe goddess," I corrected her.

She pooh-poohed me. "Alice was no doubt a very fine actress. It's a tough slog. I know something about that you know. Though I will never be as pretty as she or your mother was."

"Neither will I," I lamented.

"I'm dying to see them. We could play dress-up for a bit," she said excitedly.

"I should have known an actress with your taste would appreciate vintage," I smiled, though in truth I was embarrassed. No one would ever imagine Clara Bishop in get-ups like these.

"Why don't you wear one of Alicia's dresses tonight?"

I shook my head. "I'd look like a fool. I shouldn't have brought them."

"Then why did you?"

I shrugged. "It seemed the right thing to do at the time. It's all a moot point since I can't open the suitcase anyway."

She made a face and shoved her two thumbs under the clasp and tried to pry it open. It didn't budge. Then I took my index fingers and grabbed at it from the top and she kept shoving from the bottom, but still it remained clamped shut.

"It must be so old it's stiff as a corpse," she said, puffing a little from the exertion.

"I can't use pliers or anything harsh because Marjorie would kill me if I broke it," I pointed out.

"I guess dressing up will wait."

I sat on the bed, feeling the pull of jet lag on my eyelids. "That's fine by me. Jeans will forever be my staple."

CHAPTER ELEVEN

The gastro pub was in an ancient brick building on the corner near the tube station. The large wooden hand-painted sign had a rearing white horse on it, and as I got closer I saw the pub was called The White Stallion. It was the very place Niall Adamson had mentioned. The brick was painted a dark red with yellow trim on the eves and shutters. But the bright exterior belied the establishment's darker tone on the interior. The wood plank floor was polished but uneven, and its deep brown colour matched the wood panels along the wall. Wooden dividers separated booths and tables; each divider had beautifully crafted wrought-iron tree branches and leaves running along the top. But as delicate as it looked, each leaf and twig came to a sharp point like dozens of tiny daggers. The wrought-iron motif was repeated throughout the room in lighting fixtures and chandeliers, as though the whole place were wrapped in barbed wire, while white sheer fabric billowed down from the ceiling, creating a canopy. It was like stepping into a fairy tale gone wild.

"I half expect to see Little Red Riding Hood and the Big Bad Wolf," I whispered into Trinity's ear when we reached the long ebony bar that stretched nearly the width of the pub.

"I can promise you both," she said cheekily and patted a bar stool. I sat obediently. Trinity's mobile rang. "I have to take this. My agent.

I won't be long. Order us something cold." She dashed out the door. There didn't seem to be anyone around, so I grabbed a drinks list that was lying on the bar. Just then, out of the corner of my eye, I saw a sudden swoosh of red flash past me. I whirled around but whatever or whoever it was had already vanished. Suddenly, the front door opened and a slew of well-dressed men and women filed in one after another as if school were out. Then I saw it again. Only the swoosh wasn't a blink of red, it was like a flag in a bull-fighting ring in the form of crimson jersey. The jersey was clinging to the shapely silhouette of a woman. Long cascading strawberry blonde hair should have clashed with the dress but didn't. She was beautiful in the way that women with large blue eyes, a turned-up nose and a strong jawline often are—like the offspring of an aristocrat who mated with a showgirl. I instantly disliked her for no other reason than that she was a young, sexy waitress like Amber. And young, sexy waitresses like Amber were public enemy number one. If that sounds bitter, it's because I *was* bitter. I grabbed the drinks menu and held it up to my face like a spy, a cowardly spy.

"You that Hollywood friend of Trinity's?" she said archly as she waltzed behind the bar and pulled a wine glass down from the rack. I squirmed in my seat. "She told us you were coming. So you're wanting a drink on the house, then?"

"I can pay," I objected.

She rolled her eyes impatiently.

"Can you drink wine?"

"Yes, sometimes without spilling it," I answered dryly.

The sexpot waitress grabbed a bottle of something red and poured me a glass. Guess my options were limited.

"Here you go. A nice Malbec," she said and slid the glass in front of me before disappearing through a swinging door, which I assumed was the kitchen.

"I see you've met Saffron," Trinity said, standing behind me, her phone still in her hand.

"She's a sweetheart," I said sarcastically and wondered what kind of parents called their kid Saffron.

"Just get a move on, love!" a woman called out cheerfully as she came out of the kitchen and stood behind the bar. She was much older than Saffron and wore a sweet expression beneath a crown of short, wavy salt-and-pepper hair.

"Milly Goodge, this is Clara Bishop," Trinity introduced us. "She's the friend from Hollywood I told you about. She's a screenwriter."

I held out my hand. "Nice to meet you, Milly."

"What have you written? Anything I've seen?" she asked the usual question and started wiping the bar with a dishtowel.

I was about to give the answer all unproduced screenwriters gave, "not yet," but decided it was time to come clean. "I'm not really a screenwriter." I could feel the scowl on Trinity's face. She was sort of like Marjorie that way, never wanting me to give up. She was about to speak when her mobile rang yet again. She stamped her foot. "Sorry, will be right back."

When she was gone, I turned back to Milly. "I'm a journalist. Celebrity stuff."

"Tabloid, eh?" she said breezily and continued cleaning in silence. "You didn't have any of that phone-hacking business in America, did you? Just teasing." She burst out laughing.

"We did not," I said proudly.

"You Yanks are smarter. I bet you burned the evidence before you got caught out," she said and winked at me. She was the type of merry barmaid made famous on shows like *Coronation Street;* the type people poured their hearts out to. I bet she had plenty of stories, maybe even some advice on how to win back Dean.

"So Milly, how long have you been the bartender here?" I asked.

"I'm not the bartender," she corrected me in her fizzy manner. "I'm the owner of The White Stallion. The bartender quit, bloody bastard he was." She winked again.

"Oh," I said, my curiosity piqued. "I take it he left on bad terms?"

"Not exactly." Milly began to wave the dishrag so close to my face that I could smell the mopped-up beer. "He found a better-paying job at a swishy hotel. The Savoy. Couldn't blame the chap, had a whole brood of kiddies to support."

I felt my face turn white. The Savoy was where Dean was staying. Of all the hotel bars Milly could have mentioned, it was the only one that mattered to me.

"I always wanted to go to The Savoy," I said, trying not to sound shaken up.

"I bet you've stayed at your fair share of fancy hotels, what with being from Hollywood," she said and stopped wiping the bar to fix her eyes on me. "What are you drinking?"

"A Malbec," I said. She picked up the bottle Saffron opened and shrivelled her nose. "That's the cheap stuff. Let me get you something nicer."

"Do you know how to make a sidecar?" I asked hopefully.

"I do," she said. "I haven't had a customer ask for one of those in years."

I grinned and turned to face the room once more. The place was now brimming with well-scrubbed men and loads of fashionable-looking career girls. The crowd seemed a mix from every walk of life. I got the impression that everyone from bankers to shop girls to garage mechanics came here. Tufnell Park must be an eclectic area, I thought. And everyone was drinking their faces off. Saffron glided throughout the room like a butterfly in a meadow, hovering elegantly just long enough to enchant before flitting away. The men's eyes poured over her like cream on ripe berries. They sat straighter too and hung on every word like it was poetry, and not the daily special, she was reciting.

"She's quite the flirt," I said sourly to Milly. Every time I looked at Saffron I saw Amber.

Milly looked past me to the dining room and grinned maternally. "Saffron is a pretty girl, and everyone loves a pretty girl, don't they?"

"Do they?" I said. "Half those men are probably married."

"So what if they are," she chortled. "She's serving them beer, not performing lap dances. Here's your sidecar."

Milly stood watching me as I took the first sip. It was perfect. "Delicious!" I announced and she beamed.

"What's that?" Saffron was at my side.

"A sidecar. You wouldn't like it," I said coolly. She shrugged and ordered a bottle of champagne for one table, and a pint of pale ale for another.

"Champagne will be a good bit of cash," Milly said brightly.

"Yes, need to make up for budget buddy at table nine," Saffron snipped.

Milly looked over to what I assumed was the feared table nine. But I refused to look.

"What do you expect from a poor bloke like him?" Milly asked. "He'll always be a single-pint drinker until he can find another job."

"Until that happens, I wish he'd find another spot to brood in. He practically lives here, acts like the pub is his living room," Saffron said with a pout and took the drinks away.

Intrigued, I turned and watched her deliver the pint of beer to table nine. The so-called budget buddy was unshaven and his face was covered in coarse hair that, while not exactly a beard, was slightly darker than the sandy hair on his head. He was dressed in dark jeans and a check shirt—nondescript clothes that said nothing and concealed everything. Saffron didn't spend quality time with him as she did with the other customers. The man didn't look at her either. Her charm was wasted on him. I smiled and thought how frustrating this type of man must be for all the waitresses in the world with names like Saffron and Amber. Then he looked up and caught me smiling at him. It was Niall Adamson. I raised my hand to wave but he didn't seem to recognize me. He just stared blankly. Maybe he needed glasses, or maybe as usual I hadn't made enough of an impression to be worth remembering, or perhaps I looked different without my arms around a toilet bowl.

"You okay?" Trinity had returned from her phone call.

"I'm fine," I said as Milly shook the cocktail shaker. "Just looking at the man seated all alone back there. The scruffy blond guy."

Trinity looked over at the table and shrugged. "He's always here. Doesn't seem to have a home, if you ask me. Do you know him?"

"Met him at a press junket in LA. He writes freelance for the *Daily Buzz*," I explained. "But he doesn't seem to remember me at all."

"Do you know him, Saffron?" Trinity asked the waitress who had returned to the bar to pick up an order.

"Niall?"

"Yes, him."

She shrugged. "Lives around here. But don't know much other than he thinks tipping is a city in China."

I laughed at her joke and she smiled at me. Maybe all pretty blondes weren't the enemy. Trinity only shrugged and took a sip of my sidecar, then made a face like she'd sucked a lemon. "Milly, can you make up one of your signature G&T's?" she gasped.

I chuckled and slowly my gaze returned to Niall. He was reading a newspaper, immune to the charms of sexy waitresses.

CHAPTER TWELVE

The sky showed no mercy. Blackening clouds battled overhead and lashes of rain scraped like a cat's tongue. I stood on a street corner, my knapsack over my shoulder, within sight of the set for *Come to Daddy*. At least I had an umbrella. Trinity had been asleep when I'd tiptoed out of the flat. I didn't tell her where I was going because I didn't want to hear all the reasons I shouldn't try to see Dean. I wanted to talk to him. If he saw me again—far away from LA and Amber—maybe he'd come to his senses.

The set was a large warehouse in an area called Shoreditch. Walking from the tube station, I had gathered the area wasn't especially affluent, but it was a neighbourhood on the verge. Dotted among the working warehouses and auto shops was the right amount of edgy art galleries and hipster cafés to justify the zone's claim to cool. Yet in all its sorrowful glory, this pile of bricks and mortar was the perfect setting for a lurid reality show. I imagined the set for *Come to Daddy* was like all the others Dean made—a giant loft with multiple bedrooms and communal areas designed and decorated to make the most of sexy young things who were out to snag a man, in this case a dirty old rich one.

Large white production trucks sat outside on the pavement like mechanical sculptures, orange pylons bookending each vehicle, as security men paced up and down, clutching damp collars to their faces to stave off the rain. Car tires splashed through the waterlogged road behind me, and I ducked in front of one of the trucks like an assassin. A chauffeured sedan rolled through the rain and stopped about ten feet away. It could be another producer or some of the English cast members or nobody at all, but it could also be . . .

The driver jumped out and opened a black umbrella to shield his mystery passenger from the rain. But I'd recognize those long legs anywhere. Dean unfolded his lanky frame from the back seat and stood rubbing his hands together for warmth. He always had the manly slouch of Gary Cooper. I swooned at the sight of him, like the college girl I was when we met, which was followed by an overpowering urge to wipe the rain from his forehead, to touch him again. Being so close sent my anxiety packing, and for the first time I felt like things would be okay, like we could get back to a normal life. It would take time to forgive the affair, but we would still be together. It would be one of those crazy episodes you hear about in an otherwise stable marriage.

I was about to step forward, ready to forgive and forget, when Dean's next move stopped me dead. Instead of rushing indoors, he waved off the umbrella and extended his hand. I heard a loud gasp as Amber, in sizable heels, short coat and even shorter skirt, stepped out from the car like a gazelle, grabbing Dean's hand and giggling all the while. Then I heard another gasp as he took the umbrella from the driver and held it gallantly over Amber's beautiful head. I realized then that the loud gasps were all mine. He quickly escorted Amber inside.

I stood shivering, from the cold or the shock of seeing Amber, I didn't know which. I probably would have stood there, frozen to the ground, if it weren't for the suspicious looks from several crewmen wondering about the crazy girl hovering by a production truck in the rain. Eventually, a nervous-looking assistant director, his walkie-talkie banging against his leg, came over.

"Are you here to audition?" he asked me suspiciously.

I didn't know what to say, but I knew it was time to confront the agony head-on.

"I'm here to speak to Dean Lapointe," I answered icily.

"And you are?" he asked archly.

I smiled as sweetly as I could. "His wife."

Slack-jawed and wide-eyed, he offered no immediate response, so I continued to stand my ground and tried to gain strength from the prolonged awkward silence. After what felt like an eternity, he finally clicked into AD mode.

"I'll let him know you're here," he announced with mock authority. He then turned and trotted off, speaking hurriedly into the walkie-talkie. I didn't have long to wait before he was back. He was still fidgeting nervously.

"He says he'll be out in a moment. Can I get you a coffee?"

"No, thank you," I said politely. "I just want Dean."

He nodded and we stood there not speaking—he, rocking back and forth on his feet and whistling, and me, staring at my shoes and checking my watch. Eventually, Dean emerged from the set and stalked towards me through the rain, his face expressionless and his shoulders tense. We were face to face for the first time since he'd walked out on our marriage, and he looked like he wanted to *kill* me, and all I wanted to do was fall in his arms.

"Nice meeting you," the AD yelped before rushing away.

Dean stood in stony silence, the rain pelting out a loud rhythm on our umbrellas. I forced a smile.

"Hello, Dean," I said. My stupid smile was now a nervous tick that wouldn't go away.

"I knew you'd do this. You're always so *predictable,* Clara!"

I swallowed hard and tried to salvage my dignity. "I wanted to see London," I answered sarcastically.

"Have you seen enough?"

"Not yet."

"Why don't I get my assistant to book you on a tour bus?"

"I prefer to walk."

"Then walk away and don't look back," he said severely.

I flinched and fought to keep the steel in my voice, but that nagging tap of heartbreak was getting harder to ignore. "Why are you being this way?" I asked with an audible tremor.

Another awkward pause; this time I could see that some of the film crew was watching us. If I wanted to create a scene in front of an audience, now was my chance.

"Look, we grew apart," said Dean, giving the pat answer.

"That's not true!" I pleaded, fully aware that instead of a grand scene with me in the lead part, I was playing the role of the crazy ex. "We were trying for a baby, a family. That's all we wanted."

"It's what *you* wanted," he hissed and glared at those within earshot. They scattered away. "Look, we tried to carry on like we married out of some wild passion. But that's not what happened and we both know that. Let it go. Let me go!"

"Dean's right. He just wants you to set him free," Amber announced as she slipped in under Dean's umbrella and wrapped her arm around him possessively. He looked uncomfortable, and in his one act of decency, he didn't put his arm around her. "He was being polite. But someone has to tell you the truth. He's not in love with you, Clara. He's in love with me."

"How dare you speak to me?" I snapped. "As far as I'm concerned we've never met. You hurled a canapé at me; I don't count that as an introduction."

She laughed. "That was an accident. Fine, I'm Amber Ward."

She held her hand out but I refused to take it. She snorted with laughter. Dean looked back to the set as though wishing an AD would rescue him.

"You better go, Clara," Dean croaked. "There's nothing left for us to talk about."

Amber smirked at me. I wanted to wipe that look off her smug puss, but I was paralyzed. I had to make do with standing there like a fool as she grabbed Dean's hand and led him away. I stood there like an unwanted dog abandoned by its owner as the man I wanted to spend my life with, the man whose children I wanted to have, walked away from me. I watched them open the door to the set and vanish into the darkness.

"Are you sure you don't want a coffee?"

The assistant director held out a steaming paper cup, and I watched the rain plop in it like a pebble skipping across a pond. Where he'd come from or how long he'd been there I had no idea. But I took the coffee from him. He was the closest thing to sympathy around and I needed it.

"Thanks."

He nodded and dashed away again as though not wanting to be seen fraternizing with the enemy.

Police Station—Cirencester

"It must have upset you a great deal to see Amber with Dean like that." Hooper watched as I paced the room. The gold gown made a distinct swishing sound as I moved. My feet were killing me, but I wasn't going to ruin the effect by going barefoot.

"It did," I admitted flatly.

"Now I understand how all of you got embroiled in this mess. At least I think I do."

"You know the players," I said archly. "You don't know the plot. Not yet. What I haven't told you is that things were about to change. And I think, for the better, though I didn't know it at the time."

=CHAPTER THIRTEEN=

I held the coffee in my hand as I wandered around in the rain, the umbrella folded up and useless. I wasn't sure how far I'd walked, but eventually I sat down on the stone steps of a townhouse and wept. I was grabbing for some tissues in my knapsack when the door of the townhouse opened and footsteps slowly descended the stairs and stopped beside me. I looked down and saw a pair of expensive black brogues with charcoal pinstripe trousers hemmed just so, pink socks peeked out between, and I knew whoever he might be he was a man of good taste.

"You look lost." He spoke with a voice that went with the tailoring—crisp and masculine and very English.

"I didn't mean to trespass," I said faintly.

"Good grief! This isn't the Wild West!" the man exclaimed. "You're soaked to the bone. Doesn't that umbrella work?"

I stared down at the black nylon umbrella that I'd closed when I left Dean's set.

"Allow me to get you a towel."

He disappeared into the townhouse, leaving the front door open. It was warm and inviting with classical music, Mozart I thought, gently wafting towards me. The hallway was covered in gold damask wallpaper with glossy white trim and held formal console tables with lamps and framed photos. This was not the home of a hipster filmmaker from Los Angeles. Nor was it the kind of place that a blonde waitress/actress/mistress would hole up in. This was as anti-Dean and anti-Amber as I could get. So I walked in.

I heard cupboard doors clanking shut and water running from deep inside the house. I followed the sound towards the back. As I walked gingerly down the hall, I saw a living room and a formal dining room to the right. The walls were painted a vibrant red, with a large white marble mantelpiece and white built-in bookshelves on either side. More framed photographs decorated the tables and shelves, and curiosity drew me closer to investigate. There was a large black and white photo of a young boy in a dark suit squished between a nattily dressed couple.

"Those are my parents."

I swallowed hard, mortified that I had been caught snooping. I turned around and at last saw the man who had been so kind standing there with a towel in his hand. He held it out to me and I took it delicately.

"You'll need to warm up too," he continued, without the least hint of alarm or irritation at having a stranger in his house. He picked up the photo and I saw now that he was dressed in a suit with a purple shirt, no tie, and that he was younger than a man in this house ought to be. He had a long nose that was noticeably crooked, as though he'd been punched several times and hard. He had dark brown hair the colour of espresso with a receding hairline on either side of his temples. His face was remarkably unlined, yet he looked like a man of forty-five or thereabouts. He was attractive without being overly handsome. Most women would find him appealing, even with his ladylike taste in décor, or in some cases, because of it.

"You look uncomfortable in the photo," I said and rubbed my hair gently with the towel. "The suit must have been wool."

"And it was a hot July day, if I recall," he added and put the photo back. He looked me up and down and I grew conscious of my appearance, which was as far from his stylish attire as one could get. "Had a bad day, have we?"

"What gave you that idea?" I asked, feigning innocence. Then he pointed to my right, where a large oval mirror was hanging. I saw what he saw. My wet hair looked matted, and my complexion was sallow, which only exacerbated the redness in my eyes. The soaking wet clothing added to the picture of a downtrodden and lonely woman. I was the shining example of a very bad day.

"I see what you mean," I admitted.

"Would you like to use the bathroom? There's a hair dryer. Not that I use it much," he said with a wink, and I followed him down the hallway and into a kitchen. It was large and white with gleaming ceramic tiles and a large glass door that opened to a luscious garden bursting with colour. But I also noticed several swords hanging on the wall, as well as a mannequin dressed, oddly enough, in an elaborate cape with a scarlet satin lining. I pointed to it. "You a vampire fan?"

He chuckled. "I collect movie props," he explained. "That was from a 1980s Dracula B movie, a very bad one. The swords came from a kung fu movie. I have an entire room devoted to such things. The plan is to open a museum one day."

I nodded and smiled but said nothing further. People who collected movie memorabilia tended to be geeky men who lived alone, and if you started up a conversation about their collection, it could take hours to shut it down. So I continued on to the bathroom and found the hair dryer and got to work blowing the water out. I wished I could blow the memory of the morning away as easily.

When I came out of the bathroom the man was gone, so I quietly slunk down the hall towards the front door, lest he invite me to tour his room of props.

"Leaving so soon?" he called out, and I saw him perched at the top of the staircase. "Would you like a cup of tea?"

I shook my head, and began to feel uncomfortable for the first time. Maybe he was some deranged interior designer.

"On second thought, you look like you could use a real drink. Let me buy you one. Where do you live?"

"I'm staying at a friend's flat near Tufnell Park tube," I told him.

"Fine. We'll go there and I'll buy you a drink. There must be a pub nearby."

I took in the soft touches throughout the house. Maybe he was a decorator. "Are you an interior designer?"

He smiled slightly but his tone was serious, "The feminine touches belonged to my wife."

"She's not home?" I asked, knowing I was being nosy.

"She's never coming home," he said darkly. Then, as if shaking a memory free, he looked at me again. "She passed away."

I felt awful having pushed the point. "I'm sorry."

"Don't be. It's been a few years now. She drowned."

"Oh, how awful!" I said and felt selfish at being so caught up in my own trouble. "What happened?"

"It was in a swimming pool. Our swimming pool. At our country estate in Gloucestershire."

"That must have been horrifying."

He nodded and walked towards the door. I followed him outside, back into the rain.

=CHAPTER FOURTEEN=

Frederick dropped me at the door of The White Stallion, then went to find a parking space. He had told me his first name but not much else. Our conversation had been routine, the stuff of weather and traffic congestion. But I didn't care. Someone was taking care of me, and at that moment that's all that mattered.

Milly was behind the bar when she saw me. She tapped Trinity on the arm, who was sitting on a bar stool sipping tea with a worried look on her face.

"What happened to you?" Trinity asked, clearly alarmed by my bedraggled appearance. "Did the umbrella break?"

I looked down at the perfectly functional umbrella in my hand and nodded. "In a manner of speaking. I couldn't get it to stay open. Must have been the wind."

She nodded in agreement, but I sensed she knew I was lying. "You just went out for a stroll, then?"

"Yes."

"In the pouring rain?"

"Yes."

"At dawn, just for fun?"

"Yes."

"You went to see Dean, didn't you?"

"Yes."

Before she could say anything further, Frederick waltzed in and stood beside me protectively like I was a stray animal he'd rescued. Trinity's concerned expression vanished once she got a closer look at the man who'd brought me. "Aren't you Frederick Marshall?"

I was taken aback. There was a well-known film producer by that name. It couldn't be. Frederick smiled.

"Yes, I believe we've met before," he said and shook her hand.

"I'm Trinity Mayberry. I've auditioned for you. I'm hoping to audition again for your new film."

"Well, I guess you two know each other, then," I said, surprised by this turn of events, and turned to Milly. "Bourbon."

"You're an impressive girl," Frederick remarked. "Make that two."

"Because I like bourbon?"

"Because you like bourbon and don't know how to use an umbrella."

I couldn't help but smile.

"Mr. Marshall is a film producer, Clara," she explained slowly, as if I were a child.

"So I've heard," I said. "You were holding out on me, Frederick."

He shrugged. "Secrets aren't just for women."

"Here's the bourbon," Milly said as Trinity gave me a *what-the-fuck* look.

"Here's *to* bourbon," I said and forced a smile. In truth I felt like hell. The confrontation with Dean and Amber was replaying in my mind over and over. And now I had Trinity falling over herself to impress Frederick, and I could tell he wasn't loving it. If that weren't enough intrigue for one day, the door opened and in walked Niall Adamson. His arrival would have been unremarkable if it wasn't for the unmistakable look of loathing mirrored on Niall's and Frederick's faces when they caught sight of each other. Yet neither spoke. Niall sat down at a nearby table and, as usual, acted as though he'd never seen me before in his life.

"Tell me something about yourself," Frederick said loudly.

"Me?" I asked with a tilt of my head. "You know enough already. I had a bad day. I cried, and you loaned me your bathroom to clean up my face."

"Oh, Clara, don't play coy with Mr. Marshall," Trinity said too eagerly. "Clara is a journalist."

For the first time, I wished she had said screenwriter, for the colour drained from Frederick's face at the word "journalist."

"Don't worry, I'm not here to work," I said quickly.

He looked relieved. "What made you cry?" he asked, changing the subject as he studied my face like a map.

The "I'm a celebrity journalist from Los Angeles whose husband just left her for a twenty-one-year-old actress/waitress" line was on the tip of my tongue, but he didn't give me a chance to answer.

"On second thought, don't tell me anything. I like a mystery," he said and downed his bourbon in one go.

"Then you came to the right place," I said and had the prickly feeling that Niall was listening to every word.

"And I'll come back. But for now," Frederick said and jotted something down on a napkin, "this is how to reach me." He handed me the napkin with his mobile number scribbled on it. "In case you find yourself crying in Primrose Hill again."

"Okay," I said and smiled.

"Till the next time, then," he said and walked away.

Trinity's eyes widened in disbelief. "How did you manage to get from Shoreditch to Primrose Hill and wind up with one of the biggest film producers in England?"

I smirked, but in truth Frederick Marshall was of little interest to me, not when I knew Amber was in London with my husband.

"Wait here," she continued. "I'm going to call my agent and make sure I'm auditioning for his next film and soon!"

I shook my head. How swiftly my problems were taken care of when Trinity had a part to land. It was time to head back to the flat and get into some dry clothes. I bent down to pick up my knapsack, only it wasn't there.

"Where's my knapsack?" I asked, worriedly.

Milly started looking around. "I don't see it. Did you bring it with you?"

Trinity returned and we all gave the pub a thorough going-over. I was beginning to panic.

"It has everything in it. My cell phone, wallet, passport, all my clothes, you name it." Then I remembered. "I bet I left it at Frederick's house."

Trinity raised an eyebrow and grinned like an evil queen. "That's good."

"Why are you looking at me like that?"

"I'm just saying it's good. Now you have an excuse to call him."

"And why is that good?"

"Because I want to be in his new film, and you're my 'in.'"

She marched out of the pub.

"That wasn't what I had in mind," I said to no one in particular.

=CHAPTER FIFTEEN=

Back at the flat, I grabbed the napkin with Frederick's mobile number and called him. Sure enough, the knapsack was in the hallway of his house. He said he'd drive it over, but not until tomorrow evening because of some big meetings he had, and would I manage without it for a night. I told him I would. Then he told me he wanted to take me to dinner in exchange for the knapsack. I told him I didn't like the way he said it. So he said it differently.

"I was teasing. I only want to have a pleasant evening with a lovely American girl, no strings attached. You will get the knapsack with or without my spending loads of money on wine and food."

I smiled, but I still didn't like it. The last thing I wanted was a date. Trinity would be overjoyed. "Okay. But nothing too fancy. All my clothes are in that knapsack and I only brought jeans."

"Isn't that what shopping is for?" Then he hung up before I got to remind him he had my wallet.

"What did he say?" Trinity was practically bouncing off the ceiling. I told her.

"Brilliant! Please do talk me up, won't you?"

"Give it a rest, Trinity. He's kind of creepy, don't you think?"

She pouted. "If by creepy you mean a man able to single-handedly make my career."

I rolled my eyes, then told her how Niall and Frederick had glowered at each other. Her face went serious all of a sudden. "Oh, that."

"What's 'oh, that'?"

She moved to the kitchen and began to make tea. "I don't know much about Niall, but it could be that he recognized Frederick and . . ." she stopped talking as if someone might strike her dead if she fessed up.

"Are you going to tell me or should I just Google him?"

She sighed and out it came.

There was the stuff everyone in the business knew about Frederick Marshall, such as he was a film producer who had made his fortune on low-budget horror movies (which explained his prop collection) and had gone on to produce and make his name on several mega-hit romantic comedies. Every British actor and actress from Hugh Grant to Kate Winslet had been in a Marshall picture. His work hadn't really garnered him any accolades in America, but it had made him rich. None of this was particularly surprising or all that interesting.

"I know all of that," I said with a shrug. "He's your run-of-the-mill big shot."

She opened up her laptop and went to Google. "Until you dig around into his private life."

The search engine went to work, and soon enough Frederick Marshall, like many filthy-rich megalomaniacs, had a story sordid enough to make for a chapter in Hollywood Babylon. It all had to do with his dead wife. Her name was Mica Glenn. She was stunning and much younger than he was, a girl known for couture gowns and a penchant for gold lamé. She was also known to enjoy the odd cocktail or ten and got a reputation for getting drunk and sounding off at parties, whining and complaining that her darling Freddie wouldn't cast her in any of his movies. She was, of course, an actress, a starving one when they met, and then a very rich one, but never in either of those circumstances was Mica a very good one. That she had failed to sleep her way to a starring role apparently nagged at her and embarrassed Frederick. And it was his arrogance, coupled with his fear of being reduced to producing B movies once again, that made him refuse her this one gift. Rumour had it that she threatened him, with what no one seemed to know, but he finally agreed to have her star in one of his films. But she died before principal photography started. When she was found dead, drowned in the pool of their country property with no one but Frederick at home, her death was initially considered suspicious and he was brought in for questioning. The toxicology results found excessive blood alcohol levels in her system, and the coroner ruled it an accident.

"He told me she drowned at home but not the rest of it," I admitted to Trinity.

"Can you blame him?" she asked. "He can't very well announce it to every new woman he meets. Imagine, 'Hi, my name is Frederick. I produce hit movies and was accused of murdering my wife. How about I buy you dinner?' Hardly!"

"You have a point."

"Did you know Mica?"

"I met her once. Stunning girl. Bit of a cow, really. It was true about her obsession with gold. She was nearly always photographed in long flowing gold gowns; silk, satin, you name it. She believed it showed off her ivory skin."

I rolled my eyes and parsed the Internet for the gory details and images. Mica was a knockout but in that vacuous way that WAGs often have. And Trinity was right about the gold—countless photos showed her swathed in the hue. One site even claimed that she was buried in her favourite gown. But what got me was her hair.

"You didn't say she was a redhead," I said.

"What difference does that make?" she asked.

"None really. Just not that common." I shrugged. "There's just something about this whole thing that gives me chills."

"It was all an accident. He's not a serial killer. Except," she hesitated.

"There's an *except?*" I asked uneasily.

"An actress friend of mine told me she was invited to his country house a year or two ago. She happens to be a redhead too. Anyhow, she said he tried to get her to wear one of Mica's gold gowns. It was all very weird. It turned her right off and she left straight away."

"No kidding," I said sarcastically.

"Trouble is some people still think he killed her."

"Because she was a bad actress?"

"Because she was a bitch."

I looked once more at the headline, "Movie Producer Accused of Murdering Mica," then I read the byline. Niall Adamson.

"Oh my God," I said. "It's Niall."

I began to click through the many stories that dealt with Mica's suspected murder-cum-accident and saw that he had covered the whole thing start to finish. He even had quotes from Frederick denying any involvement. But it was clear from the tone of the articles that Niall didn't believe him, even though the final piece he wrote stated Frederick's innocence, referring to him as "a wrongly accused grieving widower."

"Blimey," Trinity remarked.

"I wonder if that's why Niall lost his job? Maybe Frederick got him fired?"

I typed Niall's name into the search engine, and within seconds there were loads of hits, and they weren't stories written by him, they were *about* him. The headlines said it all, but I opened a few links and got the drift pretty quickly. It was all over the Internet. Niall Adamson was one of the reporters embroiled in the phone-hacking scandal. He had been accused of hacking into mobile phones, notably of a cabinet minister who wound up in prison for fraud. Niall was raked over the coals. According to reports, the authorities had no real evidence against him, but when he refused to testify against his colleagues—people the prosecutors did have proof of guilt against—he was sentenced to jail for refusing to cooperate and spent almost six months behind bars. And not surprisingly, one of the people he allegedly hacked was Frederick Marshall.

"Do you think he found evidence that proved Frederick killed Mica?" Trinity asked.

"I have no idea. And if he had evidence, why not turn it in and have him arrested?"

"Not if the evidence was gotten illegally."

I mulled it over. It wasn't pretty. But I knew better than most how newspapers worked. There was little in the way of loyalty. If the editors and management needed a fall guy to save their skins, then a crack reporter would do nicely. The higher the profile, the more it deflected from them. From what I read, including between the lines, Niall was a disgraced journalist but an honourable one.

"Poor guy. Not that he cares what I think. Niall Adamson doesn't even remember meeting me," I said.

Police Station—Cirencester

Sergeant Hooper was nodding at me, his lips pursed. "Good on you to get acquainted with Frederick Marshall. He is one of the top movie producers in all of England! That was a shame, him being suspected of killing his wife. Never believed it myself. You know he started his career with slasher films?"

"I know."

"I watched every one of them, more than once, mind." Hooper grinned slyly, as though remembering a particularly graphic scene. "So did he hire you to write a screenplay?"

I bit my lower lip. "Not exactly."

Hooper began tapping his foot on the linoleum floor; it made a dull thud. "Then what, exactly? And how does Niall Adamson figure into all this? Is he harassing Mr. Marshall again? Tapping his phone? If you know anything, you must tell me."

I shook my head and drew the trench coat around my shoulders tightly. "I'll tell you what I know . . ."

= CHAPTER SIXTEEN =

There was a knock at the door and Trinity went down the steps to answer it. She returned, slightly winded, with a cream-coloured envelope in her hand. "This came for you."

I recognized the handwriting. "It's from Dean."

"I thought as much. That's Savoy stationery. Says so on the back."

"Was that him at the door?"

She shook her head. "It was a messenger. Do you want me to leave you alone?"

"No, please stay." I carefully peeled open the envelope and slid out the single piece of paper. I read it twice.

Dear Clara,
I'm sorry for what happened today. It must have been horrible for you. But you shouldn't have come to London. I've been a coward for not being more honest, but here it goes: You were right. If you hadn't been pregnant, we never would have married. I thought I was doing the "right" thing. I was wrong. It was a mistake. I should have never proposed. I'm to blame for that, as I'm to blame for giving you hope that we could make a go of it. I am fond of you, but I never felt the same as you. I tried, but I just couldn't. Our marriage is over. I'm never coming back to you. I love

Amber and we're pursuing a life together. You should move on with your own life and find happiness however you can. I'm sorry if this hurts you all over again but it had to be said, and I hope by putting it in writing, and not some lame email or text message, that you'll understand that I'm serious. Take care, Dean.

When they say the truth hurts, they aren't kidding. I started to cry so hard and fast it was like a broken water main. Trinity led me to the sofa. Between sobs I told her at last what had happened at the set that morning—that I'd gone hoping to reconcile with Dean and instead ended up trying to confront Amber and what a fool she made of me. Trinity listened sympathetically. When I'd finished, I gave her the letter to read as a coda to my story. I mopped up the tears on my face with the back of my hand, but after reading the letter, Trinity brought me a huge bath towel in anticipation of the night's activities.

"Fond of me? 'Take care'? My whole marriage was a sham. An ode to Dean Lapointe's sense of duty."

"I'm so sorry, Clara."

"All these years I only believed what I wanted to believe, but none of it was real. You'd think I could have come up with a better fantasy than a bad marriage," I said solemnly. "I want to go home."

"Of course you do. We'll get your things back from Frederick and get you on the first plane back to Los Angeles, promise," she said kindly.

"I'm going to lie down for a bit," I said. "I need to be alone."

She nodded and handed me back the letter. I went to my room and collapsed on the tiny bed and stared up at the red ceiling fan. It spun swiftly, round and round, and I stared at it, focusing as hard as I could, hoping it would hypnotize me. If people used hypnosis to quit smoking, then it should prove equally beneficial in helping me quit being a wife.

As I lay there, knowing full well the hypnosis wasn't going to pan out, I thought back to Marjorie and Alice. Being left must have been this painful for them. I didn't remember how my mother coped when my father walked out, and I knew even less about Alice. Of course, they both had a child to look after. I could call Marjorie but couldn't bear listening to her tell me it was the family curse again. Not for the first time, I wished my grandmother were alive. Alice would have known what to do. Seeing her in *He Gave No Answer*—how she could take a slap across the face and dish one out moments later—I knew she was as tough as the stage name she chose. If that car accident hadn't ended her life, if I had had her guidance all these years, then maybe I wouldn't be in this mess.

You can't bring the dead back to life, but you can wear their clothes. Marjorie said she had found comfort in wearing them, and so might I. I stood and grasped the handle of her suitcase and hauled it onto the bed. But no matter how hard I tried, it was no use. The clasp was as jammed as ever.

Perhaps it was the frustration, anger or grief that made me shut my eyes tightly and make a wish like I was a five-year-old with a chocolate layer cake lit up with candles. "I wish you were here, Alice. I need you. And I wish I'd been there for you too. Things might have ended so differently for all of us."

Then, feeling foolish, I stepped back and felt something crunch beneath my foot. It was Dean's heartfelt note. I picked it up and tossed it across the room but it didn't get far; it swayed in the air before landing on top of my grandmother's suitcase. I didn't want anything of *his* touching anything of *hers* so I swiped it away like it was an insect. I must have struck the clasp in the process because the suitcase suddenly flew open, launching its contents in a spray of silk and satin fireworks. But that wasn't all. Sheets of white paper blew through the air along with the dresses and scattered like feathers around the room. I was stunned. I hadn't noticed any paper inside when we packed it. As the suitcase lay gaping on the bed, I saw that a thin blue "trap door" had flapped open. The papers must have been stashed inside this false bottom.

I picked up a few of the loose pages off the floor and skimmed them. The format of dialogue and scene descriptions was a dead giveaway; it was a screenplay. But for what? I gathered all the scattered papers and clumsily put them into the right order according to the page numbers. When I found the first page, I'd hoped it would have a title, a writer's name, anything to give me a clue as to what it was, but there was nothing. The type itself was uneven; the letters "t" and "s" were slightly higher than the others. It had been years since I'd seen a script that was typed on an actual typewriter. It had yellowed slightly over time, but otherwise there were no tears or folds or stains; it was pristine. I felt as though I'd unearthed an ancient artifact. There were only fifty typed pages in total, about half a movie script. I read the first scene.

EXT. HOLLYWOOD SIGN—DAY
A dark-haired man, ROD SLATER, is sitting in a
grey sedan. He's smoking a cigarette and waiting
for something to happen. Then it does.

POLICE SIRENS are coming up the hillside towards
him. Rod steps out of the car.

SIRENS getting closer. Rod stamps out his cigarette.

TWO POLICE CARS pull up in a flurry of dust.

A UNIFORMED COP and a DETECTIVE in plain clothes
exit one of the cars.

                    ROD
You took your time getting here.

                 DETECTIVE
Just like you to be in a hurry. Who is it
this time? Another blonde?

                    ROD
You're a real sentimentalist, aren't you?

The two men walk down the steep incline of the
mountain, the loose earth slipping beneath their
feet so that they have to look down as they move,
lest they get swept away.

                 DETECTIVE
                 (shrugging)
You never were one for blondes, unlike me.
I'd take a blonde a minute if I could keep
up. You still wasting time with that redhead?

                    ROD
              (coolly detached)
Red makes all the difference.

    I smiled at the wisecracks. The tone was clear. Whatever the title, it
was a film noir. But the comment about the blonde made my blood
boil. Dean was like that detective, a blonde a minute, or at least
Amber for now. I'd rather be anything but a blonde. Maybe red did
make the difference. Marjorie seemed to think a change of colour
would do the trick. Just exactly what the trick was, I couldn't say.

I put the script down and checked the suitcase to see if the rest of it was tucked inside. There weren't any more pages, but there was an old photograph stuck face down to the false bottom. I gently pried it off. And when I turned it over I gasped. It was a full-length black and white photo of Alice, one I'd never seen before. From the clapboard at her feet, it was obvious that it was from a screen test. Probably for *He Gave No Answer* but I wasn't sure. The dress she was wearing looked familiar, but it wasn't one she wore in the film. It could be from a screen test for the untitled script I'd just found. It seemed strange to think that even though the photograph was black and white I knew the dress was bright green. And I knew that because it was the bottle-green dress I'd first tried on in Marjorie's closet. I quickly fumbled around in the pile of dresses and found it. Sure enough, it was the exact dress.

I continued to study the photograph like a director lining up a shot. Alicia Steele looked great in the photo—sultry and sexy—and her hair was definitely not blonde. It might have been red.

I squinted to make out the writing on the clapboard at Alice's feet. There was a title written in chalk but it was barely legible. The date of the photo was easier to make out, December 7, 1952. I stared hard at the date. There was something about it . . . Then I remembered. My grandmother died on December 10, 1952. The photo was taken three days before the end of her life. I double checked the date on my watch. Today was December 1. I couldn't help thinking that if it were still 1952, my grandmother would be alive.

I didn't even know she was still trying to act then; Marjorie always told me Alice quit trying after she was born. But this proved she hadn't given up her dream after all; maybe she would have gotten the part had she lived. I wanted to imagine she was close to being happy at the end, before her life got snuffed out. Though I knew Alice felt as alone as I did when that picture was taken.

I walked over to a small oval mirror that hung on the wall above the dresser. My mousy hair rested on my shoulders, its normal lifeless self. That wouldn't do any longer. I resented my mother's opinion but not my grandmother's. The photo was telling, and it seemed to be telling me what to do.

I went into the living room, where Trinity was watching a reality show. She quickly switched the channel when she heard me, but it was too late. She was caught.

"I just flipped by it," she said shamefully.

"Where would any of us be without our guilty pleasures?" I waved her off and wondered where those words had come from. They didn't quite sound like me. Then again, what happened next wasn't exactly standard-issue Clara Bishop either.

"You ever dye your hair?" I asked.

She twirled one of her pigtails in her fingers. "Do you think this caramel colour is natural?" She winked. "Why?"

"I feel like a change," I announced.

It was as if Trinity had conspired with Marjorie because as soon as I'd said it, she clapped her hands together and leapt off the sofa. "Most women get a new look when they've been dumped."

"Is that so?"

I followed her into the bathroom, where she opened up the vanity cupboards beneath the sink. I saw at once that asking if she dyed her hair was a dumb question, for there were loads of boxes of drugstore hair dye.

"What colour are you thinking? Ash? Chocolate? Black?" she rattled them off, placing each box on the vanity for my inspection. But there was only one choice for me.

"Red."

She stopped her search and looked up, examining me. I must have passed because she reached into the very back of the cupboard and blew the dust off a box. "I bought this a year ago for an audition but didn't think I could pull it off. Redheads need a lot of attitude." She said it like a warning.

I grabbed the box. The colour was called "Vivacious Red," which made me snicker; "vivacious" was the last word anyone would ever use to describe me.

"You're not trying to please Frederick Marshall, are you?" she asked pointedly.

That was the last thing on my mind. "Don't be ridiculous. What I'm doing has nothing to do with him."

She shrugged.

"Let's do it," I said.

Trinity nodded solemnly, as though colouring my hair was akin to a baptism.

CHAPTER SEVENTEEN

An hour later the damage was done. But colour wasn't enough for Trinity. She had to blow-dry and set my hair too. Then she began to spray it like she was trying to kill it. "That stuff smells!"

"Just cover your eyes," she said as the onslaught of mist continued. I did as I was told.

"You look beautiful!" she exclaimed, proud of her work. "Now go have a look."

Cautiously, I went and stood in front of the bathroom mirror. I wasn't sure who the woman in the reflection was entirely. If I didn't know better, I'd say she looked more like Alicia Steele than Clara Bishop.

"What's wrong?" Trinity asked, sensing that I was spooked.

"Let me show you something."

I grabbed the photograph. The resemblance was unsettling, disturbing even. But why shouldn't we look alike? She was my grandmother, after all; we shared the same gene pool.

"Is this who I think it is?" she asked.

I nodded. "Alicia Steele."

"Blimey. You're her spitting image."

"It's remarkable, isn't it?" I said proudly. "I never thought I looked like her. Amazing what a little box of dye can do."

"Is her hair red? It's hard to tell."

I looked at the photo once more. It had to be red.

"Where did you get it? And what film is it for?"

I showed her the open suitcase and the script pages. "But there's no title page, so it's all a mystery."

Trinity walked to the edge of the bed closest to the window and bent down to pick something up from under it. "I think these are more script pages," she said and held them out to me. I practically tore them from her hands. One glance said it was far more than another page of dialogue; it was what I was searching for and then some. The title and the byline were crystal clear: *The Woman Scorned: An original screenplay by Alicia Steele.*

I was speechless. *My grandmother had written the screenplay.* Then I looked at the other page Trinity had uncovered. It was lined foolscap with handwriting on it. I studied the shape of the letters, the flowing penmanship. I'd never seen Alice's handwriting before; it was lovely and uniform like calligraphy and far from my chicken scratch. It appeared to be notes on how the story ended, and each line was a scene intent to build suspense towards the climax.

Clara vows to get even for what her husband and his mistress did to her.

Clara enlists Rod to kill her husband.

They get close, up on High Tower Court, but Rod changes his mind—can't do it.

The hoodlum, Edgar, will have to do. Clara cuts a deal with him—he wants her all to himself.

Then it all goes wrong. She is double-crossed.

Clara has lost everything . . . she gets into her car and drives into the hills to end things once and for all. She can no longer control what happens in her life, but she can control her death . . .

"What's wrong? You look like you've seen a ghost," Trinity said, alarmed.

"Not seen. But I may have just received a message from one." I handed her the pages.

"Oh my God," she said after reading them.

"I know. Not only did my grandmother write this, her main character is named Clara."

That was plenty to shake anyone, but it was the last plot point of the outline that shook me hardest—*she can control her death.* Alice never got to write those scenes because she was dead before she could finish it. Was the note in my hand the secret to her death? That instead of an accident my grandmother had controlled her death by killing herself. My grandmother, grief-stricken over her failed marriage and failed career, must have become so embroiled in writing the script that reality and story got intertwined. That must be what caused her to have the accident; she was half out of her mind. Otherwise, she would never have killed herself and left Marjorie behind. And Marjorie had always insisted that Alice had died from a broken heart. She must have known more than she let on.

"Have you read it yet? What happens?"

"I only read the first scene, and Clara wasn't in that. Though Alice did write a line about redheads making all the difference," I admitted.

"Is that why you dyed your hair red?" she asked tentatively.

I shook my head and felt the alien curls land on my face. "I don't know, maybe, probably. What's going on, Trinity?" I began to panic.

"There, there," she soothed me like a baby. "It's perfectly reasonable to want to change your hair at a time like this, as I said before. And you read that bit about redheads and saw the photo of Alicia and it inspired you."

"Fine, but what about the name Clara?"

"Ask your mum. She probably read it years ago and named you after it as an homage to Alice," she said. Her explanation made complete sense. And perhaps Marjorie simply forgot about the script, which irked me because all these years it would have been nice to know I wasn't the only aspiring screenwriter in the family. Then I remembered.

"This may sound crazy, but I made a wish for Alice to help me, and then I found all of this," I said, making a sweeping gesture across my room.

She pursed her lips as though summoning patience. "Wishes don't come true, darling. Not like that, anyway, not birthday cake–type wishes."

"Maybe," I conceded.

"You must get some rest. You've had a shock with Dean and now this script," she said soothingly. "But you mustn't worry that the ghost of Alicia Steele is haunting you, or that you're becoming her creation, some sort of femme fatale Frankenstein."

I nodded, even though that was precisely what I was thinking.

"I'm going to call Marjorie now," I said. "Can I use your mobile since Frederick has mine?"

She handed it to me. "I'll leave you alone," she said and left the room, closing the door behind her.

Marjorie must have read the screenplay and outline years ago. It explained her being so cryptic about Alice's death all these years. Her phone rang thousands of miles away but there was no answer. I tried her cell but it went straight to voice mail. I didn't bother leaving a message. In the end, I sent an email from Trinity's smart phone and asked if she wanted to meet me in London. Some things are better discussed in person. And sometimes a girl just needs her mother, even one like mine.

I lay down and obsessed about the notes I'd received unexpectedly from Dean and Alice that were like the missing pieces in the puzzle of Clara Bishop. I slowly drifted off to sleep, but the day's events didn't end there. Dreams followed, nightmares too. I was a passenger inside a convertible driving uncontrollably towards a cliff. Only it wasn't Alice behind the wheel but the fictional Clara. Or maybe they were one and the same—the redhead who made all the difference.

Then dawn came, warm and bright, through the window. I let myself awaken slowly, yawning and stretching, content to remain in bed. Only when I opened my eyes did I realize something was terribly wrong. At first I thought it was exhaustion. Or I was still dreaming. It was the kind of eerie phenomenon that if you told someone about they'd send you to a psychiatric ward. I wiped my eyes and opened and shut them repeatedly. But it was no use. That morning everything including my own skin looked different. The entire world was in black and white.

TAKE TWO:
THE FEMME FATALE

=CHAPTER EIGHTEEN=

Panicked, I leapt from my bed and whipped open the curtains, but to my horror the entire city was a sea of grey, black and white. I needed to find Trinity. I hoped she'd know what was going on. Then I caught sight of my reflection in the small mirror and stopped dead. My well-worn cotton pyjamas were no more; instead, I was wearing a long flowing nightdress complete with frilly collar and cuffs. I must have screamed because Trinity was pounding on my door all of a sudden.

"What on earth is the matter?" she shouted.

I had to calm down. "I thought I saw a mouse," I said quickly.

"Oh, not another one!"

"Another one?" I asked and panicked further. I was terrified of mice.

She remained on the other side of the door as she spoke up. "I've had this problem before. I may have to borrow Clifford, the neighbour's cat, again."

"I was probably seeing things," I said, knowing how true that was. The tone of her voice was its usual upbeat self, so I decided to test the waters. "Is everything okay with you this morning?"

"Fine and dandy," she chirped.

It wasn't what I wanted to hear. Whatever this was, it was only happening to me.

"I'll be out in a minute. I need to get dressed," I said.

"Come out when you're ready," she said. "I've put coffee on. But I have to run out for a bit."

I waited until I heard the lock turning in the door before coming out of my room. Immediately, I saw how the flat had changed. Gone was the giant shoe-shaped chair and animal-print rug. The Arborite kitchen set remained, but otherwise the furniture and art were completely different. I walked around the room and touched the sofa, the chairs and lamps. It all looked familiar even though I'd never seen it before. Then it dawned on me. I recognized the look from years of décor magazines and my mother's obsession with mid-twentieth-century style. Everything in the flat was early 1950s. I crossed the room to the window. The venetian blinds were closed tight like eyelids. I twirled the plastic wand to open them as wide as they could go, praying that the morning light would flood the room with colour. Instead, bright white strips of sunlight landed across every surface, creating a black and white striped pattern. The blacks were blacker, the whites, whiter; everything else was a shade of grey.

My anxiety rose like a pot of water boiling over. I raced to my room to get dressed, desperate to get out and find a reasonable explanation, even though I had no idea where to go for one. I practically ripped the nightdress off, but in my haste I couldn't locate the pair of jeans or any of the clothes from yesterday. I had no choice but to wear one of Alice's dresses. I grabbed the green one from the photo and slipped it on and stepped into a pair of kitten-heeled shoes. Then I noticed the handbag for the first time. It was on top of the dresser. It was delicate and feminine—a lady's handbag. I opened it and found some pound notes inside, along with a lipstick. Looking in the mirror, I carefully traced my mouth with the lipstick and ran a brush through my hair, the curls from Trinity's makeover still bouncy and full.

Armed only with my grandmother's things, I scrambled out the door and marched onto the street. I hadn't taken two steps when I noticed that I was not the only person in vintage clothes. Everywhere I looked, men were going about their business wearing suits and hats, and women were clothed in pretty day dresses with wasp waists and flared skirts. That wasn't all. The cars and buildings, the signs and sounds, were of another era, as though my life had rolled backwards. Yet everything had a fake look about it, like it belonged on a studio backlot, a living, breathing movie set. I half expected to see giant HMI lights and cranes and director's chairs in every corner. Only there weren't any. Everything and everyone seemed to be playing their part, and I was the only one who was in on it.

Alarmed, I darted down the alley that ran the length of Trinity's townhouse. A cat hissed at me and leapt onto an old trash can. I dashed further down the alley, coming to another small side street where a woman was bringing in laundry from a clothesline. I stopped and stood, panting a little from the exertion.

"Can I ask you a question?" I blurted.

She barely looked at me. "How can I help?"

"What is today's date?"

"Second of the month."

"December?"

"Course it is. What else follows November?"

I paused, knowing what I was about to ask next would sound crazy. I asked her anyway. "What year is it?"

That made her stop what she was doing and stare hard at me. "Are you all right in the head?"

"I think so," I answered.

She looked me up and down and seemed to decide that tricksters, criminals or the insane didn't dress in bouclé and kitten heels, and that whatever was wrong with me wasn't going to beat her to death or steal her life savings. That didn't stop her from snatching the last article of clothing from the line and holding her basket in front of her like a shield. "It's 1952," she snapped, then rushed away towards her house.

I reeled from her words. What she said was impossible, and yet everywhere I turned was evidence that backed her up.

Shaken, I slowly made my way back home, taking the high-street route, and wondered if I was still dreaming or insane with grief over losing Dean. Maybe it was some sort of hallucinatory post-traumatic stress disorder. But as I walked, I took in every sight and sensation, indulging in the beauty of a city sculpted from shadow and light, where everything from people to cars to buildings had a sharp silhouette, as though the great cinematographer Gregg Toland had lit the entire world for Orson Wells' next picture. If this were all a dream, part of me didn't want to wake up, not yet.

There was no one at the flat when I returned. I turned on the radio to Doris Day singing *Sentimental Journey*. I adjusted the dial only to find Rosemary Clooney. I turned it off and went back to my room where *The Woman Scorned* glared at me from the desk. Maybe there was a clue in its pages.

"I guess you want to be read." Curled up on the bed, I devoured the screenplay, and when I was finished, I didn't know what to make of it. The plot and characters were haunting, the script full of eerie coincidences that were tough to ignore. As I'd suspected when I first found the unfinished script and her notes, Alice's fictional Clara could have been me, the jilted wife. But that's where the similarities ended. I wasn't a vengeful woman. Her Clara sought revenge in the harshest way possible: murder. She plotted to kill her husband and was attempting to persuade Rod, the private detective, to do it. I turned once more to the page of notes that Alice had jotted down and felt that same chill shoot through me as it had done the first time I'd read them.

Then I heard the door open and my name called out. "Clara?"

It was Trinity at last. I raced out to the living room and there she was. Only she wasn't her usual self. Like the rest of London, she was clothed head to toe in a costume; hers was a pale suit with a matching hat pinned to her hair. Under normal circumstances, I would have said the look suited her. But there was nothing normal about it.

"You okay? Were you sleeping?" she said and stepped closer.

"Must have been," I said and stepped back. From the looks of things, she wasn't aware anything was amiss. "You look nice."

"Thanks."

"Does anything look different to you?" I asked. She gave me a puzzled look.

"Everything looks fine." Concerned, she surveyed her flat, then smiled slyly. "Did you buy me a present? A new lamp or something?"

I shook my head. Then she saw the script in my hand. "Is that the screenplay?"

Relief washed over me. Some things were evidently the same. Maybe I was on the verge of waking up after all. "So you do remember our talk from yesterday?"

"Only that you still have to get me the audition with Frederick Marshall. I assume that's his movie script in your hands?"

Whatever was going on, the same people, Trinity and now Frederick, had made the trip back to 1952 with me. Only I seemed to be the sole person aware of it.

"I'm destined to star alongside David Niven," she said excitedly.

"David Niven?" I exclaimed.

"He's so suave," she said, as though it needed explaining. "By the way, this came for you just now. The boy caught me when I was coming through the front door."

It was a telegram. I'd only ever seen them in the movies. The point of origin was LA.

"It's from my mother," I said, rattled by the turn of events, not to mention the century. It must be her response to the email I'd sent last night. I supposed it made sense that yesterday's email would be today's telegram. I opened it, hoping to be told she was on the next flight to London. What I got shocked me enough that I had to sit down.

"Is everything okay?" Trinity asked, alarmed.

There was no way I could share the contents of the telegram with Trinity.

"Everything's fine. I'm just tired. If you'll excuse me, I'm going back to lie down."

"Okay, I'm going to draw a bath. I'm still so thrilled to have a flat with its own bathroom!"

"What do you mean?" I asked her. The flat had a bathroom all right, but I wasn't sure why it was worth noting.

"You Americans are spoiled," she said cheerfully. "You probably all have bathrooms, one for each person! We just got them over here; only modern flats and houses have them."

She went into the bathroom and I heard the water running. I read the telegram again to be certain I got it right the first time. I had.

Dear Miss Clara Bishop,
I'm responding on behalf of Marjorie. You asked her to meet you in London, England. You must have meant another Marjorie. My Marjorie is only five years old, and believe me, she has no friends in England. Signed, Alicia Steele. December 2, 1952.

It was from my grandmother, and she had signed it using her screen name. She was alive. Of course, if this was 1952 London, she was across the ocean in 1952 Los Angeles. My mother was at this moment a little girl. The grandmother I never met just sent me a telegram. I read it several times over before I focused on the most significant part of all. December 2. She would be dead in eight days. She would be dead in eight days unless I stopped her from driving over that cliff, but how? I clutched the screenplay in my hand and returned to my room and picked up her screen-test photo. Standing in front of the mirror, I saw once more the resemblance, and it was more than the wardrobe and hairstyle. Like me, Alice was in mourning over her husband's betrayal. And like me, winning back a lost love could set things straight, but there wasn't a weapon or potion invented to make a person love you. But a woman needed more than love, she needed to be something, just like Cora did in *The Postman Always Rings Twice*.

From that moment, I knew what I had to do. It was so simple. I had made a wish, and part of that wish was to have been able to help Alice, if only I'd been around in 1952. Now here I was. I would save her and, in return, she would save me. So I connected the dots. Alice wanted to be a star. If she'd got the role in whatever film the screen test was for, then maybe she wouldn't have taken her own life. Or maybe had she finished *The Woman Scorned* and sold it, she would have been satisfied with that success. Either scenario might have given her something to live for and made her realize she wasn't a failure, instead of being pushed beyond the brink and leaving her child alone in the world.

I would get her a movie role, a starring one if possible. I would also finish her script and try to sell it. And I knew the man who could make it all happen.

=CHAPTER NINETEEN=

When the telephone rang a few moments later I knew who it would be.

"Do you want me to answer it?" I called out to Trinity. I could hear her splashing about in the bath.

"Please do, darling."

Still clutching the telegram, I picked up the receiver.

"Hello?" I said cautiously. Just as I expected, it was Frederick.

"Good afternoon, Miss Bishop," he said politely; 1952 seemed to have softened his edges. "I assume we're on for this evening? You must be anxious to get your things back."

My knapsack! How I wanted to believe that life would return to normal when I got my knapsack and all its contents, the real Clara Bishop, back. But I had a job to do, and instinctively I knew that how I acted from now on would be vital to ensuring my plan's success, so I said sweetly, "How nice of you to remember."

When Trinity emerged from the bath in a fluffy robe, she asked about the call. I admitted it was Frederick and that we had made plans to meet that evening. She chattered on about his film, though I only half listened.

"Don't forget about me. I want a part in that movie!" She winked, as though she were joking.

I smiled. "I remember. But I need your help with my hair, and I need to borrow some makeup. Frederick has all of mine."

"Sure!"

"We don't have much time," I said, checking the clock on the wall.

Hair and makeup aside, there was the matter of what I would wear. Judging by the contents of the suitcase, my grandmother wasn't big on slacks or casualwear. I was pretty much restricted to dresses and skirt suits.

Then a long satin gown caught my eye, glistening in its whiteness. I ran the satin through my fingers; it was sleek and soft. There was a familiarity to the gown that got to me. But unlike the green dress, what I recollected wasn't from a photo. It was the very same satin slip dress that Alice had written about. I flipped through the script until I found the part.

INT. A GRAND HOTEL—NIGHT
Clara stands in the lobby surveying the space.
It is packed with PARTYGOERS dressed in their
finery. But even among the City of Angels'
wealthiest and most famous, Clara knows she isn't
about to blend in. She steps forward wearing a
long white satin bias gown that makes her red
hair look like it has caught on fire; a dress
some would call virginal, but not with her body.
Her body is killer. She finds him leaning against
a giant marble pillar and smiles in her way.

Rod, despite being a private dick, is as vulnera-
ble to her as the next chump, but he knows enough
not to smile back. Not yet.

CLARA

Am I late?

ROD

Time stands still when you're at the end
of it.

That was the dress all right. I grinned, undecided if Alice's script was all corn or all classic. I slipped on the dress. No sooner had the bodice and skirt slid into place than an icy draft blew through the room sending the satin swirling into shimmering pools at my feet. I raced to the window. The temperature had fallen suddenly, and as I peered into the night sky I saw fog rolling in, like a distant smoke signal. I latched the window shut, but it was too late. The room itself seemed hazy now and the cold was biting. I searched around for some kind of cover-up. A mink stole was lying on the floor begging to be picked up and cuddled. Wrapped in satin and mink, I was over-dressed for dinner, no matter how rich and successful Frederick was. As I made final preparations to leave, there came over me another feeling, one that masked all the fear and confusion. It was courage gained from having nothing left to lose.

= CHAPTER TWENTY =

"You look like Rita Hayworth!" Trinity gasped. Her jaw had dropped when I entered the living room. "When is Frederick picking you up?"

"He isn't. I'm meeting him," I said. When he'd called, I'd asked him when and where. He told me when and told me to pick where. I didn't know London, but that didn't stop me. There was one place that stuck out in my mind, and I told him without hesitation. Perhaps it was madness to go there, or perverse pleasure and curiosity, I couldn't tell which.

"All right," she said, though I could tell she thought I was daft. "I'll call a taxi. Where to?"

I hesitated, knowing the reaction that was sure to come but finding the confidence to not care all that much. "The Savoy." I purred.

"The Savoy?" she repeated. "Where Dean and Amber are staying?"

"That's the one," I said casually.

"What in the devil are you up to, Clara?"

The devil, as the saying goes, is in the details. The Savoy was smack up against the River Thames. Its name in skinny neon letters glowed above the entrance, which was set back from the road. The building itself was grand in the way that architecture from the Victorian era tended to be. Nothing subtle about it, it stood as a testament to class and tradition, a bygone exclusivity that time had carved through to make way for vulgar meritocratic new money.

As I stepped out of the cab, The Savoy appeared all the more grand in the high-contrast light and darkness of black and white. I'd never noticed shadows as much before. But they were everywhere. Giant pointy ones, round swirly ones, menacing square-shaped ones. Even the fog had a greater weight to it, as though it had rolled in just for me, like a red carpet at a film premiere. There was also a storm brewing in the sky, and it lent an air of drama to the scene.

"Good evening, miss," said a uniformed doorman as he opened the door for me.

I paused in the lobby like the scene from the screenplay; only there wasn't a sea of people, just a few scattered about. But there were enough to take note, and instead of shrinking away, I began to take pleasure in it. I stopped at the concierge and rang the bell. A uniformed man in his fifties showed up fast and efficient.

"I want to send a telegram to America," I said.

"Yes, miss," he said and gave me the form to fill out. I stared at the blank form and tapped the pencil on the counter. What did a granddaughter write to the grandmother she never met? Part of me wanted to pour my heart out, but the smart part of me knew better. Clara Bishop didn't exist to her, and if I was going to save her life, then I needed her to trust me and not have her think I was a crazy person. So I wrote:

Dear Alicia,
Forgive my error with the name. I meant the invitation to go to you obviously. You can call me a fan. Loved you in He Gave No Answer. *I'm a*

Hollywood screenwriter in London making a film. You might be perfect for a part in it. Will set up screen test soon.

I hesitated at signing my name. Her character was Clara. Would that seem odd to her? I decided my name wasn't that uncommon and signed it *Yours truly, Clara Bishop.* I prayed it would be a kernel of hope for her. The concierge told me he'd send it immediately.

We were meeting in the American Bar inside the hotel. It was crowded, mostly with men who looked like they either worked for a bank or wished they did, with a few beatnik types dressed in black speckled among them.

"I'm meeting Frederick Marshall," I announced to the hostess, a dull brunette with a smile that seemed stuck on with wallpaper paste.

"He's waiting for you," she said, and I followed. As I moved through the room, I was aware that dozens of eyes were gawking at me, wondering where I'd been or where I was going. I was the beautiful mystery who distracted them from their Scotch and soda, and what started out as glances turned into a tunnel of hard stares. On the other side was a light that came from the look of satisfaction on Frederick Marshall's face, like a man who had just eaten filet mignon cooked blue. And he stood up when I got to the table. Dean had never stood up for me.

He looked pressed and polished and untouchable. The fifties suit was cut to perfection. Yet, in black and white, he looked like a stylish ghoul and had a roughness that simmered below the dandyism. His cheekbones were more sunken than I remembered. It didn't help much that the candle on the table lit his face from below like a campsite ghost storyteller, which did little to erase the image of him as a suspected murderer.

"You look lovely," he said.

"Not the most original compliment, but it will do for a start," I found myself saying. The tone of *The Woman Scorned* seemed to have found its way into my attitude as well as my getup. I liked it that way.

"I'm with the most beautiful woman in the room," he offered up instead.

"That's more like it," I said.

"I've brought your train case," he said.

"Train case?" I asked, confused. He lifted a train case off the floor that perfectly matched my grandmother's suitcase. It had to be hers: the very one that had been destroyed in the car accident. I stared at it, which seemed to annoy Frederick.

"What's wrong? You afraid something is missing? Go on, open it."

I did as I was told, knowing that there would be nothing inside that belonged to me. Sure enough, there was everything that a girl in 1952 needed: lipstick, mascara, bobby pins, extra silk stockings and, perhaps unsurprisingly, a package of cigarettes. But there was no passport or cell phone.

"Thank you," I said and shoved it beneath the table, out of view.

"Did you want bourbon?" he asked.

"I'll have a sidecar," I said. "That is, if this dump can make one." I began to remove my gloves, meticulously, one finger at a time, as I searched the bar for Dean. He was nowhere to be seen. I had to admit my heart sank a little, which annoyed me.

"We shall see," Frederick said gravely as he studied the drinks list. I studied him.

"The lady will have a sidecar, please," Frederick told the waiter. "That is, if the bartender at this 'dump' can make one?" He winked at me.

"I will check with the kitchen. Lemons are still rationed, but we may be good for tonight," the waiter explained and scurried away.

"Rationed?" I asked. Why was there rationing in 1952? "The war is long over," I pointed out.

"The government still rations certain items. We have a huge debt to pay your country for its help in the war," he said and seemed none too pleased about it. "Lemons don't grow on trees in London like they do in your native California. We're still recovering, you know. Despite what your fellow American said about us."

"What American?" I asked.

"I thought England was broke, but the whole damn city is crawling in Rolls-Royces, Bentleys, Daimlers and expensive blondes," Frederick quoted.

"Who said that?" I asked, wishing it had been me.

"Raymond Chandler," he answered.

The server returned with my sidecar, containing the precious lemon juice.

"I'll have a Scotch over ice," Frederick ordered. "Make it a double."

When the server raced off, Frederick arched an eyebrow at me. "You seem to be in a bad mood."

"A friend of mine is in trouble," I said and ran my fingers through my hair in a blatant act of flirtation that any film heroine would be proud of. "But you don't want to hear about it."

"Try me," he said as his drink arrived on a silver tray. "To making troubles disappear."

We clinked glasses. "If only it were as simple as that," I said furtively.

"I can't make you tell me, but maybe it would make you feel better. Maybe I can even help."

"That's the sticky part," I said and held his gaze. "You can help me very much. But I don't feel right asking."

I was comforted by how he looked intrigued by, not wary of, what I'd said.

"Go on. I'm used to people asking me for favours."

I bristled at this, but it was now or never.

"My friend's an actress. She needs a job badly. I think she'd be terrific in your movie," I said.

He rolled his eyes. "Don't bore me," he sighed. "If you're trying to get me to give the lead to your friend Trinity . . ."

I shook my head and kept going. "No, not her," I said, very aware that I was betraying my friend, but I'd worry about that later. "The actress I'm talking about is an American. Her name is Alicia Steele."

"Never heard of her," he said dismissively.

"She starred in a film noir a few years ago—*He Gave No Answer,*" I said and waited for a sign he'd seen it. No sign came. "You should watch it. She's terrific in it."

"I suppose I can see if there's a print lying around town," he said and started to scan the room for livelier conversation.

I wasn't going to give up that easily. "All I ask is for you to let her audition." I paused, knowing what I really wanted would seem outrageous, but I had to say it. "And give her the starring role, of course."

"That's all, is it?" He raised an eyebrow at me. "Let her play the leading lady just like that?" He paused. "What's in it for me?"

I didn't know how to respond. And if that wasn't awkward enough, at that precise moment, Dean and Amber strolled past our table. Deep down I knew they had joined me on this crazy journey. So I shouldn't have been shocked to see them wearing period clothes, yet I flinched a little. Dean wore a suit and fedora like it was routine, and Amber was downright demure in a cocktail-length dress with cap sleeves. The hostess seated them on the other side of the bar. But they saw me. They saw Frederick. And Frederick saw them and saw me watching them.

"Do you know that couple?" Frederick said. His expression was unreadable.

"Yes." I cringed at the word "couple." "You could say that."

"He's here making a new show, *Daddy's Girls.*"

"You mean *Come to Daddy?*" I asked.

"I mean *Daddy's Girls.* It's a new talent show. Young girls sing their hearts out in front of a live audience each week. The audience picks the winner. You seemed overly interested when he walked by."

"Did I?"

I considered lying. But it was easier to tell the truth.

"Dean is my husband, and he left me for that blonde."

It was Frederick's turn to recoil. And it pleased me that he seemed surprised.

"That's awful," he said. Then he laughed. That didn't please me so much.

"I'm glad you find it amusing," I said and finished my sidecar. The great thing about luxury-hotel bars is that the servers anticipate your needs, and my glass was no sooner drained empty than our man was back with a refill.

"I'm not laughing that Dean Lapointe left you," he said and leaned in once more. Only this time I chose to remain ramrod straight in my chair.

"You know his name?" I asked, shocked. Maybe Dean *was* making an impression in London.

"I'm laughing because Dean Lapointe has been trying for the past week to meet with me about directing my next film," he said scornfully. "By the look on your face, Clara, you share my sense of the ironic. Had he treated you with respect, he would have been able to come by our table and say hello. But because he's been a complete cad, he knows he can't approach me. He'll wonder if I'll even take his calls, let alone hire him."

I was stunned by this strange twist of events.

"That's, that's . . ." I didn't know what to say, but the situation began to amuse me, especially after the second sidecar flowed through my veins. "That is . . . actually . . . very funny."

And we both laughed, perhaps too loudly, but loud enough that Dean and Amber could be in no doubt we were having a good time. It was up to them to decide if it was at their expense. They must have guessed correctly, for within minutes Dean and Amber left the bar, choosing to walk the long way around so as not to pass by us again.

"We frightened them off," I said, still amused. It was the first time I felt in control since Dean had left me. And at last I understood the rush of revenge that the fictional Clara had coveted so badly. It felt good. Too good. Yet what I said next felt like the real Clara, coming out from under all the glamour.

"You should meet with him," I said to Frederick. "He is a great director. Very underappreciated."

Frederick studied me a moment, trying to decide if I was joking. "If you think I should, I will meet with him. There is a talent show element to the movie script, which was the only reason I was considering Dean."

"You should," I said again.

He raised his glass to me. "You are a gracious woman, Clara Bishop from Hollywood."

I raised mine and drank. I was many things that night but gracious wasn't one of them. He watched me closely and ran his tongue over his lips.

"Your hair is exquisite, Clara. The colour is so alive, your skin so pure and fair, you're like a Raphael painting." He drank some more. It unnerved me that he could speak such romantic flattery and not sound like a geek with a college crush. Then his expression changed and went dark like the night sky. "On second thought, you're the perfect vision of a dangerous woman. A Rita Hayworth, able to twist a man's affection like a lock of hair." He reached over and stroked the hair trailing over my shoulder. "You wouldn't try that with me, would you, Clara? I wouldn't dare if I were you."

He was dead serious. I swallowed hard and brought the conversation back to what mattered.

"Alicia Steele is a redhead too. I know how much you like them."

He stopped. "You don't say?"

"But she's in Hollywood."

He sighed loudly. "I am not. I'm in London."

"Yes, but Hollywood actresses do screen tests all the time for foreign producers. Surely you can fly her over here to audition. She'll have to come once filming begins, anyway."

"That's very expensive for an unknown entity," he said. "A casting director friend of mine is over at Paramount doing screen tests for another British film. Maybe this Miss Steele can read there."

"But flying here would be better. You can meet her," I pleaded, knowing it was me who wanted to meet her, knowing somehow that if Alice came to London she would be safe.

"You act like it's a matter of life and death," Frederick said.

"It is."

His face widened into a large smile that seemed to swallow his face. "If I do this for you, she'd better be good."

I finished the sidecar. "She's great."

"I want something in return." He smiled.

I didn't much care for the sort of grin he wore but knew I had no choice but to make another promise I wouldn't keep. "I'll do anything you ask to make it happen," I said.

"Come away with me for the weekend."

I gulped. I wasn't expecting that. "You never asked me what I do," I said, stalling.

"Okay, what do you do?" he said disinterested.

I waited a beat, then said it loud and clear but with a hint of hoarseness thanks to the lemon juice. "I write for *Hollywood Hush*."

Frederick glowered at me, and for a second I caught a glimpse of a man who could do murder. There was no way anyone could convict a man on looks alone, and yet he had an intensity to him that gave the impression he could be capable of anything. He certainly was big enough and strong enough to hold a woman's head under water until her life slipped away. I tried to shake the mental picture. It must be tough if you were innocent to know that some people wondered if you had murdered your spouse and gotten away with it.

"You never said you were a gossip columnist."

I swallowed. "I thought I'd write up a lot of stories in the press about you and the film. Drum up interest in America," I offered.

He swatted at me like I was a fly. "I already get all the press I need professionally. More than I want personally."

I assumed the death of his wife, Mica, had occurred as before, just decades sooner. "You must be referring to your wife's unfortunate accident," I said provocatively.

"I was. And to be clear, you are never to bring her up again."

He glared at his glass of Scotch as if it might bite.

There was little choice in the matter and I knew it. If I could save Alice's life, then there was no price too high. "I will come with you," I said. "If you give Alicia Steele the lead part."

"I underestimated you, Clara." He leaned across the table and squeezed my hand. "You're not such a nice girl after all. Redheads usually aren't." He pulled me towards him, and, startled, I knocked our glasses to the floor, where whatever alcohol was left soaked into the plush pale carpet. Frederick didn't care who was watching; he drew me closer and kissed me on the mouth so hard I felt his teeth grind against mine. When he let me go, I slumped back in my chair, rubbing my wrist where he'd gripped it so tightly. The server with the impeccable sense of timing appeared and cleaned up in silence.

"The lady accidentally spilled our drinks. Bring us two more,"

Frederick ordered, not taking his eyes off me. "Don't look so surprised, Clara. You needed to be kissed."

I looked him in the eye and planted a sultry look on my face, the kind that Rita Hayworth held the copyright on, and told him point blank, "You have no idea how much it means to me that you will help my friend Alicia. I would never steer you wrong."

He leaned over the candle and I wondered if the heat burned his chin, but he seemed impervious to it. "You wouldn't do that. You're not that stupid."

"Here are your drinks." The server was back, and I was thankful for the timing.

"I need to go to the ladies room. Please excuse me." Frederick stood for me, and I marched away as quickly as I could. I needed to catch my breath. The night had taken a turn in a direction I hadn't anticipated. I'd had no time to process seeing Dean, and now I was making a deal to spend the weekend with a man I didn't like. I was churning it all over in my head when Amber ambushed me from behind a potted plant.

"We need to talk," she said crossly.

I stopped in my tracks. She was almost luminous in black and white. The high-contrast lighting that had brought out the best in The Savoy's architecture worked equal magic on her crisp cheekbones and sculpted nose and chin, giving gravity to the paleness of her hair and skin and eyes. Though it wasn't just her beauty I noticed as we stood face to face; something inside me snapped so hard I was convinced even Amber could hear it.

"Well, if it isn't the mistress who stole my husband," I said haughtily.

"What do you think you're doing here?" she barked. "Trying to win him back? It's pathetic! Do you think showing up with Frederick Marshall when you know Dean's trying for a meeting with him will help you?"

"I had no idea Dean was trying to meet Frederick," I said mildly.

"Dean thinks you're trying to wreck his chances. He doesn't want you here."

"You've got quite a mouth on you for someone so young and inexperienced," I said.

"Is that so? You're nobody, Clara. Don't get in the way of Dean's success," she snapped.

I smiled a moment, savouring the opportunity. "Don't mess with me," I warned her calmly. "I could ruin you before you even begin. You need to be taught some respect."

She flinched. It was a far cry from our first interaction on Dean's set and I loved it.

"You can tell Dean that Frederick is going to meet with him. I asked him to and he agreed, though I don't know why I bothered," I said coolly. "Now hurry along. It's past your bedtime."

I stepped away without a backwards glance. But my breathing was rapid, as though I'd run a great distance. After turning a corner, I stopped in front of a hallway mirror. The reflection was of a seductive and powerful woman, a woman who was in control. Yet I knew it was more than an image, beyond what I'd created with makeup and pretty things made of satin and mink and beyond the fog and black and white. It was a sensation, one I felt far below my skin and hair; I felt it in my bones. It was Alicia Steele's noir underworld swallowing me whole at last. In that moment I knew that both the fictional and the real Clara were one and the same and that she was a hell cat.

CHAPTER
TWENTY-ONE

Frederick insisted on driving me to the flat, which was just as well considering I had the train case to contend with. It sat balanced on my lap in the passenger seat of his curvy convertible Jaguar. The interior was pale, might have been tan, might have been ivory, but that was tough to confirm and wasn't worth asking. It was an arrogant but classy automobile, and that suited him. We didn't speak much. An opera singer howled from the car stereo as I watched London whir by in a streak of white lights, when he swerved to miss some drunken revellers who stepped off the curb in front of us. He cursed and the train case landed with a soft thud at my feet.

"Bloody punks!" he yelled. "You okay?"

"I'm fine," I said and stared down at the train case.

He pulled the car up in front of the townhouse and made like he was going to get out to open the door for me.

"Don't bother getting the door," I said with a polite smile and looked up at the warm glow in the windows that belonged to the flat. "Looks like Trinity's waiting up for me. You know, she should audition for you too." There, I'd kept my promise and it served two purposes; it would make Trinity happy that I'd tried, and it also made Frederick want to get away as fast as possible.

"I'll give it some thought. And we will figure out a weekend soon. I have production matters to deal with," he stated.

"The weekend only happens if Alicia gets a part," I said smoothly.

He grinned in a way I didn't like and goosed his engine. "Have a good night. I will ring you."

"Sure," I said and got out of the car. That was a benefit of the times: without smart phones and computers it would be much easier to play hard to get.

I waited until his car had disappeared around the corner before heading along the front walkway. Something caught my eye in the hedgerow and I stopped to investigate. It was a leather case the size of a large briefcase that someone had abandoned. It was old and banged up and had that worn quality to it that vintage leather has. It was beautiful. I flipped open the clasps and lifted the lid. To my amazement there was a portable typewriter inside. The body was dark plastic, not quite black, maybe mahogany. The keys were all there and it still had a ribbon in it. I couldn't fathom why anyone would toss it out. I decided to take it with me. It was heavy, and with the train case, I had my hands full, but I was determined to balance them both. I must have been very focused not to have heard the footsteps.

"You're the most glamorous thief I've ever seen."

I whirled around and found Niall Adamson standing on the sidewalk a few feet away like a sentry. As with most of the men I'd seen today, he was wearing a fedora, and perhaps because of the chill in the air and the brewing weather, he also had on a trench coat. Any way you looked at him, the clothes classed him up, and that made him more handsome than ever, like an old movie star.

"I'm not stealing exactly. Someone tossed it here because they didn't want it," I said self-consciously. "How long have you been watching me?"

"Long enough. What was in the case? Not a lover's head, I hope."

"It's a typewriter."

He lit a cigarette and walked towards me.

"Stay where you were. I'm not interested in your line," I said tartly, enjoying how words that I once could only write now slid off my tongue like melted butter. It was as if I'd been talking to strange men in foreign lands my whole life.

He smirked and kept walking. "But I've been practising my line all the way over here," he said dryly.

I gestured to the patch of ground a few feet away where he'd been standing.

"All that way? You must be exhausted," I said back as fast as a strike on a match. "Say, are those American?"

"How can you tell?"

"The smell." I had experimented with smoking in high school, but I could never get through a drag without coughing. But now, the scent of Marlboros made me homesick for LA, and I lifted my chin and breathed in the aroma. "Marlboro?"

"You know your fags. Have a go."

Next he held the cigarette out for me to take a puff—it had touched his lips and then would touch mine—a strange kind of kiss. I took the cigarette and drew in the smoke, expecting to look as glamorous as Lauren Bacall in *The Big Sleep*. But the glamour was short-lived as I coughed up a lung just like in school.

"I take it you don't smoke much," he said.

"It's been a while."

"If you like, we can go up to your flat and get you a glass of water?"

"I'm fine," I said, sputtering, but finally able to inhale without gasping. Was that a come-on? Water glass instead of etchings?

He continued to smoke like Humphrey Bogart, and as he looked at me I detected a small wave of recognition in his eyes. "This may seem like another line to you, but haven't we met?"

I felt an immense sense of relief that the man remembered me. I wondered if he also remembered how we knew each other and, more importantly, when.

"We have," I admitted. "At The White Stallion. I was at the bar. You probably didn't get a good look at me."

He ran his blue eyes over my face like I was a lost lover he'd been reunited with after a war. "I've seen you somewhere else." Then he snapped his fingers, grinned and pointed at me. "The Beverly Hills Hotel. You're Clara Bishop! I was in Hollywood to interview Jane Russell."

"That must be it," I said flatly. It was official: I was the only person who travelled back through time with their memory intact. "Now, if you'll excuse me, I want to go to bed."

But he kept talking . . .

"Tell me something. Do you always act like you're in a film noir?"

"Excuse me?" I asked, taken aback that anyone besides me would spot it.

He chuckled. "Your dialogue, how you look and your attitude are straight out of central casting. If you're the femme fatale, who are you going to double-cross?"

"I'm sure I don't know what you mean," I said nonchalantly.

"There's always a double-cross. I hope you've got yourself a worthy target."

"I don't have a target," I denied, thinking of Amber.

He contemplated this a moment before saying, "Then you're a fake femme fatale. How disappointing."

I wasn't sure if I liked him or hated him. If he hadn't helped me out with the You-Know-Who interview, I'd tell him to shove off. He rummaged around in his pocket and pulled out an old-fashioned cigarette case. Marjorie had one that belonged to my grandmother. She kept it on the mantel beneath the movie poster. I'd not seen another, except in movies, until now.

"I didn't think they still made those," I said, gesturing to it.

"They don't," he said.

"My grandmother had one," I said.

He nodded. "My father gave me this." He smoked and I just stood there, the typewriter at my feet. "I should get going. It's late."

"Allow me to carry the cases upstairs for you. They look rather cumbersome." He bent down and picked up the typewriter.

"Please don't bother," I said. "I'm perfectly able."

He placed it on the walkway and he spoke again. "You don't fool me, Clara."

"I'm sure I don't know what you mean," I said, mildly irritated.

"You act like a tough dame, but in truth you're nothing but a damsel in distress," he said. I was about to object when he put his finger on my lips to hush me. I felt my face flush. "I happen to like rescuing damsels."

"What gives you the idea I need rescuing?" I asked, again taken aback, but allowing myself to give a little. "But you're not wrong. I've had it rough lately."

He blew smoke out of the corner of his mouth in that way smokers have, thinking they can somehow prevent it from landing in someone's face. It never works, and I felt the smoke sting my nostrils. "I'm sorry. I shouldn't have teased you." He spoke earnestly. "Is there something I can do to help?"

I pulled the mink tighter around my shoulders. "I wish there were."

He continued to hover like there was something he wanted to get off his chest. "I'd like to buy you a drink sometime," he said. "That is, if you need someone to talk to about things . . ."

"I'd like that very much," I said, surprised to discover it was true.

"What's your telephone exchange?"

For some reason that made me giggle. "You know, I haven't the slightest idea? This isn't my flat. I'm only visiting. Why don't you write down yours?"

"How about we agree to meet tomorrow night at The White Stallion? About eight?"

"That would be swell," I said and immediately covered my mouth with my hand. Had I uttered the word *swell?* Next I'd be saying Jiminy Cricket.

"Until tomorrow night," Niall said and touched the brim of his hat like a salute and disappeared into the fog.

Walking up the steep flight of stairs to the flat dressed in heels and an evening gown, while carrying a heavy typewriter and train case, wasn't so easy, and I regretted not taking Niall up on his offer. But I would see him again tomorrow night. If only I had spent the last ten years acting like I had tonight. Tonight I'd discovered the pleasure of making a man do whatever I wanted. Frederick and Niall would be fun to play with.

When I entered the flat, I found Trinity asleep on the sofa. I would have left her there if I hadn't noticed her reading material. Piled neatly beside her on the floor with a few loose pages clutched in her hand was the screenplay from my room.

Maybe it was the time of night, the sidecars or the new-found steely attitude, but I snatched the papers from her grasp and she awoke with a start.

"What are you doing reading this?" I snapped.

"You scared me to death!" Trinity sat up and snapped back.

"Well, what of it?" I asked, aware that I was overreacting.

"Calm down, Clara. I didn't think you'd mind, really. I went into your room to give you an extra blanket and it was there. At first I thought it was for Frederick's movie, only it wasn't. But I kept reading it anyway. I couldn't help myself. I'm an *actress* you know. Sorry."

I felt like a fool and slumped down onto the sofa beside her.

"I'm the one who's sorry. I don't know what came over me. It's been a strange night." I forced a smile. "What did you think of it?"

Trinity pursed her lips. "Alicia Steele is a fine writer."

I paused, unsure what to reveal. "Don't you remember what I told you about her?" I studied Trinity's face for any ounce of recognition, but none came.

"Not really. Is she a famous screenwriter? What's she done?"

No matter what the era, that was always the first question anyone ever asked. "It's her first script. She's a friend of mine in Hollywood." I thought retelling the truth about her being my grandmother would be too much for Trinity to bear. Thankfully, my explanation was enough.

"I figured you two know each other very well. It's like she was writing about you. There are a lot of similarities."

"I suppose there are," I said vaguely, tired and not wanting to drudge it all up again.

"Are you Alicia Steele?" she asked pointedly.

The question caught me off guard. In some ways I supposed I was Alicia, but there was still plenty of Clara Bishop to go around, just a new and improved version. "No, I'm not," I said and yawned. "She's back in LA."

"So you gave her your story?"

"Not exactly. I'd say she gave me hers too."

"So you're co-writing?"

"You could say that."

"What's in the case?" she said, noticing it for the first time.

"It's a portable typewriter I found."

She nodded and looked at her watch.

"Bloody hell. It's that late? Time to go to bed." She held out the script to me and I clutched it to my chest.

"I'm sorry I acted so intensely tonight," I said.

"Don't think twice about it," she said and smiled. "How was your night with Mr. Marshall?"

"It was good. I told him he should hire you."

"You didn't!" she beamed.

"I did. Now the rest is up to you." I smiled back. "By the way, you didn't tell me how thick the fog got around here at night. It was almost impossible to find the house!"

Trinity gave me a very odd look that penetrated me to the bone.

"What?" I asked.

"You must be tired," she said softly. "It was a gorgeous clear night with a full moon. Not a stitch of fog in sight."

Police Station—Cirencester

I stopped talking and waited. Sergeant Hooper cleared his throat a couple of times as though trying to delay saying something, delay making a conclusion. I decided to say it for him.

"I knew you wouldn't believe me. But I'm telling the truth." I stood up and moved around to the back of his chair and leaned forward so when I spoke he'd feel my warm breath on his neck. "Everything was upside down. I was frightened and alone."

He trembled a little, and I returned to my chair and gave him a searching look.

"I can't even write that part down," he said at last and tossed his pencil on the table. "The whole police department will think I've come unhinged."

"I know the feeling," I admitted.

"So you're trying to tell me that you became someone else after you started wearing your granny's clothes and reading her screenplay? And that you saw only in black and white and went back in time? And what about the others?" he asked. "Were they 'in' on this act of yours?"

I bristled at the accusation. "Like I just told you, it was as if my life and the people in it were transported back to 1952. But I was the only one who knew it. They carried on as if they were meant to be there, in that time, in that place. As for seeing things in black and white, that seemed to only happen to me."

"Did your plan to save Alice work, then?" he asked and cleared his throat like he meant to clear his head. I knew what he really wanted to know: Was Alice alive and living out her final days at some old-age home for actors in California? I wasn't about to tell him. He needed to hear the whole thing or none of it would make sense. He continued, "That is, assuming any of what you're telling me is true."

I smiled. "The truth is stranger . . ."

"Than fiction. Yes, I know that one," he said impatiently.

The smile fell from my face.

He took a deep breath and rocked slowly in the chair, his foot against the table leg for leverage. I had a feeling I knew what he was thinking.

"And I didn't become someone else exactly. I just started to act differently, but I'm not going to lie . . ."

Hooper removed his foot from the table leg so that the chair smashed hard on the floor. He leaned forward and pointed his finger at me. "No. You are not going to lie to me."

I parted my lips into a tiny smile. A smile that could be read a dozen ways, and I wanted Hooper to take his pick.

"What I was about to say was that I liked it. Whatever 'it' was, it felt good."

"To be in control, perhaps?" he suggested.

"That's part of it," I said.

"*To be what, then?*"

"*To be less predictable.*"

We looked at each other, and for a moment nothing was said, neither of us made a move. Then he shuffled through the yellow papers looking for something and skimmed his handwriting. When he found what he wanted he glared at me suspiciously.

"*Do you still only see in black and white, then?*"

"*It's more complicated than that.*"

"*Complicated how?*"

"*I'm getting to that part.*"

"*I want to believe you, Clara . . .*"

I raised an eyebrow.

He coughed, "Miss Bishop. But it isn't sounding good."

I tossed my head back and the trench coat fell onto the chair behind me, leaving my shoulders and décolletage bare. I took my time retrieving the trench and covering up again. Hooper looked like he was starting to perspire.

"*Go on,*" *he said.* "*I want to hear your side . . .*"

"*I went to bed just like I said. I figured it was all a dream and I'd wake up with a hangover . . .*"

CHAPTER TWENTY-TWO

The morning of the second day of my life in black and white, I dressed in a dove-grey tea dress, though I was fairly sure it was pale pink. I set the typewriter up in my room on the tiny desk and fed a sheet of paper into the carriage. I hadn't tried to write a movie in years; I wasn't sure if I knew how anymore. The machine sat there like an *objet d'art*, daring me to bring it to life and give it purpose. It wasn't difficult to empathize with the fictional Clara's emotional state. All I had to do was replay the events of the past few days. Dean and Amber making a fool of me on his set. Dean's note telling me he never loved me. Dean and Amber parading through The Savoy. Amber's attempt to intimidate me in the hallway of the hotel. Like the husband and mistress in the screenplay, Dean and Amber shouldn't be allowed to escape unscathed either. I would come up with something. In the meantime, a little make-believe revenge would be cathartic. My fingers hovered over the keys as though they were burning coals until a scene formed in my mind, and then I let it unfold on the page.

INT. FORMOSA CAFÉ—NIGHT
Clara and Rod sit in one of the red leather
booths by the bar, a couple of highballs between

them. She's wearing a red dress to full effect.
He's acting like he doesn't notice she's trying.

                    ROD
        You said it was urgent. Now you've got me
        here, what's on your mind?

                    CLARA
        Did I say urgent? I suppose I did. I need
        your help.

                    ROD
        You don't look like the kind of dame that
        needs my help.

                    CLARA
        What kind of dame do I look like? Or don't
        I want to know?

                    ROD
        So tell me, what do you need?

                    CLARA
        I'm in trouble up to my neck. Can I trust
        you?

There. My first scene was complete. I smiled and bopped up and
down in my chair with excitement. I yanked the page out of the
typewriter. I was holding in my hands a piece of fiction created by
my mind but also by my body. The physical act of typing made me
feel like an artist, this white sheet my blank canvas. A computer does

the job, but it's too easy to make mistakes disappear. I'd learned the hard way that mistakes in judgment don't go away at the touch of a keystroke. From now on in life and in writing, my decisions would be made with precision.

I spent the rest of the day carefully hanging, folding and pressing the garments until every item from my grandmother's wardrobe was ready for its close-up. It felt like I was preparing for something, like an army officer getting ready to go to battle. Which was fitting, because after writing and thinking about the script, and my own situation, I had enough anger smoldering inside me to start a war. I had Plan A, land Alicia Steele a starring role in Frederick's new movie, and Plan B, finish the script and get him to buy it. But there was also Plan C. The more I thought of Dean and Amber, the more I despised the two of them. Where I'd been distraught and depressed before, I was now seething and ready to boil over at any moment. I had come up with something special for them. And like the screenplay, I'd need some help. It would involve Niall. Even though he wasn't a detective like Rod in the script, he was an investigative reporter, at one time anyway, and that was close enough to be useful for what I had in mind.

Yet, like in the scene I'd written, I wasn't sure if I could trust Niall. But I did know there was only one red dress in Alice's collection. I remembered what it looked like when I could see colour. It was a dark red, almost burgundy, with three-quarter sleeves and a lace overlay. The hem was scalloped and reached just below my knees. It was demure on the hanger, almost schoolmarm, but once on it morphed into a sexy, clingy thing, the sort of dress a woman wore when she couldn't risk a man saying no. Or, as in the script, it was a garment to be worn "to full effect." It would do nicely for my eight o'clock drinks at The White Stallion.

When it was time, I dressed in the red dress and did my own hair. Turned out that hot rollers weren't anything to be afraid of. I used the makeup that was in the train case, and when I was done, I spun around for Trinity's approval. She wolf-whistled, but I could sense she didn't entirely approve.

"I don't see why you're going to meet that Niall fellow. Not when Frederick seems so taken with you. He's a much better catch," Trinity said.

"I'm not interested in catching anyone. And you're just saying that because you want to star in the film."

She grinned. "Not star; I'd be happy with the second lead."

"That's very gracious of you," I grinned back. "How do I look?"

She stared a moment, then said with the tiniest note of suspicion, "Like a woman on a mission." She stuck out her lower lip. "My agent still hasn't heard if I got the audition."

I recognized the pleading in her voice and knew what she was getting at.

"Don't worry about that. Believe me, I will be seeing plenty of Frederick Marshall, more than enough to constantly badger him about you."

She perked up. "Brilliant!"

I shivered at the thought of the getaway weekend. I would find a way to ensure it never happened. I was in control now, not Frederick.

CHAPTER
TWENTY-THREE

I walked through the door of The White Stallion and was struck by the transformation of the place. The décor was completely different. The spiky ironwork and gauzy ceiling canopy were no more; instead, it had the well-worn feel of a stable but without the stench. This pub was warmer, more welcoming, and wasn't trying too hard to be so-hip-it-hurts and was the better for it. But that wasn't all. A visible haze hung in the air from cigarette smoke. There were no anti-smoking campaigns in 1952; on the contrary.

Then I saw Saffron. She looked like a cigarette girl without the tray of bad habits around her neck. She breezed by with a quick smile of acknowledgment. Niall was at his usual table in the back and stood up as I approached just as Frederick Marshall had done.

"A girl could get used to good manners," I said as he pulled the chair out for me to sit down.

When Saffron fluttered to our table, for once I wasn't resentful of her beauty. I hardly noticed it at all.

"Don't you two look cute." She smiled at me.

"Two bourbons please," Niall ordered.

Saffron looked to me and turned on her charm. "Is it true you write for *Hollywood Hush?*" she asked boldly.

"I used to," I said. I was purposefully evasive. Now wasn't the time to discuss my favourite interview or weirdest celebrity story or whatever question readers of tabloids, even 1950s tabloids, usually wanted to know. Her face fell a little.

"You know I'm an actress . . ." she began. Perhaps it was my disdainful expression, or maybe it was Niall's timely cough, but she stopped talking and changed tactics. "Nice dress," she nodded approvingly, like that was what she had intended to say all along, and turned on her heels.

"Was I rude?" I asked. Niall shook his head.

"I suppose you get that a lot?"

"I get my fair share of actresses wanting me to get them press," I admitted sourly.

Niall leaned in conspiratorially. "Saffron is right, though. That is a killer dress."

I looked up at him through my false lashes and smiled. "This old thing?"

The drinks arrived and Niall raised his glass like he was going to make a toast, but his hand hovered over the table hesitantly.

"You going to make a toast?" I asked.

"That would seem like the thing to do. I'm just not sure to what!" he said.

I thought a moment, then raised my glass. "Allow me. Here's to better days." I closed my eyes and sipped the bourbon like it was honey.

"Why better days?" he asked. I could hear the concern in his voice. "You hinted at rough times last night, and I haven't stopped thinking about it." He bristled a little, like he was revealing more than he should.

"You did call me a damsel in distress," I reminded him with a smile. "You really want to know?"

"I wouldn't have asked if I didn't," he said.

"Can I trust you?" I asked, repeating the line I'd written. It was time to lay on the sad, lonely and in-need-of-being-saved-by-a-man act, and lay it on thick.

It took exactly two and a half shots of bourbon for me to pour out my story to him. I tried to tell him in a tone of cool detachment, like it didn't matter all that much, it was just something that happened. I didn't want him to think I was a hysteric. The whole sordid mess with Dean and Amber was served up like a plate of cold scrambled eggs. I'd left out that Dean confessed he only married me because I was pregnant. I didn't tell Niall about the pregnancy or the miscarriage. I told him about Amber and the confrontation last night. I skipped the part about my grandmother. That was none of his business and was too far-fetched for anyone to believe. When I was done talking, he polished off his drink and wiped his mouth with the back of his hand like he was trying to forget how it tasted.

"Husbands leave wives all the time," he said with a trace of bitterness. "Sometimes not soon enough."

It wasn't the reaction I was hoping for, and I said as much. "I guess you only want to rescue damsels who are carrying heavy typewriters or broke a nail on the way to tea?"

He snickered. "I'm just not sure you need rescuing. I get that you're upset. But if you want my opinion, your husband seems like a first-class jerk. You're better off without him. And, well, the girl's name is Amber. Isn't that enough revenge?"

I grinned my approval of his joke. "Who said anything about revenge?" I asked.

He leaned forward. "Women always want to retaliate. They just can't let go."

I bristled and took a swig of bourbon to douse the smoldering inside. "Perhaps you're right. I don't want either of them to get away with it. Toss me aside like I'm yesterday's news."

"Or last week's *Hollywood Hush*," he interjected with a wry grin.

"Clever," I admitted, then continued. "Men should never lie to women about loving them, about wanting to spend their lives with them. He's a coward. And I hate women who sleep with other women's husbands. It isn't nice. It's not ladylike."

He whistled, long and low. "Ladylike? From where I sit, women have been screwing each other over for centuries. You can't stop it. As for men lying to their wives, you can't stop that either."

"That's what I admire about you, Niall Adamson, your faith in the goodness of humankind."

He smiled out of the corner of his mouth. It was now or never, and I chose now.

"You said you wanted to help me," I began. "And I have an idea how."

"Go on," he said cautiously.

"I want to hire you to write some scathing articles on Dean's show, maybe even write a scathing article on Amber."

Niall sat back and took it in. I continued, "You could go on set and interview him and then write about how bad the show is, how mean and manipulative he is to the contestants and how he yells and bosses everyone around. It's all true; you should see the stuff I've seen. We could create a scandal that sends him packing back to LA. Maybe you find something only someone with your special *skills* could."

I saw immediately that Niall's face had hardened like cement.

"I see where this is going. You've got the wrong guy," he shot at me.

"C'mon, Niall. Are you saying you wouldn't dig around, maybe exaggerate a little for a big story?"

He was silent. I knew when to shut up, so I shut up. Took a deep breath and tried again.

"I've got the right guy," I said, trying to sound as soft and helpless as I could. "I looked you up."

"I went to prison, as I'm sure you know. I was a fall guy. Plain and simple. The cops know it. Scotland Yard knows it. That doesn't make me some two-bit criminal for hire. Do your own dirty work."

"I'm sorry," I said softly. "I don't mean to say you're not honest. You're impressive, that's all I meant."

"You get impressed by strange things," he said. "And no offence, but until this wiretapping scandal erupted, I was a serious reporter. This movie star beat is all I can get these days."

I nodded sympathetically. "I know. You once covered crime and politics . . ."

"And the war. I was on the front for the BBC. Real news," he said.

And I was a screenwriter, I wanted to say, but thought better of it. "All I'm asking is for you to do what I can't," I said. Then I remembered what he'd said to me back in LA about wanting to work for American magazines. We all want something. I pulled the ace out of my deck of cards. "I've got all the contacts you need to start over. I can make you the most sought-after freelancer in London. Every editor in America will beg you to write for them."

"Just what I want. To write about movie stars for the rest of my life."

"It's an honest living."

"Like I said, you got the wrong guy."

Then Saffron was back with her tray, standing over us like some Victoria Secret overlord.

"Another round, kids?" she asked.

"Just the bill," I said.

"Not a problem. I brought it with me just in case." She smacked the bill on the table. "I can always tell when a couple is finished."

"You don't say," I retorted, but she had twirled away. Niall and I both went for the bill.

"It's on me," he said.

"I should object," I said slyly, but I was pleased. My mother always said when a man offered it was a good sign he would do anything you asked.

He got up to leave. But there was one more thing I wanted to know.

"Niall?"

"Yup."

"How well do you know Frederick Marshall?"

"Why do you ask? Did he invite you to his country place for a midnight swim?"

"That's not funny."

"No, I suppose it's not."

"I was curious. Wondering what sort of character he is."

"You mean, do I think he killed his wife?" Niall stood looming over me. His expression was tough to read.

"Maybe," I admitted.

"He was never charged and was cleared after the investigation. It was in all the papers, so he must be innocent," he said tersely.

"I read what I read, but that doesn't mean it was true. You reported on it extensively. Was there ever anything truly incriminating? Did you ever get any photos or anything on tape?"

"Maybe I did. Maybe I didn't. If I did, I wouldn't tell you." He tipped his fedora to me. "Let's just say that Frederick Marshall is one man who was content to see my reputation destroyed and me serve time. You could say we don't see eye to eye. It's been lovely getting to know you better. You're quite the girl."

"Just a damsel in distress," I said gently. "Please, think about what I'm asking you to do? It's not unheard of for a gossip columnist to get back at someone through a story."

He smirked and walked away, slowly and deliberately, but as I expected, he took one final glance at me over his shoulders before walking through the door.

Saffron whirled by and hovered at the table. I sensed she wanted to tell me something. "Typical," she sighed. "If you ask me, you should find a date with more manners. Leaving you here like that."

"He's not really a date."

"That's good."

I looked at her and raised my brow. "Why? What's wrong with him? I know he spent time in jail. He maintains he's innocent."

"Then I guess you know all there is to know. If it's not a date, then none of it matters anyway." But she still didn't budge. Instead, she sat down where Niall had been.

"I can't help it, but I overheard some of what you were saying," she confessed. I narrowed my eyes at her. I had no idea how much she'd heard, but I didn't like it.

"Go on," I said.

"I have a friend. He's a journalist like you. Writes for *Talk*," she said. *Talk* was a tabloid broadsheet like *Hollywood Hush* only even more trashy. I tapped my fingernails on the table. "What exactly did you hear?" I asked her.

She shook her head. "Hardly anything. Just that you wanted to write about a new television show and you couldn't. I assume because you're busy?"

"That's right," I agreed quietly.

"If Niall won't help you, my friend might." She sat there looking like there was more to the story, but I wasn't about to find out.

I bit my lower lip. If I couldn't count on Niall to help me, then I needed a backup plan.

"What's his name?"

Saffron beamed. "Lawrence Hayward. But everyone calls him Larry."

CHAPTER TWENTY-FOUR

Saffron had been good to her word and called Lawrence Hayward at the end of her shift.

I wore a peplum skirt suit the colour of wet cement, complete with hat and gloves, to meet him the next day, the third day of my life in 1952, at the garden gate entrance to Kensington Palace. I walked through Kensington Gardens along the Broad Walk. It was a sunny day, and it pained me to miss out on what were even in winter elegantly landscaped gardens. Instead, through the prism of black and white, one of London's most beautiful sites was made to look drab and forlorn.

He was sitting on a bench reading and looked up when I approached. I knew the type—in the future he would be a lonely man with an immense Blu-ray collection who spent Saturday nights watching *Citizen Kane*. In 1952, he was a bookworm. As I got closer, I could see his Adam's apple move up and down his throat as he swallowed, hoping that the redhead in the suit that hugged her like cellophane was the writer from America. When he stood up, I saw he was much shorter than me and wore scruffy trousers and a faded striped shirt that needed to take a step closer to an iron. He was innocuous, unthreatening and average. The perfect look for a tabloid reporter. Then he smiled, a lopsided toothy smile. I looked at the book he was reading: Dale Carnegie's *How to Stop Worrying and Start Living*. Clearly I wasn't the only one with a crisis.

"I'm Clara Bishop," I said and held out my hand. He took it, held it longer than I liked, then kissed it longingly.

"I'm Henry Taylor," he said.

I snatched my hand from his.

"I'm Larry Hayward," a shrill male voice called out. I turned away from Henry, whoever he was, and saw a tall, wiry young man skipping down the path towards me. He wore a suit that looked too big on him and his hair was greased back with pomade.

"I'm sure it's my loss, Henry," I said dismissively and walked towards this bouncing ball of energy.

"You must be Clara," he said and looked me up and down like he was buying me.

"That's right," I said and smiled coolly as we shook hands.

We sat down on a bench, and I wondered whether Henry Taylor might have been a better choice.

"So how do you know my cousin?" he asked me.

"Cousin?"

"Saffron's my cousin. Didn't she tell you?"

"No, she didn't mention that," I said and wondered why she hadn't.

"I'm the family embarrassment," he answered bluntly. "She's the star of the clan. Always going on and on about making it big one day. She recites Shakespeare and Chekov at Christmas. Used to put on plays for the whole family."

He snickered, but I thought it was sweet and imagined a little girl Saffron, already a beauty, playing Juliet beneath a Christmas tree in her pyjamas.

"Between you and me, she can't act her way out of a paper bag," he continued, clearly enjoying running her down. "She keeps asking me to write about her. Has she asked you?"

I nodded. Saffron had made me promise to get her in the press in exchange for the introduction. I promised to try, even though I knew that selling a story on an unknown actress was next to impossible.

"Thought as much," he snorted. "She's a wily one that Saffron. Is she a friend of yours?"

I shook my head. "We only just met, and she knew I was looking to find a writer and said you were . . ." I hesitated.

"A friend?" he snorted again. "Saffron's only real friend is Saffron. Let me tell you this. Her only motivation for hooking us up is so I help you with this assignment and then you'll write about her, because she knows I won't."

"I'm sure she's not that calculating," I said doubtfully.

"You want to know what she told me about you?" he snorted.

I wasn't sure I did, but he didn't wait for an answer.

"She said you were a lonely American who had just been dumped by her husband and I'd have a chance with you if I helped you out."

"If that's what you're expecting, I'd better leave," I said and stood up. Larry grabbed my wrist to stop me. I didn't appreciate being touched by a stranger. Hated it in fact. But I didn't struggle or call out; I simply glared. It must have been enough, as he let go.

"Sorry," he said. "I shouldn't have grabbed you."

"No, you shouldn't have."

"I didn't think this was a date," he said quickly. "I just wanted you to know the truth. That's what we journalists do, isn't it? Tell the truth."

"Except on occasion," I pointed out. "So, will you help me?"

"I might do," he said, then a sly grin crept across his face.

I explained to him that the stories he'd write for me would run in *Hollywood Hush* in America after *Talk* had first dibs, and every story about Dean afterwards too. He was anxious to be published in America, so my promise had him practically drooling. He told me his editors at *Talk* let him write pretty much what he wanted as long as it was salacious and lurid.

"The show I wanted you to write about is *Daddy's Girl*," I finally told him.

He was impressed. "That's just filming! I'll be ahead of the curve on that one. What's your access?"

"The producer is my husband. Dean Lapointe. We're estranged."

He rubbed his chin again, trying to decipher the information. I decided to help him along. "He left me for another woman. I want someone to cover his show, so to speak. You get my meaning?"

"I get your meaning. You're after a wee bit of payback."

"We understand each other. You'll have no problems getting on set. Dean will want *Talk* covering him. He has big plans over here."

"What sort of big plans?"

"He's trying to direct a film. Have you heard of Frederick Marshall?" Larry snorted like I was an idiot for asking. "Dean is meeting Marshall about his next picture. You can ask him if you like. He'll want to talk himself up."

"I'll get on it. Sounds like fun."

At first I'd regretted suggesting to Frederick that he meet with Dean. But the more I thought about it, the more I schemed and dreamed up this plan to ruin him, the more I realized it could be useful if Dean felt he stood a chance. He'd talk himself up to the heavens. Hell, even if he got the job, I'd find a way, somehow, to ensure he lost the job too. The bigger they are . . .

"Clara?" Larry said and snapped his fingers. "You vanished there."

"Sorry about that," I said, feeling self-conscious. "Where were we? Oh, yes. And while you're at it, see what you can dig up about Amber Ward. She's an actress. She's also his mistress."

"The same girly who stole your husband?"

"You're a smart man, Lawrence Hayward," I said and got ready to leave for real this time.

"Has she played any big roles?"

"About the same as Saffron," I said flatly.

When I got home, there was a telegram waiting. I practically tore it in half opening it.

Dear Miss Bishop,
I would be lying if I said I remember you. But happy to hear from a fan and thrilled by audition. Looking forward to hearing from you soon. Please let me know when I can expect to fly to London and get the script for my screen test. Kindest regards, Alicia Steele.

I felt the first wave of happiness in a long time. Of course, I didn't have a copy of the script for Frederick's film—yet.

By the end of the day, Larry's editor had given him the go-ahead. We agreed to meet back at Kensington Gardens, near the pond, after the interview the following morning. I didn't want to risk phone calls or meeting closer to home. This deception had to be old-school fool-proof. Besides, I hadn't heard from Niall, and considering his disapproval, I couldn't be too cautious.

It was all going according to plan until Trinity came home that evening from the theatre. I'm not sure what made me tell her what I was up to, but I regretted it as soon as I opened my mouth.

"You're doing what?" she said, her eyes wide in disbelief. "What in bloody hell has got into you? Get even with Dean?"

"You make it sound so bad. You know he deserves it. And it's not like he's never had a bad review," I said snidely.

"Fine. If a critic watches the show and tears it to shreds that's one thing, but you're actually hiring a writer to bash him for revenge. It's not what women like us do."

"Women *like us?* You mean women like *you*. I've grown a backbone, Trinity. And I'm sick and tired of being treated like a doormat by men like Dean."

She went quiet. "What do you mean 'men' like Dean? What other men are you referring to?"

I bristled at her question. In truth, I didn't have an answer. I didn't know what I meant by "men." There hadn't been many men before Dean and certainly none since, not yet. Before I could respond there was an odd clicking sound. It kept up for a few seconds.

"What was that?" I asked.

"What was what?" Trinity asked.

"That clicking sound."

She shook her head. Then it happened again. It kept on longer this time.

"I don't hear anything," she said dismissively. "It's probably that mouse again."

"It's the typewriter," I gulped as the sound stopped abruptly. I rose from the sofa and tiptoed to the door.

"You're being ridiculous," Trinity said, crossing the room with me on her heels. She banged on the door.

"Why are you knocking?" I hissed. She took a step back like I'd frightened her. I flung it open. The room was empty. The typewriter sat where I'd put it, taking up most of the tiny desk.

"See? All good," Trinity pointed out.

I approached the machine; it was just as I'd left it. There was the sheet of paper in the carriage. I expected to find a cryptic message, but it was white as snow. I yanked it out, startling Trinity.

"You're making me jumpy now!" she gasped.

I cast my eyes about the room, searching for a clue. The window was open, the curtains billowing in from a strong breeze.

She frowned. "I think you need to rest, either that or a good stiff drink," she suggested. "You've been a complete wreck, and I know you have reason to be, but I'm worried about you."

When she'd gone from the room I moved to close the window and my arm knocked the script off the desk. It fell like a cascading deck of cards. As I bent down to gather the scattered pages, I saw that the outline lay on top of the pile. I reread the first note: *Clara vows to get even for what her husband and his mistress did to her.* I thought of what Larry was set to do tomorrow. It was a start.

The typewriter sat in silence. Had I imagined hearing its keys? The more I stared at it, the more it beckoned me. I inserted a fresh page into the typewriter and a new character came to me . . . he would be a rich man, but a dangerous one, not unlike a certain film producer . . .

INT. FORMOSA CAFÉ—NIGHT
Clara is waiting at her usual table when a well-dressed man named EDGAR enters. He is a local gangster with a pack of hoodlums and some cheap floozies on the payroll. Edgar walks over to Clara and, not waiting for an invitation, sits down. As far as gangsters go, he is all right, polite to the ladies and ready to please.

                    GANGSTER
     So you're the redhead I've heard so much
     about?

                      CLARA
     What of it?

                    GANGSTER
                    (smiling)
I heard you need my help to . . . shall we
say, get rid of an inconvenience?

                     CLARA
If you mean put this inconvenience, as you
call it, in his place, then yes, you heard
right. And to be clear, the inconvenience
belongs to me.

                    GANGSTER
I thought as much.
          (looking her up and down as
           though she were naked)
I think we can work together.

                     CLARA
Not so fast. You haven't named your price.

                    GANGSTER
Haven't I? How foolish of me. I believe
a few days together at my place in Palm
Springs might be a start.

Clara stares at him and sips her drink.

                     CLARA
I've never been to Palm Springs.

The gangster smiles.

I stopped when Trinity knocked on my door. "It's flipping past midnight, Clara! Quit your typing."

"Sorry!" I called out and heard her pad back to her room. I reread what I had typed. That made it two scenes I'd completed. It had been far too long since I'd written something worthwhile and not some snarky article about celebrity weight loss or baby bumps. It helped that *The Woman Scorned* was already half written. It could be my transition back into the business I'd regretted leaving behind. But it was much more than that: it was also an heirloom from the grand-mother I never knew and a far more desirable family legacy than unfaithful husbands. If it was the new millennium, there was little demand for an old-school film noir script, unless it had superheroes or vampires in it. But here in 1952, it would be an easy sell, and that's what I was counting on. I would write all day tomorrow and the next until the script was finished and Frederick could read it.

CHAPTER TWENTY-FIVE

The next morning brought me five days closer to Alice's car crash and one article closer to the start of my revenge on Dean. Trinity was still asleep when I woke up. I got dressed and stepped outside to buy a newspaper. The air was thick with fog. I found it difficult to see more than a few feet in front of me. If I didn't know it was morning, I would have thought it was after dark, for there was no real daylight. A man passed by, and he held a handkerchief over his mouth. A woman dashed around a corner and into a store, her eyes squinting in the mist. I entered the local newsstand and bought the *Daily Mirror* for December 5, 1952. The front-page headline told me that for once it wasn't all in my head: *Great Smog Blankets London.* I quickly scanned the article: apparently, a cold snap had caused Londoners to use more coal to keep warm, and there was some atmospheric phenomenon called an inversion that trapped the air so that it hung low and deep across the city.

"They're thinking of cancelling buses," the newsagent told me when he saw me studying the page. "The airports are all closed."

"Closed?"

"Can't fly in this! Worst pea-souper I've seen and I'm nearly sixty," he said.

I looked out the window of the shop and saw people scurrying indoors, their faces covered. One couple were nattily dressed save for the surgical masks they wore. If this smog lasted more than a few days, there would be no way for Alice to fly here in time.

"This is awful," I said, feeling panic grip my insides. I wondered if what had been happening to me was in any way responsible for this. "How long will it last?"

The newsagent shrugged. "No one knows."

I would have to think of another way. I remembered Frederick's suggestion that Alice do her screen test in Hollywood and he'd get the footage sent. It would have to do. I was to meet Larry in half an hour—his interview with Dean would be over by now.

The cab dropped me off, and I raced to the meeting place. It was hard to breathe, but I pressed on, covering my mouth with my hand. As I grew closer, there stood Larry, holding a battered umbrella, wearing a grey flannel suit and long black trench coat, his hair slicked back.

"This bloody smog will be the death of me," he said and spat into a handkerchief. I tried to hide my disgust.

"Well, what happened with your assignment?" I asked.

He started to walk and I followed him. We turned up to the duck pond, where we were alone. I felt like a spy in a Cold War novel. The ducks were barely visible but for a faint outline of them skimming the surface, searching for food. They looked cold. Then again, in a world without colour, everything appeared frozen and bleak like the Arctic.

Larry told me he had been on Dean's set early in the morning and welcomed with open arms. As predicted, Dean had talked his ear off and spoken endlessly of wanting to direct feature films and, more specifically, of working with England's powerful producer, Frederick Marshall.

"Apparently, it's a screwball comedy," Larry explained.

"Of course it is," I said, thinking how appropriate given the way my life usually went.

"David Niven is the lead. Blimey, he's suave."

"So I hear," I said impatiently.

"I met the girl, Amber Ward," he said at last. "She's a knockout!"

I glared at him. He coughed. "I mean, she's okay looking. If you like blondes with big assets . . ."

"Did you get anything interesting on her?" I asked.

"I spoke with her a bit. She said she was going to audition around town. Trying for meetings with producers and the like," he continued. I didn't like the sound of that, but in a city with as much acting talent as London, a girl like Amber didn't stand a chance. "What is she auditioning for? Did she say?" I pressed.

"I would have gotten more except another reporter came around and chatted her up," he said. "And he had her monopolized the whole time."

"Who was he?" I asked, trying to come across like I didn't care all that much, that I was merely curious.

"I was surprised to see him. I mean, Amber has as much experience as Saffron, so why the interest? Maybe she's a bigger deal than you think? And it wasn't the usual tabloid hack either but a famous, or should I say infamous, writer. You probably haven't heard of him, he was in jail for a bit . . ."

"Niall Adamson." I spoke his name like shooting bullets. Larry nodded like a fool.

"Yeah! Him!" He was pleased until puzzlement took over. "How did you know that?"

"Lucky guess," I lied.

Larry shrugged and continued, "I have a great headline for the story on her. 'Ward of the States,' America's Latest Blonde Bombshell Becomes Britain's Newest It-Girl!"

"That's very witty," I said, but I'd already stopped listening. Niall hadn't been in touch since our talk at The White Stallion. Yet he obviously decided to help me, at least I hoped that was why he'd bothered to show an interest. I wondered how long I'd have to wait before he reached out. Or would I just read about it in the paper?

"So what about it, then?" Larry said and looked at me expectantly. I hadn't heard anything he'd said.

"About what again?" I asked. He looked annoyed.

"I want to get some decent photos of Amber for the story."

"I don't want you doing a story on Amber Ward," I said tersely.

"I'm going to write about Dean like you want," he objected. "But she's pretty. I could get an article or two out of her if, like she says, she's auditioning. I can follow her around. 'A Day in the Life of an Almost Starlet.' Has a lovely ring to it, don't you think? My paper loves a profile and photo of a pretty girl," he explained unnecessarily.

"No," I said even more bluntly. "She's not to get any press from you or me."

"You're insane, Clara. If she gets a part in something over here, there will be loads of press itching to find out who she is. You can't hide her, not a girl with her looks. Like I said, Adamson was already on the job!"

"She'll never get a part!" I said defensively. I intended to add, "She's a slutty server destined to work in strip bars," but instead what came out of my mouth was "She's a soda-shop waitress and that's that. She'll hoof it back to America and disappear." In the meantime, all I could think of was Niall and what he was up to.

"I'm going to get proper photographs done, real classy stuff in a studio," he continued. "Amber Ward may be a star one day! I can say I discovered her . . ."

I no longer cared what Larry was saying. Amber had about as much chance of becoming a movie star as I did. I said goodbye with some promise of his to meet me at the flat in a day or two. Right now I didn't care if I ever saw or spoke to Larry Hayward again. I hailed a cab immediately and fell into the back seat. I needed to reach Niall, but I had no idea how. He wasn't on staff, so that left ringing the editor's desk. Then there was Frederick Marshall. This fog might stop Alice from flying here, but I couldn't let it stop him from casting her.

CHAPTER TWENTY-SIX

The fog was so thick I could barely make out the townhouse from the road where the cabbie let me out. I picked my way along the walkway, and my fingers were just touching the key to the lock in the front door when I was grabbed on the shoulder. I was about to scream but a hand clamped down over my mouth. My assailant spun me around and I saw that it was Niall. He released me immediately.

"What the hell are you doing?" I demanded, my heart racing.

"I didn't want you to scream bloody murder," he explained, a little too nonchalantly for my liking.

"You wanted to give me a heart attack instead?"

"I wasn't worried. You're tougher than you look."

I gave him the once-over. It amazed me that despite everything that had happened, the sight of Niall excited me as much as it infuriated me.

"How was your visit with Amber?" I asked sharply.

He seemed surprised that I knew about it; then, in a flash, that wry grin he had was back. "Larry Hayward!" he said and snapped his fingers. "You didn't hear from me so you got yourself mixed up with Larry."

"I'm not mixed up," I argued. "He was willing to help, unlike you. I need a reliable man."

"What did you promise him?" He smirked as he said it. "Your undying affection? You have to be careful with a bloke like Larry. He's lonely. I'd hate to see him get hurt."

The accusation enraged me, probably because of how close it came to the promise I'd made to Frederick. "How dare you accuse me of such a thing? He didn't want anything of the sort," I said. "I may have told him a few facts to write about Dean so he'd get a scoop. And he'll get some bylines in the U.S., like I promised you."

"You've got it all covered," he said, still smiling as he shook his head.

"Why would you give that girl the time of day?" I couldn't resist asking.

His smile vanished. "Your jealousy is giving me a bad taste in my mouth. I interviewed her out of curiosity. See what about her gets up your crumpet so bad. She's just a kid."

"She's sleeping with a married man! My married man. There's a code between women and she broke it. I would never do that," I said. "What is it about blondes that men can't resist?"

He looked offended. "I didn't say I couldn't resist her." He grabbed my arm and pulled me towards him. What had gotten into men all of sudden that overpowering a girl was the thing to do?

"You're the second man to grab me like that and I don't like it." I tried to pull away, but Niall was too strong, and he pulled me closer until I disappeared into his arms. As I lifted my head to breathe, his lips landed on mine and he kissed me. His kiss wasn't as violent as Frederick's. It was tender, passionate and, what's more, I *did* like it. When he was done kissing me, he shoved me away. I wiped my mouth so he would think I *didn't* like it, that I wanted to erase the taste of him.

"You should learn to *let* a man kiss you. It's less repellent than you think."

He walked away, but he hadn't gone two steps before he stopped abruptly and turned back to face me. "By the way, that husband of yours, Dean?"

I stood rigid and stuck my chin in the air to take what was coming. What else had Dean done to me? "What did you find out?"

He grunted disdainfully. "Only that he's not worth any of this. Just a hunch." Then he turned away and disappeared into the fog.

By the time I got to the flat, I was desperate to call Frederick and prayed that Trinity was out somewhere. No such luck; she was stretched out on the sofa reading a magazine. There was a half-empty bottle of cheap wine on the coffee table and two glasses; one used, one not.

"So glad you're back!" she slurred. It wasn't like her to be half-drunk during the day.

"Are you okay? Did something happen?" I asked. "What's with the wine?"

"I wanted to celebrate. I have an audition for Frederick Marshall's new movie! The second lead. I may borrow one of your dresses," she said, bubbling over with excitement.

"Of course," I said, equally excited for her. "That's wonderful news!" It was a relief that she got the audition. She'd be happy, and it was one step closer to showing me that Frederick could be trusted to do what I asked of him.

"Yes, I'm going tomorrow. Will have to leave early what with this fog and all."

"Yes, damn stuff," I agreed. I wanted to call Frederick to get an update on Alice's audition and see how far he'd gotten with that part of our deal, but I couldn't talk to him with Trinity in the room. It would take too much explaining as to why I was trying to get another actress a part. She wouldn't like it; even though my plan was for Alice to have the lead, she'd still view it as competition. So out I went, making my way back through the swelling cloud of coal dust to the phone booth on the corner. A man answered, only it wasn't Frederick, and judging by his officious tone he was either his accountant or his butler.

"I'd like to leave a message. You'll need to write it down," I said by way of warning that what I had to say wasn't short or sweet.

"I'm quite capable, I assure you, madame," the voice boomed.

The message was about Alice's audition at Paramount. I wanted to know what Frederick wanted her to read, a monologue or scene from another screwball comedy like *Bringing Up Baby*. I also wanted to find out precisely when it was going to happen, so I could send her a telegram as soon as possible so she had plenty of time to prepare. My voice picked up speed and intensity with each syllable. I felt like an agent closing a deal.

"Got all that?" I asked when I was finished talking.

"Of course," he said. Only he wasn't finished with me. He had a message too. "Mr. Marshall was expecting your call," he said, which shouldn't have surprised me. "He wanted to let you know he is meeting with Mr. Lapointe this afternoon. He said you should start packing because your trip is imminent. Good day, Miss Bishop." Then the man hung up on me.

CHAPTER
TWENTY-SEVEN

The next morning the fog hadn't lifted; if anything, it was worse. I went to the newsstand and bought *Talk* and flipped through the pages until I found what I was looking for buried inside in the entertainment section. Larry's writing was brief and to the point: *American-style variety show* Daddy's Girls *shows little class to showcase English girls' singing talent. Cheap sets and lousy lighting make it look like the producers scraped the bottom of the barrel for this one. Hollywood's Dean Lapointe, the show's so-called producer, wants you to watch his show, but he really wants you to know he'd prefer to direct* real *movies (his words). His lack of respect for the variety genre makes this reporter want to turn off . . .*

Ouch. It didn't get any better after that. A wave of guilt rushed through me in such a hurry it was gone before I knew it. It was one story, and as I knew all too well from years in the tabloid trenches, one tiny article wasn't going to change anything. But it would embarrass him. And that was just the beginning. I had big plans for Larry to roll out a whole series. Wait until I got the story wired to *Hollywood Hush* . . . But then another item caught my eye. It was a tiny "upcoming" ad and it made me mad as hell: *Gentlemen, You'll Prefer this Blonde. The latest bombshell from Tinseltown is in London and set to start a fire in the hearts of Englishmen. Read my in-depth feature on a day in the life of Amber Ward in tomorrow's paper. Zowie!*

That son of a bitch! He was going to do it. I quickly flipped through the pages of the *Daily Buzz* looking for a byline of Niall's, but there was nothing . . . yet.

Furious, I tucked the papers under my arm, intending to march back to the flat as fast as I could, but I was slowed down by the air itself. I coughed and covered my mouth with the papers to try to filter out some of the pollution. This was worse than the worst LA smog. I made it back, nearly bumping into several other pedestrians. I threw open the door and startled poor Trinity, who was quietly reciting her lines for the audition.

"What on earth?" she exclaimed.

I then showed her the pieces in *Talk*. She sighed. "I told you nothing good would come out of this vendetta of yours."

"How can you say that? I did nothing wrong. I was a good wife to that man. If Amber hadn't gone after him, he'd still be with me."

"Tsk tsk," Trinity scolded me. "You don't know if your marriage would have lasted. It's the fifties now, and divorce is more common than you think! Now I have to rehearse, so unless you're going to run the lines with me," she hinted for me to get lost.

Fuming, I sat at the desk in my room and stared at the typewriter. Alicia Steele's notes were clear. Clara would enlist Rod to kill her husband. He had it coming and she was as cold-hearted as they come. But the bit in *Talk* about Amber got to me, and I read it over and over, then stared at it until I was completely consumed by thoughts of her. What happened next made perfect sense, and I was sure Alicia would approve of a slight change in the plot. I began to type . . .

EXT. HIGH TOWER COURT—DUSK
Clara makes sure she is obscured by the overgrown
bougainvillea that spills over the neighbour's
fence into the tiny pathway. She waits for him.

The HIGH TOWER ELEVATOR would speed up the process, but she doesn't want to take a chance that
one of her neighbours would see him.

The SOUND of leather shoes SCRAPING the cement
steps catches her attention. The FOOTSTEPS are
heavy and dragging, like it is a great effort,
which of course it is, with the hundreds of steps
climbing from Camrose Drive to High Tower Court.
And there is no mistaking that the footsteps
belong to a man.

Clara steps back further into the bougainvillea.
She peeks through the vines and sees with a mix-
ture of relief and nervousness that it is Rod.
She emerges into the fading daylight.

                    CLARA
          You came.

                    ROD
          I said I would. Next time I'm taking the
          elevator.

Clara smiles. He walks towards her and sweeps her
into his arms and kisses her. She struggles, only
barely, to be set free, giggling like a teenager
with a crush on the high school quarterback.

                    CLARA
          Going back down won't be so bad.

> ROD
>
> I'm tired of all this. Let's forget about
> your husband. Let him rot up here in his
> clapboard mansion with that woman to care
> for him. We can run away.

Clara shoves him away from her and marches down
the path towards the elevator. The stone bell
tower stands out against the night sky like the
ruins of a Gothic castle. Rod follows patiently
and stands behind her, so when she stops, she
can rest her head on his chest.

> CLARA
>
> You know we have to pay a fee to use this
> elevator. When it breaks it's a son of a
> gun. I've always been afraid of falling
> down the shaft.

She walks to the elevator door's glass window.
The elevator car is at the bottom of the shaft.
She shivers even though it's eighty degrees out-
side.

> CLARA (CONT)
> I'm terrified of heights.

> ROD
> So why do you live way up here on top of the
> hill?

                    CLARA
          My husband wanted to. He never cared about
          what I wanted.

                    ROD
          Another reason to run away. I'll always
          care about what you want.

Clara turns to him and kisses him long and
soft, like she was stroking his lips with a silk
scarf.

                    CLARA
          I've invested my whole life with him. He's
          filthy rich and I deserve a piece of it.

                    ROD
          Isn't that what divorce is for? Alimony.

She laughs.

                    CLARA
          I was a foolish girl in love when I mar-
          ried him. I'm no longer foolish or in
          love.

                    ROD
          You love me, don't you, baby?

She tears up just enough to make him want to do
anything to stop her from crying.

                    CLARA

        You know I do. But how are we going to be
        together?

She turns back to the elevator shaft and shudders
once more.

                    ROD

        You're not asking me to kill your husband,
        are you? A guy can get the chair in this
        state for murder.

                    CLARA

        Kill my husband? Whatever for? I will see
        him in divorce court. No, Rod, her. She's
        the one I want out of the picture. That's
        why I asked you to come here tonight. I
        wanted to show you how I think we should
        do it.

                    ROD
             (with a look of distaste)
        The dame? I don't kill women.

Clara smirks and peers down the hollow shaft.

                    CLARA

        A girl would die if she fell down there,
        wouldn't she?

Rod strokes her hair.

                              ROD
        She would. It wouldn't be tough to imagine
        such an accident happening.

Clara glides away towards the path from which
they came. She turns to him. The tears are gone.

                             CLARA
        I imagine it all the time.

I stopped typing and pulled the page out of the machine. I didn't need a mirror to know I was grinning ear to ear. The femme fatale always gets the bum rap in film noir. She never gets away with it and usually gets whacked by the hoodlum or even the leading man. In the postwar era, no one liked their women to be tough and independent and act like men; if they were, they paid for it with their lives. But *The Woman Scorned* was from the femme fatale point of view, and I'd be damned if I'd let the fictional Clara be destroyed by the time the end credits rolled. I was writing the screenplay now, and the mistress would die a horrible death at the hands of Clara. It would be a happy ending of a sort.

The phone rang in the other room, and I could hear Trinity answer it. She put on an act so thick with honey, it had to Frederick. I leapt out of my chair and dashed to the living room. She nodded.

"Yes, Mr. Marshall, she's right here. One moment please." Her hands were shaking when she handed me the receiver.

"Hello, Frederick," I said. We didn't speak long; what he had to say wasn't much other than he had arranged for Alicia Steele to do a screen test in LA because of the fog. She could read from anything she wanted. It was up to her. I was disheartened because it meant I wouldn't meet Alice, and I worried if I could keep her safe from such a distance. I didn't ask him how his meeting with Dean went, and he didn't offer up any information. There would be time later to find out. I could imagine Dean sucking up. Whatever the outcome, I'd find a way to use it against him.

By early afternoon Trinity was off for her audition, her head wrapped in a silk scarf to protect her face and lungs from the onslaught of smog. Equally shrouded in a hat and scarf, I headed over to the local telegraph office, which had been a grubby Internet café, or rather, was destined to become one. Alice would just be waking up. I pictured her in our house on Camrose Drive, as Lyle and Lillian were no doubt lying together in some other bed somewhere in LA. Alice would be making breakfast for my mother. I'd seen photos of Marjorie when she was five. Beautiful and innocent, unaware of the horrible fate her equally beautiful mother had in store. Not if I could help it; if it were up to me, things would be very different. Fortunately, miraculously, fate seemed to be in my hands. I wrote the telegram.

Dear Alicia,
I understand your audition is soon. I regret more than you know not being able to fly you to London. What the English are calling the Great Smog has grounded all aircraft. The film's producer, Frederick Marshall, asks you to choose from whatever script you wish and use it in your audition. Good luck. You're going to be a big star. Warmest regards, Clara Bishop.

I paid the man to wire the cable and walked back onto the street. The sign for The White Stallion appeared through the dense air and, still reeling from Larry's stunt, I wanted nothing more than a stiff drink despite it being pre-cocktail hour.

Saffron was on me the second I strolled in. I didn't have much time for her either.

"I'm sorry for Larry," she sputtered. "He told me who Dean is, and I was stunned to read such horrible things in *Talk* this morning."

I waved away her concerns. "Don't bother about that part of it. He did what I wanted in *that* story."

I sat down at the bar and she poured me bourbon without my having to ask.

"You wanted him to write bad things about your husband?"

"Don't be so surprised. He's kind of a heel," I said, still taken aback by my unintentional fifties vernacular. It started to occur to me that eventually the era might swallow me whole, just like the Great Smog had swallowed London. I took a big gulp of the bourbon.

"But you're right about one thing, Saffron. I am livid with your cousin," I said tersely. She stood there, waiting for me to continue. "He's about to publish a gushy article on this untalented no-good actress named Amber Ward when I told him not to. You should be angry as the devil too. She has less experience than you. Why hasn't he written about you?"

My missile hit its target. Saffron was enraged now. "That rotten son of a gun!"

"And while we're on the subject, I wasn't too thrilled to find out you told Larry that I might be up for some romantic interludes because, and I quote, I am 'a lonely American'?"

She looked like she wanted to disappear into the smog, which amused me. "I'm . . . I'm . . ." she stuttered.

"Desperate to get yourself in the press?" I finished the sentence for her. She nodded.

"It was wrong of me," she said contritely. "But you must understand, I need all the help I can get. It's tough trying to get noticed."

The last problem a girl with Saffron's looks had was getting noticed. But I took her point.

"Well, *I* would have done the story on you. But now that Larry didn't uphold his end of the bargain, I'm afraid I just can't." This was, of course, a lie, but I didn't care. I wanted Larry to pay for his mistake, even if the worst thing that would happen was tension at the family dinner table at Christmas.

Satisfied, I swivelled on my bar stool and saw Niall sitting at "our table" alone. I sauntered over and tossed the newspaper down in front of him.

"Have you seen *Talk* this morning?" I asked, not even trying to hide my irritation.

"I did," he said. "You should be happy. Or do you always react to getting what you want by throwing newspaper about?"

"What Larry wrote about Dean was fine. It's the other piece. The one that's coming out tomorrow that I'm upset about. All about Amber. Like the world needs to know all about Amber!"

He pulled a cigarette out of his pocket, twirled it in his hands a moment, then lit it up.

"How can you smoke when the entire city is covered in the filthy stuff?" I asked, recalling the pack of cigarettes that remained in my train case at the flat.

"You think this one cigarette will make a difference?" he asked, perplexed.

"Haven't you heard that smoking can kill?"

"No," he said sharply and inhaled a long deep drag. "Do you want to try one again?"

After that first attempt I wasn't so sure. Still, I took one from the packet and held it in my fingers like I knew you were supposed to. Niall struck a match and held it up for me. I had no choice but to try to smoke again. I would make an excuse that the fog was getting to me to explain the coughing fit that was sure to follow. I inhaled and watched the paper burn away. Then a funny thing happened. I didn't choke, sputter or cough. Instead, I blew the smoke out of my parted lips just like any femme fatale worth her salt could do. Just like Lauren Bacall. I wondered if I looked half as good as she did.

"You seem agitated yourself," I said after we'd sat in smoky silence longer than was comfortable.

"I spoke to my editor. They won't let me cover the smog story."

"Why not?"

"That little matter of my being accused of wiretapping a cabinet minister, remember?"

"I remember," I said sympathetically, and got the point that even in 1952 Niall Adamson was a shamed journalist.

"It doesn't matter," he said, clearly not wanting to talk about it. "But they only want the puff stuff from me. The real news is for less controversial chaps, apparently."

"I'm sorry," I said.

"People will die from this smog," he said earnestly. "I'm not sure the NHS will keep up with the demand in heart and lung trouble that will come. It needs to be investigated and reported by decent writers."

"I've never seen you this serious," I said.

He shrugged. "The Great Depression, the Great War, the Great Smog. None of it seems great to me."

"Maybe it will blow over by morning," I suggested hopefully and for reasons of my own, still holding out faint hope of flying Alice here before December 10.

"Don't wager on it," he said, sounding as gloomy as the fog.

Then a second shot of bourbon arrived courtesy of Saffron.

"It's on me," she said.

"Thank you," I replied. When she scurried away, Niall gave me a look. "That's an expression I don't much care for," I said.

"Tell me, what are you doing getting messed up with Frederick Marshall?"

I tried not to flinch. "What gives you that idea?"

"I saw him drop you off the other night. Before you stole the typewriter," he teased.

"I didn't steal it," I reminded him, holding the cigarette aloft. "Are you spying on me?"

I was torn between wanting to tell him everything and telling him off. I chose somewhere in between.

"If you must know, I need Frederick's help."

He snorted. "With what? Don't tell me you've got acting aspirations too?"

"A friend of mine is in real danger," I said, and my tone was serious enough that Niall wiped the sarcasm from his voice.

"What kind of danger?"

"I can't get into it." I shook my head. "But Frederick has the power to change things for her."

He sat back and flicked his cigarette into the ashtray. "I didn't know you were so noble," he said, and this time he did sound sarcastic.

"I'm not some tramp with a grudge. I'm a wronged woman."

"Out for revenge!" he chastised me. "How petty."

"Is that so?" I felt my voice shake and I fought it. "Tell me, Mr. Adamson, when does revenge become something noble? When avenging the death of a loved one, perhaps?"

He sat up. "Perhaps. But there's nothing noble in going after some poor sap with bad taste in women." I bristled and he smiled and said, "Present company excluded, of course."

"If you must know, I *am* avenging the death of a loved one. But I can't say more than that. You just have to trust me."

I could tell from his expression he didn't. But it was the truth, in a manner of speaking. Getting even with Dean was in some way getting even with Lyle. And punishing Amber was like punishing Lillian. My revenge was Alicia Steele's—just like in the screenplay.

As I turned my head and blew the pale smoke into the air, I watched it form soft patterns like paintbrush strokes against the darkness of the room. I shivered a little as though I could sense the spectre of the fictional Clara circling. It all made sense to me.

Niall furrowed his brow and pummelled his cigarette out. "I'm just wondering what's next for Clara Bishop? Now that she's gotten even with her husband."

"You'll just have to watch me." I smiled at him innocently. He wasn't buying it.

"For the record, Amber Ward is not in love with your husband," he said and pulled his notepad from his jacket pocket, plopping it down in front of me.

My ears pricked up. "What makes you so sure?"

"She's after a career upgrade. He's her first stepping stone. She'll leave him at the first sign of a better offer. She's a Bette Davis fan, which tells you something, although she apparently relates more to Marilyn Monroe."

I was outraged. "She couldn't touch Marilyn Monroe. Who does she think she is?"

"She's a nobody and she knows it. But she's ambitious."

"She seems to have charmed you," I said, irritated. "So you would have done the same. Walked out on me to start a new life with Amber."

He studied my face again, and this time I made sure there were no clues for him to find. I wanted to be a blank slate—no past to regret and no future to predict—just a redhead playing dress-up in her grandmother's dress.

"If you were my wife, I'd never let you out of my sight long enough to notice a meaningless blonde."

I gazed at him, surprised by what he said.

Niall stood up and stepped beside me. Then he took my chin in his hand and wrenched my neck up none too gently until I had no choice but to look up at him. It was rough and invasive and, what's more, I enjoyed it.

"You going to kiss me again?" I taunted him, knowing I wanted it.

"Don't flatter yourself," he said coldly, releasing me.

Then he put on his fedora. "Good luck getting your friend out of her jam," he said. "Remember, I'm an investigative journalist. It may come in handy if your friend is truly in danger."

"I'll keep it in mind."

Then he walked away. I rubbed my neck and ground my cigarette into the ashtray.

CHAPTER
TWENTY-EIGHT

By the time I got back to the flat, Trinity had popped open a bottle of champagne.

"We celebrating something again?" I asked innocently.

"You are the best friend ever!" Trinity screamed in delight and ran over and threw her arms around me.

"Thank you, but what happened?" I asked, hugging her back.

"I got the part!" Trinity shouted.

I let her bounce up and down as she poured two glasses of bubbly. "I can't tell you how difficult it was to get champagne."

"Let me guess, it's rationed."

"It is! But I have connections," she said with a wink. "We movie stars have to be resourceful!"

"To you landing the part of a lifetime!" I said cheerfully, thinking how fast the casting process was. Usually directors and producers deliberate for days if not weeks. "They must have loved you to make such a quick decision."

"They did. Frederick Marshall took one look at me and knew I was right. Although I did remind him we were friends, hope you don't mind," she said sheepishly. "I just wish David Niven had been there to read with me."

I wondered if I was the reason she got the part so quickly. Frederick had dreams of a dirty weekend with a redhead, and I was that red-head. But Trinity wasn't part of the deal.

"Of course I don't mind," I said and felt that now she was cast I could tell her about Alice. "Another friend of mine is reading for the lead in the next day or two."

She frowned at this. "That's odd. I thought he said he'd found his star already."

I felt the blood drain from my face. "What do you mean? Who?"

"I'm not sure. Some unknown girl."

My heart was thumping in my chest. Was Frederick really going to double-cross me? Or was the unknown girl Alicia Steele? That had to be it. We had a deal. For an instant, I shuddered at the thought of his hands all over me.

"Is the girl local?" I pressed her for more details.

She scowled. "Actually that much I do know. She's from America. Can you imagine casting a foreigner like that and her not being a big star already?" she said, sounding offended on behalf of all English girls. But for me it was glorious news. It would make sense that Frederick would be preparing the other cast members and his crew that he'd found some unknown American actress. No one but me knew she hadn't read for the part yet. I had complete confidence in her talent. Once Frederick saw her read, he'd be so taken with her. The audition was just a technicality.

"That doesn't seem fair," I said to be conciliatory.

"Not when there are loads of great actresses in England!" she continued. "You know, I feel like going out. Despite this smog business, let's gussy ourselves up and head to The White Stallion for some delicious pub fare," she said. I smiled; gastro pubs were a long way off, so simple plain food would have to do. "I'll buy!" Trinity joked. "A movie actress needs to be seen, you know."

The decade I'd spent chasing after celebrities dining out at restaurants in order to get a lame story came flashing back. "Oh, I know all about *that*," I said and smiled.

We left the flat and entered the street cloaked in total darkness. The glow from the street lamps barely lifted the gloom, but we used them to guide us towards the pub. The townhouses lining the street appeared to close in on us like a canyon, and our footsteps echoed on the concrete. Up ahead, a shadow crossed our path and we heard talking. But as we grew nearer, one voice was familiar. Then the figure stepped out of the shadow into the sparse light up ahead.

It was Niall, a lit cigarette dangling from his mouth. He was leaning up against a street lamp, talking to a group of teenaged boys. What I noticed was how the boys were dressed, long Edwardian overcoats with patterned waistcoats and suede shoes. Each had his hair slicked into a quiff at the front like a pompadour. It was a look that I'd call rockabilly and was in stark contrast to Niall.

"Who are those boys?" I asked.

"Beats me," Trinity said. "They're just a bunch of Teddy Boys. Not sure what you call them in America."

I knew the term. Teddy Boys were youthful gangs that listened to American rock 'n' roll and played in bands and otherwise caused trouble for English society. "We call them teenagers," I said plainly.

They were far enough away not to notice us, and I watched Niall point his finger at one of the boys angrily. He was always so intense. I wondered what had happened.

The group dispersed and the boys scrammed around the corner, and Niall disappeared in the opposite direction. We carried on to the pub.

CHAPTER TWENTY-NINE

Our celebration at the pub was in full swing, and for the first time in a long time, I'd forgotten that anything was wrong in my life. Cocktails and laughter had that effect on me, I guess. But the good time was cut short by the arrival of a lanky man in a dark grey suit. I froze. It couldn't be . . . He removed his hat and my jaw fell open. It was.

"What is it, Clara?" Trinity asked, worried.

I pointed to the man in the doorway and whispered, "Dean."

She looked up. "So it is."

"How did he know where to find me?"

Trinity's guilty expression gave me the answer.

"He rang while you were out, looking for you. He begged me. I told him you'd be here. Please don't be angry."

Before I could object, she stood to leave and put her hand on my arm. "Besides, you two have a lot to discuss." Then she was gone.

I watched Saffron approach him like a jaguar stalking an antelope. His lips moved and her eyes darted in my direction. Dean started to walk over, but I looked the other way, like I hadn't a care in the world. That drinking cocktails alone in a pub in London was precisely the sort of thing I did.

"Clara?"

I looked up, refusing to give him anything but a blank stare. I wondered why he'd come. Was it to discuss the divorce? Or was he coming back to me, as I had wanted so badly before the world turned upside down?

"May I join you?"

"It's a free country," I said and sat quietly, wanting him to do the talking.

"Can I get you something to drink?" Saffron asked, arriving at our table with her bosom heaving for effect.

"I'll have a sidecar too," he said, pointing to my drink. He still was my husband, after all. I waited for him to ogle Saffron, but he didn't give her a second glance, and that irritated me. Saffron was far prettier than Amber, but it was as though she was a mouse in his eyes.

"She's a beautiful girl, isn't she?" I said, my voice cool. He shrugged.

"I didn't really notice," he said.

"Why not? You're still a man, aren't you?" He didn't flinch.

"Pretty girls are routine in my line of work. You know that. I didn't come to argue with you."

I breathed deeply. Let him talk, I told myself over and over, but myself wouldn't listen to reason, so out it came. "Why are you here?"

"I wanted to thank you," he said.

It wasn't the answer I was expecting, not in any of the scenarios I'd thought up. "Thank me for what?"

"Frederick Marshall called me, and we met to discuss his new picture," he said with a smile. "He watched *Daddy's Girls* and said I have an eye."

"How wonderful," I said half-heartedly.

Saffron appeared with our drinks, but she didn't leave right away.

"You must be Dean Lapointe," she said and painted on her best smile.

"Yes, this is Dean," I said. "This is Saffron. She's an actress."

"Nice to meet you," he said. "Good luck with your career." I always could tell when Dean was unimpressed. He never liked wannabes hitting him up for work—until Amber, that is.

Saffron flared her nostrils and hoofed it away.

"Did you see the piece in *Talk* this morning?" I taunted him.

"I did," he shrugged. "But it's nonsense. You know as much as I do that kind of rot doesn't last beyond the day. And besides, I got lucky. The only thing people care about right now is this damn smog."

He had a point, which was disappointing considering the lengths I went to to get the story to run.

"Look, I don't want to take up too much of your evening," he said. I bristled at this.

"You can take all the time you need," I said sarcastically. "I'm your wife."

He sipped his sidecar and pursed his lips from the sour taste of the lemon.

"I wanted to thank you because I know Frederick Marshall had no intention of meeting me before we ran into you at The Savoy. Amber said you would ask him to, and while I didn't believe it at first, I appreciate it. Given all that happened between us, well, you're a first-class lady, that's all." He sucked back his drink.

I sat there trying to settle the shaking that had taken over my body; I prayed he couldn't see it.

"You didn't have to hunt me down to tell me that," I ground out. "You could have just sent me a text."

He looked confused, like he hadn't heard me right. "A what?"

I rolled my eyes. "A telegram," I snapped. "You could have sent a telegram or a thank-you note, like that other note you sent."

He recoiled. "I wanted to thank you in person. We're friends, aren't we?" he asked stupidly.

"Like the wolf and the lamb," I said.

"If that's how you feel, then why did you help me out?" he asked like I'd offended him.

"Frederick asked me what I thought of your work. So I told him the truth. I said he would be crazy not to meet with you."

"Well, he won't be sorry."

I laughed. "No, you're right about that," I said. "*He* won't be the one who's sorry."

Dean pulled some cash from his wallet. "Let me get these."

"I won't stop you," I said.

Then just like that he was gone. The shaking got worse and the tears came flowing down my face. If that wasn't a rotten enough feeling, Niall strode in like a prize bull and plunked himself down in the chair that Dean had vacated.

"You don't seem happy to see me," he said sarcastically.

His words irritated me enough that the tears stopped. He gave me a handkerchief, and I made sure to wipe as much mascara on it as possible before blowing my nose. I gave the dirty cloth back to him with a smile.

"You have mascara on your nose," he said matter-of-factly.

Mortified, I grabbed a napkin and wiped my face but he shook his head.

"Allow me," he said and pulled another handkerchief from his pocket. He dipped it in my sidecar and proceeded to wipe the makeup from my face. I felt about three.

"What did your husband want?"

I drank the sidecar. It tasted bittersweet, maybe from my mood or the handkerchief. "All he wanted was to thank me for getting Frederick Marshall to meet with him."

Niall nodded. "Did he get the job?"

"Not if I have any say," I said darkly. "I could use another of your cigarettes."

He took out two, one for each of us, and lit mine for me. I took it and inhaled the rotten smoke so deeply I could feel it in my toes.

"Why do I get the feeling you have plenty of say?" he said.

"You know," I said, remembering Cora in *The Postman Always Rings Twice*. "I'm not really a hell cat."

Niall stubbed his cigarette out and leaned towards me. I held my head up; my lips were in perfect alignment to graze his.

"Hell cat enough for me," he said and kissed me, this time like he meant it. And I didn't resist. The more I thought of Dean, sitting across from me to thank me, the harder I kissed Niall.

"We could go to your place," I suggested, the smoke from my cigarette creating a halo over him.

"And leave this dump?" he teased. "Let's go to yours."

I frowned. "My flatmate."

"We'll be as quiet as mice."

I smiled, thinking of the eerie typing that I'd blamed on the mouse. Trinity was probably asleep by now.

"That will do fine," I nodded.

I lay naked in the fold of Niall's arm, feeling guilty that I'd succumbed to the moment. I had more serious business to contend with. Getting caught up in passion and desire wasn't my usual forte, not that waltzing around the foggy streets of London wearing tight-fitting dresses with peekaboo hair and red lipstick was. I wondered if Alice or Marjorie would have done the same. Looking at Niall's bare, firm chest, I decided they would have. I kissed his arm and ran my fingers through his wavy blond hair. I wanted him to shield me from everything.

"Do you like me, Niall?" I asked quietly.

He kissed me some more. "You're one of a kind." Then his face screwed up like he had something on his mind, like he was about to ask if I'd ever had an STD. "You don't have any kids, do you?"

I went numb and withdrew my caresses from him. Staring at the ceiling fan, which was equally annoying in black and white, I said plainly, "I was pregnant once. But I had a miscarriage. To be honest, it was far more devastating for me than for Dean. It's all I wanted, a baby of my own."

He held me tight. "Sorry, that was wrong of me to ask."

"Don't be sorry. It's part of getting to know someone. Intimacy."

I could be wrong, but I thought I felt him squirm.

"Enough of that kind of silly talk," I said, wanting to shake the past loose a little while longer. "What do you like for breakfast?"

"Breakfast? Is it morning already? You can't tell with the smog."

"It's still nighttime. I'm thinking ahead. I'm used to being a wife, remember? Let me take care of you."

He eased upright. "What about your flatmate?"

I sat up too, and instinctively pulled the covers up to my chin. "We're grown-ups. I'm sure she won't mind."

"I can't, Clara."

"Why not?"

"I've got an early day," he said. I started to protest, but he quickly covered my lips with his hand. He released me and kissed me again. "I've got to go." He got up and dressed in the dark as I lay there watching yet another man leave me alone in bed.

— CHAPTER THIRTY —

The next morning was December 7, the day of Alicia Steele's screen test. The date had been etched in my memory ever since discovering the black and white photograph. The twist of fate that the very screen test in the snapshot was something her granddaughter had arranged was inexplicable, magical, and I hadn't the faintest idea what it meant. Yet I wasn't surprised when I opened the closet to see that the green dress had vanished. I knew where it was. It was back in Hollywood getting steamed and pressed for an audition—the one light in a long, dark tunnel smeared with deception and betrayal.

I was disappointed that I'd let Dean and Niall distract me from my mission. Today was going to be the start of settling the score for my grandmother and subsequently my mother and me. The family curse would be broken and we would find happiness.

I scurried as fast as I could to the telegraph office. The bell rang when I entered, and the little old man came out of a back room.

"Let me guess. Another cable to California?" he smiled.

"How did you know?" I smiled back at him.

"Your timing is impeccable. This one came for you late last night," he said and handed a telegram to me. It was from Alice.

Dear Clara,

I've prepared for my screen test. Even have my outfit picked out—a dress that I made for another film but it was never worn. It was designed for the femme fatale role—I'm hoping it will weave its magic on the casting director. I wanted to thank you again. No one has gone out of their way for me before. I can't tell you how much this means to me. Wish me luck. Signed, Alicia Steele.

I could almost hear the excitement in her voice, the optimism and hope. It made everything I'd done up till now worth it. To hell with Amber and Dean, to hell with Frederick and Niall, to hell with anyone who stood in my way.

"Any reply?" the old man asked patiently. I nodded and he handed me the form. I didn't hesitate.

Dear Alicia,

The dress sounds perfect. You don't need luck. This part was written for you! I have a good feeling. So all I will say is break a leg. Love, Clara.

I quickly scratched out "love" and replaced it with "signed" and gave it to the man and paid him for it.

Trinity was up early reading the morning paper when I returned and padded into the kitchen to pour myself some black coffee.

"I don't think you're going to like the story in the paper," she said mysteriously.

"Why?" I asked and crossed to the sofa to sit beside her.

"I told you that Frederick cast the female lead."

She held up *Talk*. A giant photo of Amber took up almost an entire page, with an equal-sized story beside it. "I would kill for press like this," she sighed.

I snatched it away and read the headline. *Ward of the States: Starlet Amber Ward Lands Lead Role in New Screwball Comedy. By Lawrence Hayward.*

"That rat Larry!" I seethed, but in my head another name cried out to be condemned. How dare Frederick betray me!

"How could she have landed this part?" I asked, but it was all there in black and white for the world to read. She had tagged along with her "boyfriend," the director Dean Lapointe, for a meeting with the producer of the film, Frederick Marshall, who was so charmed by her that he asked her to read.

"Apparently the camera loves her and she's got great comedic timing. I called my agent, who heard all about it, and she said Amber was the next Carole Lombard," Trinity explained. Her words felt disloyal to me. I wanted to scream.

"She prefers to think of herself as the next Marilyn Monroe," I said sarcastically. I stared at the photo; there was no doubt that the camera adored her. It was a Hollywood-style portrait that would have made George Hurrell proud; the kind of perfectly executed old-school glamour shot, like Dietrich and Garbo posed for. Amber's blonde hair and ivory skin gave her an angelic quality that certainly wasn't present in the 3D version. Her blue eyes cast a pale intensity over the image. Her lips looked soft and dewy, and I imagined they were painted blood red. Red was the only colour I could see. How had my plan backfired like this? Of course I knew how—good-girl Clara encouraging the meeting—well, good girls finished last. I needed to see Frederick immediately. But I was too furious to speak. The tension rippled through my body and I began to crunch the paper in my fist.

"Hey, I was reading that!" Trinity said.

I released the paper. Then out of nowhere came the clicking sound from my room that I'd heard the other night. The typewriter was summoning me again. I looked at Trinity, but she was calmly buried in the newspaper. She hadn't heard it. I went to the door and listened. It stopped. I went inside. As before, the machine was alone, untouched and silent. I sat down, my fingers poised over the keys.

EXT. HIGH TOWER ELEVATOR—NIGHT
Rod waits for Clara to show. Instead, he hears
her HUSBAND and his MISTRESS walking below from
their garage to the elevator. Then the elevator
begins to CHUG AND CHURN as the chains pull it
up from the ground floor. Rod ducks behind some
brush and waits. The door opens.

                         HUSBAND
          You need to pack for Hawaii, sweetheart.

The mistress laughs like a little girl. Rod hears
a scream but doesn't move.

                         MISTRESS
          What is she doing here?

Rod peers through the brush and sees Clara block-
ing their path to the house.

                         CLARA
          Get away from my husband!

                         HUSBAND
                    (to his mistress)
          Go into the house. I'll take care of her.

CLARA

You're not going anywhere until I tell you.

HUSBAND

What are you doing with a gun?

At these words Rod jumps out into view. Clara is
startled and the husband tries to grab the gun.
There's a struggle. Rod grabs a rock lying nearby
and smacks him on the head with it. The husband
crashes to the ground and doesn't move. The mistress screams, then faints, falling hard onto the
cement walkway.

CLARA

Is she dead?

Rod squats by the body and feels for a pulse. He
does the same with her husband. He looks up at
her and shakes his head.

ROD

Not yet. They're both alive.

Clara races to the elevator and shoves the rock
in the door to prop it open. She presses the
button and the elevator chugs and churns down to
the bottom, leaving the shaft empty.

ROD

What are you doing?

> CLARA

This is what we planned. We shove her down.
Let her fall. She won't feel a thing.

> ROD

Are you crazy? We can't do that now. He saw
you. He'll call the police. You'll get the
death penalty.

Clara smiles and stands over the mistress's
unconscious body.

> CLARA

After what she did to me, I already have a
death penalty.

> ROD

You're not talking sense.

> CLARA

Nothing about this makes sense. Are you
going to help me? If you won't, then turn
around and walk down those stairs and drive
away and don't look back.

> ROD
> (swallowing hard)
> I'll help you.

Clara nods solemnly.

CLARA
You do love me? Like you said you did?

Rod nods. They pick up the body and drag it to
the empty elevator shaft.

I stopped typing. I didn't want to write the rest of it, not yet. In my grandmother's notes, Rod would stop Clara from committing murder because he loved her. Then Clara would drive off in her convertible, and she would speed along up through the zigzagging hills to the Hollywood sign and that would be where it ended, just like it had ended for Alicia. I didn't like it, not one bit. It was too close to home. Sitting here, reeling from the news that Amber Ward not only stole my husband but also the role that may have saved my grandmother's life, I felt the level of despair that Alice must have felt, the hopelessness and the realization that all is lost, and for the first time I was afraid of what might happen. I didn't want to end up where Alice ended up. I didn't like how my life was imitating her art.

But I didn't have long to obsess over it because the telephone rang. I could hear Trinity speaking like a fool, so I knew it was Frederick.

"She's right here, Mr. Marshall. Goodbye and thanks again." She held out the receiver.

"Hello, Frederick," I said with enough ice in my throat to freeze the smog into solid blocks. "Yes, I have some things to tell you too."

I rang off. He wanted me to come to his house as soon as I was able. I was able.

I stamped my feet hard as I marched up the hill through the heaving mass of smog to the Tufnell Park tube. I shoved and got shoved by other pedestrians on the sidewalk. Up ahead I saw the faint roof light of what might have been the only black cab on the road. I was about make a dash towards it when a hand grabbed me through the fog and pulled me into a shop doorway. It was Larry.

"You son of a bitch!" I snapped. He shoved his paw over my mouth and wouldn't let go until I stopped fidgeting. I calmed down and he removed his hand. I wanted to bite it.

"Look here, I checked with a buddy in New York, and he said my story on your husband didn't run."

I raised an eyebrow and smirked at him. "So? We had a deal and you broke it."

"Our deal was I'd write a negative profile of Dean Lapointe, and I did that. You were going to get me published in America. You broke the deal. I told you I was going to write about Amber and I did. And good thing too. Just like I said, she's going to be a star."

It took all the willpower I had not to spit in his face. "Well, I've changed my mind. Your story on Dean wasn't up to par. You're not good enough for American papers." It wasn't true but it would do.

"You're a bloody American tart is what you are," he said nastily. "I have a mind to write about you. The scorned wife out to get her husband."

"You wouldn't dare," I hissed.

"Try me, Clara Bishop," he jeered back. "Amber told me you were out with Frederick Marshall."

I went cold. "It's a lie."

"She told me you were at The Savoy with him. What's that about then?"

"Stay out of my way, Larry. You don't know who you're dealing with," I threatened and felt a fiery rawness whip around me despite the shelter of the doorway, as though I could conjure the fictional Clara at will.

"Amber told me that Dean didn't get the directing job. Marshall's hired an Englishman. Maybe you had something to do with that, then?"

"Don't be ridiculous. The only reason Frederick met with Dean was because of me."

"Is that so? I bet Dean won't see it that way. Maybe I'll ask Frederick Marshall myself."

"I'd stay away from Frederick if I were you," I warned. "He's a man prone to violence."

"You haven't fallen for those idiotic rumours, have you? He didn't kill his wife. She drowned."

I shrugged, wanting to be vague, hoping that if nothing else, pointing out how getting outside Frederick's good graces would be bad for his career. "If you say so."

Larry rubbed his chin. "You know something the rest of us don't?"

"Maybe," I lied.

"If you have info on that case, then I'm all ears."

"Like I said, leave him alone. Don't stick your nose into his business, or else he won't let you near Amber or any of his stars."

Larry kept rubbing his chin like it was itchy. "Don't be messing with me. Remember, I'm as expert at digging up dirt as you are," he said warily. "I'd say we're equals."

I saw the black cab sitting there in the haze like an apparition. I turned back to scraggly Larry. "That is one thing we are not."

Then I made a run for it and, grasping the handle of the cab door, I dove into the back seat.

"Primrose Hill, please."

CHAPTER THIRTY-ONE

I hadn't been to Frederick's house since I'd wandered in off the street. That day, standing in the rain being dressed down by Amber, seemed another world. Today the house loomed through the mist like a fortress etched from clay; its grey mass appeared to undulate with the waves of murk. I asked the driver to wait for me, and he agreed for a princely sum.

The front door was slightly ajar, so I let myself in. Seeing the interior through my lens of black and white gave every object and angle a severity it didn't have in colour. Gone was the air of femininity. Instead, the corners of the walls soared sharply above me, while the mantelpiece and the slew of picture frames appeared razor-edged. The furniture and objects were lighted from the chandelier and sconces like a Caravaggio painting. A decorative oriental screen was backlit and cast a series of stripes at canted angles across one wall. It was into this pattern of shadows that Frederick materialized. He was drinking from a fine bone china teacup.

"Lovely of you to arrive so promptly," he said politely. "Have a seat."

I sat down on a pale chaise that looked like a fainting couch. Judging by its worn fabric, it had been well used for that purpose.

"I hear you've been busy casting your movie," I said.

He grinned. "Your friend Trinity read well enough. I'm not sure she's best for the role, but I wanted to make you happy."

I snorted my disgust. "Happy? You double-crossed me."

He sighed and sat on a Queen Anne chair. Its delicate curves made him appear giant and utterly ridiculous, like a grown man taking tea at the kiddie table. "You saw the article in *Talk?*" he asked and I nodded firmly. "I was afraid of that. Larry Hayward is a no-good hack. I've never trusted him. You know he wrote the most scathing things about me when I was under investigation for Mica's death." He shook his head.

"From what I know, he wasn't the only one," I said, silently referring to Niall.

"True. I had more than a few reporters chasing me, trying to prove my guilt and, thankfully, my innocence. A few of them paid for it, though, in the end."

I shifted uncomfortably on the couch at the cloaked reference to Niall's time in prison, and wondered whom else Frederick got even with. "Then you got lucky," I said, provoking him.

"Luck had nothing to do with it. Innocence prevailed. Good triumphs over evil," he said flatly.

"Does it? Well, I know Larry; he's good at what he does." Again I was goading him.

He eyed me suspiciously. "You *know* Larry? Is he a friend?"

"We've worked together. You know how it is with us tabloid reporters; we talk to each other, look out for each other. Get it?"

"I'm sure that I don't." He eyed me suspiciously. "But I had hoped to see you before you read it, so we could chat."

"Well, I didn't, and I'm here, so cut to the chase," I said. "You can't cast Amber. We had a deal."

He laughed like I had said something highly amusing. It annoyed me. He took two long sips from the teacup and placed it down on

a side table with the carefulness of a jeweller returning priceless dia-
monds to their glass case.

"I'm sorry you feel that way. But I'm a successful producer for a
reason. Amber was right for the part, better than right, she knocked
my socks off. And to top it off, she's a sweetheart of a charmer. She
knows how to play the game, if you know what I mean."

I did and recoiled. I knew enough about Frederick to know being
irate wasn't going to work, so I softened my tone. "But you haven't
even seen Alicia Steele's screen test yet," I pleaded. "What if she's
better than Amber?"

He shrugged. "I doubt it."

"That's not fair. You could at least watch it before signing Amber's
contract."

"I'll watch it, but it won't change things. You know, I did screen *He
Gave No Answer.*"

My heart lifted a little. "And? She's great, isn't she?"

"She's good. I'll give you that. But I didn't see her comedic side. If
anything, she's a dramatic actress. Maybe in my next film . . ."

"But there's not time for that!" I shouted, then took a deep breath
when I saw his displeasure at my outburst.

He picked up his teacup and drank again. "As you are aware, her
screen test is today. That much I will do for you."

I felt a surge of hope return. "Will you promise not to sign Amber's
contract until then?"

"Too late, I'm afraid. I signed it this morning. She's the star. Another
discovery by Frederick Marshall. David is thrilled to act opposite her."

"David Niven?" I asked.

"Who else?"

"I heard you didn't hire Dean?"

"He's not up for the job. So no," he said plainly. "How did you
find out?"

"Larry, who else?" I said it to provoke him. "He's quite tight with Amber."

"That won't continue. I can assure you."

I stood and moved to a sideboard where an array of framed photos was displayed. One in particular caught my attention. It was Frederick with Marilyn Monroe. The actress was wearing a white fur coat and a high-wattage smile no other actress could match. Certainly not Amber. Even with Marilyn's troubled life and rotten work ethic, she was heads and tails above Amber. Few actresses around could survive such rumour and innuendo, which got me thinking. Amber may worship Marilyn, but the world didn't need two.

"You met Marilyn Monroe," I said.

"Yes, in Hollywood last summer. She's extremely smart and witty. Now that's a talented actress."

"I couldn't agree more," I said and smiled, regaining my composure. "I thought of a way for you to make this up to me."

He laughed out loud but I ignored him. "I'll get my contacts in the press to write all about Amber during rehearsals and also after filming begins. The adoring public will know where she shops, what she likes to eat, even who she dates," I gulped, thinking of Dean. "I can make her a household name. Not a bad thing for publicity, no matter how successful the producer is."

I looked at Frederick. I could tell I had his attention. "Go on."

"Only once filming begins, the stories start to change. They'll focus only on her diva behaviour: not showing up on time, if at all, arriving drunk or on drugs, how the director and cast hate her. How she thinks she can get away with what Monroe does. The public will turn on her. It will be such a fall from grace that you'll have no choice but to fire her. She'll flee to LA with her tail between her legs. The only acting role she'll ever get again will be in porn. You'll still benefit. You know what they say, there's no such thing as bad press."

"You really hate this girl that much?" he asked.

"I want Alicia Steele to get the part that much," I said sternly.

He shifted in his chair. "Need I remind you that to fire a star once filming begins is expensive. The British film industry isn't Hollywood, Miss Bishop. We're not made of money."

"No? Too bad," I said. "Then you should do the right thing and fire Amber now and cast Alicia."

He sighed impatiently. "No."

As I turned to face him, I knocked one of the framed pictures to the floor. It was a silver filigree frame, and the glass shattered into a few large pieces on the hardwood.

"Oh, I'm sorry!" I exclaimed. I kneeled down and carefully picked the pieces up. Frederick rushed to the sideboard and stood over me like I was a scullery maid. I cautiously turned the frame over, wary of the glass shards poking out, and saw that it was a photo of his dead wife, Mica. He held out his hand and I gave him the photograph.

"Your wife was very beautiful," I said.

"She was on the outside," he said coolly. "Mica was troubled. She was also trouble. But most women are."

"Still, it must have been awful seeing her lying in that pool," I said, wanting to see his reaction, anything that would allude to guilt or innocence.

He didn't satisfy me. Instead, he turned the photo over on its face and stared at the backing. "You know there are people out there who still think I killed her?" He stared straight through me until I took a step back.

"I may have read something like that," I admitted cautiously. I didn't like how the power between us had shifted. He was like a mobster in that way; no matter how tough a dame I was, he was tougher.

He took up residence again in the armchair, with the oriental screen drawing its perfect stripes across him. This time I skipped the chaise and sat in a wingback chair opposite him, allowing the light to cast its canted slats across me too.

"So, my dear Clara. As I was saying, Amber will star and that is that."

"That's your final decision?"

"It is."

"Then our deal is over."

Then he smiled and held it there. It unsettled me.

"I give up," he said at last.

I sighed deeply, relieved. "So you'll do it?"

"I give up," he repeated. "On this little game of ours. It was amusing for a while. I admit, I adore the chase, but now you're too much trouble."

"What do you mean?" I asked anxiously.

"What I mean simply is that London is full of gorgeous redheads. You're a dime a dozen, and I no longer covet you as a lover. It's too bad, really. We would have had such fun."

I didn't know what to do or what to say. There was no doubt that I had become embroiled in a mess, a dirty rotten revenge of my own making. But what of it? My grandmother's life mattered more than anything else. Even if I was in over my head, there was only one way to go, and that was all the way. I had to take a chance and use the one piece of information that Niall had let slip and that I'd filed away for safekeeping; it was now or never.

"I think you will change your mind," I said and rose to leave. "Because if you don't, then I'll give the photographs to the press."

"What photographs?" he scoffed.

"Only the photographs a certain journalist secretly took at your country house. It's quite scandalous stuff. Enough to reopen those rumours about Mica and how she died. Enough to make people despise you and boycott your films. You'll be back to making cheap slasher films."

His eyes went dead. "I don't believe you."

"Don't you?" I walked to the door with him on my heels. I opened it and saw the reassuring sight of the black cab. Frederick saw it too. "Do you really want to take that chance?"

"There are no photos. This is absurd!"

"Suit yourself. But I'd think good and hard about it, especially once you see how amazing Alicia Steele is."

Without waiting for an answer, I stepped into the street, the air thick with charcoal smoke, and got into the cab.

Police Station—Cirencester

Sergeant Hooper was sucking on his pen.

"Are you saying Frederick Marshall did in fact murder his wife? If you have proof, you must tell me; otherwise, it's obstruction of justice!"

"I'm just getting started. Now, if you'd let me finish."

Hooper was practically tearing the pen in half with his teeth, like a wolf with fresh-killed meat.

"You know that you can get thrown in jail for blackmail?"

"You know what sort of man Frederick Marshall is. He had it coming to him."

He threw the pen on the desk with a force that was intended to startle me, only the pen wasn't cooperating and rolled off the desk onto the floor. Hooper fumbled about to catch it, but he missed and resorted to crawling under the table to retrieve it. I took the opportunity to uncross and cross my legs, knowing the slit on the side of my gown would provide ample viewing pleasure of my upper thighs. He took his time, and when he re-emerged, his face was beet red, from embarrassment or exertion or both.

"Find your pen?" I asked.

"Tricky bugger," he said and sat back down. "Where were we?"

"I got into the cab . . ."

CHAPTER THIRTY-TWO

I wrapped my coat tightly around me and curled up in the corner of the back seat. The driver rolled the car slowly away from the curb. There wasn't much to look at but for a few abandoned cars. The streets were clogged with people, their faces covered, fighting their way through the murkiness. It was a living nightmare, and I was glad to be safely tucked inside the cab.

"You're a brave girl," the cabbie said, peering at me through his rear-view mirror. "It's not the best time to be out and about."

"No," I agreed. "Then why are you driving today? Isn't most of London covered in soot?"

"Aye, it's true. Doing my civic duty, that's all. Saving damsels in distress." He winked and I turned away to stare into the mist. That's what Niall called me. Thinking of my hubris moments ago, I'd never felt less like a damsel. Why can't a woman fight for good any way she sees fit? If that meant sometimes doing wrong in order to do right, then it was perfectly justified. After all, Niall had implied there might be evidence of some sort; photos were a possibility. I chose to believe there were. I could rewrite the truth to suit my needs. That's what reporters like me did with a nugget, an innuendo, a whisper; we turned it into a full-blown story, fit to print. Once out there, it became true, for the most part, or at least long enough to place doubt.

Yet despite my momentary bravery, the encounter with Frederick had taken its toll and I was shaking when I got to the flat, from fear or the cold, I didn't know and I didn't care. There was little that I could do except sit around and wait for him to come to his senses. Trinity was getting ready to leave for her physical. Every movie production requires the major players to get a doctor certificate for insurance purposes.

"I hope I can get there in time," she said anxiously.

"There's a lone cabbie out stalking the streets looking for damsels in distress," I said with a grim smile.

She was about to respond when the phone rang. I nearly jumped out of my skin. It had to be Frederick. She grabbed the receiver and put on a perky New Yawker accent like she was a switchboard operator wearing a headset and smoking a cigarette. "Mayberry residence . . . Aha . . . Clara Bishop? Sure, she's here. Just a moment please."

I snatched the receiver from her hand as she covered her mouth to hide her giggles. "This is Clara." It wasn't Frederick. It was Niall.

"Oh, it's you," I said and momentarily pictured him naked in my bed. But the lousy way he walked out on me made me indignant.

"You sound disappointed," he said. "I'm across the street at The White Stallion. Can I come up?"

"Whatever for?" I asked.

"I need to talk to you."

"Fine, I'm here." I rang off. "Niall is coming over."

Trinity was practically out the door. "Don't mind me, I'm making myself scarce. Toodle-oo."

Niall was there in a flash. He went to kiss me, but I turned my head so that his lips planted one on my cheek.

"Say, it's colder in here than it is on the North Sea. Well, have it your way," he said with a shrug. "I just got a call from your friend Amber Ward."

I rolled my eyes. "What did the dear girl want? A playmate?"

"I don't know what's got into you," Niall said. "But you should know she got a part in that Frederick Marshall picture. And not just any part, he gave her the lead."

"That's old news," I said and showed him Larry's story.

"I thought you'd be knocked flat by this development," he said and flopped on the sofa.

"Why don't you make yourself comfortable," I said sarcastically.

"Don't mind if I do. You want to know why she called me?"

"I'm on the edge of my seat."

"She wants to give me the exclusive story on her rise to stardom. I get to follow her around, go to costume fittings, read-throughs and visit the set, all of it." He paused and lit a cigarette, then another, and held it out for me. I took it. "I must have charmed her that day on set."

"How wonderful," I answered, watching the smoke rise in front of my eyes like a veil. "Though you should know she's also chummy with Larry. Perhaps she's playing you two against each other."

"I'm not worried, put it that way."

In truth, it would be very useful if I had to implement my plan. Niall's articles would go far in making her a star, and I wouldn't have to ask him to do it. He'd write them because the *Daily Buzz* wanted the exclusive story, and then when the time came, when Amber was the picture of the sweet, dedicated and talented actress, using a pseudonym, I would leak just enough information to set the media wolves on her. I'd sit back and watch them tear her apart piece by piece. Even Niall would have to follow the story of her destruction.

He drew long and hard on his cigarette. "And the funny part is Amber has you to thank for it." The whirring machine of revenge stopped dead when he said it. "She said she only got to audition because she went with Dean to his interview. An interview she told me you arranged."

"Is that what she told you?" I let out a fake laugh. I went to the kitchen and drowned my cigarette in a half-empty cup of coffee, hoping he wouldn't press me further. He did.

"What are you up to, Clara?"

I wouldn't look at him. "Oh, are you still here?"

"Listen," he said and leapt off the sofa and grabbed me around the waist tight enough that I couldn't wiggle out. "You asked me to help you once. Tell me what's going on and I'll help you now."

I thought about the threat I made to Frederick. I thought of Alicia Steele on the other side of the world practising her lines. Of Marjorie, a little girl about to lose her mother. And I thought about Dean and Amber celebrating her role of a lifetime. But I also thought of how sick to death I was of being alone in all this mess, so I told him as much as he needed to know.

"My friend, the one who's in trouble, she's an actress and Frederick was supposed to cast her, not Amber. She's in a bad way, Niall. Desperate and alone. If she doesn't get this part, I'm not sure what she'll do. Kill herself maybe."

I expected him to react with concern, but he took his time mulling it over. "Kill herself because she didn't get a part in a movie?" he repeated skeptically.

It wasn't the reaction I wanted, and I told him as much. "It's not just the movie. You see, my friend, she's lost everything. Her husband walked out on her, her career is going nowhere, she feels she has nothing to live for. Now do you understand?" I pleaded.

He bit his lower lip. "Are you sure you're not talking about yourself, Clara?"

I glared at him. "I'm not. Alicia Steele is her name. She's an actress in Hollywood and she works in the wardrobe department at a film studio. In fact, she made this," I said and gestured to my dress. He nodded, appropriately impressed.

"Where is she now?"

"She's in California. But she's doing a screen test tomorrow for Frederick. I'm convinced once he sees it he'll fire Amber, and if not, he'll fire her anyway because I'm going to make him. I told him I could get my hands on photos that implicate him in the murder of his wife."

I stopped, my chest heaving. Niall stared at me, but when he spoke he was calm, deliberate. "What photographs? Is this something to do with Larry?"

"No," I snapped. "I made them up. I blackmailed him with the idea there *are* photos. As a matter of fact, I got the idea from *you*."

"Me?"

"You once insinuated there was more about the case than ever got published. At least, I took it that way."

"I didn't think you would take me seriously. I was just sounding off. There are no pictures. Never were any pictures," he said and practically shook me.

"You mean you only tap phones?" I taunted him.

"Don't try to be provocative, Clara, it doesn't suit you. And it won't work. I'm long past being tormented by my mistakes."

I shoved him away. "Is that so? Are you saying Frederick is an innocent man?"

"The jury thought so. Listen, I just never got a good feeling from him. The day she died, the servants said they had a huge row over a role for her in his next movie. He didn't want her to do it. Sure he could've killed her, but did he? Only he, his wife and God know for sure."

"But a reporter of your stature has finely honed instincts, and you still sound like you suspect him." I was getting more and more worked up. "That's good enough for me. Good enough to put doubts in his mind of what I might have on him. Even if he didn't do it, he knows how manipulative reporters are with editing. We could reopen all those doubts."

He grabbed me again by the elbow. "Look, Clara, you don't know who you're messing with. Frederick Marshall is a powerful man, and powerful men can be dangerous."

"Don't worry, I won't be going with him to the country for a midnight swim," I laughed, repeating Niall's sarcastic comment to that effect. "Now, let me go!"

He dropped my elbow and pulled out another cigarette.

"There has to be another way to cheer up your friend," he said calmly.

"Cheer up!" I repeated. "Cheering up is for a child who has dropped an ice cream cone. Alicia Steele doesn't need cheering up. She needs to be saved."

"Calm down, Clara. There has to be another way."

I wasn't calming down; if anything the hysteria was increasing. "There isn't, Niall . . ." Then, despite myself, I leaned into his chest. After a moment, he reached up and stroked my hair. We stood that way for a few moments, and for the first time since this nightmare began, I felt reassured and safe and not alone—until there came more clicking sounds from my room.

"Do you hear that?" I asked him. But the clicking had stopped.

"I don't hear a thing," he said.

I pushed free of his arms and walked to the door of my room. "You didn't hear the typing?"

He came and opened the door. The window was wide open and the curtains were billowing frantically. He shut it quickly and stopped at the typewriter.

"You writing an article?"

"No," I said and cautiously moved to the desk. "A screenplay. I'm co-writing a screenplay."

"What's it about?"

"It's a film noir," I said. "Lust, betrayal, the usual."

I forced a smile, then I saw it. On the floor below the typewriter was a small grey lifeless piece of fur. It was a dead mouse. I screamed like a schoolgirl.

Niall calmly took a handkerchief from his pocket and picked it up by its tail.

"Maybe this was your mystery typist," he said and took it away. Wait until Trinity found out. To think, after my inventing a mouse, there really was one.

When he came back, he found me still staring at the floor where the mouse had been.

"I feel sad that it died. Poor thing," I said. "And in my room."

"With this smog, I'm not surprised. People are dying too. The hospitals are full of respiratory cases."

"Are you working on a story about it after all?"

"I am. I don't care if they publish it or not, but I'm going to write about it. The government has let coal burn like there's no tomorrow, until now there may be no tomorrow. It's corrupt and it must stop, or I'm afraid we'll have many more days like this."

I thought for a moment. "You know, if you can't sell it here, I might be able to get someone in New York or LA to buy it. If it is an in-depth environmental report, and you get officials on the record." I felt like a broken record, promising more than perhaps I could deliver to Larry and now Niall. With all this time-travel nonsense, I wasn't even sure who, if anyone, I would know in the media circus of 1952.

He smiled boyishly, like I'd given him a new baseball mitt and the afternoon off school. "You'd do that?"

"Sure, why not? You're one of the few who haven't betrayed me."

CHAPTER
THIRTY-THREE

A half-hour later we were back lying naked in each other's arms, crammed tight into my tiny twin bed. I felt less guilty about the second time. Maybe because I felt more in control of fate, or I was getting used to succumbing to desire, or it could have been that I liked Niall more than was good for me. He was one giant step away from Dean and that couldn't be bad.

"I might fall asleep," Niall yawned. I could see why. The smog turned day into night, and surrounded by such gloomy darkness, bed seemed the only reasonable place to be. I was about to tell him so when I heard Trinity run into the flat like she was being chased.

"Clara!" she yelled. I leapt out of bed and grabbed a robe, but I wasn't fast enough. She whipped open my door and saw us there, the robe clutched in front of my naked body, Niall's bare chest on full display, his modesty protected by the sheet. He folded his arms behind his head and grinned.

"Hello, Trinity," he said.

"Hello to you too," she answered; whatever she had on her mind seemed momentarily forgotten. "I'm sorry for blasting in like this. I wasn't expecting . . ."

I shook my head. "Don't worry. Give us a second and we'll be right out."

She turned away, and I noticed she held a file folder in her hand.

Dressed now, Niall and I walked into the living room, where Trinity was pouring three shots of Scotch.

"We'll all need a drink," she said and gestured to Niall. "At least the ladies will, but I poured one for you anyway."

"Good God, what happened?" I exclaimed. "Are you all right?" Given she'd just returned from her physical exam, I thought the worst.

Her eyes looked to the file folder on the counter, the one I'd seen in her hand a moment ago. She thrust it at me. I opened it cautiously. My first instinct was that Trinity was dying of some awful mid-twentieth-century disease, but as I scanned the report, my throat constricted. I tried to swallow, but there was no saliva in my mouth, just a dry sensation as though the life had been sucked out of me.

"Amber is pregnant," I announced, not making eye contact with either of them.

"How did you get her medical chart?" demanded Niall, always the reporter.

"The entire cast went to the same doctor," Trinity said, then went on to explain how she had been left alone in the exam room and got bored waiting so she nosed around and caught sight of a pile of folders. She snuck a peek and saw that they were for all members of the cast. She poked through them and then she found Amber's file. She couldn't help but look more closely—after all, it was Amber—and there it was: pregnant. She didn't wait for her exam but stuffed the folder into her purse and got dressed, telling the nurse she'd forgotten an urgent meeting and would return tomorrow. Then she hoofed it home.

"I don't know what to say," I said, still in shock.

"That makes two of us," Trinity agreed. "Better drink this." She handed me the Scotch and I shot it down in one gulp. She poured me another. "I'm so sorry, Clara. I know how much you wanted Dean's baby. How long you tried."

"There's no turning back the clock," I said, knowing the irony was lost on them. "He will marry her now."

"You don't know that," Trinity said.

I nodded. "Oh, I do. He married me when I was pregnant, only because I was pregnant. He'll do the same. He'll want to do the so-called right thing."

I wanted to cry. If any occasion called for tears, surely it was this, but none came. The thought of *that woman* carrying my husband's child was too much. I'd longed to have Dean's baby, mourned the one that was almost mine, and now this.

Niall cleared his throat like he had an important announcement to make, and when he spoke, he was all business.

"This may prove to be in your favour," he said and grinned in that slightly wicked way he had. "Frederick won't make a movie with a pregnant woman."

Slowly, the same wicked smile unfurled across my face. "I hadn't thought of that," I said. My blackmail was unnecessary. A pregnant leading lady wouldn't do. He would have to fire her now if he wanted to keep on schedule.

"She can do the film, you know. They can hide her stomach with costumes," Trinity said as though what she said helped.

I shook my head. "Frederick won't want a pregnant ingénue. He wouldn't stand for it. It's not like she's a big star already and they'll wait another year for her. He'd have to recast." And recast with Alicia Steele, I thought gleefully, relieved that at last my plan was taking hold. "I wonder if he knows she's pregnant."

"The medical report is supposed to be confidential," Trinity added.

"The doctor would have to tell the production company," Niall pointed out. "Anything that could affect the film being made on time and on budget would be disclosed."

He was right. And given it was 1952 and women's rights weren't up to snuff yet, there would be no penalty for firing a woman because she was pregnant. Niall checked his watch.

"I've got to go," he said and grabbed his coat, kissing me softly on the forehead. "Be good."

"I won't make any promises I can't keep," I said and watched him walk out the door.

"So I take it you're over Dean?" Trinity said and pointed to the door. "Niall Adamson is your new lover?"

"Lover?" I repeated. "I like the sound of that. Yes, I suppose he is. As for Dean, what choice do I have? He's going to be a father to another woman's child."

There was a knock at the door. To our surprise, it was Saffron.

"Well, look what the cat dragged in," Trinity said. "Do come in."

She barely smiled.

"Have a seat," I offered. She sat down demurely with her legs folded and her handbag on her lap.

"What brings you by, Saffron?" I asked. "We run up a tab at The White Stallion?"

She shook her head. "I was on my way home and wanted to know if you've heard from Larry."

I raised an eyebrow, recalling the altercation in the doorway and how he'd threatened me, but when I spoke my tone was polite. "Not a peep. Why?"

"He's not returned my calls. I wanted to give him a piece of my mind."

"That could be why he's not calling back," Trinity pointed out.

"I asked his mum, my auntie, and she said he was supposed to come home last night but she hasn't heard from him."

"He lives with his mother?" I asked. She nodded. Oh brother. "Maybe he got lost in the fog."

She dropped it then and asked Trinity more details about the film, and I let my mind drift away. Perhaps Larry was doing another photo-op with Amber. That is, assuming Frederick hadn't found out about her pregnancy yet. I wished I could see his face when he found out. I crossed to the window and saw a tough-looking kid dressed head to toe in the Teddy Boy uniform standing below. I wouldn't have thought much about it until Niall showed up and the two began to argue.

"Guys, come take a look," I said, and Trinity and Saffron came and peered at the scene unfolding on the sidewalk.

"What are they saying?" I asked.

The window was open just a crack, but we didn't dare make it wider in case they heard us. A few words wafted up to us.

"I will tell her if you don't!" the teenager said angrily.

"Sam, you don't know what you're talking about!" Niall snapped.

I didn't like how quiet Saffron was.

"Saffron, do you know who that boy is?"

"Don't you?" she asked, surprised.

"No, I don't," I said, feeling suspicious all of a sudden.

"I thought you knew," she said as though reading my mind. "I tried to tell you, but you said you knew about him."

"What are you saying?"

"That's his son. Niall is married."

I felt the floor sway beneath me. How had I become a mistress? Why had he lied? Not that I ever asked him if he was married. I hadn't. But he knew what I'd gone through with Dean. Were there no decent men left in the world? I knew Trinity and Saffron were watching me, waiting for me to speak, scream or otherwise react. But I just stood staring out the window and wondering what type of wife she was—the type to turn a blind eye, or was she biding her time, waiting for proof or the courage to confront him. Or perhaps she was a wife like me, someone who never saw it coming, but believed that because she loved him he must love her.

CHAPTER THIRTY-FOUR

I'd managed several hours of fitful sleep when the phone rang. Trinity was already out, gone to her rescheduled physical and to return Amber's file. She was going to ask as subtly as she could when the doctor reported the cast's results to the insurance company and the producer. I crawled to the phone feeling like hell. It was Frederick Marshall at the other end. He wanted to talk to me about my proposition and gave me an address to a pub in the east end. He told me to be there in an hour and not to keep him waiting. I didn't like his tone; gone was the flirty lilt, his voice drained of even rudimentary friendliness, but then again, I had threatened him. I didn't know whether Frederick knew about the pregnancy or not, and I decided it was best if I kept my mouth shut on the topic to see how it played out.

I took my time getting ready. I chose a snug-fitting dark dress with lace sleeves and a lace panel that covered my décolletage but provided ample cleavage viewing. I knew it was necessary to come to this meeting fully armed.

Once outside, I heard my name and Saffron came through the mist at me.

"Sorry to bother you," she said. I could tell she was worried. Her face was devoid of makeup, and her normally perfectly coiffed hair was dishevelled and, more to the point, she was in flats.

"I'm off to an important meeting," I began, then thought about it. I was the one in charge, not him. Frederick could wait. "Is something wrong?"

"It's Larry again," she said. "I know you don't like him much, but he's disappeared. His mum said he still hasn't turned up."

"Have you tried his editor at *Talk?*" I asked. I didn't like Larry and wasn't sure why Saffron thought I would know anything of his whereabouts.

"We rang him and Larry hasn't filed a story or checked in since day before yesterday," she said.

"Maybe he's with a girl," I suggested, biting my tongue rather than suggest she check a brothel.

"That's unlikely. You've met him," she said and smiled faintly. "I know he was working for you . . ."

I waved her off. "No, he wasn't. He did one story, but after that Amber feature we broke off our agreement. I can't help you. Sorry. I'm sure he'll turn up."

I watched her walk away and disappear, her face covered in a pale silk scarf. I started to make my way to the tube station. But I hadn't gotten far when I saw the faint glow of a black cab.

"Why, it's you again," I said as I stepped into the cab. The same driver was behind the wheel. "You're always here when I need you."

"It just works out that way, love," he said and smiled. "Where to?"

I looked down at the scrawl I'd made on a piece of paper. "Some place in the east end, Whitechapel? In a pub called The Ten Bells?" I said.

He looked concerned. "That's not a nice part of town, miss. Are you sure?"

"It's what he told me," I explained, a wave of foreboding washing over me.

"Well, if you're meeting a gentleman, then I feel better taking you," he said.

I smiled and settled into the back seat.

"It's quite far, will take us some time in this fog," he explained cheerfully.

"So be it," I said.

It did take ages to get there, and the closer we got the worse the landscape looked. Still recovering from being bombed out in the war, there was much rubble where buildings had stood and had yet to be rebuilt. Shop windows were boarded up too. I remembered studying how the King and Queen had toured this area after the Blitz, visiting homeless families. There didn't seem to be many homes now either. Even the trees and shrubs looked forlorn and neglected. The people we passed wore depressed expressions to match the surroundings.

When we pulled up outside The Ten Bells, the cabbie whistled. "This is the place," he said. "Strange spot for a date."

"It's not a date," I explained and stepped to the curb, but his remark got my attention. "What makes it strange?" I asked as I looked up at the pub; it looked like every other pub in London.

"This is the neighbourhood where Jack the Ripper murdered his victims," he said ominously. "The Ten Bells was where two of the women drank their last ales before he stabbed them to death."

Without another word, he drove away, leaving me alone in the street. I wrapped my scarf around my head and shivered. Was Frederick meeting me here intended as a macabre joke, or was he trying to frighten me? My fingers were clasped around the door handle when I hesitated; it felt as though someone was watching me. I looked slowly side to side, but in the fog you couldn't see more than a few feet in any direction. Taking a deep breath, I went in.

He was waiting at a back table. I removed my coat and scarf at the door so that I could display my figure to full advantage as I walked towards him. His eyes never left me, but he definitely wasn't pleased to see me. His manner was cold, but it was the menace I sensed the most as I sat down. I wasn't accustomed to making people angry with me; I had always wanted people to like me. Though my behaviour of late belied that trait. Besides, if he despised me, our fledgling friendship was a sacrifice I was willing to make.

"You don't seem very happy to see me," I said and was rewarded with a blank stare for my efforts.

"Your little stunt the other day took all the romance out of it." His tone was all business, like we were in a penthouse boardroom in a glass office tower, not a tight-fitting table for two in an East End pub with a notorious past.

Frederick ordered for us—two English ales. I despised the taste and the smell of beer, but I had my reservations that The Ten Bells could produce a sidecar. When it arrived, I picked up the enormous frosted glass with foam on top thick as cream. One sip was unable to alter my opinion of the drink, and so my glass stayed on the table fully committed to remaining untouched. Frederick had drunk half of his tankard before at last he got to the point.

"I want those photographs."

So he had bought my lie.

"Not until you fire Amber," I said sternly, looking for any indication that he knew about her condition. "And cast Alicia Steele."

He drank more of his beer, somehow managing not to get even a whisper of foam stuck to his upper lip. The foam was probably too afraid.

"Your friend's audition was done yesterday," he said icily. "I'm prepared to give her a small part in exchange for the photos. I won't even bother looking at the screen test."

The light from the rudimentary pendant lamp overhead cast a large shadow across his face. His small black eyes never wavered from me. He just stared, unblinking, giving the impression he didn't have eyelids.

"I hope you don't feel I pushed you too far?" I asked and shoved a dose of the demure female into my voice, wondering if he had looked at his wife the night she died like he was looking at me now. Had she pushed too far?

"Amber Ward got the lead because she was that good. She read like a pro and, better still, she looks like a star," he said, those dead eyes daring me to contradict him.

"Is that so?" I asked as irritation won the battle with my self-restraint.

He pulled out a cigarette case, and for a moment I was reminded of Niall. I wondered what he'd think of me being here, ignoring his warnings to stay away from Frederick. I took a cigarette. I leaned forward so he could light it for me and sucked in the nicotine and did my best not to blow smoke in his face. "As for your new proposition, no dice. Lead role and we have a deal."

He smirked. "I'm not going to fire Amber," he said.

I kept quiet. I was convinced that Frederick didn't know about the pregnancy. This was merely gamesmanship. I understood why actresses like my grandmother coveted the femme fatale part. It was fun.

"Your silence impresses me," he said calmly. "I can't read you at all. It's what I like about you."

He didn't speak for a moment, but his eyes wandered about the room as though surveying it, scrutinizing it. Then he fixed his glare on me once more. "This is my favourite pub, though not fashionable enough to entertain movies stars. Mica despised it. I stopped coming here when we were married because she found it eerie. After she died," his voice trailed off, lost in a stream of thought he wasn't going to share. Shaking it away, he said with a note of finality, "Now I come alone. Except today."

"Seems quite far from your house."

"I hate that house. Mica wanted it, not me. As you pointed out when we met, there is little there that speaks to the kind of man I am. I will sell it after the film wraps and buy a home around here."

"I appreciate all the personal information but I think it's time for me to go. You need to think things through."

"As do you," he said. "I can assure you that those pictures would not damage me in the slightest."

I shrugged and stood up. "Then why do you want them so badly?"

He swallowed. "Perhaps this bit of blackmail has aroused me more than I care to admit, as much as your silky red hair. I will get what I want, Clara Bishop. I always do."

I turned away, about to retrieve my coat and scarf, when he spoke again.

"Be careful out there, Clara. All that fog, a girl can simply turn a wrong corner, and, well, you get the idea."

I didn't look back as I grabbed my things and walked through the door.

CHAPTER THIRTY-FIVE

I realized as I started to walk away from The Ten Bells that I hadn't the faintest idea how to get home. The streets were narrow and twisty, and it wasn't long before I became disoriented. I kept looking over my shoulder thinking that someone was following me, but there was no one. Not even the faithful cabbie appeared. Then I saw a young man on a delivery bicycle and I waved him to stop.

"I need to get to Tufnell Park," I explained, aware of how anxious my voice sounded.

"I can give you a lift to the Thames if you like. You can catch the tube from there," he said kindly.

I looked at the giant flat basket on his bicycle. It was designed to carry dry goods, not passengers. It wouldn't be easy and it wouldn't be ladylike, but it sure beat being lost in Jack the Ripper's hunting ground. Especially after Frederick's parting words. Within a few moments we were off, and he speedily navigated the streets with me bouncing behind him like a sack of flour. Then through the fog came the smell of the river and I knew we were close. He pulled up on a corner for me to get off his contraption, which I did with minimal grace.

"Just follow this road. It will go to the Victoria Embankment and you can take the Northern line," he explained and smiled. Only then did I notice he was missing a front tooth and how ragged his clothes were. I dove into my handbag and found a five-pound note and placed it in his palm. It must have been a lot, for he removed his hat and practically bowed at me.

"Thank you, miss!" he grinned and got back on his bicycle, waving at me like a schoolboy, which he probably was.

I walked along the embankment, taking in the stench of the Thames, not daring to look over the side. What was most certainly a cold, black body of moving water had no appeal to me. I was spooked enough already. I kept my pace up but my shoes were starting to pinch, so after a while I sat down on a bench. That's when I saw a sign for The Strand. Good God, I was within walking distance of The Savoy. It was like returning to the scene of a crime. Amber was probably safely tucked into the luxury loo, puking her guts out from morning sickness as Dean proudly ordered tea for three. I was tempted to waltz into the American Bar and order a sidecar for one. I'd earned it. But no sooner had I made the decision than I saw a woman coming towards me out of the fog. I ducked behind the bench because she looked all too familiar, and as she grew closer I saw at once that I *did* know her. It was Amber. Only it was a different sort of girl who made her way through the mist in a full-length trench coat and cloche hat. Certainly hers was not the face of a budding actress on the verge of stardom. Maybe between my leaving The Ten Bells and here, Frederick had gotten word and fired her. I wanted to tell her to cheer up; at least she was carrying the child of a man we both loved. I crouched down even tighter so she wouldn't see me, but there was no need. Amber walked past like she was in a trance. Her tempo and carriage weren't those of a person on a casual stroll. Hers had purpose and direction.

Curiosity and my years of celebrity stalking got the better of me and I followed her. She was hard to keep pace with, not least because she was wearing smaller heels. Mine were killing me, but I made sure not to lose sight of her in the fog. She turned up a small street away from the Thames and then down an even smaller street, almost an alley really, that came to a dead end. I waited on the corner and watched her knock on a large wooden door. She didn't have to wait long before someone opened it. I couldn't see who was inside, so I waited a few minutes, then dashed back down the alley. The door was unmarked, not a name or business sign in sight. I stood back and looked up to the windows. The blinds were closed but lights were on like it was Christmas Eve. There was a sign on the building next door. *Smith's Textiles and Tailoring.* My best guess was that Amber was up there getting a wardrobe fitting; perhaps the buildings were connected by a hallway or something. There was no point lurking in the alley, so I found my way back to the embankment.

I was contemplating removing my shoes and going barefoot when a car horn blasted through the air. I whipped around, panicked that I'd ended up in the middle of the road, only to see the usual cabbie pull up beside me.

"Need a lift?"

"How did you know I was here?" I asked, baffled.

"I didn't. Dropped someone off at The Savoy and was coming around to go home when I saw you."

"I'm awfully glad you did." I practically fell into the back seat, my feet were burning so badly. "I sure wish this fog would lift."

"It's brought the whole city to a standstill. Buses have been shut down entirely."

He turned up The Strand and we drove past The Savoy. A shiver ran up my back. "So who did you drop off there?"

"Just some chap. He said he was in the movie business." The shiver returned and then some. Had Frederick gone to see Amber?

"Was he English or American?" I asked.

"To be honest, I'm not sure. He was a stern fellow."

We rode the rest of the way in silence as I rubbed my stocking feet, but when we arrived at the flat, Niall was standing outside.

"I've changed my mind, keep going," I instructed the driver.

But it was too late. Niall jumped in front of the cab, and the driver had no choice but to stop. "Just drive over him!" I yelled, but obviously he didn't listen. Niall ran around to the passenger door and tried to open it.

"Clara! Come out or let me come in!" he said and pressed his face against the window.

"What shall we do, miss?" the driver asked. I sighed.

"I'll get out," I said and paid him. I stepped out in my bare feet, my shoes hanging from the fingers of my left hand.

"What happened? You hurt yourself?" Niall asked.

I ignored him and shut the cab door. Then I marched up to the front of the townhouse and fumbled for the key. Niall was behind me.

"Saffron told me what happened. That you saw me with my son," he said with urgency in his voice. "Will you listen to my side?"

"Let me guess, you forgot to tell me?" I asked and at last found the key. I opened the door and let him follow me up to the flat. Once inside, I saw that we were alone and sat on the sofa as if I didn't give a damn. I also put my shoes back on, cringing as I squeezed my feet into them. There was something about a confrontation that required proper footwear. He moved to a spot on the sofa beside me, but I waved him off.

"No one said you could sit down. You won't be staying that long."

He shook his head. "I didn't forget. I didn't tell you I was married on purpose."

"What a surprise," I said sarcastically.

"My marriage is over. My wife, Gloria, she had an affair. Couldn't take the scandal I got messed up in, I guess. The only reason I'm still living with her is my son, Sam."

"You're a martyr! How wonderful for you."

I rose up from the sofa and began to pace across the floor. I liked how my heels sounded on the parquet. Maybe I'd take up tap dancing when this was all over. Niall kept spilling it.

"Sam needs a strong parent. His mum spoils him. He's just got in with that bad lot you saw the other day, wearing that getup. He's joined a rock 'n' roll band!"

I rolled my eyes. "Not that!" I said sarcastically. Niall kept going.

"There's a part of me that felt I deserved the unfaithful, unloving wife. I'd broken the law; why should anyone want to be with me?"

"If you or she were that unhappy, one of you would have left. Remember, I have experience in this area. You could say I'm an expert."

"Dean is a first-class chump," he said and that made me laugh.

"Pot. Kettle. Black," I said harshly.

This stopped him for a moment. "I suppose that's a fair assessment," he continued. "I wanted to tell you, but after we slept together, how could I?"

That got me. "How *could* you? How *couldn't* you? I told you about Dean. You should have told me from the get-go, but once you saw where we were headed, you owed it to me. How dare you make me party to an affair? I'm not Amber Ward. Not every woman willingly sleeps with a married man."

I stood rigidly, my arms folded, my foot tapping on the wood floor like a drummer in a military parade, the pain momentarily forgotten.

"The gist of it is I'm married with a teenaged son but I'm falling for you, Clara," he said and rushed over and tried to kiss me.

What I did next was pure reflex and one-hundred-percent instinct and, well, perhaps a dose of Alicia Steele too. I swung my right hand back and slapped him once across the face, good and hard. I was stunned. He was stunned too and stood rubbing his face. Does it make me a bad person to say it felt good? Then I'm a bad person. I was also sick to death of being played with by men like Niall, Dean and Frederick. To hell with the lot of them.

"If you think I'm going to apologize," I stated firmly.

"I deserved it," he agreed, and that disarmed me a little. "You got to know I'm going to ask for a divorce. Gloria won't be surprised."

I turned away from him, not knowing what to believe. It was another couple's drama, and I had enough of my own to contend with.

"You have to trust me," he pleaded.

"I don't have to do anything!" I said. "Goodbye, Niall. I'll see you in the funny papers, or at least I'll read your byline."

CHAPTER THIRTY-SIX

It was nearly midnight when I heard Trinity come home. She rummaged through the fridge; finding nothing to eat, she poured a Scotch.

"How did it go?" I asked.

"I'm healthy as a horse."

"Did you find anything out?"

"That doctor is a cad. Wouldn't tell me a bloody thing, not even when my report gets filed with the production company. You can tell whose payroll he's on."

"You were gone a long time," I said.

"Had to do wardrobe fittings."

That reminded me. "Say, where was that? Some tailor off The Strand?"

She looked puzzled and shook her head. "No, up near Notting Hill. Why?"

"No reason," I said. The mystery of where Amber went continued. The phone rang, cutting through the air like a foghorn.

"It's bloody late for a phone call," Trinity whined.

"I'll get it," I said and picked up the receiver. It was Saffron and she was in a state. "We'll be right there," I told her.

"Who was it? Where are we going? It's nearly midnight!" Trinity demanded.

"It was Saffron. We're going to the hospital. They found her cousin Larry. Someone beat him nearly to death."

"Oh my God! How awful!" she said and put her coat and hat on. "Who could have done that and why?"

As we ran down the stairs and out the door, I kept thinking I knew who did and why.

The hospital was only two blocks away and we were there quickly. Saffron was in the hallway outside Larry's room when she saw us and came running towards us.

"He's in bad shape," she explained tearfully as we followed her into his room. We slowly approached his bed. Larry lay there, his eyes swollen shut. His whole face was covered in bandages; his swollen and bloody lip protruded from the gauze as if he were pouting. One arm was set in a plaster cast. His body looked battered and lifeless. If I didn't know he'd been beaten, I would have guessed he'd been in a car accident.

"The doctor says he's concussed and three ribs are broken and an arm," Saffron sobbed. "He could be such a rat. But he didn't deserve this."

"There, there," Trinity said soothingly. "Have the police come?"

She nodded and blew her nose. "But he's been sedated so they couldn't do much. If he wakes up, they hope to get a statement."

"He'll wake up," I said, wishing it to be true more than knowing it was true.

"Course in this bloody smog, chances are he didn't even see anyone coming. Couldn't defend himself. The police said there's been a rash of muggings and such since the smog. But I don't know, in his line of work, he angered a lot of people."

"No one would target poor Larry," Trinity said. I kept my mouth shut.

"I'm just so grateful you both came. I didn't know who else to call. He doesn't have many friends, though he mentioned how excited he was working with Clara to get his name in the Hollywood press."

"Would you like a tea?" I offered Saffron, wishing she'd quit saying I worked with Larry. I wanted to forget all about it. "Or want us to walk you home?"

"I'd like tea," she said. "My mum and auntie are on their way, so I'm going to wait for them."

"I'll stay with her," Trinity said.

I made my way down the sparse hallway, which looked identical to *Call the Midwife* and every other BBC period medical drama, where I'd noticed a sign for a commissary. I felt lousy about Larry. It also occurred to me that he might spill our little arrangement to the cops, and then I'd be dragged into the police station for questioning. I didn't think I'd broken any laws, but then again I wasn't up on my British justice system circa 1952. I was deep in thought, churning every possible scenario over and over in my head, when I turned a corner and ran smack into Niall.

"What on earth?" he exclaimed.

"It's you," I said coldly. He was the last person I wanted to speak to. "Now, if you'll excuse me, I have to fetch tea for a friend."

"You're going the wrong way," he said calmly. At that moment I despised his calmness. "It's that way." He pointed down another hall. "Go through those double doors and make the next right. But first tell me, why are you here?"

"I don't owe you an explanation," I hissed.

"That's true. But tell me anyway. Is it your suicidal friend?" he asked. I couldn't tell if he was being sincere or mocking.

"She's in Hollywood," I said.

"Right, yes, you did mention that."

"If you must know, it's Larry Hayward. Someone beat him half to death."

He expression went grave. "Did he tell you who did it?"

"He's out cold," I shook my head. "You told me Frederick was dangerous. Do you think he did this?"

Niall raised an eyebrow. "Do you?"

I started to shake and tremble so much I didn't object when Niall put his arms around me. "Frederick must have thought Larry had the photographs. I never said who had them, but I told him I knew Larry. I may have exaggerated how closely we worked together," I admitted reluctantly. "And I also hinted to Larry that I had something on Frederick. That's probably what happened. They must have put two and two together and got five."

"This is quite the dilemma you've got yourself mixed up in," he said. "And potentially poor Larry."

"It's all my fault," I said, on the verge of tears.

"Let's wait and hear what Larry has to say first," he said soothingly.

I sniffled a bit and he gave me his handkerchief, which I blew into loudly. I gave it back to him, and he took it, hesitating a moment before stuffing the soggy mess into his pocket. I smirked a little.

"What are you doing here?" I asked when I came up for air. "Chasing ambulances?"

"In a manner of speaking. I've been following up on some smog deaths here and interviewing doctors and family members," he said. "Come along, let's get that tea and I'll walk you home."

CHAPTER THIRTY-SEVEN

It was four days into the Great Smog, and only one day before my grandmother's official date of death. Niall had escorted us home from the hospital, and Trinity and I had gone straight to bed. I was surprised at how deeply I'd slept; sheer exhaustion, I suppose. Trinity was already sipping tea and studying her lines when I came into the room.

"Any news about Larry?" I asked.

"It made the papers. Well, it made *Talk*." She showed me the article. It was, of course, sensationalized, and they blamed it on a random act of violence and warned all citizens to be on their guard against such "smog monsters." I had my doubts.

"Oh, I almost forgot. When I bought the paper there was a telegram for you from Hollywood," she said and handed it to me. "Must be your friend."

I tore it open.

Dear Clara,

Once again I must tell you how grateful I am for the opportunity. The audition went well enough, but the casting director told me for certain that the part had already been cast in England. I am, of course, devastated but appreciated the opportunity immensely. I will go back to trying to finish a screenplay of my own. It's probably easier if I write myself a role! Best of luck with the production. Warm regards, Alicia Steele.

I read it over and over. How could this be? Frederick must know by now that Amber was pregnant.

"Your friend after you to finish the script?"

"Something like that," I said.

I went back to my room and stared at the walls. I'd failed my grandmother. Maybe I'd even made matters worse. She said she was devastated. Instead of helping, maybe my interference would push her over the edge.

I will go back to trying to finish a screenplay of my own. It's probably easier if I write myself a role! They were her words and my Plan B. If I finished the script and got Frederick to buy it and produce it, then that would work. Of course, realistically, he couldn't produce it in one day, but he sure could read it and buy it. That is, if there was a finished script. It was still early morning and that gave me some time.

EXT. HIGH TOWER COURT—NIGHT
Clara steps back from the body of the unconscious mistress. She waits for Rod to pick the woman up and drag her to the elevator shaft. Rod picks the woman up and carries her, her head and limbs limp. Clara smiles.

                         CLARA
        Let me pry open the door to the shaft.

Rod stands rigid. He doesn't smile back. Looks down at Clara's husband, also still unconscious.

He kicks the man gently in the ribs. The husband
groans. Rod shakes his head.

                    ROD
    No, sweetheart. I'm not a murderer.
    I'm carrying her up to the house and then
    I'll drag his sorry carcass there too
    if I have to.

Clara's smile turns off like a switch.

                    CLARA
    You son of a bitch. How dare you double-
    cross me?

He walks towards the house.

                    ROD
    Get yourself another chump to do murder. It
    ain't me.

Clara watches him carry the mistress away. Her
husband moans. She looks down at him, hatred in
her eyes, and kicks him the ribs much harder than
Rod had.

INT. FORMOSA CAFÉ—NIGHT
Clara and Edgar the gangster are halfway through
their third cocktails. Clara is resigned. Edgar
is stern.

                    EDGAR
     I can get rid of her, but you are the pay-
     ment. You get it?

Clara sips her drink and nods silently.

                    EDGAR
     Then we understand each other?

Clara forces a smile.

INT. EDGAR'S BEVERLY HILLS MANSION—NIGHT
Clara has finished another drink. Edgar stands
by his bedroom doorway. His tie is undone and he
unbuttons his shirt but says nothing. Clara walks
towards him. She is drunk, but she can still
manage a straight line and a sex-kitten sway. She
pauses in the doorway. They look at each other.
Edgar takes off his shirt and tosses it on the
floor. They don't smile and they don't talk. Clara
goes through the door. A large king-size bed is
visible in the background. Edgar smiles for the
first time, a thin, crooked smile, and follows
her. He shuts the door.

   After I finished the scene, I took a deep breath and exhaled loudly.
I wasn't sure how much I liked fictional Clara sleeping with Edgar. It
made my sleeping with Frederick seem predestined. I cringed at the
thought. But it was the right thing to do for the script, and it might
be the only thing to do for me. It was chilling how much the script

mirrored my own life right down to the last detail. Which brought up the matter of the ending. Alice's notes were clear: *Clara has lost everything . . . she gets into her car and drives into the hills to end things once and for all. She can no longer control what happens in her life, but she can control her death . . .* Yet I couldn't bring myself to write such a scene. Not knowing what I knew, not feeling what I felt, and certainly not wanting to end up in the same place myself. I took a break and sat beside Trinity who was studying her script and barely looked up when I came in.

"I'm nearly finished *The Woman Scorned*," I said. "I just don't know quite how to end it."

"Oh, that. Good for you. That will please your writing partner," she said, though I sensed she was too preoccupied to really listen. "How do you think it should end?"

"Alicia, my co-writer, wants the femme fatale to kill herself by driving off a cliff," I said, trying to sound professional and not like the granddaughter of a dead woman. "But I'm thinking she should just kill her husband's mistress and get away with it. Start a new life or something."

Trinity scrunched up her face as if concentrating so hard pained her. "Femme fatales always die, though, don't they? You shouldn't fiddle with audience expectation."

I hesitated. Her comment irritated me, even though she was only echoing what most every producer would say if they read an altered ending. I wondered what sort of producer Frederick was. "I'll think about it," I said. Though I knew the ending must change. My femme fatale would survive. Exactly how she ended up, punished or recalcitrant or remorseful, remained to be seen. Her fate was in my hands. It was more than just a resolution to a film noir saga. It was the finale to my film noir life.

CHAPTER
THIRTY-EIGHT

I spent the remainder of the day unable to commit to an ending. I wrote several and tore up every last one of them. The story wasn't playing out. But by the late afternoon it wasn't the only thing that plagued me. I had yet to hear from Frederick. His silence disturbed me. Maybe after having Larry roughed up, he'd realized I was bluffing about the photos. He'd already made it clear that sleeping with me wasn't enough motivation to cast Alicia. Yet I sensed something nasty was afoot; the sensation hung over me like the smog.

Trinity had gone to the hospital with Saffron. The inside of the flat was as dreary as outside, so I switched a lamp on and was pouring myself a drink when there was an urgent knocking on the door to the townhouse. Whoever it was wanted their presence known and then some.

I opened the window and called down. A figure stepped out onto the sidewalk but the mist concealed him, then a once-yearned-for voice cut through the fog like a swift stroke from an executioner's sword.

"It's Dean."

He stood on the street below me like a ghoulish Romeo. Through the grey haze, I could make out an outline. He was wearing a long black trench coat that flapped open in the wind as he held tight to the black fedora on his head.

"Clara, please let me in. I need to talk to you."

Something in his voice was off. It was imploring and sombre. I swallowed hard and felt the knot in my stomach twist tighter.

"I'll come down," I said.

Once inside the flat, he removed his hat and flashed me a brief smile that was the type to make teenage girls swoon. I remember when it had the same effect on me.

"Have a seat," I said and made a sweeping gesture towards the sofa. I hung up his coat and hat and took up residence in the pale slipper chair by the window. Despite the window being closed, the draft was palpable.

Dean clutched his shirt collar tightly around his neck. "Don't you find it cold?"

"Not especially," I shrugged and waited. The thing with awkward set-ups like this is that no one wants to be the first to spill. I could make it easy on him and tell him I knew all about the pregnancy, but I could see how nervous he was, upset even, and I can't lie, I enjoyed it. If leaving me didn't make him uncomfortable, then this certainly did. He rubbed his hands together and blew on them like he was starting a campfire.

"Want marshmallows to go with that?" I teased without smiling.

"Funny," he said.

I could sense myself fidgeting, and there was one way to stop it. I finally had a reason to open the pack of cigarettes that were hiding in the train case. I went and got one and lit it.

"Since when do you smoke?" he asked me. He seemed disappointed. I liked that.

"Since you walked out on me," I said bluntly. "Next."

More rubbing of hands. I rolled my eyes. It was too painful to take.

"What do you want, Dean?" I asked and blew smoke above his head. We watched as it circled and swayed between us before dissipating into invisible particles. Kind of like our marriage.

"I didn't know who else to turn to," he stammered.

"What's the matter? You and Amber fighting over baby names?" I said cruelly. By the look on his face, I could tell he didn't think I knew. "Yes, Dean. I know all about it."

I expected a vitriolic attack at worst or an apology for the delayed announcement at best. Instead, he hesitated, though it was obvious he had something important to say. At last he spoke.

"There is no baby," he said.

"What do you mean?" I asked, not expecting him to say that. "Did she miscarry?"

"She had an abortion," he said matter-of-factly.

I didn't know where to look or what to say. I wasn't one to judge, but to give up a baby . . . She must be torn up about it. Then I thought back to yesterday afternoon near The Savoy, my following Amber down that dead-end road. She must have gone to some backroom quack. The poor, fool kid. Maybe if I'd spoken to her . . .

"She got the lead part in Frederick Marshall's movie. She was so excited, but then she found out she was pregnant," he stopped talking and looked at me. I raised an eyebrow like it was attached to a crane and said nothing. He continued. "I tried to tell her that Marshall could schedule the film shoot to accommodate her changing figure. You know the drill. But she said she needed to be free to work on her career. That a baby would be in the way."

He stood up and began to pace. "Turns out she never loved me. She was using me to get her career going. You should have seen her flirting with Frederick Marshall. It sickened me. I only put up with it because, well . . ."

"Because you wanted him to hire you too," I said. I knew him so very well. "You need a drink? We have some bourbon that might pass the test." He nodded. I got up and crossed to the kitchen cupboard and took down two old-fashioned glasses and opened the bottle. My mind started to target Frederick. He must have convinced her to do it. He was a dangerous and powerful man, just like Niall had said. Putting Larry into the hospital and now this. I poured the bourbon out neat and went back into the living room, carrying the bottle under my arm. Dean took the glass from my hand and shot it back.

"Good thing I brought the bottle," I said coolly and poured him another. This time he sipped.

"I'm sorry" was all I could think to say.

"I knew you would be. Despite all the bad things I did. How I hurt you. I knew you'd have sympathy."

"You knew I still loved you, you mean?" I said.

He nodded. "Do you?"

I let the bourbon burn a trench down the inside of my throat.

"Clara, I'm so sorry for what I did to you. You didn't deserve that," he said softly, and he put his arms around me, burying his face in my shoulder, his voice muffled by my hair. "I know the pain I caused. Can you ever forgive me?"

"Yes," I choked a little. He sensed he was squeezing me too hard and he let me go. We stood there eye to eye. Then he kissed me. Gently at first, like a brother kisses a sister, but then it went on too long to be chaste, to be a note of affection between old friends. The kiss quickly became passionate, and I felt the comfortable rhythm of his tongue lashing against mine. It was like a dream. A colourful dream come true set against the background of a black and white nightmare. Then we were apart again and his eyes seemed alive once more. That smile that could make teen girls faint was let loose, only I didn't feel a swooning sensation run up my spine.

"Can I come back home?" he asked, and a boyish grin spread across his face. "I've been wrong. I took you for granted, how much you loved me. No one will ever love me like you do."

My eyes widened. I had fantasized about this moment once, what seemed like a long time ago, and now here it was and it was all wrong. He was still the selfish man I married. It was all about him. I turned away from him and buried my face in my hands, even though no tears came.

"Clara, I'm sorry if what I said repulses you," he said and grabbed my shoulders. "I shouldn't have said it. Not after everything. But you need to know I've changed. I can finally appreciate you."

I couldn't face him. I thought of the typewriter sitting on the desk, waiting for my fingers to touch it, to finish the script and end this torment.

"I don't know what to say," I told him. At least that was true.

"You don't have to answer me now," Dean continued, but another loud rapping on the front door interrupted us.

"Busy night," I remarked. I flew down the staircase to the door and opened it only to find Niall shivering in the doorstep.

"Niall!" I whispered and stepped outside. I balanced on the step so that if Dean happened to look out the window he couldn't see either of us. "What are you doing here?"

"I found out something, about Amber," he said.

I closed my eyes and spoke slowly. "She had an abortion."

"Why am I always the last to know about Amber?" he asked flatly.

"The real question is how do you know?" I asked.

"She called me. Trouble with her boyfriend, apparently, *your* husband. I'm the only other person she knows." He smirked and lit a cigarette. "Discounting Larry, of course. And he's in no condition to offer advice to the lovelorn." He took one drag, then offered it to me. I shook my head.

"You need to go away," I said urgently. "Dean is here."

He looked taken aback. Then he crinkled his eyes so tightly they nearly disappeared. "I guess this makes things pretty neat for you."

"I don't like what you're implying," I said and lifted my chin to the sky in defiance.

"You'll like this," he said and grabbed me tight and kissed me. Despite how furious he made me, I found myself kissing him back. He shoved me away from him with the same vengeance he'd grabbed me with.

"Are you sure you're finished?" I asked sarcastically. It was a dumb thing to say, for he grabbed me and kissed me a second time and tossed me back against the door even more harshly than the first time.

"Now I'm sure," he said with a glint in his eye that deserved another slap to get rid of it. "So let me guess? Dean wants to come home to mother?"

I stamped my foot in indignation. "I'm not his mother."

"You aren't his lover either," he said rudely.

"Don't you have to go back to your wife and son?" I snapped.

"Oh, that's the other thing. Seems she preferred her lover to me. She hightailed it out of our place this morning. Sam's moved in with a bandmate."

I was dumbstruck. He was so cold about it all. He might as well have been discussing his library dues.

"I'm so sorry. I had no idea," I said, softening my tone.

Before he could answer, Dean called down from the top of the stairs.

"Clara?" he said. "I have to get back to the hotel. Amber doesn't know I came here."

Niall smirked at me. "Good work, Clara, you got him lying to the mistress."

"Go stand in the next doorway," I pleaded. "He can't see you."

Niall did as I asked, and when he was safely out of sight, I opened the door.

"It was neighbourhood kids selling papers," I explained. Dean walked down towards me with his coat and hat on. He grasped my chin in his hand and kissed me again. My mouth felt cold against his. I could still taste Niall.

"You don't have to answer me tonight," he repeated. "But I'm going to end things with Amber and move into my own room at The Savoy."

He lifted his head and stroked my face with his right hand.

"Goodnight, Clara."

"Goodnight, Dean."

I watched him slump away into the fog. From behind me came the scraping of Niall's shoes on the damp pavement. He popped his head over my shoulder.

"Goodnight, Dean," he repeated and waved at the fog.

"Oh, shut up," I said and went upstairs. He followed. I didn't stop him, but I didn't want to encourage anything either.

"I'm in no mood for romance," I said sharply. "If you think we're sleeping together again."

"Hush," he cut me off. "I wanted to make sure you were all right."

Before I could answer, there came another loud bang on the door.

"Again? What is this? A flophouse for cheating husbands?"

"That's not funny."

"Says you," I answered. "Stay here. Maybe Dean forgot something."

I went downstairs for the third time that night and without hesitation swung open the door. He stood there grinning like he was giving me a cheque for a million bucks. From where I stood, it felt like someone had tied a noose around my neck and cinched it tight.

"Good evening, Clara. It's time for our getaway. I've been longing to show you my country place."

It was Frederick Marshall.

CHAPTER THIRTY-NINE

Breathing wasn't an option; the wind was knocked out of me and I hadn't even been socked in the gut. Frederick eyeballed me for a moment, then laughed like we were playing a scene from one of his screwball comedies, only I wasn't in on the joke.

"You never mentioned we were going to your country house," I said, immediately fearing the worst. Only a madman would play such a game.

"You look frightened, my dear," he chuckled. "I can't understand why you're surprised. Where else would we go?"

"Tonight's been full of surprises," I said, trying to think fast but coming up empty. "Dean came to see me, for starters." A sound overhead caught my attention, like a window being thrust open. It must have caught Frederick's ear too, for he stepped back and looked up at the building. Thankfully, the fog was too thick for him to see what was probably Niall listening in. Giving up on finding anything amiss, Frederick fixed those small black eyes of his on me. I decided to give staring back a try.

"Why didn't you tell me she was pregnant that day at The Ten Bells?" I asked bluntly.

He shrugged as though he had neglected to inform me that Amber wasn't a real blonde.

"What difference would that have made to you? I told her she had to *fix* her condition or else she'd lose the part. It wasn't difficult to convince her that being such a young mother would ruin her career. Young girls are easy to handle that way."

"So you are to blame. If it had been her choice, that's one thing. But to practically force her. You disgust me," I seethed.

"I wouldn't judge me too harshly. It wasn't much of a discussion. I told you once before, she knows how to play the game."

"I assume by playing the game you mean you're sleeping with her?" I asked, hoping it was true and that he'd lost interest in that part of the deal.

"Don't tell me you're jealous?"

"Don't get your hopes up."

"In any event, I thought you'd be happy about Amber moving on. I wouldn't be surprised if that man came crawling back to you," he paused and gave me the once-over again. "By your manner, I'd say he already has." He smiled. "Not to fear, I will have you back in your husband's arms before you know it. Mind you, you never know, you may prefer me to him."

He stepped down onto the sidewalk and looked up at the house again. I kept my eyes focused on him.

"Why should I come with you?" I said abruptly. He stepped back onto the landing and thrust his gaunt face into mine.

"Why must I constantly remind you?" he asked impatiently. "I always get what I want. Photos. Redheads. Photos of redheads." Then he chuckled again.

I should have told him then and there that the pictures didn't exist and ended the charade. I didn't want to end up like Larry or, worse, Mica. But now was not the time to revert to reliable and predictable Clara Bishop.

"What about the screen test? My friend's part; you didn't keep your side of the bargain."

"Oh, not that again." He spoke like he was bored.

"You have no plans to cast her in the film, do you? You let me think you did, but you lied," I accused him.

"You're taking all the fun out of our weekend," he said, deadpan. "Now go get the damn photographs and get in the car, or else I'll come upstairs and look for them myself. And that won't be anywhere near as fun."

Something was keeping him from barging into the flat and turning it upside down. I couldn't put my finger on what, but it gave me hope that there was still room for negotiation.

"Photographs for a screenplay," I said abruptly.

It got his attention.

"What was that?"

"I will come with you, and I will bring the photographs, but we need a new arrangement," I said as calmly as I could. "I have a script. It's a film noir. I want you to read it and produce it."

"You disappoint me, Clara. After all the pleasure we've had playing our little chess game, you are only after a screen credit. Typical and predictable."

I recoiled at the word "predictable." If only he knew how untrue that was.

"It's a great script. Alicia Steele and I wrote it together. It's called *The Woman Scorned*."

He frowned. "Why does that sound familiar?" Then he raised his chin and studied me.

"Fine. Give me your script." Then he stroked my hair, like he had that night at The Savoy. "I don't know if you're Lucrezia Borgia or Donna Reed. But I'm longing to find out."

"I'm sure there's a compliment in there somewhere," I said dryly.

"Indeed. It's all part and parcel of the seduction."

I pulled my head back so that his fingers were no longer in my hair.

"You should know, the script's not finished," I said.

"You're giving a producer an unfinished script?" He seemed insulted, which made me smile.

"I'm not sure how it should end," I said truthfully but tried to sound wry.

He rolled his eyes. "My car is still running," he whispered. "Go upstairs and get the photos and the script. I won't ask a second time."

"But I haven't packed," I whispered back, thinking of Niall upstairs.

"You don't need anything where you're going," he said ominously. "I've taken care of everything."

"I need my handbag," I said firmly.

"You don't need money."

"But I do need lipstick," I said. This made him laugh again.

"A woman always needs to look glamorous." He smiled. "You have one minute. Don't make me come and get you," he said, the smile gone from his face. I flew up the steps and into Niall's arms. He had been listening by the window and heard everything.

"What have you got yourself into, Clara! You can't go with him," he insisted. "I won't let you. It's madness. It's obvious he's threatening you, and for what? Photographs that don't exist?"

"I don't want to go with Frederick," I admitted. "But I have to. You would never understand why."

"Let's confront the bastard together. Straighten out this whole mess."

I smiled faintly. "It's my mess and only I can straighten it out." There was no way I could tell him about my grandmother—that I would do anything, even sleep with Frederick, to save her.

I checked the clock. I'd been longer than a minute and knew that any second Frederick would be banging on the door. I picked up the script and my handbag. Checked that my lipstick was inside in case Frederick got nosy, and headed to the door. Niall tried to block me.

"You can't go. I'm going downstairs to tell him," he announced and made for the door.

I beat him to it and grabbed the doorknob. "No, Niall. I have to do this my way."

He was much stronger than me, and it took everything I had to stop him from opening the door enough to slip through it. It was a tug-of-war until out of the blue the typewriter keys began to click away. And this time I wasn't the only one who heard it.

"What's that?" he said. Distracted, I turned and released my hold on the doorknob, and the door flew open at him and he was knocked out cold, crashing to the floor in a giant heap. The typewriter went silent.

"I'm so sorry, sweetheart," I said, then bent down to make sure he was still breathing. He was. I kissed his cheek and stepped over him and down the steps to Frederick's waiting car. He smiled at me like we were on a date.

"This fog puts me in a romantic mood. In fact, I'm craving a midnight swim. How about you?"

Police Station—Cirencester

I held my lower lip between my teeth and bit down till it hurt. Sergeant Hooper was staring at me.

"You sure you want to hear the rest? You must be bored," I suggested hopefully. "We've been shut up in here nearly the whole day."

"It's my job, listening to stories."

"So I shouldn't expect to leave any time soon?"

He shook his head. Between the black and white vision, time travel, assault and blackmail, I didn't stand much of a chance. "Frederick Marshall isn't the kind of man I thought he was," he said. "But I haven't heard enough to lock him up. On the other hand, when it comes to you, Miss Bishop, I've got pages."

I smiled. "Call me Clara."

CHAPTER FORTY

He drove the car like it was a sunny summer day on a racetrack and it terrified me. The smog hadn't abated, and each turn and curve proved one step closer to killing someone or being killed.

"Slow down!" I cried. "You can't see where you're going. We could hit someone."

"Don't fret!" he shouted over the engine's roar. "This is fun for me. Relax and enjoy the thrill of being out of control. Wait until we drive by the cliffs!"

"Cliffs!" I yelped. I checked my watch; it was nearly midnight on December 9. One day away from losing my grandmother once again and yet here I was veering closer and closer to a similar catastrophe. I closed my eyes briefly but it only frightened me more.

We left London behind, and the drive through the countryside was a blur of grey and shadow. The car headlights barely cut through the fog.

I sat curled up against the door as far from Frederick as I could get without falling to my death. He didn't speak for the remainder of the drive. He stared ahead with a vacant expression, his fingers clutching the steering wheel tightly so that the bones of his knuckles gleamed white. He had me where he wanted me and there was nothing I could do. As the car tore along the country roads, I thought of my grandmother. She was out there in Los Angeles. A city I remembered in Technicolor reds, yellows, greens and blues. If I succeeded in saving her life, would my own be altered in the future? One thing was clear; I didn't see Dean with me. I finally saw him for his true self. Reliving the last few weeks, past, present and future, he was a heel. A self-absorbed, arrogant heel. And I could do better. In fact, as we careened through tight turns and roundabouts and narrow roads with sky-high hedges, the only man I wanted near me was Niall. I hoped he was okay. I felt bad leaving him lying there. I knew Trinity would find him when she returned. The bodies were piling up all right. I was in over my head. Or I had lost my mind and was totally bonkers. Trinity had been right. I was someone else's creation. I was Alicia Steele's femme fatale Frankenstein. And I knew what lay ahead wasn't going to be a happy ending. What was I thinking writing a film noir from her point of view? A femme fatale is no damsel in distress; she's wicked and despised.

It was getting colder with each mile. I drew a blanket around my shoulders. It was a check pattern. Damn black and white vision! Who knew what colour anything was.

We turned up a very rough road that was framed on either side by giant oak trees with boughs so low they seemed to want to shake hands. I ducked to avoid a beating. Then suddenly there were lights in front of us, and as we drew near, I saw with a start what looked like a castle. It was made up of odd angles and sharp points with small narrow windows, hundreds of them it seemed, and an enormous black door that resembled a giant gaping mouth set to devour its guests. It was the kind of place that Frankenstein, even a femme fatale version, *would* have; it was ghastly and, naturally, it was Frederick's country manor.

The car screeched to a halt on the gravel and Frederick yanked the parking brake up.

"Welcome to my home," he said proudly.

"What do you call it? Xanadu?" I asked tersely. He was a filmmaker; surely he'd seen *Citizen Kane* a few dozen times.

He laughed for real, a good-natured guffaw. This unnerved me even more. He got out of the car, and I waited for him to come around and open my door. For an instant, I considered dashing away into that crazy oak forest we drove through, but I'd seen enough Hammer horror films to know how that might end up. Even out in the middle of nowhere I was as trapped as I would be in a jail cell. I stepped out of the car. My legs felt weak.

Frederick walked up the stone steps. He didn't even look over his shoulder because he knew I'd follow him. As we moved through the mist, a trace of an odour caught my nostrils. It was familiar, though slightly different from what I was used to. The saltiness was distinct, and I knew then that we were by the sea.

"The ocean," I said matter-of-factly.

"The house sits on a cliff. You can see the sea crashing against the rocks below if you follow that path there." He pointed into the darkness. There was no point trying to see a thing in the pea soup we were standing in. "I'll take you there tomorrow. It's beautiful."

"And dangerous," I added. Just what I needed, a cliff.

He frowned. "Yes, I suppose it is if you get too close. That doesn't happen often."

"Often?" I asked nervously.

He ignored me and turned the key in the lock. The giant black door rattled and screeched open as if it hadn't been disturbed in decades. I wanted to suggest he buy some WD-40 but realized it hadn't been invented yet. It seemed to take all his strength to push it.

"Butler's night off?" I asked sarcastically.

"As a matter of fact, it's his weekend off," he answered snidely.

The door fully ajar, I followed him inside. The foyer resembled a mausoleum and was flanked by two towering columns with a grand staircase that wound up to another storey. It really was a castle. The floor and columns were made of rough and uneven stone. It was cold and drafty too. The only light came from a few small table lamps, while a giant chandelier loomed impotently overhead, its bulbs dark and useless.

"That doesn't work?" I asked and pointed to it.

"Of course, give me a moment," he said and disappeared into another room. Within seconds the chandelier twinkled and shone, but its mangled curves and spiky shards of glass gave it a Gothic air that might have been impressive if it wasn't so ominous. I swallowed hard. He returned looking pleased with himself.

"Nice pile of bricks," I lied politely but noticed my feet wouldn't budge. I was crippled with fear.

"I will pour us some champagne," Frederick said, leering at me. My dress was fitted in all the right places. Funny how "all the right places" in certain circumstances can be all the wrong places at the same time. "I'll get it from the cellar. Go into the sitting room and wait for me."

"Can you give me a map?" I said tartly.

He smiled. "You are a wit." I rolled my eyes. "It's down that hall, first door on your left. The butler should have left a lamp on. I will join you in a moment and light a fire."

He vanished down a hall on the opposite side of the house. I shuddered again and, looking down at my frozen feet, willed them to move. They did. I had taken one step on the stone floor when I heard a woman scream.

CHAPTER FORTY-ONE

My head instinctively jerked in the direction of the scream. Not surprisingly, it was the same direction that Frederick had gone. I knew better than to investigate such matters alone, so I remained where I was, aware that my feet had refrozen to the stone beneath them. I waited for more screams. My heart was thundering in my chest as I thought irrationally that perhaps Mica was either still alive like Rochester's lunatic wife in the attic or else she was haunting the joint. Then I heard a loud crash, more of a smash really, and that was enough to get me moving. I was at the door in a flash, but it took all of my strength to pry the giant blockade even a few inches, not enough to squeeze through. I kept clawing at it, and stuck my foot in the crack to force it open. Then without any warning it flew open with such impact that it sent me tumbling to the floor.

"Where do you think you're going?" Frederick stood on the threshold towering over me, a suitcase in his hand, his hat askew and his tie and shirt rumpled like he'd been attacked.

"How many of you are there?" I asked pointedly and rubbed my neck.

Frederick grimaced and offered his hand to help me to my feet. "I'm the one and only. I went through the servants' entrance to get this," he said and, putting his suitcase on the floor, wiped the sweat from his forehead with a handkerchief.

"I heard a scream and I got scared," I explained warily. "You sure your wife's name wasn't Bertha?"

"You're full of one-liners aren't you, Clara? No, I'm afraid I've not locked my dearly departed Mica up in the attic. It was a real woman and she shocked me as much as she did you."

"A maid gone wild?"

He was about to answer when I heard footsteps walk up behind me. They were small, dainty steps, and by the sound they made on the stone, the shoes were definitely heels.

"Not a maid, an actress," said a familiar voice.

My blood went cold as I turned around to see Amber standing not two feet from me. Even in shades of grey she was still the golden girl; her long wavy hair was platinum and fell about her shoulders in loose waves, her skin alabaster and her eyes pale and intoxicating. Her lips were glossed to a shine that twinkled as brilliantly as the crystal fobs hanging from the chandelier. Her dress was only a shade darker than her skin, and its satin fabric picked up the candlelight, illuminating her every curve. She looked otherworldly, some might say angelic, but I knew better.

"Don't be too upset, Clara," she said. Her voice still sounded like a truck-stop waitress smacking a stick of gum. "If I'd known you were having a romantic tryst with Freddie, I would have stayed in London. To be honest, I am surprised. But I guessed as much when I saw you two at The Savoy. Dean wouldn't believe me. Trouble is, you've played the heartbroken wifey so long no one would have thought you were sleeping around."

"I wasn't playing anything," I said. "I'm still his wife. And Frederick and I are just friends."

She snorted derisively and gestured to Frederick, who was standing behind me in silence. "By the look on his face I'd say he has a different view of things. But don't worry. I'm not the jealous type. There is plenty of Frederick to go around."

I looked at Frederick. He glared back.

"Did you know Amber was going to be here?"

"Certainly not," he said. "To enter the cellar I have to cross through the kitchen. When I flipped on the light, she shrieked like a banshee and flew at me like a madwoman."

"How did I know it was you?" Amber whined. "I couldn't figure out the light switch and I was hungry. You scared *me!* That fridge of yours needs some stocking up, I might add."

"You neglected to mention how you got into my home," he said, annoyed.

"The butler did it," she said and then snorted again, this time with laughter, and turned to me like we were co-conspirators. "I've always wanted to say that." She looked back to Frederick and her features softened, and she became the pretty young thing once again. She rushed up to him and rested her head on his chest like a child.

"Dean kicked me out of The Savoy. I had no place to go but here. You weren't at your house. I checked. I knew you spent weekends here and, well, I am your new star," she said through batted lashes.

"What a performance!" I said sarcastically. Amber gave me such a harsh look that her eyes practically spun around in her head. "You don't scare me," I said and stood my ground as she clung to Frederick.

She was about to respond when Frederick cleared his throat and picked up his suitcase. "I've had about all I can take of listening to women's troubles, and certainly enough about Dean Lapointe. Now, we'll just have to make do with the three of us tonight. Tomorrow I will drive Amber to the train station and arrange a room at another hotel. In the meantime, I'll show both of you to your rooms."

That shut us up, and we followed him up the grand staircase. What he couldn't see was Amber and I vying for top spot behind him. My long legs outstepped her shorter ones, but she "accidentally" bumped my elbow to send me off balance and into the railing. In retaliation, I grabbed the skirt of her dress and pulled her back behind me. I was tempted to knock her down with my handbag. We continued this absurd competition until we reached the top. By that time we were perspiring and out of breath.

"Amber, you may stay in the room on the left. And for tonight, Clara, you're to have the second master bedroom at the end of the hall."

"Why does she get the big room?" Amber complained.

"Because I'm a grown-up," I answered.

She glowered at me but kept her trap shut and stormed into her room. I smiled, satisfied.

"You women," Frederick sighed, exhausted. "It's after midnight. Let me show you your room." He swung open the door. Inside was the largest canopy bed I'd ever seen. A huge wooden armoire took up residence across from it, and a mirrored vanity stood on guard by a large picture window.

"There should be a fresh toothbrush and other such things in the bathroom. The butler was supposed to have left it so," he explained. He moved to the bed, where a long pale swath of fabric was lying across the bottom. He lifted it up, and I saw at once that it was a satin gown, and I didn't need to see in colour to know it was gold. He had to be kidding.

"Ah, my man remembered to steam the dress for you too," he said and ran his tongue over his lower lip.

"I'm sure that wasn't necessary," I said. "I'm fine with how I look in this."

He shook his head. "It is a nice dress. But it won't do."

"We going to a black-tie affair or something?" I asked sarcastically.

He smiled as though I was flirting with him. "I want you to put this on."

He came over and draped it over my arm. I nearly dropped the script. Placing the screenplay and my handbag on the bed, I moved to the armoire as if to hang up the gown. There was no way I was wearing it.

The armoire was packed with dresses and furs. I pulled open a drawer full of flowing silk nightdresses and whistled.

"You must abduct lots of female guests who don't have time to pack," I said and felt ill at the thought.

"You weren't abducted," he said dryly and moved to the door. "This was Mica's room and those are all her things."

"How sweet that you've kept them all," I said, trying not to let the terror I felt seep into my voice. When his back was turned, I tossed the gown on the bed like it was dirty socks.

Ignoring me, he opened the door and stood on the threshold. "You have one hour to prepare yourself."

"Prepare myself for what?" I asked, even though I knew.

The creepy smile was back on his face. "When I return, I will have read your screenplay. You will hand me the photographs. Which, I assume, are in your handbag. Unless you've found other, more delightful, places to hide them."

I looked at the square black bag on the bed. He smiled.

"And after those two items of business have been dispensed with, we will enjoy each other to my satisfaction."

CHAPTER FORTY-TWO

The sound of the sea churning and the harsh wind whipping through the trees were enough to keep me on tenterhooks as I sat on the bed trying to figure out what to do, but the creaks and moans of the castle were what kept me on high alert. Each groan or squeak could be Frederick. I'd checked, and the door only locked from the outside. And the descent to the ground from the bedroom window was a fatal one. I was a prisoner.

It was nearly one o'clock in the morning on December 10. Was the date as ill-fated for me as it had been for Alice? The sudden knock on my door wasn't the answer I was hoping for. I watched in terror as the doorknob turned slowly and the heavy door creaked open. I had a fairly clear mental image of Frederick wearing a velvet smoking jacket with matching paisley slippers and carrying two glasses of champagne as a "pick me up." But it was Amber who crept through the narrow slit. The door closed behind her. She was in some sort of frothy nightie with a matching flowing robe that left nothing to the imagination; on her feet were marabou mules. I tried not to picture her in this getup in bed with Dean.

"You get lost?" I asked contemptuously.

She put her fingers to her lips to shush me. "We should whisper," she whispered. "In case Freddie is awake."

"Trust me, he's awake," I said, relieved not to be alone. I would use Amber as my human shield if need be.

She tiptoed in the marabous all the way to the bed and sat down beside me like we were having a sleepover. I scurried to the other side of the bed.

"No one asked you to make yourself comfortable," I hissed.

She rolled her killer pale eyes like it was a bother to do so and sighed. "I'm not your enemy."

"Who said you weren't?" I said and ran my fingers through my red hair.

"I'm sure you're quite satisfied with yourself," she said accusingly.

"About what?" I asked stiffly, not wanting to have this conversation when each second brought me closer to Frederick's naked bulk.

"That Dean ended things with me," she said and sniffled.

"Oh dear, you're not catching cold are you?" I asked with fake warmth in my voice. "You better take care of yourself because you're going to be a big star."

"Look, I know you don't like me," she said.

"Whatever gave you that idea?"

"But Dean wasn't happy in your marriage, and he told me he was already separated when we met," she explained, then paused.

"Go on, you have my attention," I said and began to twist the satin duvet into a tight ball in my fist.

"He lied to me too," she said with a shrug. "Maybe we're both better off without him."

"And what about the baby?" I asked.

"I had no choice," she explained, and I thought for an instant there was regret in her voice. The drapes were open, and I could see the clouds were brewing a rolling mix of charcoal and ebony that moved hastily, signalling an approaching storm. Perhaps it would clear the air. When I looked back at her, she had placed her hand on mine. I snatched it away like she was a leper. Ignoring my reaction, she continued unemotionally.

"It had nothing to do with the film. I'd already had the procedure when Freddie came to the hotel. I just let him think he was forcing me to do it. I figured I'd have something on him this way, you know, in case he tried to fire me from the movie. You know I don't have much acting experience."

"You don't say?" I resisted telling her how close she had come to being fired because of me.

"And I could blame him if Dean found out." She shrugged like it was no big deal. "Which, unfortunately, he did. You win some, you lose some. We can switch back if you like. I'll take Freddie and you can have Dean all to yourself."

I was stunned. I had underestimated her; she had out-femme-fataled me and then some.

"You're awfully young to be so diabolical," I said archly.

"These days a girl can't be too careful," she observed. "Right now I want to focus on my career. My only regret is that Dean found out. The doctor, the man who did it, called the hotel and spoke to him. I guess he figured Dean knew."

This last part was too much for me, and despite not wanting to share my feelings with her, they came pouring out. "Do you know I tried for years to have Dean's baby?" I said, knowing full well she didn't give a damn. "I almost did, you know. But I lost the baby. It very nearly destroyed me. It was all I wanted. And you had it and you threw it away?"

She pursed her lips. "That's sad what you went through. When you want something so badly and it gets taken away and you have no control, it's the worst. But I'm not you."

I breathed in deeply. "I firmly believe it is your right to do what you want with your body. But you let everyone believe you were forced to do it."

"Yes, well, now you know. The real question is are you taking Dean back?"

I bristled. "That's none of your affair."

"Oh, but it is, it's entirely my affair," she said bitterly.

"I don't know what I'm going to do," I said simply. "You can't possibly convince me you're still in love with my husband."

"I'm not going to try. But you should know that if I wanted him back, I'd get him back."

"Of all the nerve! You deserve a good slap across that china complexion of yours."

I remembered how satisfying it was to slap Niall; it would be even more so to smack Amber. Perhaps sensing I wasn't kidding she leapt off the bed just out of reach. I flew across the bed and managed to snag a piece of her filmy housedress.

"Let go of me!" she shrieked.

I was on my feet and about to give her the slap of her life when the door flew open and Frederick stood looking at us with a grin on his face the size of Texas, a tray of canapés in one hand, a bottle of champagne under his arm. We both froze and I let go of Amber. She grabbed her housecoat and bundled herself up inside it.

"My, my, who would have thought two rivals would be such close friends?" he breathed. "Having you both here isn't such a bad idea after all."

"She's hardly my rival," I said bluntly. "And don't get any ideas."

"What she said!" Amber added.

"That's what I do. I'm an ideas man," he said with a chuckle. "Now go to bed, Amber. I have business to discuss with Clara."

I could tell that Amber wasn't having any of it, and for once, I was cheering her on.

"Why does Clara get the midnight snack? I'm starving!"

"I'm sure she'd love a saucer of milk," I said acidly. Amber glared at me.

Frederick sighed. "Very well." He came into the room and placed the tray of canapés on the vanity. Amber practically leapt on top of it.

"Careful, Frederick. Amber can be pretty clumsy with hors d'oeuvres."

She scowled but continued to stuff her face. Frederick looked about the room, and I knew for what. But I had hidden the handbag in the armoire among several others that belonged to Mica. The dress was still on the bed. His fingers grazed it longingly.

"Clara, about that business we discussed," he said, then began walking about, growing more agitated.

"What about it?" I asked, knowing I was safe as long as Amber was near.

"That screenplay of yours. It's quite good," he said.

I fought the urge to smile or clap my hands or in any way show my pleasure. My whole adult life all I wanted was to write a good script and have a producer want it, even one like Frederick. There was so much I could have said had the circumstances been different, but they weren't. I didn't matter right now. What did was being one step closer to saving Alice. So all I said was, "Now it's you that sounds surprised."

"I was. And don't be offended; I'm notoriously picky. But I'm considering producing the screenplay. I've never made a film noir. Who doesn't love a glimpse into the underbelly of society with all its dark and brooding tough guys and desperate, mysterious femme fatales, eh?"

Try living it.

"Have you decided how it will end?" he asked.

"Not yet." Then I got an idea, call it self-preservation, but I decided to appeal to the artist in him. "I would love to hear how you think it should end."

That got him to finally end his search of the room, at least for the moment.

"You could give it the routine ending: Clara gets killed."

I felt a chill rush through me, hearing my name and "killed" in the same sentence.

"But I don't like routine stories," he continued, enthused. "Clara could knock off the mistress."

At this Amber lifted her head from the food. "Huh?"

"Go on, I'm *loving* that idea," I said, even though it was what I'd already wanted to do. "You are a genius, Frederick." He beamed at the flattery, and continued speaking excitedly about the script's potential.

"We can decide later. But if I do produce the film, your friend and co-writer, Alicia Steele, would be first in line to play Clara," he said.

"Who's Alicia Steele?" Amber asked suspiciously. "Why can't I play Clara?"

I was aghast at the thought of Amber in the part. How dare she grasp at every role she heard about? "You don't have the *gravitas*," I said coolly.

She looked at me blankly as she chewed on a piece of cheese. Then after swallowing she said proudly, "I may not have gravy-ass now, but I can buy it if I want it. After my first film, I'll be rich! Tell her, Freddie."

He and I exchanged knowing glances, and we let the subject drop. He cleared his throat. "And it was very clever of Alicia to use scenes from it for her screen test."

It was my turn to be stunned. "She did?"

"Didn't she tell you she was reading from it? Funny, when you told me the title I knew it sounded familiar," he chuckled. "Which reminds me. I brought the film canister with us. It's in the boot of the car."

My whole body was trembling now from excitement, nerves, everything. "I thought the smog grounded all flights?"

"To London, yes," he said. "But I had it rerouted to Paris. It came over on the ferry. You know the saying; the show must go on. I watched it yesterday. She's a looker, you were right about that."

"How much of a looker?" Amber demanded competitively.

"Of course she read the Clara role." He winked at me as we both ignored Amber.

"May I see it?" I pleaded demurely.

"Don't you have something to give me first?" He raised an eyebrow.

"After I see it," I said firmly.

"We will compromise," Frederick answered brusquely. "I read the script. Now you change. Then we watch the film."

"Change into what?" Amber looked thoroughly confused. "What does she have to give you?"

There was no getting around it. So I dutifully picked up the gown and went into the adjoining bathroom to slip it on. I emerged moments later, feeling like an elegant corpse. Frederick looked at me salaciously, like I was a centrefold come to life and about to climb onto his lap, which he probably expected. I walked towards him.

"What's with the getup?" Amber said, clearly feeling left out.

"You're stunning," he breathed, then went to the door. "Come along."

Amber started towards the door but I shoved my arm in front of her. "Not you."

She scowled and looked to Frederick, but he shook his head.

"Stay here Amber, that's a good girl," he said.

As I followed Frederick through a maze of hallways, I regretted not having Amber with me. But seeing the screen test was so personal, and I didn't want to share it with anyone, least of all her. Besides, as long as Frederick thought I had the photos hidden, I was safe. He led me into a giant windowless room with soft red velvet chairs that faced a sky-high back wall. An elegant walnut desk with a green lamp and telephone on it sat behind the row of seats.

"Welcome to my private screening room. I'll go thread the film. Sit down."

I did as I was told, but the anticipation was a severe test of my patience. All of my scheming and persuading had finally paid off in a strip of celluloid. My heart was beating so fast I felt I might faint when I heard a loud click and the screen lit up. I watched the numbers count down from ten to the final sync beep, and then it cut to the clapboard, the very one from the photograph. At long last I could read every word. December 7, 1952. *The Woman Scorned.* The clapper snapped the board shut and there stood Alicia Steele in the green dress, her eyes brazen, and even though it was in black and white, I knew her hair was the same shade of red as mine. She spoke the lines in a voice more husky and assertive than in *He Gave No Answer.* This Alicia Steele was a tough dame. The scene was the one where Rod and Clara meet for a second time. The male actor was off-screen and sounded like a casting director.

                              ROD
          You said it was urgent. Now you've got me
          here, what's on your mind?

                             CLARA
          Did I say urgent? I suppose I did. I need
          your help.

ROD

You don't look like the kind of dame that
needs my help.

CLARA

What kind of dame do I look like? Or don't
I want to know?

Her delivery was pitch perfect, vulnerability, sensuality and a heart of steel all at once. Then a second scene came on screen, the one on High Tower Court, when she first tells Rod she wants to murder someone.

CLARA

I've invested my whole life with him. He's
filthy rich and I deserve a piece of it.

ROD

Isn't that what divorce is for? Alimony.

She laughs.

CLARA

I was a foolish girl in love when I married
him. I'm no longer foolish or in love.

I sat motionless, dazed by seeing my grandmother moving and speaking. The best part came in the few seconds after the casting director called cut and Alicia stood and smiled. She wasn't acting then; she was being herself. The woman I'd never met was suddenly alive in front of me. What I noticed was how authentic the smile was too. It wasn't the smile of a woman on the verge of driving off a cliff. She looked like she had a million reasons to live. Tears streamed down my face as the short film ended, turning the screen into a blazing light of emptiness before the room went black. Then it was all over. Frederick returned and switched on a light.

"What did you think?" he asked me.

I couldn't look at him. I stared at the screen and wept.

"I guess you thought she was pretty good, judging from your reaction. I happen to agree. She's got talent. I'll send the casting director a telegram this morning telling him I want to option the script and that she should play the lead."

I tried to speak, but my throat was so dry nothing came out. I swallowed and tried again. "Are you sure your telegram will reach her in time?"

"In time for what?" he asked.

I shook my head. "I only meant, are you sure she'll get it today?"

"I'm sure he'll tell her."

"Can we call him now? Make sure?"

He rolled his eyes. "What are you so obsessed about? Is she paying you or something?"

I wasn't sure how to answer at first, and then I said simply, "I owe her."

Frederick reluctantly dialled long distance to LA as I stood over him.

"I'll leave a message." When he was done, I felt a giant wave of relief sweep over me, and I wanted nothing more than to go to sleep. It had to work. It had to be enough to stop her from doing something rash. But my sense of solace was short-lived because Frederick knew he'd done his part, and he wanted payback.

"Now, what about those photographs," Frederick said and backed me against the wall. He stroked the satin straps of the gown, his fingers brushing my skin underneath. It was time to come clean; he'd done everything I asked. "Let's go back to the bedroom and play hide and seek some more."

"I have a confession," I blurted.

He was agitated. "Which is?"

"The truth is I made them up. There aren't any photographs."

He scrutinized me. "I don't believe you."

"You've got to. It's the truth. I was desperate you see. I needed you to help my friend and you did and I'm grateful," I said in a rush.

"I want the pictures, Clara," he persisted, his breathing growing rapid.

I started to panic, thinking of what happened to Larry and what might happen to me. "I made it up," I told him. "I read about Mica's death and you told me once how people still suspected you and so I made it up." I stood there, turning my face away from his as he leaned over me, his breath hot on my cheek, when it occurred to me that if he was so sure there were photos, and he was so frantic to get his hands on them, then maybe he wasn't so innocent after all. And I wasn't the only one to come to that conclusion.

"Oh God. Are you saying he did kill her?" It was Amber. She had crept into the screening room and heard everything. Frederick's temper was nearing its peak.

"You stupid cow, I told you to stay put!" he yelled. Amber shrank from his voice.

"He didn't kill anyone, Amber," I said, more to convince myself than anyone. "I needed him to think there was evidence so he'd do what I asked, and he did and everything's fine."

"It's not fine!" Frederick pounded his fist into the wall by my head. I leapt away and stood by Amber.

"Don't be so sore, Freddie. Listen to Clara, there are no photos. And besides, if you did kill your wife, we won't tell. Will we?" She looked to me. I shook my head. It was the wrong thing to say.

"I didn't kill anyone!" he shouted. "Come with me. Both of you." He shoved us in front of him and pushed us along through the maze of hallways until we were beneath the giant chandelier in the foyer. There was a loud crack of thunder and Amber screamed.

CHAPTER FORTY-THREE

Frederick continued to shove us up the stairs to the bedroom, where he expected the photographs to be. I tried to think fast. How could I explain why the handbag, when he eventually found it, was empty? No matter how things turned out, I'd never seen a man angrier than he was right then. A fact not lost on Amber.

Amber gasped. "See what you did?"

"Me?" I answered. "I was doing fine until you came into the room."

Frederick reached the top of the stairs and pounded his fists into the air. "Shut up! You two are driving me mad! I should force you to have an old-fashioned duel. You can finish each other off. Catty remarks at twenty paces."

"No thanks," Amber snapped defiantly.

"For once I agree with her," I said.

He grabbed each of us by an arm and pulled us into Mica's room. Then he began tearing the place apart, starting with the bed. Amber and I huddled in a corner, and I gestured to the door. We shuffled closer but weren't fast enough for Frederick, who slammed it shut. "Go stand by the window."

Silently, we did as we were told. With one swipe he cleared the vanity of Mica's perfume bottles and jars, the glass shattering on the stone floor. His chest was heaving now, and then he stared at the armoire as though he'd only just noticed it. "There are only so many places to hide things in here," he said and practically ripped its door off. In seconds he had every handbag on the floor and was opening them one by one, shaking out the contents of each. Mica's bags had little in them, a lipstick here, a compact there. At last he found mine. He smiled. He knew it was the right one. I braced myself against the stone wall. He opened it and his eyes widened, puzzlement followed by rage. "They aren't here."

"I told you. They don't exist," I pleaded.

"Did you remove the photos and hide them somewhere else in the castle?" he asked.

I shook my head repeatedly. He crossed the room towards me.

"Tell him where they are," Amber said in a panicked voice.

"I can't! I made them up!" I insisted. But it was no use. Frederick was practically on top of me. At that moment, the thunder returned with a vengeance and lightning struck, lighting up the sky. He glanced out the window and my gaze followed his. Below the window was the swimming pool. I caught my breath.

"I have another idea," he said. "I think we all could use a relaxing swim."

"A swim?" Amber said, missing his sarcasm entirely. "It's the middle of the night."

He ignored her, instead choosing to clasp my chin in his hand and squeeze, just hard enough to twist my lips into a pucker. "You're a reporter, Clara. I'm sure you'd love a tour of the crime scene. Just like the swarm of reporters loved seeing William Holden's corpse in *Sunset Boulevard*," he said menacingly. "I can show you exactly where Mica's body was found, floating face down in her gold dress. What a coincidence; her dress was exactly like the one you're wearing now."

I swallowed, but with the hold on my face I couldn't talk. He wasn't done spewing either. "Tell me, are you a fan of *Sunset Boulevard?*"

He forced my head to move up and down in the affirmative. "Yes? Me too. As a producer, there is always at least one point in the filmmaking process where you want to kill the writer." Then he released me.

"Now get moving, please." Then he turned to Amber. "You too, sweetheart."

"Why me? I'm not a writer."

"But you're a witness," he pointed out cruelly.

Grabbing each of us by the arm, he manhandled us out the door and dragged us down the stairs. He ushered us through the castle to a side door at the end of a narrow passageway. Just as he was to open it, there came another crack of thunder and shot of lightning and every light twitched then snuffed out, leaving the entire castle shrouded in darkness.

"The electricity is gone," Amber said unnecessarily.

"You don't say?" he answered acidly. Shoving us in front of him so we were cornered, he grabbed a garden torch that was leaning against the wall and lit it with a wooden match.

"You're kidding, right?" I said.

"We'll need light in order to see the pool in all its infamy," he answered caustically.

He yanked at the door until it creaked open. I could barely make out the stone path that bent and twisted through an English garden that might be beautiful come spring. My heels were unsteady on the stone, and I picked my way along, feeling him close on my heels, able to snatch at me if I was to try to run away. At one point, Amber clasped my hand, and I didn't have it in me to shake her off.

I felt my dress snag on an enormous hedge as we turned a corner. Suddenly, there before us was the glassy pool, the wind blowing across in fine ripples. We stood near the edge, staring into the water. It wasn't difficult to envision the body of his wife floating on such a polished surface.

"So now what?" I demanded, the nervous edge audible in my voice.

"You disappoint me, Clara. Don't you have any of your reporter questions to ask? Such as when did I last see Mica alive? Why didn't I hear her scream? I assure you, I've heard them all before. I'm sick to death of them."

I shook my head violently. "No, I believe it was an accident."

"Now that I have your attention," Frederick said, seething, "where are the photos?"

I saw movement beside me and turned to see that Amber had ventured far too close to the edge. Frederick followed my gaze and I saw him twitch. He started towards her. She panicked and her heel slipped on the wet tile. I leapt to her side and managed to grab the torch and knock it towards his face. It must have struck him because he shrieked and fell backwards, landing hard on the ground.

"You could have killed me! You're a madwoman!"

"Could have killed you? You were going to kill us!" I shrieked back.

"Don't be absurd! I was only trying to scare you!"

"Well, it worked," I said angrily.

Amber was useless, lying on the ground, watching.

"You're not going to tell me where the photos are, are you? What more do you want? Money? I said I'd produce the film," he blabbered.

He pulled himself to his feet and clambered back up the path to the house without another word. Amber and I remained where we were, too frightened and too confused to know what to do.

"You did it!" she said. "You fought him off!"

"Hardly," I said. "He didn't put up much of a fight. And you did nothing."

Amber got up and cleaned herself off and nodded towards the path. "I'll go see if he's hurt. I can't have him being mad at me, can I?"

"Just like that? You're suddenly not afraid?" I asked and followed her. "Don't be so sure he'll forgive you."

"It wasn't me who smacked him with a torch. I'll blame you."

"Why doesn't that surprise me," I said.

We moved silently along the pathway. The enormous door was ajar, and we slipped through it and down the dark hallway until we were within a few feet of the foyer. I stopped in my tracks and grabbed Amber.

"What is it?" she asked, irritated.

"Voices. He's not alone," I whispered.

We listened but couldn't hear what they were saying.

I stepped closer to try to see who was there and had popped my head into the foyer just as the lights came on. Amber squealed. The giant chandelier was lit up and beneath it stood Frederick, pale and puffing, with Niall, Trinity, Saffron and Dean, of all people.

CHAPTER FORTY-FOUR

Hearing Amber's cry, they turned in our direction and we stepped out into the light. But it was obvious that Niall and Frederick were arguing.

"How dare you set foot in my home again," Frederick charged.

"Believe me, it's not by choice, but you took something of mine," Niall fought back.

"What something of yours did I take?" Frederick sneered, irritated beyond belief.

That's when Niall finally looked at me. He pointed, his eyes taking in the gold dress, and grinned in that lopsided way of his. "Clara Bishop."

My first instinct was to run into Niall's arms, but then I thought about how long it took him to get here. "You took your sweet time!" I said to him. "I thought you were too hurt, or too angry, to rescue me."

"I have a bump on my head, but that wouldn't stop a guy like me from rescuing a damsel like you."

Before I could respond, Amber put on a big show rushing to Frederick's side. "You poor dear. I'm sure I haven't the faintest idea what got into Clara. But you have to know it was all her. I never thought you were going to murder us."

Frederick's eyes narrowed, and I recognized his default angry expression. He looked at me. I stared back.

"I was trying not to have you fall into the pool," Frederick muttered.

"And you would have saved me too, if it weren't for her."

Then she looked at Dean. Her face became soft and sulky as she moved from Frederick into his arms. He embraced her reluctantly while avoiding eye contact with me. Niall rolled his eyes. Trinity and Saffron each hugged me.

"There, there, love, it's okay. It's all a misunderstanding," Trinity said.

"How did you find me?"

"I came to the flat to tell you about Larry," Saffron explained. "But when Trinity and I got there Niall was lying on the floor, out cold. He bashed his head right proper, slipping in the entryway like he did." I swallowed and peered at Niall. He raised an eyebrow. "I threw a pitcher of water on him like you see in films and he came to."

"He told us that you'd driven off with Frederick," Trinity continued. "Of course, with the smog, we didn't know what to do."

"Then your husband turned up," Niall said. "Looking for you."

"I told Amber it was over," Dean said sheepishly. "I thought you'd be happy."

"How did you all get here?"

"Billy," Niall said, as though that explained everything.

"Who is Billy?"

"You know him well enough," Niall said, and just then in walked the cabbie who always appeared when I needed him.

"You?"

"Yes, miss. I'm an old acquaintance of Niall's. He paid me to keep an eye on you. Said you might get into trouble."

I looked at Niall. He shrugged. "I didn't realize how *much* trouble. I've said it before, you're quite the girl."

I felt myself blush. But it all seemed too easy. I turned to Saffron. "You should know that Frederick is to blame for Larry's beating."

Frederick piped up. "That's nonsense!"

"You practically confessed," I said, but Saffron cut me off.

"It wasn't him," Saffron explained. "Larry came to yesterday, and he'll be okay. Turns out he owed some gambling debts to the wrong people and they roughed him up."

I couldn't believe what I was hearing, yet in some twisted way, it all made sense. Except for Frederick. I turned to him.

"But you threatened me if I didn't give you those photographs," I said and stepped towards him. "You made me think you were going to turn me into William Holden in *Sunset Boulevard!*" I accused him.

"You bloody well blackmailed me," he retorted.

Good point.

"But if you weren't guilty of the death of your wife, why would you care about any photos?" I asked.

Frederick cleared his throat and almost seemed embarrassed; it wasn't a look I'd seen on him before. "There might have been photographs, but not of my wife. You see, on occasion, I invite ladies here to have a bit of fun, like I invited you. I dress them up in gold gowns and red wigs, we drink a bit of champagne and sometimes these parties get a bit wild. More than one reporter came here on several nights to follow up on Mica's death. Like that Larry. And Mr. Adamson, for another. He came here numerous times. I can think of at least one incident where I caught him spying through a window when I was in bed with at least three redheads."

I looked at Niall. He wouldn't meet my eyes, just stared at the ground sheepishly.

"For all I knew, there were pictures," Frederick continued. "You had me convinced. After the murder investigation, it took ages to get my reputation back on track. The last thing I need is a sex scandal."

"So you dress women up like your wife?"

"Not exactly. Despite what I told you, it isn't Mica's dress. She hated them. I always forced her to dye her hair and wear gold gowns. It's my taste," he shrugged. He must have realized how it made him sound by the stunned looks on all our faces. "I may be a pervert but I'm not a killer. Mica was an alcoholic. She was drunk and we'd had a huge fight. But I went to bed because I was fed up. She fell in the pool when she was alone. Her blood alcohol level was so high, the coroner said, that she probably passed out before she hit the water." For the first time Frederick looked genuinely sad, and I felt sorry for him.

Niall cleared his throat. "But I never wrote a story about those parties because at the time I wasn't interested in famous people's private lives. Still not."

I didn't know what to do or say next. I was done trying to write this plot in my head to a satisfying ending. The only thing that mattered was Alice. The rest was just madness.

That's when Niall spun me around into his arms and kissed me. When he let me go, he wore his stupid lopsided grin. This time it matched the lopsided angle of his fedora. But the grin didn't last, because Dean came at him, and in one swift move slapped Niall across the face so hard it knocked his hat off.

"How dare you kiss my wife?" Dean growled. I rushed to Niall but he gently pushed me aside and faced Dean.

"Did you really just slap me?" Niall asked, stunned.

"You bet I did!" Dean shouted. "You're not man enough to take a punch!"

"Is that so?" Niall said, seething.

I shoved them apart, each an arm's length from me. "Listen, boys, I'm flattered but you got to stop," I told them. "You know what they say, Niall, 'See to it you can take a slap as easy as a kiss,'" I said, repeating my grandmother's dialogue from *He Gave No Answer.*

"Then let's see if he *can* take it," Niall said, and then without warning raised his hand to slap Dean. Only Dean ducked and Niall slapped me. My head snapped to the left and back like a rubber band. The entire side of my face burned. I shut my eyes from the pain and the shock.

"Are you all right, Clara?" I heard Saffron ask. My head felt funny. I was dizzy and warm and wanted to lie down.

"My God, Clara! I'm so sorry," I heard Niall say.

"You bully," Dean said to Niall.

"You coward," Niall said to Dean.

"Stop it!" I heard Trinity say to both of them.

"I'm all right. Men always slap women in film noir," I said, with my hand to my face.

"Only when they need to snap out of it," I heard Frederick mutter snidely. He didn't say precisely what "it" was, and I didn't feel much like asking. Slowly, I opened my eyes. The room seemed brighter, although my vision was blurry. I blinked several times and opened my eyes wide until at last the foyer, the chandelier and everyone came into focus. But that was the least of it: every inch of the place was in colour, and everyone was dressed head to toe in twenty-first-century clothing. I was back.

"I didn't mean to hit you," Niall repeated.

"Don't worry about it," I said to him. I was dazed, but that didn't stop me from grinning ear to ear. I looked at Frederick. "I guess you were right. I needed to snap out of it. Just like in the movies."

Dean shoved Niall out of the way to stand beside me.

"As long as you're not hurt," he said softly.

"I'm not the one who hurt her," Niall spoke up and straightened his shoulders.

"Well, I think we've all had enough bloody fun for one day," Trinity said sensibly. "It's a little late to be heading back to town in that storm. Your little castle seems to have plenty of room, if you ask me."

Frederick slowly got up. "I keep all the bedrooms suited up in case of surprise visitors. There are three others left, one each for Trinity and Saffron, but the men have to share the third, but don't worry, it's equipped with twin beds."

"I'll stay with my wife," Dean piped up firmly and put his arm around me. Silence. Although if facial expressions have a language of their own, Niall's and Amber's were speaking volumes. Even Trinity's and Saffron's eyes were bulging.

"Of course you may stay with your wife," Frederick said, glad to be done with me.

Dean smiled and rubbed my shoulder. I had gotten what I wanted; Dean had come back to me. All I had to do was walk up the grand staircase of this ancient castle with my husband at my side and close our bedroom door and life would be exactly as it was before. But all the strange things that had happened, the clothing, the black and white, moving through decades, all of it, had changed everything. I no longer wanted life to be like it was before. Dean still didn't love me the way I wanted him to. He had cheated on me. And the other cold, hard fact was I didn't love him anymore, not like I thought I did. I also wasn't as forgiving as he seemed to think I would be. Then I looked at Niall. He was a heap of trouble in his own right. Then again, I'd become the kind of girl who got into trouble plenty, and I'd shown myself I could take a slap or a kiss and not bat an eye. I guess I was tougher than I thought. And I wanted to be tough now when the situation called for it.

"Don't I get a say in all this?" I asked.

Dean removed his arm as though I were covered in spiders. "Sure, Clara," he said and chuckled nervously. "You saying we should head back to London now?"

"I'm not saying that at all," I said firmly. "I'm saying I don't want you in my room."

Silence again. Then Dean whispered in the vain hope the others wouldn't hear, but in such a cavernous tomb that was impossible. "Can we discuss this later? I'll sleep on the floor if you prefer. Just let me come back."

I saw Amber flinch. And while it pained me to not march Dean upstairs and play the triumphant wife in front of the disgraced mistress, I couldn't do it. I didn't want him.

"You've had plenty of time to discuss our marriage and you haven't bothered to text, call, email, nothing. And when I've tried to see you, you let that girl humiliate me. I'm done with the both of you."

I didn't need to look at Niall to know he was smiling. Trinity and Saffron actually applauded. Amber took the opportunity to run up to Dean and fasten her skinny arms around his waist. But Amber wasn't smart enough to know when to quit.

"Forget her, Dean! She's like you said, cold and bitter," she hissed. I looked at Dean; the bastard wouldn't meet my eyes now.

"You said that?" I asked, my mouth quivering. I may not love him anymore but the words still stung.

"I was wrong," he said desperately and tried to shake Amber off. She wouldn't be diverted.

"Why don't you tell him the truth, Amber? That you weren't heartbroken when he left you? That the first thing you did was hightail it out here and into Frederick's bed. At least you tried to," I said. Both men looked aghast.

"That's not true!" she cried. "How dare you make things up?"

I laughed. "You really are a lousy actress."

"Oh yeah. Well, you are a crap writer, and that friend of yours? Alicia what's-her-name? She's a crap actress. I saw the screen test. She's nothing, like you're nothing."

That was too far and everyone but Amber knew it.

"Amber!" Dean snapped, looking at her with horror. "Apologize immediately."

"Don't bother," I said and walked up to her. She was still wearing the high heels, and there we stood, not quite eye to eye, the blonde in her skimpy nightie and the redhead in a gold satin gown. Even Louis B. Mayer couldn't have dreamed up a better scene, and I knew what I would have written had I been the screenwriter.

```
INT. CASTLE FOYER—NIGHT
AMBER, the blonde bombshell, stands and faces
Clara with utter defiance. The two women are so
close they can smell last night's champagne on
each other's breath and each other's Chanel No. 5.


                    AMBER
        You think you're so tough because you dyed
        your hair red and swan around in vintage
        clothes like you're Rita Hayworth. But
        you're not. You're nothing but a mousy,
        washed-up, thirty-something woman who can't
        hold on to her husband. Even if he wants to
        come back, he won't stay, Clara. Women like
        you can't keep a man.


Clara nods as though in agreement. Amber smiles
triumphantly.


                    CLARA
        I have one thing to say to you. There is
        plenty of ice in the freezer.
```

Amber's sly smile disappears into a puzzled frown.

                          AMBER
          What are you talking about? I don't need
          ice . . .

                          CLARA
                    (slight smile)
          Yes, you do.

And with that Clara slaps Amber hard across the
puss.

Only I didn't write it, I did it. Amber yelped in pain and covered
her cheek with her hand. She wanted to cry but was either too proud
or too shocked to let the tears flow, but her eyes were plenty glassy.
I surveyed the faces of the rest of them in case anyone else needed
straightening out. The women were covering their mouths to hide
their laughter. The men stood their ground but said nothing. Amber,
on the other hand, got madder and madder like a two-year-old in a
tantrum, her face equally red, but then again the colour was probably
from the smack I gave her.

"I'm going to sue you, Clara Bishop," she yelled. "I'll charge you
with assault! You and Dean will have to pay me hundreds of thousands of dollars, maybe even millions!"

"Me? Why would I pay?" Dean asked stupidly.

"Because she's your wife and you brought me into this mess,"
Amber snapped. "There may be permanent damage to my face and
that's my livelihood."

"I thought waiting tables was your livelihood?" Trinity asked ever
so politely.

"I'm an actress! I'm the star of the film, remember?" she continued undeterred. "I'm going to sue you big time!"

"I didn't touch you," I said calmly. That stopped her in her tracks. Her eyes grew wide and she practically choked.

"You slapped me."

"I didn't lay a hand on you."

"Don't try denying it, Clara. I have a room full of witnesses," she stated and grinned like she had me.

"I didn't see anything," Trinity said.

"Not a bloody thing," Billy the cabbie tossed in.

Saffron shook her head.

"Me neither," Niall said and moved to my side.

"Huh! I'd expect as much from you lot," she went on. "But Dean and Freddie saw too."

"You're not in America anymore. The English don't sue over every slight to our character," Frederick said smoothly. "And besides, I didn't see Clara touch you."

"But, Freddie, I'm your star." She spoke with genuine panic in her voice. "You said so, you discovered me yourself."

He looked embarrassed. "I may have over-exaggerated that. You're a beautiful blonde with an ugly personality. And after everything I've heard and seen tonight, I have one word for you: recast."

"You wouldn't dare!"

"I may like redheads in gold gowns, but I don't appreciate being played, and you played me for a fool," he said flatly. "And to top it off, I don't admire cruelty, and you, my dear, are a first-class bitch."

Her whole face was red; indeed, so was her décolletage. That left her one man standing. My husband.

"Dean?" she pleaded.

He shook his head. "Clara didn't slap you, Amber. You must have fallen asleep in the sun and got a slight burn. It will be gone by morning."

"Sunburn! This is fucking England! That does it. I'm leaving now, even if I have to walk back to London." She stormed upstairs.

"I will call her a cab," Frederick said. "There's a lovely inn in the town, not more than a few miles away. It will do for the night."

"Don't bother, mate," Billy piped up. "I'll take her." He nodded to us all and walked out the door.

"I think it's high time we turned in for the night," I said, exhausted yet oddly satisfied.

Trinity came with me and we walked down the hallway, past Amber's door, where we could hear the muffled sounds of her packing, cursing and otherwise harrumphing about.

"You did good," she said to me when we reached my door.

"Remember what you said about my being Alicia Steele's femme fatale Frankenstein?"

"Yes, sorry about that."

"Don't be. It was true," I said. "And I want to hang on to a bit of her."

"Don't kid yourself," she said, touching my arm. "Every one of us gets trampled by life at one point or another. Sometimes more than once. You're just as tough and just as beautiful as any screen heroine, you just never realized it."

"Maybe anti-heroine is more like it?" I said and smiled. "But as much as I tried to be her, the real me shone through loud and clear."

"How do you mean?"

I thought of Larry's injuries, the door clunking Niall, Frederick's ludicrous behaviour by the pool, the accidental slap and every other misplaced and misunderstood moment from the past week and said, "I'm just a screwball comedy in film noir clothing."

She grinned and hugged me before heading to her room. I went inside and leaned against the door to shut it, only it wouldn't budge, so I put my whole weight against it when I saw a hand creeping in. I screamed. It was Niall.

"My God, why didn't you knock?" I said. "You shouldn't creep around in a place like this. It's scary enough."

"Sorry, Clara," he said. "I did knock. Damn door is so thick you obviously didn't hear me."

"Well, what do you want?" I asked, feeling very exposed in the thin satin dress so close to that giant four-poster bed. Why did he have to look so irresistible?

"I came to apologize. I shouldn't have kissed you. Especially not in front of a crowd. I was quite out of line. I'm sorry."

I flicked my hair over my shoulder and back again. "I accept," I said and felt myself step closer to him despite my best instincts. "Only next time do it in private." And I brought my lips to his.

CHAPTER FORTY-FIVE

When I woke up, it was mid-morning on December 10. Niall was still sound asleep as I tiptoed to where his jacket was folded over the back of a chair. As I searched his pockets for his smart phone, I felt nothing but trepidation. I needed to know one thing. One vital thing. I found the phone and went to the browser and typed in my grandmother's name. There it was—an IMDb entry for *He Gave No Answer*, which gave her date of birth and date of death.

"Everything okay?" Niall asked, his eyes half closed.

"Sorry I woke you," I said. "I needed to check a date."

"Did you find it?"

I nodded and turned away. I had my answer. Alicia Steele, Alice, my grandmother, had died on this day in 1952. I hadn't changed a thing. The tears were about to tumble down my cheek and it wasn't something I wanted to share; tears required explanation, and I needed to reflect on the information in private, at least for now. Niall lit a cigarette and shoved his grandfather's case back into the pocket of his trench coat. He took a puff, then held it out for me. I frowned at it.

"Why not?" I said and shrugged. I put the cigarette to my lips and inhaled deeply, only to have the smoke retaliate and come back out of my mouth in a fit of coughing. Niall rushed into the washroom for a glass of water, and I threw the offending cigarette out the window. Smoking like Lauren Bacall was truly a thing of the past.

"I think I just quit," I managed to say.

"I think it quit you," he teased.

Then we heard a high-pitched noise off in the distance.

"What's that sound?"

Niall opened the window. He looked concerned. The sound grew louder and louder, and there was no mistaking its source. "Police siren," I said. "More than one."

We stood and watched as two police cars tore up the drive to the front of the castle.

"Better get dressed," he said.

But they were too fast. We heard a kafuffle downstairs, followed by loud steps beating a pathway to our door.

"Police."

I had no choice but to slip into that gold gown once again. When I opened the door, two uniformed officers looking none too happy were there to greet me.

"Clara Bishop?"

I nodded.

"You're under arrest for assault."

Niall gave me his trench coat for warmth, and they led me down the staircase and out the front door. As I was being stuffed into the back of the police car, I saw Frederick wailing at another officer as he too was being forced into a car.

"I can't believe this is happening again! Don't you people have anything better to do?"

Everyone else, Saffron, Dean, Trinity and Niall, were asked to come in for questioning. No doubt as witnesses. I sighed. Amber wasn't going away quietly.

Police Station—Cirencester

"And that, Sergeant Hooper, is that." I took a sip of water and waited.

Hooper stared at me.

"I told you it would be tough to believe. But everything I said was the truth." I couldn't blame him if he didn't buy my story.

He scowled. "So you admit to slapping Miss Ward across the face, then?"

"I do," I said. "But she deserved it."

He shifted around on his chair. He had amassed quite a pile of yellow foolscap pages, and he shuffled them like a deck of cards.

"How do you account for all this? It's bloody impossible," he said.

I nodded. "I agree. Impossible. So what are you going to do?" I asked. "That sure is a lot of paperwork."

He clasped the lot of it in his hands.

"And it's been a long interview," I added.

He took up the pile of papers and in one swift motion ripped them in half. I flinched at the sound. He then scrunched the two halves up and tossed them in the wastebasket. Then he pulled up a new piece of paper and scribbled furiously.

"Sign this," he instructed me and showed me a single paragraph that stated I had slipped and fallen into Amber, accidentally striking her across the face. Given my history of such clumsy mishaps, it was really quite reasonable, far more so than the truth. "None of your friends will corroborate Miss Ward's side of things. You and Frederick Marshall seem to be victims of her bitter temper."

"Yes, that's true," I said, shocked by the sudden turn of events.

"You're free to go, Clara." Hooper stood up and opened the door. I followed him, pausing at the doorway.

"Thank you," I said and kissed him on his cheek. He blushed.

"You're very welcome," he said and smiled. "I would hate to see you

taken in by the likes of her. You got to be careful of her type. You know
what they say, 'Hell hath no fury like a woman scorned.'"

"That's right," I agreed and walked out the door.

Niall was waiting outside the police station for me. I still had his trench coat over my shoulders as we walked towards Billy and his cab. It was dark, and there was thick fog again.

"I'm sick to death of this fog and mist all the time. I can't wait to be back in sunny California," I said with a sigh.

"You plan on leaving soon?" he asked. I detected the disappointment in his voice.

"I have to go home sometime," I said.

We were silent for a bit, and then Niall grinned and said, "You're not going to tell me that this is the beginning of a beautiful friendship, are you? I know how you love those film noirs."

I smiled and shook my head. "No, Niall. For one thing, I like you more than as a friend. And for another, *Casablanca* isn't a film noir."

He stopped and chewed on this as I raced to the cab. Billy held the door open and I jumped in. Then Niall climbed in beside me and we kissed.

CHAPTER FORTY-SIX

I grinned all the way through the streets of London, taking in all its colours from the back of the taxi. A city never looked so vibrant. The sun had at last made an appearance, so that every shop window, bus stop and park bench, even the sidewalks, appeared to twinkle. Trinity's flat was bright and airy like it had been when I first arrived. My tiny room looked happy and full of light. The closet was as I'd left it, overflowing, and the typewriter sat looking forlorn on the tiny desk, the same blank sheet of paper drawing me in. Part of me was afraid to go near it. As much as I admired the land of film noir, I was in no hurry to make it a permanent relationship. I wasn't sure where the magic began and where it ended, the clothes on my back, or the suitcase, or the unfinished screenplay—the thing Alice started that I was supposed to finish. But one thing was missing—the train case. Though I wished that the matching set of luggage had stayed together and intact, it made sense that the case had vanished, destroyed in the car accident.

"Clara, let's go to the pub," Trinity called out from the living room. "We told Niall and Frederick four o'clock and it's nearly that now. I can't keep my producer waiting."

"I'm coming," I said and took another glance at the time-worn machine. *A Woman Scorned* was one scene from *The End* and I still couldn't finish it.

We had put our coats on and were about to open the door when the typewriter keys began to click. I stopped cold and looked at Trinity. She heard it too.

"What is that?"

We tiptoed to the room, but this time the door was wide open, and we didn't have to get too close to see what was going on. There on top of the typewriter was a ginger cat. It walked back and forth along the top, its paws punching a different key each time.

"I can't believe it!" I burst out laughing. "Whose cat is that?"

"It's Clifford. He lives downstairs. That's the cat I borrow to kill mice when I need to. He's a great mouser."

I sighed. That explained the mysterious typewriting and the dead mouse. "Maybe he can finish the script," I joked. My cell rang. It was a Los Angeles area code but it wasn't Marjorie's number. I was anxious to talk to her and had called a couple of times since leaving the police station but hadn't been able to reach her.

"Hello," I said. The woman at the other end of the line was professional, concise and spoke with all the warmth of an iceberg.

"Your mother had a heart attack. We've admitted her, but her condition isn't stable."

When the plane landed at LAX, the air was the colour of toast. The drive to the hospital seemed to take forever. I'd called the nursing station from the baggage carousel, and Marjorie's condition had improved; she was considered stable, but she was quite weak. Weak enough that they wouldn't let me speak to her. I rarely took cabs in Los Angeles, and the driver apparently thought I was a tourist. Eventually, we wound our way through the traffic on La Cienega and into the vast complex that is Cedar Sinai Hospital. I raced down the corridors like you see on television, the robin's egg blue suitcase banging and knocking into me the whole way.

"Where is Marjorie Bishop?" I asked, out of breath. The nurse looked me up and down.

"Are you her daughter?"

I wanted to ask who else I'd be but just nodded. She picked up a file and walked around the nurse's station and down the hall. I followed. She looked at the suitcase.

"Been away for a long time?"

"It feels that way."

"Did you go far?"

I smiled at this. I wanted to say all the way to 1952 but instead said simply, "London, England."

"That is far." Then we reached Marjorie's room. The nurse opened the door for me and I walked in cautiously. She was lying on the bed fast asleep. Everywhere were tubes—up her nose, coming out of her arm; she looked very, very ill.

"I've never seen her sick before," I said to no one in particular. But the nurse nodded politely.

"I'll leave you alone with her. She'll wake up soon."

I sat on the edge of the bed as carefully as I could and held her hand. "Mom?" There was no reaction. "Marjorie?" I said softly. Slowly her eyes opened. They were rimmed with red. She looked at me, and a weak smile drew the corners of her mouth up.

"Clara," she said faintly. "You're back."

"Yes," I said. "I'm back. I came as soon as I heard. I wanted to make sure you're okay."

"I'm fine. Just had a little trouble with my heart," she explained.

I felt the tears come to my eyes. She looked at me and shook her head. "Don't cry, sweetheart. I'll be fine."

I swallowed hard. She was studying me. Then I remembered. "How do you like my hair?" I asked and tossed my hair so the curls tumbled down. She brought her chin up higher and gave me the once-over.

For a moment, I thought she was going to cry. "Do you hate it?"

The weak smile came back. "You look very pretty. Like your grand-mother."

I was taken aback. "That pretty?" I asked. Marjorie nodded.

I watched her eyes roam over my outfit. "You're wearing her dresses?" she asked.

"I haven't stopped since I left," I explained. "I guess they've grown on me."

The door opened and my mother smiled, a little stronger this time. I turned and in walked my father. I stood and hugged him. He held me and kissed the top of my head.

"I didn't know you were here," I said.

"He's been here every day," Marjorie said with as much slyness as she could muster.

My father ran his fingers through his white waves of hair and smiled. "You were away and, well, we were married once."

"Oh God, don't explain to me!" I said, feeling badly. "I'm glad you're here."

For the next few hours the three of us stayed together. It was almost like a family. He teased her. She teased him. And I sat there wonder-ing what had gotten into them. At one point I must have yawned, perhaps more than once, because my father stood to leave.

"I'll drive you home," he said and put his arm around me.

"But I don't want to go," I said.

"You need to rest. I will pick you up in the morning."

"Don't worry, I'm fine," my mother reassured me.

We walked down the corridor together and out to the car park. The haze had lifted as usual and the sky was white hot. I squinted and dug for my sunglasses in my handbag. I'd never been so happy to see the California sun. It was a contentment that I wasn't going to mess with.

"Don't take me to the apartment," I said. "I want to go to mom's house."

My father turned the ignition key. "That's a good idea," he said and kissed my cheek. "Tidy it up for her."

We chatted about Marjorie's health and when she could possibly come home. And then my trip came up and that topic took us all the way to Camrose Drive. Of course, I had to leave out the bits about the enchanted suitcase full of magical clothes, the screenplay that belonged to my grandmother and being thrown into a living, breathing black and white film noir. So mainly I told him about Trinity getting a big break and which bars made the best sidecars. I also neglected to mention Niall.

CHAPTER FORTY-SEVEN

I didn't unpack. As soon as my father had dropped me off, reassuring me that he'd call if anything changed during the night, and despite my jetlag, I set up the antique typewriter in the great room, facing it towards the mantel and the giant movie poster starring my grandmother. I poured a shot of bourbon and raised the glass at the poster. "Okay, Alicia Steele, you wanted the story to end. I'm going to end it, but in exchange, you're going to take care of Marjorie. Deal?" My grandmother's expression remained unchanged. "Good," I said as though she were in agreement. "And no funny stuff either. You're going to stick with me, right in the here and now." I shot back the bourbon and poured another and started to type.

It was dawn by the time the screenplay was finished. I had to admit it felt good. And the world still appeared to be in colour and in the right century. Exhausted, I stumbled away from the typewriter and onto the sofa. It was soft and deep and that was the last thing I remember until my cell phone rang. I scrambled to my feet and dug it out of my handbag. It was my father.

"How is she?" I asked, dispensing with pleasantries.

"Good. She's much better today. The cardiologist says she's out of danger."

Tears of relief flooded down my face and I sniffled. "I'm so happy. I'm going to shower and come down."

"Take your time," my father said. "She's going to be fine."

I hung up. It was nearly one o'clock in the afternoon. I'd slept away the entire morning. Marjorie would think I'd forgotten about her. I ran into the bathroom and took a shower. I went to the suitcase for clothes but the lock was jammed again. The tiny key that had worked faithfully seemed to stick in the lock yet wouldn't turn. I tried a dull kitchen knife to gently pry it open, but it was no use. It was exactly as it had been when I first went to London. No matter what I did, it wouldn't be jimmied, and it was far too delicate and too precious to bash open with a hammer. I ran into my old room and, sure enough, a pair of skinny jeans and some T-shirts were stuffed into a drawer. My hair was another story. The past several weeks involved a set of hot rollers. There was no time for that, so I left it straight and drove to the hospital, leaving the screenplay on the small table beside the typewriter.

"You look fabulous!" I said to Marjorie and hugged her gently to avoid tangling up the various tubes. She did look better than yesterday. Her eyes were bright white again and her complexion had life to it and, despite the tube in her nose, she'd managed to apply lipstick. That was my mother through and through.

"Thank you, darling," she said; her voice had gained strength too. "Sorry I scared everyone so much."

"Don't think about that," I said. "Besides, it brings us closer. Dad's been hovering around you like a lapdog."

I'd rarely seen my mother blush before, but there was no other way to explain the rosy glow that materialized on her cheeks.

"I prefer to think of myself as a working dog," my father said. I turned to see him in the doorway with a cup of coffee in his hand and the newspaper. "A German shepherd or Rottweiler."

"You're more Dalmatian or golden retriever," I teased, then turned my attention back to my mother. "I was just telling Marjorie that sometimes these moments test us and make us closer, and then you appeared, so I must be right!"

My father coughed. "You want to tell her or should I?" he said cryptically. I felt my stomach fall again.

"What is it?" I asked in a panic. "I thought you were going to be fine!"

"Hush, I am fine," Marjorie said. "This is what your father means." She raised her left hand. I could see the ugly IV needle stuck in her blue vein; the gauze had a tiny circle of blood on it.

"You have to wear the IV at home?" I guessed. Then more blushing from Marjorie.

"Are you blind, Clara?" she said and laughed. "Not my hand, my finger. Your father proposed to me again."

My jaw dropped. Sure enough, my mother had quite the chunk of ice on her ring finger, a platinum setting to boot. Somewhere behind me someone wolf-whistled.

"Geez, that's quite the rock, Marjorie." It was my friend Sylvia with a giant vase of roses. "Sorry to muzzle in on intimate family moments, but this thing weighs a ton."

My father took the flowers and set them on the bedside table. I was thrilled to see my friend and we embraced. Finally, I got it together enough to speak.

"That's fantastic. It's crazy but fantastic," I said. They were the kinds of words you said when you didn't know what to say. I'd never known my parents married. They split up when I was so young. "And congratulations!"

Somehow the three of us managed a group hug, another first, as Sylvia, never without some form of photographic equipment, snapped us with her smart phone.

"Oh, I almost forgot," Sylvia said. "I brought you a welcome-home gift, Clara."

"You didn't have to," I said kindly.

She stuck her head out into the hall for a second. "Actually, it was something you picked up in London but left behind. You've got to learn to pack more carefully."

Before I could react, Niall walked into the room.

"Hello, everyone," he said and looked respectfully at my parents. "I'm Niall Adamson. Trinity told me which hospital you were in. And Sylvia found me waiting outside the door."

"I told him not to be so English and polite, and to just follow me," Sylvia explained cheerfully.

"I hope you're feeling much better, Mrs. Bishop. And pleased to meet you, Mr. Bishop." He shook both their hands as they looked at him with a mixture of confusion and friendliness. He was back in his slightly wrinkled, striped button-down and dark jeans. His hair was its normal wavy blond mess. And he was sexy as hell. I felt all sweetness and swooning and knew I was smiling. A reaction not lost on my parents.

"I take it he's a friend of yours?" my father asked pointedly. Maybe he had some Rottweiler in him after all.

"A friend?" Marjorie scoffed. "From what I see, this young man is in love with Clara and she's in love with him."

Now it was my turn to be in full blush mode. I had no choice but to stare at my feet. I expected Niall to be the same shy retiring type that I was, but he didn't seemed fazed by my parent's bluntness.

"That is true, Mrs. Bishop," he admitted with a sort of glee in his voice. "Though I'm not sure she loves me."

I looked up, unsure what to do. Where was the fictional Clara when I needed her? As if sensing my dilemma, Marjorie shook her head.

"Clara, what's gotten into you?" she said. "You don't need those clothes to make you behave like the woman you are. Just be yourself."

I locked stares with Marjorie. What did she mean exactly? She gave me a knowing nod. It was enough for me to know to ask more later. I stood up; my hair had dried into long loose waves and now flowed down my shoulders. The clothes were different, but the attitude was the same if I let it be. So I let it. I walked across the small floor space and stood practically on top of him; our noses nearly touched.

"What took you so long?" I practically purred.

He smiled that lopsided, cheeky grin of his. "To tell you I loved you or to arrive from London?" he teased.

"Either. Both," I said playfully.

"The flights were booked tight so I had to fly standby," he said.

"And the other thing?" I asked.

"I wanted to make sure you weren't taking your husband back," he said and looked at my parents. I checked too. Marjorie was smiling; my father was glaring.

"I won't be doing any such thing," I said and grabbed his hand. "You can count on that."

"This is all very romantic," my father said after he had cleared his throat. "But your mother needs to rest. Shall we all go to dinner?"

"I'd love that!" Sylvia said. We all looked at her. "That is, unless it's strictly a family thing."

"Of course you may join us," my father said, then looked Niall up and down more carefully. "I take it you're an Englishman?"

Niall nodded. "Yes, sir."

"And what is it you do?"

"I'm a reporter, like your daughter."

"Clara is a screenwriter," Marjorie corrected him.

Niall nodded politely, and he, Sylvia and my father padded out of the room, with me close behind. Marjorie called me back.

"Clara, how is the writing going?" she asked me. I stopped and turned back to her.

"Mom, even from a hospital bed you're asking?"

"Well?" she asked again. It was like she knew. Only she couldn't possibly.

"As I matter of fact, I did finish a new script," I admitted.

"Can I read it?"

I hesitated. Back in film school she was my most severe critic. When I think about it, she was partly to blame for why I stopped writing. After everything I'd gone through to finish *The Woman Scorned,* the last thing I needed was her cutting it to shreds. But this one was as much hers as mine. It was part of the family. It was time she knew what happened to me while I was away, and how I'd done everything in my power to alter fate and had failed. I could have said any of that, but all I said was "Of course. I'll bring it to you tomorrow."

"Tonight," she said emphatically. "After dinner go home and get it."

"But you should rest," I pointed out, a little alarmed by her intensity. She shook her head. "I've done nothing but rest for three days now."

"You'll have it tonight," I said and kissed her on the forehead.

CHAPTER FORTY-EIGHT

The next week passed without either Marjorie or me mentioning *A Woman Scorned*. She remained in the hospital, and I kept busy trying to adjust to life as I knew it. I wanted to hold on to my new-found confidence and ensure I didn't slip into old ways and old insecurities now that I was home. It turned out not to be such a difficult task to accomplish after all.

For starters, uninspired by my beloved jeans and T-shirts, I went shopping. I'd grown accustomed to the traditional fabrics and precise tailoring of Alice's clothes. You could say I'd discovered my feminine side, and I wasn't going to give it up. Since I couldn't open my grandmother's suitcase, I scoured local vintage shops on Melrose Avenue. When I couldn't find what I wanted, I splurged on new dresses and pencil skirts and retro shoes and bags. Sylvia wondered what had come over me, and I could never tell her the truth, but she appreciated the clothes nonetheless and even bought herself a few things. And I also managed to pick up some perfect retro pieces for Niall, who kept busy trying to drum up freelance work, which was a good thing because he'd given up smoking, as much to please me as from seeing my mother's ill health.

I also wrote handwritten letters to Trinity, Frederick and Saffron. I felt that I owed them an apology for some of my behaviour. I admitted and regretted the worst of my single-mindedness in my quest to save Alicia Steele. A noble and acceptable cause, but not one I could reveal. I never told any of them about the journey we'd been on together. I didn't understand myself what had happened; that there had been some version of a parallel universe was the best I could come up with. Try explaining that. No one would believe it.

I also sent Frederick the completed script, which I had no choice but to retype into Final Draft and send via email. Before I left London, he restated that he was interested in optioning and producing it, but only if the ending worked.

Trinity and Saffron wrote me back. Each of them not only forgave me, they thanked me. Apparently, both had benefited from riding the crest of my self-absorption. Frederick kept Trinity as the second lead in the new movie, and as for Saffron, well, someone had to replace Amber. It appeared that my stab at altering Alicia's fate had in fact altered many others' fate instead.

Some nights, there would be dreams where I was back in London in 1952 and, to be honest, I didn't always want to wake up. There was something about that Clara I missed. In my waking hours, I would try to capture some of the mood and tone but wasn't always successful.

"You want to come to the school with me on Saturday? See the kids? It's the start of the new session," Sylvia had asked me when she was helping me clean my mother's house.

"That would be swell," I said, then wiped my brow. "What a dirty rotten job this is! Let's quit for a sidecar at the Formosa. I happen to know that dump pours a good one."

Sylvia just stared a moment, then burst out laughing. "Clara, you're right out of Old Hollywood."

"What's funny?"

"The way you just spoke," she giggled. "Like you're a character in an old movie. A really bad old B movie!"

She kept giggling and I grew annoyed. "That's how we all spoke in London," I explained sulkily.

Not every element of the femme fatale Clara could be kept.

We went to the school and the kids seemed thrilled to see us. It was a whole new group, with one exception.

"Clara!" Pilar ran over and grabbed my hips and hugged me tight. "We missed you!"

"I missed you too," I said and knelt down so we were eye to eye. "You're taking the class again?"

She nodded. "I want to make more movies!" she gushed.

"Then welcome back." I said it as much for me as for her. I was back, this time without the vengeance.

"I brought you a present," she said and handed me a small paper bag. Inside was a dog-eared, second-hand copy of *The Postman Always Rings Twice*.

"Is this your father's?" I asked, worried she'd taken his copy without his knowledge.

She shook her head. "He found another one and said you should have it for inspiration."

"Tell him thank you, and thank *you*," I said. She ran off to where the equipment was being laid out. Sylvia leaned over my shoulder and wolf-whistled.

"Maybe you need to explain to Pilar that women shouldn't be hell cats?" She was teasing me.

"Why would I do a thing like that?" I grinned slyly.

"Because she needs to know that a woman won't get anywhere in life with that attitude," Sylvia explained carefully, as though I didn't understand what was at stake. "Femme fatales are only for the movies, not the real world."

"I'm not so sure," I answered. "I've never met one I didn't like. Besides, in the right hands, a hell cat can be domesticated."

Niall stayed with me at the house while Marjorie recuperated in the hospital. In between romantic dinners and moonlit strolls, I finally told him about my grandmother, how she died, how it may or may not have been a suicide and how her death haunted my mother and me. I explained to him about the script that I'd finished, and how much my mother thought I'd failed her and Alice. He listened carefully and sympathetically but said little. Not that I'd expected much. What mattered to me was that I told him everything. Including all the intimate and gritty details that informed my life, stuff that even Dean never knew.

A few days later, when I came home loaded down with shopping bags, he was waiting with an envelope.

"I brought you something," he said. "Before you open it, I want you to know that I really took a chance."

I was curious and ripped open the envelope like it was Christmas morning. Inside was a single paper. It was a hard copy of a PDF from *The Los Angeles Times*. "What is this?" I asked, even though I somehow knew. It was the story I'd heard about my whole life, but I'd never seen the actual newspaper copy. I sat down and read it. The police report was the same. The witness, an aspiring actress named Betty, described how the convertible flipped over and over before coming to its final resting place.

"It still doesn't prove whether my grandmother killed herself," I said grimly.

"There was an eyewitness," he pointed out.

"Yeah, some actress named Betty who's probably long dead by now." I sighed. "But it means a lot that you found it for me. Thank you."

. . .

The other event that occurred during this time was my giving up the apartment. Dean wanted it after all. Early cuts of *Come to Daddy* had been screened by all the American networks, so he was already gearing up a stateside version. I went with Sylvia and Niall and cleaned out my things. The clothes I'd probably never wear again were stuffed into bags for Goodwill. The collection of DVDs was packed in boxes along with books and other items I wanted to keep. All in all, I left more than I took. I guess I wanted my past to stay where it was and start fresh.

That afternoon Niall got a phone call and disappeared for a while. I didn't think much of it until he returned, excited. I assumed he'd gotten a job offer.

"I need you to come with me tomorrow morning," he said.

"Where?" I asked.

"You have to trust me."

That's how I found myself in the passenger seat of a car parked outside a home for aging actors. "What on earth are we doing here?" I asked. He was about to answer when I cut him off. "I know, I have to trust you."

He led me through the low-rise building to an outdoor courtyard where half a dozen men and women in their seventies and eighties sat poolside. Niall made for an elderly lady sunning herself in a chaise longue. She looked up when she saw us coming. Niall pulled up an empty chaise beside her and sat down, and gestured for me to do the same. I did.

The old woman removed her oversized sunglasses. She had soft wrinkled skin with loads of sun damage, but her eyes were bright and lively. She smiled at me. "Is this her?" she asked Niall.

I looked at him for a clue. "Clara Bishop, I'd like to introduce you to Betty Simpson. Betty, this is Clara." I shook hands with Betty, and the reason he'd brought me became crystal clear.

"You're the same Betty who witnessed my grandmother's accident all those years ago, aren't you?" I felt my voice shake.

Betty nodded and wouldn't let go of my hand. "That's me, dear. Your boyfriend here tracked me down, I have no idea how, but he explained to me how upset you are about Alicia Steele. How you wanted to know how and why she died."

I could only nod. The moment felt unreal, more than any second I'd spent in that black and white world of 1952. Betty kept talking. "You see, back then things were different. It was tough for a single girl in Hollywood, tougher than now. I came here when I was seventeen, from Iowa, believing I was going to be a star. But in the beginning, I never got a break, only rejection. Men expected everything and gave nothing. Eventually, I'd had enough with struggling. I didn't think I could go back to Iowa a failure; it would have been so humiliating for me. So I drove to the Hollywood sign prepared to jump. I stood at the foot of the 'H' scared witless but determined to end things. But then your grandmother's car came up the mountain. I was high up on the hill and could see for miles. Including another car that was coming around a blind corner towards her; that car was going very fast, out of control, you might say. Your grandmother slammed on her brakes to try to swerve out of the way, but it was impossible. The other car gobbled up the road and Alicia didn't stand a chance. I can still hear the sound of the crash, and of the metal crunching down the mountainside. It was horrible. The other driver just kept going; maybe he didn't see what happened. The police came and I was too afraid to tell them why I was there. I didn't want trouble. I told them I was out for a hike, but they kept questioning me about why I was so close to the sign. Other starlets had leapt to their death, and they threatened to take me to a psychiatric ward. I insisted I was fine and diverted them by inventing a bigger story about Alicia's accident. I never told them about the other car. I let them think, made them think, that she had driven off the mountain intentionally. But it was a lie. Her death was an accident." Betty's voice trailed off. "Her death haunted me all these years. I never thought of the consequences of my lies to her family . . ." Betty looked at me, forcing a weak smile. I couldn't return the gesture. "I want you to know that after watching her perish, I decided I wanted to live. And live I did. I never became a big star but I got parts, tiny ones. Eventually, I joined a touring stage company and did some singing and dancing for the next thirty years. It may not sound like much, but I was happy, happy to be alive. That's what your boyfriend found out yesterday. I hope it gives you some closure."

Not sure how to react, or what to say, I hugged Betty and thanked her for being honest now. Niall drove me home, allowing silence between us. It was a beautiful gift he'd given me; I wasn't sure he knew how special it was. Part of me was furious with Betty for nearly taking the truth to her grave, but she was an old woman, and it happened so long ago. Besides, her story didn't change anything. My grandmother was gone. What mattered was that there was enough time for me and Marjorie to make peace with the facts.

"You okay?" Niall asked me when we got to Camrose.

"Thank you. I'm very grateful for this, truly I am."

"I told you sleeping with an investigative journalist would pay off," he teased.

"You never told me that."

"I should have. It's my best line!" he laughed.

I kept the news about Betty to myself until Marjorie got healthy enough to come home. When she did, we threw a small welcome-home party for her. There were the usual tacky balloons and streamers, a shiny "welcome home" sign taped over the door. The food was top-notch though, sushi, salads, loads of healthy things. But

red wine was also on the menu, and we all had a glass to celebrate
with her.

The only downside was that now that my mother was back, Niall
was returning to London. Like me, he had a divorce to contend with,
and he wanted to see Sam, who had signed a small record deal with
his punk rock band. The long-distance thing was going to have to
do for a while. So as happy as I was for my mother and father, I was
melancholy knowing Niall was leaving.

On Niall's last night, my father and he were cleaning up in the
kitchen and I was sitting with Marjorie.

"Nice dress," she observed. "Is it new?"

"It is," I answered. It was one of the many new things I'd picked
up. "It's my signature look, don't you know. I sound like I write for a
fashion magazine."

We both laughed.

"I think you should stick to screenwriting," she said and winked
at me.

I raised my eyebrow. "So you did read it?"

"The night you gave it to me," she said.

"You haven't said anything."

"I was waiting for you to ask me my opinion," she said and swirled
the wine in her glass.

"Did you really think that would happen?" I asked defensively.

"Now, now, I'm recovering," she teased.

"Sorry." I hesitated. "What did you think?"

"I liked the ending," she said. "Quite a lot."

"Really? It's not the usual film noir," I admitted. "Not sure Alice or
Alicia Steele would approve. Hell, I'm shocked you would approve.
It's not like you, Mother."

She tilted her head. "Where did that come from?"

"I'm sorry, forget what I said." But in that moment I couldn't forget any of it. I gathered my courage and continued. "A lot happened while I was away. I guess I'm standing up for myself more."

She nodded like she understood. "I suppose I have been hard on you. But it was only because I wanted you to avoid the pain I had and the bitter disappointments."

"I don't think anyone is safe from those." We sat awhile, but I knew it was time to tell Marjorie the truth about everything. We went into her giant walk-in closet and sat down.

"You should know I didn't write the script by myself. I had help."

"Anyone I know?" she asked.

Then I explained about finding the screenplay and the photograph. She nodded, but I couldn't read her expression. "Wherever she is, I'm sure she's happy her story has been finished," she said at last. "Maybe she can finally rest in peace."

We sat quietly, both of us having our own private thoughts about Alice. "Can I show you something?" I said. "That is, if you're not too tired."

"Of course," she said.

I opened the closet where I had returned the suitcase, its contents still locked up, and pulled it out.

"You know about the suitcase, don't you?" I asked, no longer feeling the need to hide what had happened.

"What about it?" she said coyly.

I sighed. Maybe I'd been wrong, maybe it was just me. "You're tired, you should go to bed. Sorry I mentioned it."

I had picked up the suitcase when her hand closed down on mine. Marjorie met my gaze, her expression soft and revealing.

"When I was much younger than you are now, when you were a child, after your father left me for that tramp, I was very angry. Just like you were when Dean left you for Amber. And I'm positive Alice was equally angry when my father left her. I wanted to get even. It started with the green dress, you know, the first one you tried on."

I nodded, transfixed.

"At first I followed your father around for days, begging him to come home. I even got into a real knock 'em down fight with the tramp."

"You did?"

She nodded. "You aren't the only tomboy in the family."

"Now you are shocking me," I said with a smirk. She smirked back.

"Your father loved that, I might add. But at some point I stopped caring. The clothes changed my grief into anger, and then the anger made me tough. Somehow I became tough enough to raise you on my own."

"But you gave up your career," I pointed out. "Because of me."

She watched me carefully, and I shifted from foot to foot, worried I'd upset her.

"It wasn't because of you," she said slowly. "Is that what you thought all this time?"

"You've said as much," I said and felt the old hurts and childhood emotions getting the better of me.

"I was wrong to have done that," she said quietly. "I didn't have a career to give up. I was a lousy actress. There, I've said it. It took me thirty-odd years to admit, but there you go."

"I'm sure you weren't that bad," I said, trying to catch up with the revelation.

"I stank. I suppose it was easier to tell people I gave up acting to be a good mother rather than admit that I was terrible, and that I got nothing but rejections. I was pretty. That's why I got the extra work, a nice platinum blonde to linger in the background."

"Let's stop talking," I said, seeing how emotional she had become. "You're tired. You've been sick."

"No. It's good to talk. I think what happened to me and to you, well, I like to think it's Alice helping us, watching over us."

I pondered this a moment. It was a nice thought, Alice watching over us. I gestured to the locked suitcase. "I can't open it. It's broken or something. Look."

I grabbed the key from the dressing table and shoved it in the tiny lock.

"I turn it and nothing . . ." Only this time the lock opened. "It didn't work. I'm telling you the truth."

"I believe you," Marjorie said and together we opened the lid. Her eyes lit up at the sight of the clothes. "These gave me the confidence I needed at the time." She gave me a knowing smile and began to hang them up in the closet where they'd been before I left for England. Once again, the clothes were only clothes, no magic, no enchantment, just lots of silk and satin.

"Now Alice is home again."

I helped with the unpacking. The clothes brought back so many memories, a blend of two centuries and two different women with an identical problem.

"I want you to get an agent again and sell *A Woman Scorned*," she said suddenly. "You're a great writer. And you and Alice should share the credit. It would be a wonderful way to honour her memory."

"I have news about that," I said. "I was waiting for the contract, but since you brought it up. That British film producer I met, Frederick Marshall? He's optioned it and wants to make the film."

"That's wonderful!" She hugged me tight, then smiled proudly. There was one dress left to hang up. It was the bottle-green bouclé, the dress that started the whole thing. I knew it was the right time to tell her.

"Mom, there's more," I said.

"What is it?"

"Let me get the article," I said and went to retrieve it. I returned with the printout that Niall had given me, and I let her read it. She grew upset, and I was concerned that the news would bring on another heart attack.

"I know you always said she died of a broken heart . . ."

"I always believed that she killed herself," she said softly, admitting it at last.

"You need to know the truth," I said and sat beside her and told her everything that Betty had told me. "Alice swerved to miss another car that was speeding, and she drove off the edge. She never wanted to die."

Marjorie was crying now. "This means more to me than you can know."

I rubbed her shoulder. "I can only imagine. It must have been hard to think your mother killed herself when she had you to take care of."

"I thought she abandoned me. That she didn't love me enough. This means the world to me."

We held on to each other tightly. I couldn't think of the last time Marjorie and I were so close. She gently pulled away.

"And Betty, she was going to kill herself?"

"Yes. Betty was planning to jump off the Hollywood sign, but when she saw the car roll down the hillside and knew that Alice was dead, she decided she wanted to live."

"Alice saved her life, then?"

"You could say that. But the point is that Alice was happy. She should have lived a long life but fate got in the way," I said.

Marjorie held on to my hand. "Doesn't it always?"

We sat there remembering Alicia Steele as best we could from one movie and a screenplay.

"What should we do with this?" I asked her and gestured to the suitcase.

"Save it for your own daughter," she said.

I felt the blood drain from my face. "I don't think I can get pregnant," I said.

"Nonsense," she said with a shake of her head. "You and Dean just weren't meant to be. It's good you didn't have a child with him. Then you'd be stuck with him your whole life."

"Maybe I've broken the family curse by finishing the screenplay like I did," I said, still reeling from the pang of emptiness I got every time I allowed myself to want a baby. "Look at you and Dad."

She smiled and touched her engagement ring. "Exactly. The curse is broken," she said. Her words astounded me; after years of battling her conviction that we were jinxed, she was letting go. "Believe me, one day your daughter will carry the suitcase and wear these clothes to be pretty, not to be a tough dame who can take a slap as easy as a kiss," she grinned.

CHAPTER FORTY-NINE

She went to bed and I took Niall for a walk up to High Tower Elevator. It was a cool evening, but the lights from the houses and their gardens gave the pathway a warm and sensual glow.

"I'm glad you finally brought me here," he said. "Though after reading *A Woman Scorned* I'm a tad frightened that you mean to shove me down the elevator shaft like the fictional Clara planned to do."

"Don't worry. I wouldn't dream of killing you, unless we're married."

"How reassuring!" he said and grabbed hold of me.

"But only if you leave me for a blonde," I said and poked his chest hard with my index finger. "Or a brunette or another redhead, for that matter."

"I promise you won't need to worry about that with me," he said. "Though despite what happened, your father made his way back in the end. You better not take Dean back when you're old and have had a heart attack."

"Never!" I answered with a laugh. "Though I must say I'm happy for my parents."

"You should be," he said.

I walked towards the staircase. "I want you to come somewhere with me," I said.

"Anywhere you say," he answered.

I smiled at him. "We're going for a drive."

We hopped into my father's two-seater coupe and headed for the hills. Not just any hills either; I drove expertly along Mulholland Drive where it gets wild and unyielding east of the 101. When I'd driven as far as I could, I stopped the car. We were just short of security camera range.

"That was quite the drive," he said, looking a little green. "Lots of twists and turns."

"This is where the Hollywood sign sits," I told him and got out of the car. "We can't get closer than this, but you get the drift. You've read the script."

He stepped towards the edge of the road and peered over cautiously. It was so black outside you couldn't see the bottom of the canyon. He shivered. I took the script out of the car and turned to the last page.

"You're not tossing it over the side are you?" he asked, alarmed.

"Don't be silly," I said. What I was going to do could be considered as silly, though not to me. "I'm going to read the last scene out loud. My grandmother died on this road. She never got to finish the screenplay, and I want her to hear how I ended it."

His head moved up and down ever so slowly. "Would you like me to sit in the car?"

"Please stay and listen. I want to share it with you."

"I'd be honoured."

I stepped off the road onto the dirt. The ground felt loose and unstable beneath my feet; then again, the side of a mountain wasn't optimum footing for high heels. I turned on the flashlight and started to read. The breeze picked up my words and carried them across the cool air and down the canyon.

EXT. HOLLYWOOD SIGN—DAY
A dark-haired man, ROD SLATER, is sitting in a
grey sedan. He's smoking a cigarette and waiting
for something to happen. Then it does.

POLICE SIRENS are coming up the hillside towards
him. Rod steps out of the car.

SIRENS getting closer. Rod stamps out his cigarette.

TWO POLICE CARS pull up in a flurry of dust.

A UNIFORMED COP and a DETECTIVE in plain clothes
exit one of the cars.

                         ROD
          You took your time getting here.

                       DETECTIVE
          Just like you to be in a hurry. Who is it
          this time? Another blonde?

                         ROD
          You're a real sentimentalist, aren't you?

Rod moves down the side of the mountain with the
detective, always several feet ahead, anxious and
tense. The two men stop abruptly at the foot of
the letter "H."

The detective wipes his forehead and scowls.

                    DETECTIVE
        I was right. Another blonde. What a shame.

Rod looked down at the broken body of the YOUNG
WOMAN. His expression of fear turns to relief.

                        ROD
        It wasn't who I thought it was.

He began to climb back up, passing TWO POLICEMEN
with a stretcher heading down.

INT. ROD'S APARTMENT, LAUREL CANYON—NIGHT
Rod is staring at a small pink envelope on his
kitchen table, an empty bottle of Scotch beside it.
He's finally drunk enough to open it. The handwriting is neat, feminine, and the letter is brief.

Dear Rod,

*By the time you get this, I will be long gone. I took your advice and left
this God-forsaken place. This hell they call the Golden State. I know
you'll worry. I heard about a woman leaping to her death from the Hollywood sign, and knew you'd think the worst. It could have been me, once.
But you saved me. You showed me that I didn't need my husband or his
money, or revenge. I didn't kill him, and I didn't harm her, because you
asked me not to. Now I'm free. And I want you with me. Take a plane to
Mexico. The exact address is on the other side of this note. We can start
over. I love you. Your redhead, Clara.*

Rod folds the note and goes to his closet. He
takes down a suitcase. He starts to pack.

EXT. OCEANSIDE CLIFF—MEXICO—MAGIC HOUR
Clara is standing in a long satin evening gown
alone by the ocean. She is drinking champagne.
She smiles when she hears footsteps. She turns
around to see Rod walking towards her in a
tuxedo. They embrace.

THE END

I looked at Niall. "She doesn't die. I gave her a happy ending," I
said triumphantly.

"Everyone deserves a happy ending. Even the femme fatale," he
agreed.

═CHAPTER FIFTY═

Two Years Later

Clara had finished pitching her story and drinking her second sidecar. She loved happy hour at the Formosa. The producer looked like he enjoyed the pitch.

"That's a remarkable story," he said and sucked an olive off its toothpick.

"I like to think so," Clara answered. She wanted desperately to check her watch but knew it would look bad.

"Frederick said I should meet you and he was right," the man told her with a formal-looking nod, like a butler who was taking an order from his master. It made her think of that night at the castle and the gold gown that Frederick's butler had laid out on the bed. She shivered. "I enjoyed your script for *A Woman Scorned*. Wish I'd had a chance to bid on it but I was out of town."

Clara smiled. She had sold her first screenplay only eighteen months ago, but it seemed like a lifetime. "I wrote that with my grandmother."

"With her? I thought she was dead," he said, then abruptly apologized. "Sorry, that was insensitive. I meant, I thought you finished it after. At least that's the story I heard."

"That is correct," Clara said. "This one I just pitched you is all mine."

He nodded and drank more of his martini. Clara had lost count but she thought it was his fourth.

"I like it. The whole magical suitcase full of clothes that sends the lead back in time so she can solve her grandmother's mysterious death is brilliant. When can I read it?"

"I'm nearly finished the first draft. My agent will have it in another week or two," Clara said, not sure if she should admit why it was so late.

"I want the exclusive on it. Will you give it to me? No one else in town reads it before me?"

Clara grinned. "I don't see why not."

Clara got home just in time. She opened the door to her and Niall's house to be greeted by the sound of her infant daughter wailing like the house was on fire. Niall was trying in vain to feed her from the bottle. Marjorie was shaking her head at him.

"Sorry I'm late," Clara rushed in and kissed Niall and the baby on the forehead. "I'll take her."

"We have to get changed," Niall said in a panic. "We have to be at the theatre in half an hour."

"Don't worry, it's on Hollywood Boulevard. We could walk there if we had to," Clara explained and cooed at her baby.

"Not in your shoes," Niall said playfully and dashed off to the bedroom to change.

"Let me take her," Marjorie offered, and Clara gently placed the baby into her arms.

"I'd better get ready," she said and disappeared down the hall.

The couple emerged not long after; Clara in a deep purple satin gown, Niall in a bespoke tux, no tie, and a pair of purple velvet loafers.

"You two look positively radiant!" Marjorie exclaimed.

Clara tiptoed over to the bassinette, where her daughter was now fast asleep.

"Have a lovely evening, Alicia," she whispered to the infant.

"Have a good time," Marjorie said. "Your father will be here with takeout any moment."

Clara and Niall left the house and got into the waiting limo, and it took them down through the narrow twisty streets to Franklin, then down Sycamore to the security check on Hollywood Boulevard. They walked from there and onto the red carpet.

"How's this for two former entertainment journalists being on the other side of the paparazzi?" Clara whispered to him.

Before he could answer, they heard a wolf whistle and saw Sylvia, also on their side of the red carpet, waltzing towards them in a long black gown.

"Have you seen the cast yet?" she asked.

"Some of us are right behind you," joked Trinity.

The four walked down the carpet until Trinity had to go off and pose for photos alongside Saffron, who looked just like the movie star she was about to become. Frederick Marshall was off to the side in the background, overseeing the premiere. He saw Clara and smiled briefly before going back to the behind-the-scenes chatter.

"I hope the film is good," Sylvia whispered.

"I liked it at the screening," Niall said.

"Ooh, so says the newly minted film critic," she teased. "Big shot now, are you?"

"Stop taunting him," Clara joked. She headed along the crowd barrier towards the theatre. Clara was a few steps from the theatre door when she caught sight of a familiar face. It was a pretty face. She knew it instantly. Amber was watching her enter the theatre. It was supposed to be her premiere, not Saffron's, and no doubt she would blame Clara for it. And Clara knew that on some level she did have something to do with how it all unfolded. Then again, she wasn't really herself at the time. And there was just the right amount of the hell cat left inside Clara to make her not regret a moment of it. Past or present, no matter whose past it was.

Fade Out

ACKNOWLEDGEMENTS

No one said that being a writer is easy. And it would be much more difficult if it weren't for my friends and family, as well as the publishing professionals, who helped guide and encourage me throughout the process.

In particular I'd like to thank Suzanne Boyd, Vivian Vassos, Arlene Stacey and Athena McKenzie, for reading the earlier drafts and providing invaluable feedback. The editing talents of Jennifer Lambert and Harriet Bourton are not to be underestimated, and a giant thank you to them for pushing me to make each page better and better. Of course, this book would not be in your hands were it not for the dedication of my agents, Diana Beaumont and Grainne Fox. Thank you both for continuing to believe in me as a novelist.

And special thanks to Jamie Mayer and James Combs for the use of their lovely apartment in the Hollywood Hills, complete with a copy of *The Long Goodbye*, and where the first draft of this novel was written. Not to mention for showing me the way to High Tower Court and its elevator.

I'm also grateful for the many talented people who worked on this novel at HarperCollins Canada and at Hodder & Stoughton in the United Kingdom.

And finally, my heartfelt gratitude and love to Richard, for being there all the way.